STRANGE
TROPICS

STRANGE TROPICS

Uncanny Tales from Warmer Climes

Edited by Chad Arment

COACHWHIP PUBLICATIONS
Greenville, Ohio

Strange Tropics: Uncanny Tales from Warmer Climes
© 2023 Coachwhip Publications
Cover image: Ishita Nigam Garg

CoachwhipBooks.com

ISBN 1-61646-574-3
ISBN-13 978-1-61646-574-2

Contents

Ballairai Durg
Anonymous (1886)

Dinner had been over for about an hour at the mess-house of the little station of Mudnoor in the Deccan, on the night of the fifth of May a good many years ago; and though a few were playing pool in the billiard-room, the greater number of the officers were clustered in the wide verandah, smoking and talking and making merry, for the afternoon had been overpoweringly sultry, and the low dark mess-house, in spite of the swinging punkahs, was close and stuffy as a ship's hold.

Outside it was cooler. A heavy storm was raging on the edge of the ghàts many miles to the west, and though for a while the night wind blew in heavy puffs hot as from the mouth of a furnace, it soon died away, and a cool, refreshing breeze, growing every moment damper and more chill, came stealing in from the west. The orderly officer, clinking in after visiting his guards, put his head through the billiard-room window, and called out to the players, "Come out of that hole, you fellows, and smell the rain."

"By Jove, how jolly!" cried a number of those gay young warriors, clustering round the window, while the click of the balls ceased, and the dull voice of the marker, "Black lost a life, Green's the player," fell unheeded even on the ears of Green, as with swelling nostrils and open mouths they drank in that most pleasant of all scents, the smell of thirsty ground soaking up the early rain. Soon by the blaze of the frequent lightning the dark line of the coming shower was seen in the distance, and great drops began to patter on the verandah with a sound like hail.

"I say," cried an officer of the Irregular Cavalry, "here's our C. O. coming in, let's go and ask him if he's got any news of pig,"—as the commandant of the Irregulars, who happened also to be field-officer of the day, was seen by the flashes cantering down the road which led to the mess-house, with the rain squall pelting close behind him as if in pursuit. In another moment he dismounted, threw the reins of his game little Arab to the syce, unbuckled his heavy sword (cased in the wooden scabbard which kept it sharp and serviceable), and handing it to his orderly came slowly up the steps.

Major Thornhill was a fair specimen of the servants of the old East India Company—just and right honorable masters, who shall say that they were not well served? Standing on the steps, in the long jack boots and dark green tunic of the Irregular Cavalry, crossed by a broad gold pouch-belt, and adorned with two or three faded bits of ribbon on his left breast, and with a red cashmere shawl twisted round his lean flanks, though not a handsome man, he looked every inch a soldier. His subalterns swore by him, and his fierce Moghul troopers, when other regiments mutinied, followed him without wavering against their brethren; and on the dark day, when he at last met the soldier's death which he had often courted, they died in heaps across his body. A quiet, somewhat solitary man, not often moved to conversation or mirth, but, on the rare occasions when he did speak, speaking well and simply, and with a wide experience and knowledge of the country, of the natives, and of human nature; hence his judgment was in great request for the decision of the usual mess-table arguments, which for the most part are begun with dogmatic assertion and met by flat denial—each party in the quarrel being not unfrequently equally ignorant of the subject in dispute. On such occasion he would give wise counsel in few words; but, if he liked the combatants, he would sometimes illustrate his rulings by stories, which he told simply, but so effectively, that astute subalterns were reported sometimes to devise sham disputes with a view to drawing forth these good stories, for he was a single minded man, without guile, and fell readily into a trap.

"Any news of pig, major?" cried young Gordon, the subaltern who had last spoken. "I hear that you sent Maryanne out to Culmaisa."

"No," replied he, "but I told him to come here for orders after mess." Here the major's orderly, a fine-looking Pathan, although his straight black beard parted in the centre and brushed upwards towards his ears gave him a somewhat catlike aspect, stepped up to the break of the verandah and saluted.

"Well, Hyat Khan, what is it?" asked the major in Hindoostanee.

"The Huzoor's [literally, the presence] shikari Murriana, sahib, waits the Huzoor's orders."

"Very good, send him here."

The orderly went off, and speedily returned, bringing the redoubted Murriana, or "Maryanne" as he was generally called by the youth of the station.

Murriana was a Mahratta by caste. Though somewhat past middle age, he still looked full of work; the muscles stood out like whipcord from his lean, half-naked limbs, and his large black eyes glistened bright in the lamplight, as he stood with hands advanced and both palms joined, waiting respectfully for his master's orders.

"Murriana," said the major in Hindoostanee, "you are to go out to Culmaisa to-morrow and try if you can get any news of pig, and a horseman shall go with you, whom you will send back with news."

"Very good, great king [maharaj, a common Hindoo term of respect], I heard just now in the bazaar that the grey boar of Monagul has come down to the Culmaisa jungle; if it is true, the sahibs will have good sport."

"Bravo, Maryanne," cried half-a-dozen voices. "We've been after that old boar for the last three seasons; it will be a great disgrace to you if you don't run him to earth now;" and then some one struck up the well-known Deccan hunting-song of "The boar, the mighty boar," to the old English air of "My love is like a red red rose," and every one, even the major, joined in the familiar chorus.

The boar, the mighty boar's my theme,
    Whate'er the wise may say,
My morning thought, my midnight dream,
    My hope throughout the day,
Then sing the boar, the mighty boar,
    Fill high the cup with me,
And here's to all who fear no fall,
    And the next grey boar we see.

Youth's daring spirit, manhood's fire,
    Stout heart, and eagle eye,
Doth he require, who would aspire
    To see the wild-boar die.
Then sing the boar, the mighty boar,
    Fill high the cup with me,
And here's to all who fear no fall,
    And the next grey boar we see.

We envy not the rich their wealth,
    Nor kings their crowned career,
The saddle is our throne of health,
    Our sceptre is the spear;
Nor envy we the warrior's pride,
    Deep stained with purple gore,
For our field of fame's the jungle-side
    Our foe the grim grey boar.

When age hath weakened manhood's powers,
    And every nerve unbraced,

The joys of youth shall still be ours,
    On mem'ry's tablets traced:
And with the friends whom death hath spared,
    When youth's bright course is run.
We'll tell of the dangers we have shared,
    And the spears that we have won.

CHORUS.
Then sing the boar, the mighty boar,
    Fill high the cup with me.
And here's to all who fear no fall,
    And the next grey boar we see.

When the uproar had subsided, Murriana again joined his hands in supplication and said: "If it is permitted to this slave to speak, there are two panthers in a cave in the old fort of Culdurg, close by Calmaisa. Shall I tie up a goat?"

"All right, Murriana," said Major Thornhill; "but I'm glad that you've got over your fear of old forts. No Shaitāns [devils] in Culdurg, I hope? Hur hur Mahadeoeh,* eh?"

"Oh," cried Murriana, waving his hands deprecatingly, "the sahib must not say that word. It is not lucky; and this is the very night, so many years ago."

He was evidently shaken by some unpleasant memory, for he trembled visibly, and his dark brown face turned to a ghastly greenish yellow.

"All right, Murriana," said his master kindly. "You have permission to go."

And Murriana made obeisance, and left the premises.

"What was that about the Shaitāns and the fort, major?" asked a young officer. "Murriana didn't seem to like it."

"Oh, nothing," replied he. "An old story; Murriana thought he saw a ghost once."

* The Mahratta war-cry.

"And did he?"

"I don't know," said he rather shortly, and smoking in quick puffs. "He thought he did."

"I say, Dr. Daly," asked a young infantry officer, winking at the same time to his fellows, addressing the doctor of the Irregulars, a big, raw-boned Irishman, and a terribly hard rider, to whom the major did greatly incline, though he "sat upon" him about seven times a week, "do you believe in ghosts?"

"Yes," replied he; "don't you?"

"No, I don't."

"Why not?"

"I never saw one."

"Oh! That's a good reason. Do you believe that there was such a person as Julius Caesar?"

"Julius Caesar be blowed!"

"With all my heart; but do you believe in him?"

"Of course."

"But you never saw him."

"What's that got to say to it? It's only uncivilized races who believe in ghosts; Mahrattas and Tipperary men, and such like. Now I'll bet you two to one the major doesn't believe in them. Do you, major?"

"You're too fond of betting, Gordon. I'm not sure that I don't. I'll tell you a story" (and the two conspirators exchanged a triumphant glance):—

"It's a good many years ago. I was a subaltern in those days, and promotion was even slower than it is now, as you will readily believe when I tell you that there were then ensigns of fifteen years standing. I was quartered in the Mysore country, and had got two months' leave to go on a shikar trip to the western ghàts. Maryanne, as you call him, was my shikari then as now. We marched to Chickmugloor in the Nuggur Division, and then we left the main road and marched to Wastara; there I left my bullock-cart, and hired a gang of fourteen Lumbanies (the same wandering caste whom you call Brinjaries here) to carry my little tent and scanty baggage. From thence I struck across the hills through a beautiful wild country for twenty-two miles to Sultanpet, a village at the foot of the great hill-fort of Ballairai Durg.

"Sultanpet was an insignificant village, inhabited for the most part by Baders, manly, good-natured fellows, as I have always found them in the Mysore country, and excellent sportsmen. There were a few families of Mussulmans, scowling, ill-conditioned brutes, and an opium-sodden scoundrel, who called himself the kiladar [fort-commandant], for the fort of Ballairai Durg had once been an important outpost, in Tippoo's time, and a gaol for State prisoners; and indeed one of my reasons for going there was that a favorite cousin of my grandfather's (who was then alive, though a very old man) had been taken prisoner in General Matthews's ill-fated attack on Nuggur in 1783, and was reported to have died, or been made away with at Ballairai Durg, and my grandfather had asked me to go there and try if I could get any information about his fate.

"Sultanpet lay half-way up the ascent to the Durg, which is an isolated peak, flanked to the northward by frowning cliffs, looking most picturesque in the short May twilight, with the mist-wreaths wrapped round them like a girdle.

"Shortly after sunset I heard the sambre belling in the wooded ravine above me, and the sharp bark of the jungle sheep almost from within a stone's throw of my little tent, which was pitched outside the village; and I could see my Lumbanies (who are great lovers of flesh) squatted on their haunches by the edge of the jungle, licking their chops, whilst they pounded some mess in a great wooden mortar.

"'That people,' said Murriana, who came up smiling to my tent door, 'is very happy.'

"'Why so?'

"'Sambre,' replied he curtly. 'They are pounding curry stuff. They know that the sahib's luck is good.'

"'Is there good news of game, Murriana?'

"'Very good, maharaj.'

"'What?'

"'Listen, maharaj. This side, sambre; that side, jungle sheep. Listen,' said he again, his dark eyes glistening as he held up a finger. 'That's cheetul [spotted deer]; he's frightened at something. No wonder—did you hear that?—bagh!' [tiger], as a long-drawn sound, half-grunt, half-sigh, came up the ravine over which the evening mists were stealing, answered from the opposite hill by a like but hoarser roar. 'Two,' said Murriana, holding up two fingers. 'Surely the sahib's luck is good.'

"'How shall we get up to the top of the Durg, Murriana?'

"'Oh, there is a winding path. Didn't the sahib see it as he came up the ghàt?'

"'Can the coolies bring the things up?'

"'Without doubt; but this is a very good place for camp.'

"'But we shall be nearer to the game above; and if there's any young grass, you know, it will be full of sambre and bison in the early morning.'

"'It is true word.'

"'Well?'

"'The cooly people won't stay on the top.'

"'But why?'

"'I don't know, maharaj; maybe 'tis too cold.'

"'Cold, what nonsense! You know that the Lumbanies don't mind cold, nor you. Do you want another blanket? If so, go to the bazaar and buy one.'

"'Oh, the sahib is always good! I have blankets enough. I'll go wherever the sah'b goes.'

"'Then what's the matter with those confounded coolies?'

"'The place is bad, maharaj. There are Shaitāns in that fort, they say. They are a foolish folk!'

"'Listen, Murriana. We'll go up early, and we'll kill them a couple of sambre, and you go and get hold of the arrack-seller. If that old kiladar wasn't half drunk this evening I'll eat the tent pole. We'll give the Lumbanies and the Baders a feast, and they'll stop with us till all is blue.'

"'It is a very good word, maharaj,' said Murriana, grinning. 'I will try.'

"Murriana and I started before the false dawn, with two coolies carrying the guns. I left orders with my boy Barabbas, an energetic but perhaps not entirely truthful domestic (though a Christian, as may be gathered from his name), to follow with the camp at daybreak. The winding path was steep and breath-compelling, so that I hadn't much attention to spare to the scenery, more especially as I felt that I hadn't had enough sleep after the long march of the day before. Day had nearly broken before we reached the hilltop, for the pointers of the Southern Cross had just gone under; those well-cursed stars, you know them, all of you, on the march, and how the day won't break till they are gone.

"It was a sight to see. I can see it now, through the mists of fifteen long years, as if it were yesterday. The day hadn't fairly broken, and the valleys were still black as night, but all the mountain-tops had caught a rosy stain, like that of the inside of a shell, a color such as no painter on earth could match. I've seen the sun rise often enough, worse luck! but I've never seen anything like the daybreak on those hills. I don't know if any of you chaps have?"

"No, major," said the doctor, "we haven't; but 'twas seen and described long before your time, and by a blind man too. 'Pon me soul, you're not blind—I wish you were sometimes.

ʼΗμος δηριγενεια φυνη ροδοδακτυλος ʼΗως,

says old Homer; 'When the rosy-fingered morning, daughter of the dawn, appeared.'"

"Did he now? It's none of your chaff, is it?"

"No," replied the doctor, "I can't chaff in Greek; I wish I could."

"Ay," said the major, "rosy-fingered, that's just it; touching the hilltops and dropping a little light on them, till peak after peak grows bright, and blushes in the morning. That was what I saw, and then the mist rolled back to the valleys; Kalasa shone out close by; Coodery Mook [the Horse-Face], some seven thousand feet high, to the northward; the Baba Boodens behind me; and in front the sea, dark by the shore, with the plains and jungles of Canara for many miles between, but on the horizon catching a streak of light away from the shadow of the hills.

"Well, I didn't do much that morning. I shot a couple of sambre for the people; there were a good many about on the edges of the ravines, but they were rather shy and wanted stalking. We found fresh tracks of bison, and marked the place for next day, and then I went and viewed the fort. It was all in ruins; but the western curtain was still standing and formed a good shelter from the weather, and there I was minded to pitch my tent.

"The view was wonderful. There was no ditch to the west, indeed the strength of the place lay in the difficulty of the landward approach. The ground in front sloped away like a lawn for half a mile, and then fell sheer, and in all the ravines below the jungle clustered crisp and thick, the tops of the trees only showing to the edge, whilst beyond them, mellowed by the distance, the plains lay simmering in the summer haze, and beyond the plains the great mirror of the glittering sea.

"Hallo! you chaps, you're not smoking. Well, I agree with you; it's time to turn in."

But here there was a general shout, "No! No! major. Go on, we want to hear about the ghost."

"Ghost!" said he; "I didn't say anything about a ghost. I never saw a ghost in my life, I'm only telling you what happened."

"All right," said the doctor, nudging his neighbor. "He's on. Slip a little more whiskey into his tumbler when he's not looking. That's the shtuff."

"Well, all right. I'll go on if you like, though there isn't much to tell. Barabbas and the coolies came up and pitched the tents, and half-a-dozen Baders, with bows and arrows and matchlocks, came with them, keen shikarries all of them, and good trackers. We sent them out for the sambre, which they soon brought up in triumph, and then they dressed them for a royal feast, reserving a portion for the servants and me.

"My khālāsi, Ghulām Hoosein,* wouldn't touch his share, as the beasts hadn't been properly halalled;† but he asked if we were going after bison next day, and said that one of his brethren would come up and show us a sure find, and would come with us to make certain that the last offices were duly performed for the dead. I told him he might come himself and do it if he chose, but that I didn't want any of his brethren, as I didn't like the look of them, at which an evil-looking Mussulman, who was lurking behind the baggage, and whom I had not noticed before, made a gesture of contempt and spat upon the ground. I thought it best to pretend that I had not seen this behavior, though I was greatly minded to kick him.

"The Lumbanies pitched their tents some distance away from the walls, in the direction of the landward gate, and held high revel in the evening after I had served them out a tot of arrack apiece; but the Baders took their meat away, and could not be persuaded to pass the night on the hill. Murriana slept under one of the wing-walls of my little tent, and Barabbas and the khālāsi in the cooking-tent close by. The night passed quietly. I slept the deep and soundless sleep of the weary, but Barabbas, I suspect, had a drain at the arrack bottle, and the slave likewise (pious Mussulman though he was), for Barabbas was late with my tea, and the slave seemed more stupid than was his wont; but Murriana waked me as usual at four.

* The slave of Hoosein, a common Mussulman pre-
nomen.
† Made lawful by cutting their throat, and repeating
the words "Bismiilah el rahyman ul rahim" (In the
name of God the merciful and gracious).

"The Lumbanies, when I sent for one of them to carry a spare gun, were not to be found. Their camp was standing, their cooking-pots and scanty baggage were in their places, but not a man was to be seen. Murriana could not say what had become of them. They were all there when we had turned in, as merry as crickets, talking in their peculiar patois, and singing through their noses to the strumming of a sitar. Murriana said he thought he had heard some kind of a row in the night, but he evidently knew no more what had become of them than I.

"'Perhaps they wanted more drink, and ran down to the bazaar for it,' said I.

"'Perhaps,' replied he doubtfully, but he seemed thoughtful, and evidently did not agree with me.

"'Well, never mind,' said I; 'we mustn't lose our whole morning looking for those fellows. Pick up the guns, and come on.'

"So we started for the ravine where we had found the bison track, and as soon as day broke we were rewarded by the sight of a magnificent solitary bull, feeding on the young grass, not more than two hundred yards away from the edge of the jungle.

"'Come on, sahib,' said Murriana, 'we'll get round that hill, and into the jungle to the lee-side of him, and he'll feed right on to us.'

"'Good,' said I, and off we started. We got to the ravine in about ten minutes, without any trouble, and squatted behind the fallen trunk of a great tree. The path, beaten down through the long grass and marked by bison tracks without number, led past our hiding-place at a distance of about twenty yards, and the great beast was feeding quietly, drawing nearer to us as he fed. I felt rather like a murderer in my ambush; he looked such a grand harmless beast, that I thought it a real shame to kill him just for sport—not that it came into my head for a moment to let him off. It looked, nevertheless, as if I had been reckoning my chickens before they were hatched, for when he had grazed on to within one hundred and twenty yards of us, up went his nose into the air without a moment's warning, and instead of bearing down on us, he went off at a tangent in a smart canter to another ravine some five hundred yards away.

"My pity now quickly turned to rage. I drew a bead, as well as I could at that angle, behind his shoulder, and hit him, for he staggered but didn't stop, and soon reached the shelter of the friendly wood.

"'Ah!' said Murriana. 'It's that hill people, whose mothers and grandmothers are quite unfit to conduct girls' schools, who are themselves brothers-in-law of quantities of degraded people, whose aunts are never seen in decent society, who are, besides, the children of owls, whose fathers' mouths are full of the stock in trade of sweepers;' and so on, as you can guess for yourselves, while he fairly danced with rage, and shook his fist at some of our poor Lumbanies, who were coming gaily over the hill to windward, little recking of the evil which they had done.

"'Come on, Murriana,' said I, 'let's take up the tracks. Ah! I knew I had hit him; here's blood.'

"'Oh, those animals have any amount of blood,' replied he crossly. 'Ah! the Huzoor is right. 'Tis red blood—froth. His life will go! Come on, Ghulām Hoosein. Is your knife sharp?'

"'Yes,' replied the slave, grinning and feeling its edge with his thumb. 'Bismillah!'

"We followed the tracks easily through the jungle, the footmarks, large as they were, looking strangely small for so great a beast, with the toes pointed and in contact, like a deer's, and not spreading out like those of a domestic cow. Then we came to a bare, stony hill, where we lost them. The blood-marks had ceased for some little time before. Here the Lumbanies joined us, with a Bader who was said to be a famous tracker, and Murriana, though he eyed them askance, was too good a shikari to make any unnecessary noise.

"'He's gone over the hill, no doubt,' said I. 'Ask the Bader what's at the other side?' But that crafty woodsman pointing to a broken twig some six feet from the ground, in the direction of a little ravine to the right rear of the hill, and saying in

Canarese, 'The water is there, your wisdom,' trotted off confidently in that direction. Well, to make a long story short, we found the poor beast at bay, and I gave him the *coup de grâce*. Ghulām halalled him in the orthodox manner, and as the Lumbanies, being Hindoos, professed themselves unable to eat beef however savage, I told Ghulām to take as much as he wanted for himself and his brethren, and to bring home the head and marrow-bones for me—for if any of you have never eaten bisons' marrow-bones you have yet to learn to what a height of lusciousness marrow can ascend. I then continued my stalk, and shot three stag sambre and a jungle sheep, so that the village was amply supplied with meat for some days to come.

"When I got back to camp I found Barabbas sober, and breakfast ready, and after a good bathe in a beautiful little mountain stream, I had a quiet smoke, and a read, and then I think I went to sleep.

"Before dinner I had a long stroll over the hills, enjoying the cool air mightily. When I came back it was just dark, and I found Barabbas and Ghulām Hoosein hanging about the tent door, with some dusky figures in the background.

"'What does he want, Barabbas?' I asked.

"'He says the kiladar is not well in body, sar.'

"'Sorry to hear it. Tell him to stop making a beast of himself with opium and arrack.'

"'It is a true word, sar,' said Barabbas, grinning.

"'He has no appetite, Huzoor,' said the khālāsi, coming forward and salaaming. 'His health is very bad.'

"'That's likely enough. He has no appetite, that's the first symptom. Next, he'll see snakes. He'd better look out. But what is it to me whether that great pig has an appetite or not? Or to you, Barabbas?'

"'That time master giving him the bison's marrow-bones,' replied Barabbas in English, 'then he getting well soonly. He too much fonding for the marrowbones.'

"'Tell him to go and be —. He can have as much meat as he likes to take away; but I also "too much fonding for marrow-bones." Go, wild beast,' to the khālāsi, who was going to speak, 'if not, you shall eat blows;' and the slave of Hoosein went off, followed by two or three grumbling and disreputable-looking vagabonds, whom I took to be Mussulmans from the village.

After dinner I sat for a long while smoking in front of my tent. It was a beautiful starlit night and very still, and I confess that the place, with the ruins of the old fort, its crumbling bastions and fallen curtain, looked very lonely, so that I was not sorry when I saw Murriana coming round to talk to me.

"'Well, Murriana,' said I to him, 'we've come in for a good thing. There's lots of game here, and no mistake.'

"'Yes,' said he slowly, 'but the sahib will not stop here. The monsoon will soon be on, and the sahib must go to the Kooderee Mook in time. It is a better place than this.'

"'Why so?'

"'This place has a bad name,' whispered he, looking round with a sort of shudder.

"'Why?' I asked. 'By the way, why did those Lumbanies run away last night, and are they going to stop to-night?'

"'No,' replied he, 'they are all gone.'

"'But why?'

"'Shaitāns, maharaj. What can I tell?'

"'Shaitāns be blowed. Have you seen them, Murriana?'

"'No, maharaj, not here.'

"'Have you seen them anywhere else?'

"'The sahib must not talk so, it is not lucky; and the village people say that in this month, always, year by year, the shaitāns or bootahs [Canarese for wood-demons]—what can I tell?—come here to this fort.'

"'And what do they do?'

"'They fight, maharaj.'

"'Fight? All right. Let them fight; I have no objection. And that's why those fools of Lumbanies ran away. Most likely those blackguard Mussulmans have some games up here, and want to frighten the Hindoos away lest they should kill all the beasts at this season.'

"'They are a bad people, that Mussulman people.'

"'And that's why the Lumbanies ran away?'

"'For that reason.'

"'Did they see anything?'

"'Maharaj,' replied he solemnly, 'they heard something. The place is not a good place. It will be better to march to the Koo-deree Mook. The people there are Jains—very good people.'

"'Nonsense, I'm going to stop here. If you're afraid you'd better go after the Lumbanies.'

"'As the sahib pleases. I stop where the sahib stops.'

"I was rather cross at all this nonsense, and as I was sleepy to boot, I wished Murriana good-night and turned in. I have always been a sound sleeper, thank God, and am still, as some of you know, and this night, what with the cool breeze, which made the unaccustomed blanket pleasant, and the fatigue of my long stalk, I slept like the dead. About half past two or three o'clock, however, I was awakened by a hand placed on my breast, and by the voice of Murriana whispering in no dubious fright, 'Sahib, wake! Listen—listen!'

"I was drunk with sleep, and rolled over lazily. 'Oh, Murri-ana, it isn't time yet,' said I. 'Look,' turning to the tent-door, which hung open towards the south. 'See those stars; day won't break till they've set. What do you mean? Go and be banged!'

"'Sahib, sabib, wake, listen!' clutching me nervously. 'Listen to that!'

"I sat up and listened, very cross. The night was clear, a mellow, starlit night. I could see the tops of the trees showing up from the ravines and standing out of the white mists of the clouds below. It was very still, save for the monotonous, discordant chuck-chuck-chuck chul-la of a night-jar squatted on the little jungle path.

"'For goodness' sake, Murriana,' said I, 'let me go to sleep. I've heard that bird of Satan often enough. I wish you'd go and be hanged!'

"'Listen, listen,' said he.

"I listened intently, waked by his earnestness; and then, seemingly from the direction of a ruined outpost some distance away on the edge of the ghàt, I heard faint, thin cries of 'Hur, hur, Mahadeo! Boom! Boom!' mingled with sounds like the clashing of steel, and answering shouts of 'Deen! Deen!'*

"'Oh, it's only some of those accursed Mussulmans and Mahrattas fighting. Let them fight and be hanged to them; and let me go to sleep!'

"'No, sahib, no. There's no Mahratta logue here. Get up, in the name of God! See, see!' as the light from the tent-door was darkened by, as it seemed, a passing cloud, 'it's a sahib! What does he say?' And certainly it seemed to me (dazed as I was by my sudden awakening) that I heard a not unfamiliar voice saying faintly, 'Come, come quick!' So I got up, put on my slippers, picked up my gun and went forth. For a moment I stood awestruck by the beauty of the scene. The stars shone with the brightness almost of the moon, and by their light I could trace the far-away reflection from the sea. The forests and plains of Canara were dark as the grave, and the crumbling walls of the fort looked black and sinister. The shouts of 'Deen! Deen!' seemed now in the ascendant, and the Mahratta war-cry had died away; but I was startled by hearing faint cries like those you hear from the wounded or the dying, after the fight is over, from a battlefield far away.

"'Come on, Murriana,' said I, 'let's go and see what all this row is about.'

* "Religion! Religion!" the war-cry of Islam.

"'No, no, sahib,' cried he frantically. 'Come away, we have no business there. Look! there's the sahib again—he's beckoning to us;' and I looked, but though I could see nothing save a mist-wreath from the swampy ground between us and the near jungle, I fancied—it may have been fancy—that I heard the same voice crying, 'Come, come.' So I went on, following Murriana, though somewhat against my will, drawn as it were, in a manner which I did not quite understand then, nor indeed do I quite understand it now."

"Well?" cried his bearers excitedly.

"Well," replied the major, "that's all. We passed through a little strip of jungle about three hundred yards from the fort into a bit of open, and there Murriana said that his guide vanished. I never saw anything. I asked Murriana what *he* saw, and he said he saw a sahib.

"'What was he like?'

"'With respect, he was very like the Huzoor; about the same age and size.' If so, judging from my long experience of the looking-glass, he must have been a beauty!"

"Well, but—major—is that all?"

"Very nearly. I had fortunately grabbed my cheroot case in my flight, so I sat down, and after I had comforted Murriana, who was thoroughly frightened (and, mind you, I have often seen him face death, before and since, and never seen him cowed), I had a smoke and a long talk with him about Shaitāns, and such creatures; and then as the disturbance at the outpost had long since died away, and the false dawn had begun to glimmer, we went back to the camp."

"And was that all?" cried the disappointed chorus.

"Well, not quite. I thought I should like a cup of tea, and I sent Murriana to wake Barabbas, but he found him and the slave dead drunk, and when we entered the tent and struck a light, I found my little dog, a bull-terrier of which I was very fond, and which I kept chained to the leg of my cot of nights, to save him from prowling cheetahs, stone dead. When I went out, the night being chill after the plains and he a shivery creature, he had crept under the blanket on my bed, and had been there stabbed to the heart by some miscreant, possibly in mistake for me; anyhow, there were three distinct knife-cuts through blanket and mattress, one of which had gone through poor Toby."

"But who did it?"

"I don't know; possibly some of those blackguard Mussulmans, whose dignity I had wounded. Anyhow, as none of my people would stay, we marched next morning to Kooderee Mook, where we had good sport, undisturbed by man or devil."

Then arose a great strife and a clash of tongues.

"The thing is quite clear," said the doctor oracularly. "Here's a ghost with a motive at last. The spirit of your deceased uncle, major, came to warn you; and, in short, saved your life. By the way, did you find out anything touching his death?"

"No," replied the major doubtfully; "but I'll tell you a curious thing. Next day I got Murriana, though sorely against his will, to come with me to the spot where the shape had vanished. It was a beautiful little open glade, hedged round with thick jungle, and clear of all the outposts of the fort. Over this were scattered a few green mounds, and Murriana said that he thought it was an old burying-place of the Coorumbers, a wild, half-savage tribe, who wander in the jungles of Mysore and Coorg. It was on the edge of this glade, beneath a dooput tree, whose thick-woven leaves make twilight at midday, that he said the thing had vanished; and there we found a moss-grown stone, with what looked like a rude cross traced upon it and something like two Roman letters below, one of which might certainly have passed muster for a T."

"There! didn't I tell you so?" cried the doctor triumphantly. "T for Thornhill. Of course it was your grandfather, or whatever he was!"

"No," said the major quietly, "he was my maternal grandfather's cousin, and his name was Smith."

"Got you there," cried Gordon. "I should like to know how your Irish ingenuity will wriggle out of that, doctor!"

"I was about to add, when you interrupted me," said the major drily, "that it was the first letter of the two which looked like a T, and my relative's Christian name was Thomas."

"Then you believe it was his ghost?"

"I don't say that it was, and I don't say that it wasn't. I am content to say of many things, 'I don't know.' It's only you young fellows who are cock sure of everything."

The Recrudescence of Imray
Rudyard Kipling (1888)

Imray had achieved the impossible. Without warning, for no conceivable motive, in his youth and at the threshold of his career he had chosen to disappear from the world—which is to say, the little Indian station where he lived. Upon a day he was alive, well, happy, and in great evidence at his club, among the billiard-tables. Upon a morning he was not, and no manner of search could make sure where he might be. He had stepped out of his place; he had not appeared at his office at the proper time, and his dog-cart was not upon the public roads. For these reasons and because he was hampering in a microscopical degree the administration of the Indian Empire, the Indian Empire paused for one microscopical moment to make inquiry into the fate of Imray. Ponds were dragged, wells were plumbed, telegrams were dispatched down the lines of railways and to the nearest seaport town—1,200 miles away—but Imray was not at the end of the drag-ropes nor the telegrams. He was gone, and his place knew him no more. Then the work of the great Indian Empire swept forward, because it could not be delayed, and Imray, from being a man, became a mystery—such a thing as men talk over at their tables in the club for a month and then forget utterly. His guns, horses, and carts were sold to the highest bidder. His superior officer wrote an absurd letter to his mother, saying that Imray had unaccountably disappeared and his bungalow stood empty on the road.

After three or four months of the scorching hot weather
had gone by, my friend Strickland, of the police force, saw
fit to rent the bungalow from the native landlord. This was
before he was engaged to Miss Youghal—an affair which has
been described in another place—and while he was pursuing
his investigations into native life. His own life was sufficiently
peculiar, and men complained of his manners and customs.
There was always food in his house, but there were no regular times for meals. He eat, standing up and walking about,
whatever he might find on the sideboard, and this is not good
for the insides of human beings. His domestic equipment was
limited to six rifles, three shotguns, five saddles, and a collection of stiff-jointed masheer rods, bigger and stronger than
the largest salmon rods. These things occupied one half of his
bungalow, and the other half was given up to Strickland and his
dog Tietjens—an enormous Rampur slut, who sung when she
was ordered, and devoured daily the rations of two men. She
spoke to Strickland in a language of her own, and whenever,
in her walks abroad she saw things calculated to destroy the
peace of Her Majesty the Queen Empress, she returned to her
master and gave him information. Strickland would take steps
at once, and the end of his labors was trouble and fine and im-
prisonment for other people. The natives believed that Tietjens
was a familiar spirit, and treated her with the great reverence
that is born of hate and fear. One room in the bungalow was
set apart for her special use. She owned a bedstead, a blanket,
and a drinking-trough, and if any one came into Strickland's
room at night, her custom was to knock down the invader and
give tongue till some one came with a light. Strickland owes his
life to her. When he was on the frontier in search of the local
murderer who came in the grey dawn to send Strickland much
further than the Andaman Islands, Tietjens caught him as he
was crawling into Strickland's tent with a dagger between his
teeth, and after his record of iniquity was established in the
eyes of the law, he was hanged. From that date Tietjens wore a

collar of rough silver and employed a monogram on her night blanket, and the blanket was double-woven Kashmir cloth, for she was a delicate dog.

Under no circumstances would she be separated from Strickland, and when he was ill with fever she made great trouble for the doctors because she did not know how to help her master and would not allow another creature to attempt aid. Macarnaght, of the Indian Medical Service, beat her over the head with a gun, before she could understand that she must give room for those who could give quinine.

A short time after Strickland had taken Imray's bungalow, my business took me through that station, and naturally, the club quarters being full, I quartered myself upon Strickland. It was a desirable bungalow, eight-roomed, and heavily thatched against any chance of leakage from rain. Under the pitch of the roof ran a ceiling cloth, which looked just as nice as a whitewashed ceiling. The landlord had repainted it when Strickland took the bungalow, and unless you knew how Indian bungalows were built you would never have suspected that above the cloth lay the dark, three-cornered cavern of the roof, where the beams and the under side of the thatch harbored all manner of rats, bats, ants, and other things.

Tietjens met me in the veranda with a bay like the boom of the bells of St. Paul's, and put her paws on my shoulders and said she was glad to see me. Strickland had contrived to put together that sort of meal which he called lunch, and immediately after it was finished went out about his business. I was left alone with Tietjens and my own affairs. The heat of the summer had broken up and given place to the warm damp of the rains. There was no motion in the heated air, but the rain fell like bayonet rods on the earth, and flung up a blue mist where it splashed back again. The bamboos and the custard apples, the poinsettias and the mango-trees in the garden stood still while the warm water lashed through them, and the frogs began to sing among the aloe hedges. A little before the light failed,

and when the rain was at its worst, I sat in the back veranda
and heard the water roar from the eaves, and scratched myself
because I was covered with the thing they called prickly heat.
Tietjens came out with me and put her head in my lap, and was
very sorrowful, so I gave her biscuits when tea was ready, and
I took tea in the back veranda on account of the little coolness
I found there. The rooms of the house were dark behind me. I
could smell Strickland's saddlery and the oil on his guns, and I
did not the least desire to sit among these things. My own servant came to me in the twilight, the muslin of his clothes clinging tightly to his drenched body, and told me that a gentleman
had called and wished to see some one. Very much against my
will, and because of the darkness of the rooms, I went into the
naked drawing-room, telling my man to bring the lights. There
might or might not have been a caller in the room—it seems
to me that I saw a figure by one of the windows, but when
the lights came there was nothing save the spikes of the rain
without and the smell of the drinking earth in my nostrils. I
explained to my man that he was no wiser than he ought to be,
and went back to the veranda to talk to Tietjens. She had gone
out into the wet and I could hardly coax her back to me—even
with biscuits with sugar on top. Strickland rode back, dripping
wet, just before dinner, and the first thing he said was:

"Has any one called?"

I explained, with apologies, that my servant had called me
into the drawing-room on a false alarm; or that some loafer had
tried to call on Strickland, and, thinking better of it, fled after
giving his name. Strickland ordered dinner without comment,
and since it was a real dinner, with white tablecloth attached,
we sat down.

At nine o'clock Strickland wanted to go to bed, and I was
tired too. Tietjens, who had been lying underneath the table,
rose up and went into the least exposed veranda as soon as her
master moved to his own room, which was next to the stately
chamber set apart for Tietjens. If a mere wife had wished to

sleep out-of-doors in that pelting rain, it would not have mattered, but Tietjens was a dog, and therefore the better animal. I looked at Strickland, expecting to see him flog her with a whip. He smiled queerly, as a man would smile after telling some hideous domestic tragedy. "She has done this ever since I moved in here."

The dog was Strickland's dog, so I said nothing, but I felt all that Strickland felt in being made light of. Tietjens encamped outside my bedroom window, and storm after storm came up, thundered on the thatch, and died away. The lightning spattered the sky as a thrown egg spattered a barn door, but the light was pale blue, not yellow; and looking through my slit bamboo blinds, I could see the great dog standing, not sleeping, in the veranda, the hackles alift on her back, and her feet planted as tensely as the drawn wire rope of a suspension bridge. In the very short pauses of the thunder I tried to sleep, but it seemed that some one wanted me very badly. He, whoever he was, was trying to call me by name, but his voice was no more than a husky whisper. Then the thunder ceased and Tietjens went into the garden and howled at the low moon. Somebody tried to open my door, and walked about and through the house, and stood breathing heavily in the verandas, and just when I was falling asleep I fancied that I heard a wild hammering and clamoring above my head or on the door.

I ran into Strickland's room and asked him whether he was ill and had been calling for me. He was lying on the bed half-dressed, with a pipe in his mouth. "I thought you'd come," he said. "Have I been walking around the house at all?"

I explained that he had been in the dining-room and the smoking-room and two or three other places; and he laughed and told me to go back to bed. I went back to bed and slept till the morning, but in all my dreams I was sure I was doing some one an injustice in not attending to his wants. What those wants were I could not tell, but a fluttering, whispering, bolt-fumbling, luring, loitering some one was reproaching me

for my slackness, and through all the dreams I heard the howling of Tietjens in the garden and the thrashing of the rain.

I was in that house for two days, and Strickland went to his
office daily, leaving me alone for eight or ten hours a day, with
Tietjens for my only companion. As long as the full light lasted
I was comfortable, and so was Tietjens; but in the twilight she
and I moved into the back veranda and cuddled each other for
company. We were alone in the house, but for all that it was fully occupied by a tenant with whom I had no desire to interfere.
I never saw him, but I could see the curtains between the rooms
quivering where he had just passed through; I could hear the
chairs creaking as the bamboos sprung under a weight that had
just quitted them; and I could feel when I went to get a book
from the dining-room that somebody was waiting in the shadows of the front veranda till I should have gone away. Tietjens
made the twilight more interesting by glaring into the darkened rooms, with every hair erect, and following the motions
of something that I could not see. She never entered the rooms,
but her eyes moved, and that was quite sufficient. Only when
my servant came to trim the lamps and make all light and habitable, she would come in with me and spend her time sitting
on her haunches watching an invisible extra man as he moved
about behind my shoulder. Dogs are cheerful companions.

I explained to Strickland, gently as might be, that I would
go over to the club and find for myself quarters there. I admired
his hospitality, was pleased with his guns and rods, but I did
not much care for his house and its atmosphere. He heard me
out to the end, and then smiled very wearily, but without contempt, for he is a man who understands things. "Stay on," he
said, "and see what this thing means. All you have talked about
I have known since I took the bungalow. Stay on and wait.
Tietjens has left me. Are you going too?"

I had seen him through one little affair connected with an
idol that had brought me to the doors of a lunatic asylum, and
I had no desire to help him through further experiences. He

was a man to whom unpleasantnesses arrived as do dinners to ordinary people.

Therefore I explained more clearly than ever that I liked him immensely, and would be happy to see him in the daytime, but that I didn't care to sleep under his roof. This was after dinner, when Tietjens had gone out to lie in the veranda.

"'Pon my soul, I don't wonder," said Strickland, with his eyes on the ceiling-cloth. "Look at that!"

The tails of two snakes were hanging between the cloth and the cornice of the wall. They threw long shadows in the lamplight. "If you are afraid of snakes, of course"—said Strickland. "I hate and fear snakes, because if you look into the eyes of any snake you will see that it knows all and more of man's fall, and that it feels all the contempt that the devil felt when Adam was evicted from Eden. Besides which its bite is generally fatal, and it bursts up trouser legs."

"You ought to get your thatch over-hauled," I said. "Give me a masheer rod, and we'll poke 'em down."

"They'll hide among the roof beams," said Strickland. "I can't stand snakes overhead. I'm going up. If I shake 'em down, stand by with a cleaning-rod and break their backs."

I was not anxious to assist Strickland in his work, but I took the loading-rod and waited in the dining-room, while Strickland brought a gardener's ladder from the veranda and set it against the side of the room. The snake tails drew themselves up and disappeared. We could hear the dry rushing scuttle of long bodies running over the baggy cloth. Strickland took a lamp with him, while I tried to make clear the danger of hunting roof snakes between a ceiling cloth and a thatch, apart from the deterioration of property caused by ripping out ceiling-cloths.

"Nonsense!" said Strickland. "They're sure to hide near the walls by the cloth. The bricks are too cold for 'em, and the heat of the room is just what they like." He put his hands to the corner of the cloth and ripped the rotten stuff from the cornice. It gave great sound of tearing, and Strickland put his head through the opening into the dark of the angle of the roof beams. I set my teeth and lifted the loading-rod, for I had not the least knowledge of what might descend.

"H'm," said Strickland; and his voice rolled and rumbled in the roof. "There's room for another set of rooms up here, and, by Jove! some one is occupying 'em."

"Snakes?" I said down below.

"No. It's a buffalo. Hand me up the two first joints of a masheer rod, and I'll prod it. It's lying on the main beam."

I handed up the rod.

"What a nest for owls and serpents! No wonder the snakes live here," said Strickland, climbing further into the roof. I could see his elbow thrusting with the rod. "Come out of that, whoever you are! Look out! Heads below there! It's tottering."

I saw the ceiling-cloth nearly in the centre of the room bag with a shape that was pressing it downward and downward toward the lighted lamps on the table. I snatched a lamp out of danger and stood back. Then the cloth ripped out from the walls, tore, split, swayed, and shot down upon the table something that I dared not look at till Strickland had slid down the ladder and was standing by my side.

He did not say much, being a man of few words, but he picked up the loose end of the table-cloth and threw it over the thing on the table.

"It strikes me," said he, pulling down the lamp, "our friend Imray has come back. Oh! you would, would you?"

There was a movement under the cloth, and a little snake wriggled out, to be back-broken by the butt of the masheer rod. I was sufficiently sick to make no remarks worth recording.

Strickland meditated and helped himself to drinks liberally. The thing under the cloth made no more signs of life.

"Is it Imray?" I said.

Strickland turned back the cloth for a moment and looked. "It is Imray," he said, "and his throat is cut from ear to ear."

Then we spoke both together and to ourselves:

"That's why he whispered about the house."

Tietjens, in the garden, began to bay furiously. A little later her great nose heaved upon the dining-room door.

She sniffed and was still. The broken and tattered ceiling-cloth hung down almost to the level of the table, and there was hardly room to move away from the discovery.

Then Tietjens came in and sat down, her teeth bared and her forepaws planted. She looked at Strickland.

"It's bad business, old lady," said he. "Men don't go up into the roofs of their bungalows to die, and they don't fasten up the ceiling-cloth behind 'em. Let's think it out."

"Let's think it out somewhere else," I said.

"Excellent idea! Turn the lamps out. We'll get into my room."

I did not turn the lamps out. I went into Strickland's room first and allowed him to make the darkness. Then he followed me, and we lighted tobacco and thought. Strickland did the thinking. I smoked furiously because I was afraid.

"Imray is back," said Strickland. "The question is, who killed Imray? Don't talk—I have a notion of my own. When I took this bungalow I took most of Imray's servants. Imray was guile-less and inoffensive, wasn't he?"

I agreed, though the heap under the cloth looked neither one thing nor the other.

"If I call the servants they will stand fast in a crowd and lie like Aryans. What do you suggest?"

"Call 'em in one by one," I said.

"They'll run away and give the news to all their fellows," said Strickland.

"We must segregate 'em. Do you suppose your servant knows anything about it?"

"He may, for aught I know, but I don't think it's likely. He has only been here two or three days."

"What's your notion?" I asked.

"I can't quite tell. How the dickens did the man get the wrong side of the ceiling-cloth?"

There was a heavy coughing outside Strickland's bedroom door. This showed that Bahadur Khan, his body-servant, had waked from sleep and wished to put Strickland to bed.

"Come in," said Strickland. "It is a very warm night, isn't it?"

Bahadur Khan, a great, green-turbaned, six-foot Mohammedan, said that it was a very warm night, but that there was more rain pending, which, by his honor's favor, would bring relief to the country.

"It will be so, if God pleases," said Strickland, tugging off his hoots. "It is in my mind, Bahadur Khan, that I have worked thee remorselessly for many days—ever since that time when thou first came into my service. What time was that?"

"Has the heaven-born forgotten? It was when Imray Sahib went secretly to Europe without warning given, and I even I— came into the honored service of the protector of the poor."

"And Imray Sahib went to Europe?"

"It is so said among the servants."

"And thou wilt take service with him when he returns?"

"Assuredly, sahib. He was a good master and cherished his dependents."

"That is true. I am very tired, but I can go buck-shooting to-morrow. Give me the little rifle that I use for black buck; it is in the case yonder."

The man stooped over the case, handed barrels, stock, and fore-end to Strickland, who fitted them together. Yawning dolefully, then he reached down to the gun-case, took a solid drawn cartridge, and slipped it into the breech of the .360 express.

"And Imray Sahib has gone to Europe secretly? That is very strange, Bahadur Khan, is it not?"

"What do I know of the ways of the white man, heaven-born?"

"Very little, truly. But thou shalt know more. It has reached me that Imray Sahib has returned from his so long journeyings, and that even now he lies in the next room, waiting his servant."

"Sahib!"

The lamp-light slid along the barrels of the rifle as they leveled themselves against Bahadur Khan's broad breast.

"Go then and look!" said Strickland. "Take a lamp. Thy master is tired, and he waits. Go!"

The man picked up a lamp and went into the dining-room, Strickland following, and almost pushing him with the muzzle of the rifle. He looked for a moment at the black depths behind the ceiling-cloth, at the carcass of the mangled snake under foot, and last, a grey glaze setting on his face, at the thing under the table-cloth.

"Hast thou seen?" said Strickland, after a pause.

"I have seen. I am clay in the white man's hands. What does the presence do?"

"Hang thee within a month! What else?"

"For killing him? Nay, sahib, consider. Walking among us, his servants, he cast his eyes upon my child, who was four years old. Him he bewitched, and in ten days he died of the fever. My child!"

"What said Imray Sahib?"

"He said he was a handsome child, and patted him on the head; wherefore my child died. Wherefore I killed Imray Sahib in the twilight, when he came back from office and was sleeping. The heaven-born knows all things. I am the servant of the heaven-born."

Strickland looked at me above the rifle, and said, in the vernacular: "Thou art witness to this saying. He has killed."

Bahadur Khan stood ashen grey in the light of the one lamp. The need for justification came upon him very swiftly.

"I am trapped," he said, "but the offence was that man's. He cast an evil eye upon my child, and I killed and hid him. Only such as are served by devils," he glared at Tietjens, crouched stolidly before him, "only such could know what I did."

"It was clever. But thou shouldst have lashed him to the beam with a rope. Now, thou thyself wilt hang by a rope. Orderly!"

A drowsy policeman answered Strickland's call. He was followed by another, and Tietjens sat still.

"Take him to the station," said Strickland. "There is a case toward."

"Do I hang, then?" said Bahadur Khan, making no attempt to escape and keeping his eyes on the ground.

"If the sun shines, or the water runs, thou wilt hang," said Strickland. Bahadur Khan stepped back one pace, quivered, and stood still. The two policemen waited further orders.

"Go!" said Strickland.

"Nay; but I go very swiftly," said Bahadur Khan. "Look! I am even now a dead man."

He lifted his foot, and to the little toe there clung the head of the half-killed snake, firm fixed in the agony of death.

"I come of land-holding stock," said Bahadur Khan, rocking where he stood. "It were a disgrace for me to go to the public scaffold, therefore I take this way. Be it remembered that the sahib's shirts are correctly enumerated, and that there is an extra piece of soap in his washbasin. My child was bewitched, and I slew the wizard. Why should you seek to slay me? My honor is saved, and—and—I die."

At the end of an hour he died as they die who are bitten by the little kariat, and the policemen bore him and the thing under the table-cloth to their appointed places. They were needed to make clear the disappearance of Imray.

"This," said Strickland, very calmly, as he climbed into bed, "is called the nineteenth century. Did you hear what that man said?"

"I heard," I answered. "Imray made a mistake."

"Simply and solely through not knowing the nature and coincidence of a little seasonal fever. Bahadur Khan has been with him for four years."

I shuddered. My own servant had been with me for exactly that length of time. When I went over to my own room I found him waiting, impassive as the copper head on a penny, to pull off my boots.

"What has befallen Bahadur Khan?" said I.

"He was bitten by a snake and died; the rest the sahib knows," was the answer.

"And how much of the matter hast thou known?"

"As much as might be gathered from one coming in the twilight to seek satisfaction. Gently, sahib. Let me pull off those boots."

I had just settled to the sleep of exhaustion when I heard Strickland shouting from his side of the house:

"Tietjens has come back to her room!"

And so she had. The great deer-hound was couched on her own bedstead, on her own blanket, and in the next room the idle, empty ceiling-cloth wagged light-heartedly as it flailed on the table.

Some Australian Ghost Stories
T. J. B. (1890)

"So, you don't believe in ghosts? Well, you're only a 'new chum' and don't know any better. Just wait till I fill my pipe, and I'll tell you how a ghost got a man hanged up Bathurst way."

The speaker was Cockney Bill, an old shepherd at Kulnoni, on the Murray River, where they were shearing sheep, and we had all gathered round the big fireplace in the "men's hut" after our day's work was ended.

"You see," continued Bill, "a good many years ago there was a man called Fisher used to live near Maitland, a sort of 'cockatoo squatter' (small farmer), who was in the habit of going down to Sydney to sell stock for himself and his neighbors. Well, one time he gave out that he was intending to buy a lot of sheep up in the Darling Downs, and that he expected to make a large profit by selling them at Sydney, and so he went round and borrowed all the money he could, promising to pay heavy interest. Then he bid his neighbors good-by, saying he was just going to start, and that was the last seen or heard of him for some time.

"Weeks and months passed along but there was no news of Fisher, and at last the general opinion was that he had bolted with the cash that he borrowed, for by this time it had been discovered that he was deeply in debt at the time of his departure. People were beginning to forget him altogether, when one Saturday evening old Jimmy Ryan was going home from Maitland,

41

and just as he got to Fisher's place what should he see but the missing man seated on top of the three-rail fence.

"'Hello, Fisher,' says Jimmy. 'When did you get back?' But he got no answer, and Fisher walked away down the paddock.

"'Bad cess to ye,' says Jimmy, 'you're not very civil,' and when he got home he told his wife what he'd seen, and so the news was spread about that Fisher had come back.

"However, the house was still shut up, and as Fisher never called round to pay his debts, some people hinted that Jimmy Ryan had been drunk and only fancied that he had seen the missing man.

"After a little while some other men told precisely the same story about the strange appearance of the man on the fence, and so at last it came to Captain Batty's ears; and so the Captain took some of his mounted police and black tracers to the place where Fisher had been seen.

"It was a post and rail fence, and one of the rails was seen to have been broken at that self-same spot, so Cockatoo Tommy began hunting round, and in a few minutes he picked up a piece of a rail that was all stained at the end. The black fellow scraped and tasted it; then says he, 'Blood belonging to white fellow'; and he and his mates they just nosed round like a pack of hounds, and at last one of them sings out, *'White fellow been tumbled down* [killed] *and other white fellow been pull him away like it here.'* Then the police followed the trackers way down the paddock, just in the direction that the mysterious man had been seen to take, till they came to a water-hole, and then Tommy stooped down, and scooped up in his hand some scum that was floating on top of the water; then he smelled and tasted it. *'Fat belonging to white fellow,'* cried he, *'white fellow sit down like it here.'*

"So they got ropes, and the blacks just dived down, and in a few minutes they dragged out the body of Fisher with the head all smashed in.

"Of course there was an inquest, and strong presumptive evidence was brought forward against a neighbor of the dead man, and he was fully committed to jail for murder. In due time this man was tried at Bathurst, convicted, and hanged, and before the execution he confessed that he was guilty of the crime laid to his charge. It appeared that he had some money dealings with Fisher, and had gone to his place to ask for a settlement. He had found his debtor sitting on the fence, and demanded the money due him. Fisher refusing to pay, some angry words ensued, and in the struggle which followed the enraged creditor took up the piece of broken rail and struck Fisher over the head with it. To his horror, he found that Fisher was killed, and then he dragged the body to the pond where it was found.

"Now every one knows that this is all true, so you see, young fellow, there *are* ghosts," concluded Bill, triumphantly.

"Yes," exclaimed Red Jack, "sure we old hands all remember when the ghost of the Headless Shepherd kicked up such a row on King's Plains, and the people of Bathurst got the priest to go out after it with bell, book, and candle. Mickey Delany told me all about seeing it himself. You see, every night just after sundown there used to be fires lit up all over King's Plains, and kept burning all night. At first people took no great notice of them, for there were plenty of men traveling about with stock, but after a while nobody liked to pass that way after dark. Well, one night Mickey had been in town, and was going home with some clothes he'd been buying and a couple of bottles of rum, when he saw these fires springing up in every direction.

"'Bedad,' says he, 'I'll go over and see them chaps, and have a smoke and a dhrink.'

"So away he went, and as he got near one of the fires, he saw some one chucking wood on; but when he came right up to it there was nobody to be seen.

"'Well,' says Mickey, 'it's not very civil laving your fire when you see a gintleman coming, but I'm in no hurry; I'll wait a bit.'

"So with that he lit his pipe, and after a while he took a good sup out of one of his bottles. The fire began to burn low, and Mickey saw that another fire not far off was blazing up, so he took a drink and started for it. But before he reached it, he saw some one throwing wood on the one he had just left and he got mad and bawled out, 'Just wait a bit till I get hold of yez, and I'll tache you to play tricks on me!'

"With that he made a run for the fire, and all of a sudden the figure of a man with its head under its arm popped up and knocked Mickey senseless, and there he lay all night; but when he came to himself next morning his head was still sore and one of his bottles quite empty."

"Those are old yarns," exclaimed Black Tom, a stockman, "but I'll tell you what happened to me only last year. Jack Evans and I had to take down a mob of cattle from Parson Thorn's, on the Lachlan, and we came along all right till we crossed the Murrumbidger at Lang's Station. We left there just after dinner, and drove out over the Old Man Plain, where the feed was good, and the stock fed quietly along until we came to a water hole, where we camped at sun down, and rounded up the cattle by the skirt of the timber.

"We finished our supper, and I took the first watch, while Jack turned in. The Southern Cross was shining brightly, and as everything was still I just sat by the fire and smoked, and drank tea, while my horse cropped the sweet grass close by. The moon rose at last; she was nearly full, and gave a clear light, so the cattle began to draw out on the plain. I looked at my watch and found it was getting near twelve, so I jumped on my horse and started to head them back, leaving Jack asleep by the fire.

"Well, boys, I was close to the head of the mob, when suddenly they came rushing back like everything, and a man riding a bald-faced horse came scooting along past me and went on towards the camp. I thought of course it was Jack, who had woke up and come to help me; but when I got back to the fire, there was Jack, rolled up in his 'possum rug, and snoring away like a good one.

"I gave him a dig in the ribs, and asked why he went and lay down again; but Jack swore he had never been up at all, and showed me his saddle under his head, and his horse hobbled near at hand. Then I told him it was twelve o'clock and his watch; and added that I had just come from heading the cattle, but I was sure that he knew all about it, for I had particularly noticed the bald-faced horse he'd been riding.

"With that up jumped Jack in a hurry, and says, 'Tom, let's drive off the cattle as quick as we can, for something bad is going to happen to us. You've seen the ghost of the stockman that rides the bald-faced cob, and that's sure bad luck.'

"We drove on to the Edwards, and crossed it and the Murray all right, but when we got to the Campaspe it was bank and bank, and poor Jack Evans was drowned in getting the cattle over, though he was a Sydney native and could swim like a duck or a black fellow."

"Well," said the cook, "I've just come down from the Reedy Lake station, and there's a place up there where a ghost lives and no mistake. Though no one has ever seen it, plenty have heard it.

"They say that some years ago the man that owned the station determined to send a flock of sheep out on to the Maallee scrub, for the feed was getting bare near the river; so he had a hut built, and the dray went out with water and rations. The overseer left a hutkeeper at the cabin, and then met the shepherd and told him where to drive to.

"In three days the hut-keeper came into the head station, and reported that neither shepherd nor sheep had ever come to the camp, though he said he could hear a man coöeeing every evening.

"The overseers and stock men went out, and soon found the sheep, for of course they made for the river; but the shepherd

was never found from that day to this. It happened to have been
a very cloudy day, and probably the man had got twisted round
and wandered off far in the dense scrub; nobody can tell how it
was, but this is sure, no one will stop at that sheep camp. They
call it 'the coöee hut,' for every night the old shepherd is to be
heard coöeeing, and it is believed that if any one is fool enough
to go out to look for him, the searcher will get lost himself, and
perish in the bush."

"Come, boys, that's enough for tonight; it is time to turn
in and douse the light," said one of the shearers with a yawn;
and soon nothing was heard outside but the mournful cry of the
"more-pork" in the bend of the river, or the howl of the dingoes
far away in the bush.

The Mark of the Beast
Rudyard Kipling (1890)

Your Gods and my Gods—do you or I know which
are the stronger?

Native Proverb.

East of Suez, some hold, the direct control of Providence ceases;
Man being there handed over to the power of the Gods and
Devils of Asia, and the Church of England Providence only
exercising an occasional and modified supervision in the case
of Englishmen.

This theory accounts for some of the more unnecessary horrors of life in India: it may be stretched to explain my story.

My friend Strickland of the Police, who knows as much of
natives of India as is good for any man, can bear witness to the
facts of the case. Dumoise, our doctor, also saw what Strickland
and I saw. The inference which he drew from the evidence was
entirely incorrect. He is dead now; he died, in a rather curious
manner, which has been elsewhere described.

When Fleete came to India he owned a little money and
some land in the Himalayas, near a place called Dharmsala.
Both properties had been left him by an uncle, and he came out
to finance them. He was a big, heavy, genial, and inoffensive
man. His knowledge of natives was, of course, limited, and he
complained of the difficulties of the language.

He rode in from his place in the hills to spend New Year in the station, and he stayed with Strickland. On New Year's Eve there was a big dinner at the club, and the night was excusably wet. When men foregather from the uttermost ends of the Empire, they have a right to be riotous. The Frontier had sent down a contingent o' Catch-'em-Alive-O's who had not seen twenty white faces for a year, and were used to ride fifteen miles to dinner at the next Fort at the risk of a Khyberee bullet where their drinks should lie. They profited by their new security, for they tried to play pool with a curled-up hedgehog found in the garden, and one of them carried the marker round the room in his teeth. Half a dozen planters had come in from the south and were talking 'horse' to the Biggest Liar in Asia, who was trying to cap all their stories at once. Everybody was there, and there was a general closing up of ranks and taking stock of our losses in dead or disabled that had fallen during the past year. It was a very wet night, and I remember that we sang 'Auld Lang Syne' with our feet in the Polo Championship Cup, and our heads among the stars, and swore that we were all dear friends. Then some of us went away and annexed Burma, and some tried to open up the Soudan and were opened up by Fuzzies in that cruel scrub outside Suakim, and some found stars and medals, and some were married, which was bad, and some did other things which were worse, and the others of us stayed in our chains and strove to make money on insufficient experiences.

Fleete began the night with sherry and bitters, drank champagne steadily up to dessert, then raw, rasping Capri with all the strength of whisky, took Benedictine with his coffee, four or five whiskies and sodas to improve his pool strokes, beer and bones at half-past two, winding up with old brandy. Consequently, when he came out, at half-past three in the morning, into fourteen degrees of frost, he was very angry with his horse for coughing, and tried to leapfrog into the saddle. The horse broke away and went to his stables; so Strickland and I formed a Guard of Dishonour to take Fleete home.

Our road lay through the bazaar, close to a little temple of Hanuman, the Monkey-god, who is a leading divinity worthy of respect. All gods have good points, just as have all priests. Personally, I attach much importance to Hanuman, and am kind to his people—the great gray apes of the hills. One never knows when one may want a friend.

There was a light in the temple, and as we passed, we could hear voices of men chanting hymns. In a native temple, the priests rise at all hours of the night to do honour to their god. Before we could stop him, Fleete dashed up the steps, patted two priests on the back, and was gravely grinding the ashes of his cigar-butt into the forehead of the red stone image of Hanuman. Strickland tried to drag him out, but he sat down and said solemnly:

"Shee that? Mark of the B-beasht! *I* made it. Ishn't it fine?"

In half a minute the temple was alive and noisy, and Strickland, who knew what came of polluting gods, said that things might occur. He, by virtue of his official position, long residence in the country, and weakness for going among the natives, was known to the priests and he felt unhappy. Fleete sat on the ground and refused to move. He said that 'good old Hanuman' made a very soft pillow.

Then, without any warning, a Silver Man came out of a recess behind the image of the god. He was perfectly naked in that bitter, bitter cold, and his body shone like frosted silver, for he was what the Bible calls 'a leper as white as snow.' Also he had no face, because he was a leper of some years' standing and his disease was heavy upon him. We two stooped to haul Fleete up, and the temple was filling and filling with folk who seemed to spring from the earth, when the Silver Man ran in under our arms, making a noise exactly like the mewing of an otter, caught Fleete round the body and dropped his head on Fleete's breast before we could wrench him away. Then he retired to a corner and sat mewing while the crowd blocked all the doors.

The priests were very angry until the Silver Man touched Fleete. That nuzzling seemed to sober them.

At the end of a few minutes' silence one of the priests came to Strickland and said, in perfect English, "Take your friend away. He has done with Hanuman, but Hanuman has not done with him." The crowd gave room and we carried Fleete into the road.

Strickland was very angry. He said that we might all three have been knifed, and that Fleete should thank his stars that he had escaped without injury.

Fleete thanked no one. He said that he wanted to go to bed. He was gorgeously drunk.

We moved on, Strickland silent and wrathful, until Fleete was taken with violent shivering fits and sweating. He said that the smells of the bazaar were overpowering, and he wondered why slaughter-houses were permitted so near English residences. "Can't you smell the blood?" said Fleete.

We put him to bed at last, just as the dawn was breaking, and Strickland invited me to have another whisky and soda. While we were drinking he talked of the trouble in the temple, and admitted that it baffled him completely. Strickland hates being mystified by natives, because his business in life is to overmatch them with their own weapons. He has not yet succeeded in doing this, but in fifteen or twenty years he will have made some small progress.

"They should have mauled us," he said, "instead of mewing at us. I wonder what they meant. I don't like it one little bit."

I said that the Managing Committee of the temple would in all probability bring a criminal action against us for insulting their religion. There was a section of the Indian Penal Code which exactly met Fleete's offence. Strickland said he only hoped and prayed that they would do this. Before I left I looked into Fleete's room, and saw him lying on his right side, scratching his left breast. Then I went to bed cold, depressed, and unhappy, at seven o'clock in the morning.

At one o'clock I rode over to Strickland's house to inquire after Fleete's head. I imagined that it would be a sore one. Fleete was breakfasting and seemed unwell. His temper was gone, for he was abusing the cook for not supplying him with an under-done chop. A man who can eat raw meat after a wet night is a curiosity. I told Fleete this and he laughed.

"You breed queer mosquitoes in these parts," he said. "I've been bitten to pieces, but only in one place."

"Let's have a look at the bite," said Strickland. "It may have gone down since this morning."

While the chops were being cooked, Fleete opened his shirt and showed us, just over his left breast, a mark, the perfect double of the black rosettes—the five or six irregular blotches arranged in a circle—on a leopard's hide. Strickland looked and said, "It was only pink this morning. It's grown black now."

Fleete ran to a glass.

"By Jove!" he said, "this is nasty. What is it?"

We could not answer. Here the chops came in, all red and juicy, and Fleete bolted three in a most offensive manner. He ate on his right grinders only, and threw his head over his right shoulder as he snapped the meat. When he had finished, it struck him that he had been behaving strangely, for he said apologetically, "I don't think I ever felt so hungry in my life. I've bolted like an ostrich."

After breakfast Strickland said to me, "Don't go. Stay here, and stay for the night."

Seeing that my house was not three miles from Strickland's, this request was absurd. But Strickland insisted, and was go-ing to say something when Fleete interrupted by declaring in a shamefaced way that he felt hungry again. Strickland sent a man to my house to fetch over my bedding and a horse, and we three went down to Strickland's stables to pass the hours until it was time to go out for a ride. The man who has a weakness for horses never wearies of inspecting them; and when two men are killing time in this way they gather knowledge and lies the one from the other.

There were five horses in the stables, and I shall never forget the scene as we tried to look them over. They seemed to have gone mad. They reared and screamed and nearly tore up their pickets; they sweated and shivered and lathered and were distraught with fear. Strickland's horses used to know him as well as his dogs; which made the matter more curious. We left the stable for fear of the brutes throwing themselves in their panic. Then Strickland turned back and called me. The horses were still frightened, but they let us 'gentle' and make much of them, and put their heads in our bosoms.

"They aren't afraid of *us*," said Strickland. "D'you know, I'd give three months' pay if Outrage here could talk."

But Outrage was dumb, and could only cuddle up to his master and blow out his nostrils, as is the custom of horses when they wish to explain things but can't. Fleete came up when we were in the stalls, and as soon as the horses saw him, their fright broke out afresh. It was all that we could do to escape from the place unkicked. Strickland said, "They don't seem to love you, Fleete."

"Nonsense," said Fleete; "my mare will follow me like a dog." He went to her; she was in a loose-box; but as he slipped the bars she plunged, knocked him down, and broke away into the garden. I laughed, but Strickland was not amused. He took his moustache in both fists and pulled at it till it nearly came out. Fleete, instead of going off to chase his property, yawned, saying that he felt sleepy. He went to the house to lie down, which was a foolish way of spending New Year's Day.

Strickland sat with me in the stables and asked if I had noticed anything peculiar in Fleete's manner. I said that he ate his food like a beast; but that this might have been the result of living alone in the hills out of the reach of society as refined and elevating as ours for instance. Strickland was not amused. I do not think that he listened to me, for his next sentence referred to the mark on Fleete's breast, and I said that it might have been caused by blister-flies, or that it was possibly a birthmark newly born and now visible for the first time. We both agreed that it was unpleasant to look at, and Strickland found occasion to say that I was a fool.

"I can't tell you what I think now," said he, "because you would call me a madman; but you must stay with me for the next few days, if you can. I want you to watch Fleete, but don't tell me what you think till I have made up my mind."

"But I am dining out to-night," I said.

"So am I," said Strickland, "and so is Fleete. At least if he doesn't change his mind."

We walked about the garden smoking, but saying nothing—because we were friends, and talking spoils good tobacco—till our pipes were out. Then we went to wake up Fleete. He was wide awake and fidgeting about his room.

"I say, I want some more chops," he said. "Can I get them?"

We laughed and said, "Go and change. The ponies will be round in a minute."

"All right," said Fleete. "I'll go when I get the chops—underdone ones, mind."

He seemed to be quite in earnest. It was four o'clock, and we had had breakfast at one; still, for a long time, he demanded those underdone chops. Then he changed into riding clothes and went out into the verandah. His pony—the mare had not been caught—would not let him come near. All three horses were unmanageable—mad with fear—and finally Fleete said that he would stay at home and get something to eat. Strickland and I rode out wondering. As we passed the temple of Hanuman, the Silver Man came out and mewed at us.

"He is not one of the regular priests of the temple," said Strickland. "I think I should peculiarly like to lay my hands on him."

There was no spring in our gallop on the racecourse that evening. The horses were stale, and moved as though they had been ridden out.

"The fright after breakfast has been too much for them," said Strickland.

That was the only remark he made through the remainder of the ride. Once or twice I think he swore to himself; but that did not count.

We came back in the dark at seven o'clock, and saw that there were no lights in the bungalow. "Careless ruffians my servants are!" said Strickland.

My horse reared at something on the carriage drive, and Fleete stood up under its nose.

"What are you doing, grovelling about the garden?" said Strickland.

But both horses bolted and nearly threw us. We dismounted by the stables and returned to Fleete, who was on his hands and knees under the orange-bushes.

"What the devil's wrong with you?" said Strickland.

"Nothing, nothing in the world," said Fleete, speaking very quickly and thickly. "I've been gardening—botanising you know. The smell of the earth is delightful. I think I'm going for a walk—a long walk—all night."

Then I saw that there was something excessively out of order somewhere, and I said to Strickland, "I am not dining out."

"Bless you!" said Strickland. "Here, Fleete, get up. You'll catch fever there. Come in to dinner and let's have the lamps lit. We'll all dine at home."

Fleete stood up unwillingly, and said, "No lamps—no lamps. It's much nicer here. Let's dine outside and have some more chops—lots of 'em and underdone—bloody ones with gristle."

Now a December evening in Northern India is bitterly cold, and Fleete's suggestion was that of a maniac.

"Come in," said Strickland sternly. "Come in at once."

Fleete came, and when the lamps were brought, we saw that he was literally plastered with dirt from head to foot. He must have been rolling in the garden. He shrank from the light and went to his room. His eyes were horrible to look at. There was a green light behind them, not in them, if you understand, and the man's lower lip hung down.

Strickland said, "There is going to be trouble—big trouble—to-night. Don't you change your riding-things."

We waited and waited for Fleete's reappearance, and ordered dinner in the meantime. We could hear him moving about his own room, but there was no light there. Presently from the room came the long-drawn howl of a wolf.

People write and talk lightly of blood running cold and hair standing up and things of that kind. Both sensations are too horrible to be trifled with. My heart stopped as though a knife had been driven through it, and Strickland turned as white as the tablecloth.

The howl was repeated, and was answered by another howl far across the fields.

That set the gilded roof on the horror. Strickland dashed into Fleete's room. I followed, and we saw Fleete getting out of the window. He made beast-noises in the back of his throat. He could not answer us when we shouted at him. He spat.

I don't quite remember what followed, but I think that Strickland must have stunned him with the long boot-jack or else I should never have been able to sit on his chest. Fleete could not speak, he could only snarl, and his snarls were those of a wolf, not of a man. The human spirit must have been giving way all day and have died out with the twilight. We were dealing with a beast that had once been Fleete.

The affair was beyond any human and rational experience. I tried to say "Hydrophobia," but the word wouldn't come, because I knew that I was lying.

We bound this beast with leather thongs of the punkah-rope, and tied its thumbs and big toes together, and gagged it with a shoe-horn, which makes a very efficient gag if you know how to arrange it. Then we carried it into the dining-room, and sent a man to Dumoise, the doctor, telling him to come over at once. After we had despatched the messenger and were drawing breath, Strickland said, "It's no good. This isn't any doctor's work." I, also, knew that he spoke the truth.

The beast's head was free, and it threw it about from side to side. Any one entering the room would have believed that we were curing a wolf's pelt. That was the most loathsome accessory of all.

Strickland sat with his chin in the heel of his fist, watching the beast as it wriggled on the ground, but saying nothing. The shirt had been torn open in the scuffle and showed the black rosette mark on the left breast. It stood out like a blister.

In the silence of the watching we heard something without mewing like a she-otter. We both rose to our feet, and, I answer for myself, not Strickland, felt sick—actually and physically sick. We told each other, as did the men in *Pinafore,* that it was the cat.

Dumoise arrived, and I never saw a little man so unprofessionally shocked. He said that it was a heart-rending case of hydrophobia, and that nothing could be done. At least any palliative measures would only prolong the agony. The beast was foaming at the mouth. Fleete, as we told Dumoise, had been bitten by dogs once or twice. Any man who keeps half a dozen terriers must expect a nip now and again. Dumoise could offer no help. He could only certify that Fleete was dying of hydrophobia. The beast was then howling, for it had managed to spit out the shoe-horn. Dumoise said that he would be ready to certify to the cause of death, and that the end was certain. He was a good little man, and he offered to remain with us; but Strickland refused the kindness. He did not wish to poison Dumoise's New Year. He would only ask him not to give the real cause of Fleete's death to the public.

So Dumoise left, deeply agitated; and as soon as the noise of the cart-wheels had died away, Strickland told me, in a whisper, his suspicions. They were so wildly improbable that he dared not say them out aloud; and I, who entertained all Strickland's beliefs, was so ashamed of owning to them that I pretended to disbelieve.

"Even if the Silver Man had bewitched Fleete for polluting the image of Hanuman, the punishment could not have fallen so quickly."

As I was whispering this the cry outside the house rose again, and the beast fell into a fresh paroxysm of struggling till we were afraid that the thongs that held it would give way.

"Watch!" said Strickland. "If this happens six times I shall take the law into my own hands. I order you to help me."

He went into his room and came out in a few minutes with the barrels of an old shot-gun, a piece of fishing-line, some thick cord, and his heavy wooden bedstead. I reported that the convulsions had followed the cry by two seconds in each case, and the beast seemed perceptibly weaker.

Strickland muttered, "But he can't take away the life! He can't take away the life!"

I said, though I knew that I was arguing against myself, "It may be a cat. It must be a cat. If the Silver Man is responsible, why does he dare to come here?"

Strickland arranged the wood on the hearth, put the gun-barrels into the glow of the fire, spread the twine on the table and broke a walking stick in two. There was one yard of fishing line, gut, lapped with wire, such as is used for *mahseer*-fishing, and he tied the two ends together in a loop.

Then he said, "How can we catch him? He must be taken alive and unhurt."

I said that we must trust in Providence, and go out softly with polo-sticks into the shrubbery at the front of the house. The man or animal that made the cry was evidently moving round the house as regularly as a night-watchman. We could wait in the bushes till he came by and knock him over.

Strickland accepted this suggestion, and we slipped out from a bath-room window into the front verandah and then across the carriage drive into the bushes.

In the moonlight we could see the leper coming round the corner of the house. He was perfectly naked, and from time to

time he mewed and stopped to dance with his shadow. It was
an unattractive sight, and thinking of poor Fleete, brought to
such degradation by so foul a creature, I put away all my doubts
and resolved to help Strickland from the heated gun-barrels to
the loop of twine—from the loins to the head and back again—
with all tortures that might be needful.

The leper halted in the front porch for a moment and we
jumped out on him with the sticks. He was wonderfully strong,
and we were afraid that he might escape or be fatally injured
before we caught him. We had an idea that lepers were frail
creatures, but this proved to be incorrect. Strickland knocked
his legs from under him and I put my foot on his neck. He
mewed hideously, and even through my riding-boots I could
feel that his flesh was not the flesh of a clean man.

He struck at us with his hand and feet-stumps. We looped the
lash of a dog-whip round him, under the armpits, and dragged
him backwards into the hall and so into the dining-room where
the beast lay. There we tied him with trunk-straps. He made no
attempt to escape, but mewed.

When we confronted him with the beast the scene was beyond description. The beast doubled backwards into a bow as
though he had been poisoned with strychnine, and moaned in
the most pitiable fashion. Several other things happened also,
but they cannot be put down here.

"I think I was right," said Strickland. "Now we will ask him
to cure this case."

But the leper only mewed. Strickland wrapped a towel round
his hand and took the gun-barrels out of the fire. I put the half
of the broken walking stick through the loop of fishing-line
and buckled the leper comfortably to Strickland's bedstead. I
understood then how men and women and little children can
endure to see a witch burnt alive; for the beast was moaning on
the floor, and though the Silver Man had no face, you could see
horrible feelings passing through the slab that took its place,

exactly as waves of heat play across red-hot iron—gun-barrels for instance.

Strickland shaded his eyes with his hands for a moment and we got to work. This part is not to be printed.

The dawn was beginning to break when the leper spoke. His mewings had not been satisfactory up to that point. The beast had fainted from exhaustion and the house was very still. We unstrapped the leper and told him to take away the evil spirit. He crawled to the beast and laid his hand upon the left breast. That was all. Then he fell face down and whined, drawing in his breath as he did so.

We watched the face of the beast, and saw the soul of Fleete coming back into the eyes. Then a sweat broke out on the forehead and the eyes—they were human eyes—closed. We waited for an hour but Fleete still slept. We carried him to his room and bade the leper go, giving him the bedstead, and the sheet on the bedstead to cover his nakedness, the gloves and the towels with which we had touched him, and the whip that had been hooked round his body. He put the sheet about him and went out into the early morning without speaking or mewing.

Strickland wiped his face and sat down. A night-gong, far away in the city, made seven o'clock.

"Exactly four-and-twenty hours!" said Strickland. "And I've done enough to ensure my dismissal from the service, besides permanent quarters in a lunatic asylum. Do you believe that we are awake?"

The red-hot gun-barrel had fallen on the floor and was singeing the carpet. The smell was entirely real.

That morning at eleven we two together went to wake up Fleete. We looked and saw that the black leopard-rosette on his chest had disappeared. He was very drowsy and tired, but as soon as he saw us, he said, "Oh! Confound you fellows. Happy New Year to you. Never mix your liquors. I'm nearly dead."

"Thanks for your kindness, but you're over time," said Strickland. "Today is the morning of the second. You've slept the clock round with a vengeance."

The door opened, and little Dumoise put his head in. He had come on foot, and fancied that we were laying out Fleete.

"I've brought a nurse," said Dumoise. "I suppose that she can come in for . . . what is necessary."

"By all means," said Fleete cheerily, sitting up in bed. "Bring on your nurses."

Dumoise was dumb. Strickland led him out and explained that there must have been a mistake in the diagnosis. Dumoise remained dumb and left the house hastily. He considered that his professional reputation had been injured, and was inclined to make a personal matter of the recovery. Strickland went out too. When he came back, he said that he had been to call on the Temple of Hanuman to offer redress for the pollution of the god, and had been solemnly assured that no white man had ever touched the idol and that he was an incarnation of all the virtues labouring under a delusion. "What do you think?" said Strickland.

I said, "There are more things . . ."

But Strickland hates that quotation. He says that I have worn it threadbare.

One other curious thing happened which frightened me as much as anything in all the night's work. When Fleete was dressed he came into the dining-room and sniffed. He had a quaint trick of moving his nose when he sniffed. "Horrid doggy smell, here," said he. "You should really keep those terriers of yours in better order. Try sulphur, Strick."

But Strickland did not answer. He caught hold of the back of a chair, and, without warning, went into an amazing fit of hysterics. It is terrible to see a strong man overtaken with hysteria. Then it struck me that we had fought for Fleete's soul with the Silver Man in that room, and had disgraced ourselves as Englishmen for ever, and I laughed and gasped and gurgled just as shamefully as Strickland, while Fleete thought that we had both gone mad. We never told him what we had done.

Some years later, when Strickland had married and was a church-going member of society for his wife's sake, we reviewed the incident dispassionately, and Strickland suggested that I should put it before the public.

I cannot myself see that this step is likely to clear up the mystery; because, in the first place, no one will believe a rather unpleasant story, and, in the second, it is well known to every right-minded man that the gods of the heathen are stone and brass, and any attempt to deal with them otherwise is justly condemned.

Caulfield's Crime
Alice Perrin (1892)

Caulfield was the worse-tempered fellow I ever met, or even heard of, which is saying a good deal.

He was sulky and vindictive, as well as passionately violent; and yet he was a great friend of mine. People in Koorwallah said it didn't speak well for me, and made remarks about "birds of a feather," with much appreciation of their own discernment.

I suppose, now I come to think of it, that it perhaps may have looked odd for a young civilian like myself, newly landed in India, to be seen so constantly with a man who was senior major in his regiment, and getting on for twenty years older than I was.

Everyone wondered openly what we could find in common to make us such friends; they were sure we could not think alike on any one subject, and it afforded them food for a little uncharitable gossip, which is always a god-send in a second-class up-country station in the North-West Provinces.

No one in Koorwallah knew Caulfield well. Everybody seemed half afraid of him except myself, and there was no denying that he certainly was not the kind of man whose rooms one could walk into without asking, and say "Hullo!" pick up a book or a paper, wander round, looking at the photographs of his sisters, or other fellows' sisters, and then go out again. Not one of the subalterns in his regiment ever spoke to him voluntarily, none of the ladies liked him, they said he was so rude and disagreeable, and never accepted their invitations, and they were sure he had a history, which was very probable and not unusual.

As a matter of fact, he had only lately exchanged into the —th Foot from a cavalry regiment, nobody knew why, nor did he volunteer any information, which deepened the air of mystery surrounding him.

As for myself, I had struck up a friendship with him almost immediately after my arrival in the station. His bungalow was next to mine. They were both ordinary little thatched and whitewashed bachelor's houses, with narrow strips of verandah in front, where a servant was generally to be seen, either washing up plates and throwing the dirty water into the drive, or cleaning the lamps and anointing the floor with kerosene oil.

We each had an untidy square of compound, divided from the others by a dusty aloe hedge, in the roots of which lurked pink-nosed little mongooses, with their numerous and ever-increasing families.

There was very little work for me to do during the first two months while I was getting used to the language and the people, and I had ample time for sauntering over to Caulfield's bungalow to examine, with intense interest, his enormous collection of skins and horns and other sporting trophies, which were enough to make any youngster who knew how to handle a gun turn green with envy. He would sit quietly smoking in his chair, and watch me wander round, touching all his favourite treasures, and listening to my voluble chatter with irritating stolidity. He never asked me to come, or pressed me to stay, and yet, in some inexplicable manner, I felt that my visits were not unwelcome to him, except on one or two memorable occasions, when I found him in his worst mood, and he turned me out with a promptitude which caused me to show my face at his door somewhat cautiously the next time I invaded his privacy.

He certainly could not have been called an agreeable companion, and, looking back over the stretch of years which divides those young days of mine from the present, I often wonder what strange fascination drew me so persistently to seek his company. He attracted and interested me, I had a craving to be thought well of by him. I told him petty details concerning my home and family, I read him my people's letters, I confided to him that there was "a girl at home," and I cannot remember receiving anything in the way of encouragement to continue, save an occasional grunt of acquiescence, and sometimes contempt.

He never asked me questions or told me anything about himself, and yet there was a quiet strength in his manner which gave one a secure feeling that whatever confidence was thrust upon him, it would not be betrayed, however ungraciously he might choose to receive it.

Caulfield never went to church. He generally spent his Sundays out shooting, always going off by himself, and returning with a magnificent bag. He had never been known to invite anyone to accompany him, for he was madly jealous on the subject of sport, and nothing made him more angry than to hear of another fellow having shot anything that might be called game. He seemed to look upon each jheel,* and every patch of hunting-ground, in the neighbourhood of Koorwallah as his own particular property.

So it may be understood that I was fully alive to the honour conferred on me, when he unexpectedly asked me to go out with him for a three days' shoot.

"I know of a string of jheels," he said, "about thirty miles from here, where the duck and snipe ought to swarm. I saw the spot and marked it down, when I was out black-buck shooting, last week. I've made all arrangements for going out Saturday morning. You can come, too, if you like."

Needless to say, I jumped at this offer. Caulfield had the reputation of being the best shot in the N. W. P. He knew instinctively where game was likely to be found. Good sport was

---

* A large tract of marsh.

almost a certainty in his company, and, as far as I knew, I was the only fellow he had ever voluntarily invited to go with him.

I boasted about it in the club that evening, and was mercilessly squashed by two or three men who would have given their ears to know the whereabouts of the string of jheels, but who jealously warned me to be careful that Caulfield wasn't after big game, and that he did not begin the expedition by shooting me.

"He'd as soon shoot a man, as anything else," said our doctor, looking over his shoulder to make sure that Caulfield was not in the room. "I never met such a nasty, bad-tempered chap. I believe he's mad!"

And the doctor went on with his billiards, feeling that this speech had wiped off a few old scores he had treasured up against Caulfield for sundry disagreeables which had passed between them.

I left all the arrangements of our expedition to Caulfield. He requested me not to interfere when I began suggesting various things I considered might be useful; and after giving me to understand that I was to be his guest for the three days in question, he despatched a couple of carts on the Friday with a tent wherein we were to eat and sleep, various provisions and cooking utensils, a pair of camp beds, and some servants, my bedding and bearer being my only contributions to the arrangements.

We rode out the thirty miles on Saturday morning, each having sent a fresh pony on half way, and by this means did the distance in about three hours and a half. Our tent was pitched in the midst of a patch of what is called dâk jungle, clusters of stunted-looking trees with thick, dry bark, and flat shapeless leaves that clattered noisily against each other when stirred by the wind.

It was not a cheerful spot. The soil was principally "usar," that is to say largely mixed with bitter salt which works its way to the surface, and prevents anything but the coarsest of vegetation growing in it. The ground was low and marshy, and the stillness of the air was only broken now and then by the discordant cries of the large jheel birds as they waded majestically in the patches of water in search of their breakfast of small fish.

Caulfield was a different man out there to what he had been in the station. He talked and laughed and acted showman with the most intense satisfaction. He led me away from amongst the stunted trees, and showed me a great sheet of water in the distance, broken in places by little bushy islands and dark patches of reeds, and a mud-coloured native village on the top of a mound overlooking the water at the extreme left.

It was still early, as we had started before six o'clock, and the sun had barely cleared away the thick heavy mist, which was still rising here and there, and rapidly dispersing as the heat increased.

"Isn't it a lovely spot!" said Caulfield, laughing. "Beyond that village the snipe ought to rise from the rice fields in thousands. There's another jheel away to the right of this, and another joining that. We shan't be able to shoot it all in three days, worse luck, and besides it's too big really for only two guns. Come in to breakfast, we mustn't lose time."

An hour later, and we had started. Our guns over our shoulders and a couple of servants behind us carrying the cartridge bags and our luncheon.

We were both in good spirits. We felt we had the certainty of an excellent day's shooting in prospect. But, alas! Luck was against us. The birds were unaccountably wild and few and far between. Some one had been there before us was Caulfield's verdict, delivered with disappointed rage, and after tramping and wading all day, we returned weary and crestfallen with only six teal and a mallard between us.

It was undoubtedly very provoking, but Caulfield seemed to take the matter much more to heart than there was any occasion to do. He was filled with hatred of the "scoundrels," who had discovered his pet place and played havoc among the birds, and after dinner sat cursing his luck and the culprits who had spoilt

our sport until we were both too sleepy to keep awake any longer, and after our long day of exercise in the open air we neither
of us moved in our beds till we were called the next morning.

We had breakfast, and started off, taking a different direction to the previous day, but with no better luck. On and on,
and round and round we tramped, with only an occasional shot
here and there, scarcely worth mentioning.

At last, about three o'clock in the afternoon, we sat wearily
down to eat our luncheon. I was ravenously hungry, and greedily devoured my share of the provisions, but Caulfield hardly ate
a mouthful; he sat moodily examining his gun, and taking long
pulls now and then at his flask of whiskey.

We were seated on the roots of a huge tamarind tree, close
to the village I had noticed on our arrival the morning before.
We had been a very long round and had kept the yellow mud
walls, on the top of the little mound, in sight as a land-mark.
The village was a mile or so from our camp, but there was still
a good deal of ground to be shot over between the two.

The place seemed but poorly inhabited, and had a dreary,
deserted look about it. Two very old women were sitting watching us with dim, weary eyes, leaning their bent backs against
the crumbling mud wall, and a few naked children were playing
near them, while one or two bigger boys were driving a herd of
lean, bony cattle down towards the water.

Presently another figure came slowly in sight, and advanced
towards us. It was a fakir, or holy man, as was evident by the
tawny masses of wool which were plaited in amongst his own
black locks, and allowed to hang down on either side of his thin,
sharp face, the ashes which covered his almost naked body, and
the hollow gourd for alms which he held in one hand. His face
was long and dog-like, and his pointed yellow teeth glistened in
the sun as he demanded money in a dismal, monotonous kind
of chant.

Caulfield flung a pebble at him and told him roughly to
be off. The fakir fixed his wild, restless eyes on him for one

moment with a look of bitter animosity, and then walked away, disappearing behind a clump of tall feathery grass.

I felt in my pocket. I had no coins, or I should certainly have given the poor wretch whatever I might have had about me.

"Did you notice that brute's face?" said Caulfield as we rose, preparatory to starting off again. "If there's any truth in the doctrine of the transmigration of souls, he must have been a pariah dog in his former state. He was exactly like one!"

"A jackal more likely," I said carelessly. "It was the face of a wild beast."

Then we walked on again, skirting round the village, and plunging into the damp, soft rice fields. We put up a wisp of snipe which we followed till we had shot them nearly all, and then presently, to our joy, we heard a rush of wings overhead, and a lot of duck went down into a corner of the jheel ahead of us.

"We've got them," whispered Caulfield, in excitement, and we cautiously crept on till the birds were in sight, floating lazily on the still, cold water, pluming their feathers, and calling to one another in their fancied security.

"Now," said Caulfield, crouching down behind the rushes. "Fire into the brown!"

We both raised our guns, and as our fingers were actually on the trigger, there was a mighty splash in the middle of the ducks, and rising with a whir-r-r, they were out of shot in a second.

Caulfield swore. So did I. And then we both turned to see what had caused the splash.

A little way behind us stood the fakir we had seen at luncheon-time. In one hand he was still holding the fragments of the clod of earth he had thrown into the water to warn the ducks of our approach.

Caulfield shook his fist at the man, and abused him freely in Hindustani, but without moving a muscle of his face he turned slowly and disappeared into the jungle.

Words would not describe Caulfield's rage and disappointment.

"They were pintail, nearly all of 'em," he said, "and the first decent chance we've had to-day. To think of that beastly fakir spoiling it all! What a devilish thing to do!"

"They hate anything being killed, you know," I remarked consolingly, "and I expect there was some spite in it too, because you threw a stone at him."

"Bosh!" said Caulfield. "Come along, we must make haste, it'll be dark soon. I should like to try a place over by those palms before we knock off, but we may as well let the servants go back now, they've had a hard day. Have you got some cartridges in your pocket?"

"Yes, plenty," I answered, and after despatching the two men back to the camp with what little game we had got, we turned to the right and walked in silence till we saw more water glistening between the rough stems of the palms, and in it, to our surprise and delight, a multitude of duck and teal.

With our guns in our hands, we quietly crept towards the water, holding our breath, and fearing that the slightest noise might awake the ducks' suspicions.

The sun had begun to sink in a red ball, and there was a hush over the land as the air became heavy with damp, and the mist stole over the cold still waters of the jheel. Overhead came the first faint cackle of the wild geese, returning home for the night.

Caulfield raised his gun first. He was taking a very steady aim into the middle of the fluttering brown mass of feathers.

Splash! Whir-r-r! A cloud of wings rose in front of us, and wheeled bodily to the right, and the air resounded with the cries of the startled birds.

Someone had thrown a heavy stone in amongst them just as Caulfield had been going to fire.

He turned round very deliberately and looked behind him. Following the direction of his eyes, I saw the long, lanky figure of the fakir, his yellow, jagged teeth and white eye-balls glistening in the pink glow of the setting sun, and a look of fiendish triumph and exultation on his face.

Then there was a loud report, and the next thing I saw was a quivering body on the ground, and wild, terrified eyes staring wide open at me in the agony of death. Caulfield had shot the fakir.

I shudder when I recall what followed.

The man had been shot through the heart, and died almost immediately, without a sound, save one long, harrowing sigh.

Caulfield stood looking down at what he had done, while I knelt by the body trying hopelessly to persuade myself that life was not extinct. He seemed half-dazed, and it was fully ten minutes before I was able to make him realize what had happened, and the necessity for prompt action.

"You know what it means," he said, touching the body with his foot, "killing a native is no joke in these days. I should come out of it badly. You were witness that I deliberately shot that poor devil. What do you intend doing?"

He spoke in a hard, defiant voice, but there was anxiety written on every line of his features.

"Of course I'll stick by you," I said, after a moment's silence, "nobody need ever know about—about this but ourselves, but we shall have to get rid of it."

I gazed at the body with horror. The face, which was becoming rigid, looked more like that of an animal than ever. Caulfield shivered, and glanced uneasily round him.

"Look here," I said, with an effort, "we can't do anything this minute. We'd better hide it in that grass, and come back after dinner. We must get a spade or something of the kind."

"Very well," said Caulfield, humbly. All his old masterful manner had disappeared, and he obeyed me like a child.

Then, when we had performed the repugnant task, and the body had been thrust into the thick grass and covered with clods of hard, dry soil, we walked back to our camp in silence.

I looked at Caulfield as we entered the lighted tent, and could not but feel compassion for him.

His diabolical temper had led him to commit this atrocious deed, and very bitter was the reaction.

He was white and shaking, and looked ten years older than when we had started out that morning.

I gave him some whiskey, and we both sat down and pretended to eat our dinner. We waited for half-an-hour afterwards, to prevent the servants noticing anything peculiar in our manner, and then I sent my bearer outside to see if the moon had risen.

"Yes, sahib," he answered, coming back, "it is as light as day."

During the few seconds of his absence, I had hastily filled the deep pocket of my overcoat with a stout hunting-knife, which I had packed amongst my traps in case we should get any buck shooting, and also a small kitchen chopper left lying on the floor by the bearer after hammering a stiff joint of my camp bed together. I dared not ask the servants for any kind of implement with which to dig.

We left the tent carelessly, as if we were going for a stroll, and found that it was, as the bearer had reported, "as light as day." People who have never been out of England cannot readily imagine the brilliancy of Eastern moonlight. It is almost possible to read by it.

We walked slowly at first, but rapidly quickened our pace as we left the tent behind us, and we both breathed hard as we neared the spot we were making for. Caulfield stopped once or twice, and I half thought he meant to turn back and leave me to do the ghastly business alone. But he came on by my side and never spoke a word until we were close to the tall, coarse grass which hid the fakir's body. Then he suddenly clutched my arm.

"God in Heaven!" he whispered, pointing forwards, "what is that?"

I thought he had gone out of his mind, and it was with difficulty that I refrained from shouting aloud.

The next moment I distinctly saw something moving exactly over the spot where we had concealed the body. I am not what is called a coward, but I must confess that I burst out into a cold perspiration.

There was a rustling in the grass, accompanied by a scraping sound, and Caulfield and I stepped forwards in desperation. I parted the grass with my hands and looked down. There, lying on the fakir's body was a large jackal, grinning and snarling at having been disturbed over his hideous meal.

"Drive it away," whispered Caulfield hoarsely.

But the brute refused to move. Silently it sat there showing its yellow teeth, and reminded me horribly of the wretched man that lay dead beneath its feet. I turned sick and faint.

Then Caulfield shouted at it, and shook the grass, and lifted one of the clods of soil to throw at it.

The jackal rose slowly, and began to slink away. It passed close enough for us both to notice that it was an unusually large animal for its kind, and moreover had lost one of its ears. Its coat was plentifully besprinkled with grey, and was rough and mangy.

For more than an hour we worked as if our lives depended on it, using the chopper and my hunting-knife, and being helped by a rift in the ground where the soil had been softened by water running from the jheel, and at last we stood up and stamped down the earth which now covered all traces of Caulfield's crime, with the sweat pouring off our faces.

We had filled the grave with large stones which were lying about on the ground, remnants of some ancient Buddhist temple, long ago forgotten and deserted, so we felt secure that it could not easily be disturbed by animals.

The next morning we returned to Koorwallah, and the secret between Caulfield and myself drew us closer together than before. I suppose what I had seen him do ought to have repulsed and alienated me from him, but the night of that terrible burial we had sat up, one on each side of our little camp table, until daylight crept across the jheels, and Caulfield had told me the story of his life.

It cannot be written down here, but there was the burden of a cruel sorrow in it that explained much to me in his behaviour which I had never understood before.

I passionately pitied the lonely, unloved man, who had brought much of his misery on himself, both now and in the past, through his own ungovernable anger.

He shut himself up more than ever after this, and entirely gave up his shooting trips, which before had been the pleasure of his life, and the only person he ever spoke to, unofficially, was myself.

He took to coming into my bungalow in the evening and sometimes in the middle of the night, and would walk restlessly up and down my rooms, or sit in an easy chair with his face buried in his hands. At times I feared his mind was going, and I dreaded the effect upon him of the long hot-weather days and nights that were creeping gradually nearer.

The end of April came, with its plague of insects and scorching wind. The hours grew long and heavy with the heat, and the dust storms howled and swirled over the baking little station, bringing perhaps a few tantalizing drops of rain, or more often leaving the air hotter than ever and thick with copper-coloured dust.

I grew more and more anxious about Caulfield, especially when he came over to me one night when it was too hot to sleep, and asked me if he might stay in my bungalow till the morning.

"I know I may seem an ass," he said, "but I can't stay by myself. I get all sorts of beastly ideas."

I thought he meant that he was tempted to take his own life, and began to try and cheer him up, telling him scraps of gossip, and encouraging him to talk, when a sound outside made us both start. It was only the weird, plaintive cry of a jackal, but Caulfield sprang to his feet shaking all over.

"There it is!" he exclaimed hoarsely, "it's followed me over here. Jack," he continued, turning his haggard, sleepless eyes on me, "every night for the last week that brute has come and howled round my house. You know what I mean. It's the one we saw *that* night."

He was terribly excited, and, I could see, almost off his head.

"Nonsense, my dear chap," I said, pushing him back into the chair, "you've got fever. Jackals come round my house and howl all night, and all day too. That's nothing."

"Look here, Jack," said Caulfield, very calmly, "I've no more fever than you have, and if you think I'm delirious you're mistaken." Then he lowered his voice, "I looked out one night and saw it, and I tell you *it had only one ear.*"

In spite of my own common sense, and the certainty that Caulfield was not himself, my blood ran cold, and, after I had succeeded in quieting him and getting him to sleep on my bed, I lay on the sofa going over every detail of that' fearful night in the jungle again and again, try as I would to chase it from my thoughts.

Once or twice after this Caulfield came to me and repeated the same tale. He swore he was being haunted by the jackal we had driven away from the fakir's body, and took it into his head that the soul of the man he had murdered had entered into the animal, and was trying to obtain vengeance in that form.

Then he suddenly stopped coming near me, and when I went to see him he would hardly speak, and seemed to take no pleasure in my visits as formerly.

I thought perhaps he was offended because I had always laughed at his hallucinations, and treated them as, what they undoubtedly must have been, mere fancies.

I urged him to see a doctor or take leave, but he angrily refused to do either, and declared I should very soon drive him mad altogether if I bothered him much more.

After this I left him alone for a couple of days, and on the third night, when my conscience was pricking me for having neglected him, and I was preparing to go over to his bungalow, his bearer came rushing in with a face of terror and distress, and begged me to come at once. He had already sent a man off for the doctor, as he feared his master was very ill. I arrived at Caulfield's bungalow just as the doctor, who lived only across the road, appeared, and together we entered the queer museum of a house, literally lined with horns and skins and curiosities. Caulfield was lying unconscious on his bed.

"He had a kind of fit, sahib," said the trembling bearer, and proceeded to explain how his master had behaved.

The doctor bent over the bed.

"Do you happen to know if he's been bitten by a dog, or anything lately?" he said, looking up at me.

"Not to my knowledge," I answered, but the faint wail of a jackal out across the plain struck a superstitious chill to my heart.

For twenty-four hours we stayed with him, watching the terrible struggles we were powerless to avert, and which lasted until the end came, and brought a merciful peace to the poor, harassed mind and body.

He was never able to speak after the first paroxysm, which had occurred before we arrived, so we could not learn from him whether he had ever been bitten or not, neither could the doctor discover any kind of scar on his body which might have been made by the teeth of an animal, and yet there was no doubt that Caulfield's death was due to hydrophobia.

As we stood in the next room after all was over, drinking the dead man's whiskey and soda (which we badly needed), we questioned the bearer again and again, but he could tell us little or nothing. His master did not keep dogs, and he did not know of his ever having been bitten by one, but there had been a mad jackal about the place nearly three weeks before, though he did not think his master had known of it.

"It couldn't have been that," said the doctor, "or we should have heard about it."

"No," I answered mechanically, "it couldn't have been that."

It was nearly three weeks ago that Caulfield had ceased to come near me and had taken such a strange dislike to my going to his house. I began to think I must be going off my head too, for nobody but a lunatic could for a moment have seriously entertained such a notion as crossed my brain at that moment.

I went into the bedroom to take a last look at poor Caulfield's thin, white face, with its ghastly, hunted expression, and to give a farewell pressure to his cold, heavy hand before I left him, for the doctor had urged me to go home, saying that there was now nothing more that I could do to help him. I picked up a lantern after this, and stepped out into the dark verandah.

As I did so, something came silently round the corner of the house, and stood in my path.

I raised my lantern, and caught a glimpse of a mass of grey fur, two fiery yellow eyes, and glistening teeth. I saw that it was only a stray jackal, and struck at it with my stick, but instead of running away, it passed silently by me and entered Caulfield's room. The light fell on the animal's head as it entered the open door—*one of its ears was missing.*

In a frenzy I rushed back into the house, calling loudly for the doctor and the servants.

"I saw a jackal come in here!" I exclaimed excitedly, searching round Caulfield's room. "It must be in this room—I saw it go in this very minute. Hunt it out at once!"

Every nook and corner was examined, but there was no jackal, nor even a trace of one.

"Go home to bed, my boy," said the doctor, looking at me kindly. "This business has shaken your nerves. Keep quiet for a bit. Your imagination's beginning to play you tricks. Goodnight."

"Good-night," I answered, wearily, and I went slowly back to my bungalow, trying to persuade myself that he was right.

Guarded by a Ghost
David Ker (1892)

I

"Ghosts, eh? Well, there ought to be a good few of 'em on this coast, considerin' what things have been done here," said our captain, as he and I leaned over the ship's side in the unearthly splendor of the tropical moonlight. And then, lowering his voice to a hoarse whisper, he added, impressively: "And, if all tales be true, there *are!*"

I was already halfway down the formidable "West Coast of Africa" on my second voyage to the Congo, and just entering the fatal bay whose deadly climate has been aptly characterized by the homely couplet which is familiar to every Niger trader:

"Beware, beware of the Bight of Benin!
For one that comes, there were forty went in."

Since leaving Sierra Leone we had had ample proof that we were fairly in the tropics once more. Our butter at breakfast, "albeit unused to the melting mood," was rapidly becoming as soft as a drawing-room poet's head, while, by way of balancing matters, our beefsteaks, doubly-cooked by the sun and the galley fire, were as hard as a customhouse officer's heart. In spite of the fresh breeze and the awnings rigged up fore and aft, the temperature on board was already that of an August day in Egypt, and threatening to become what a British excursionist

called "more hotterer" before long; and most of my fellow passengers were chiefly engaged in helping each other to do nothing, or in imitating that renowned midshipman who "fell asleep
with the utmost energy."

But the African night fully atoned for all the shortcom-
ings of the African day. Coleridge's "Ancient Mariner," alone in
his spellbound ship amid all the wonders of that unknown sea
where no man but himself had ever been, saw no such spectacle
as that which lay before us every evening at nightfall. Beneath
the glorious tropical moonlight the calm sea outspread itself
like a mighty mirror, far as the eye could reach, while no sound
broke the deep and dreamy stillness save the low lapping of the
water against the vessel's sides. Every ripple in our wake flashed
into living fire as it broke and vanished, only to be followed by
fresh sparkles as bright and numberless as a swarm of fireflies.

Against the cold splendor of the clear moonlit sky every
strand of our lower rigging, from the topmast stay to the lowest
ratline, stood out transfigured—no longer a black cobweb of
tarred and grimy ropes, but a slender stair of enchanted gossa-
mer leading up to some fairy palace far away among the stars.
A flash of silver light shot upward suddenly from the shadowy
waters below, and fell upon our lower deck in the form of a
flying fish, shaking from its glistening wings a shower of tiny
rainbows. And then, as the moonlight began to wane, the darkening sea was lighted up with an endless procession of floating
colored lamps—shedding around them soft rays of pink, bright
green, pale gold or rich purple—in which a matter-of-fact pro-
fessor of natural history would see nothing more than "the small
phosphorescent jellyfish of the tropical seas."

On such a night any tale of supernatural wonder might have
seemed possible; and I waited eagerly for some explanation of
the weird hint with which my friend the captain had concluded
his remarks. But I waited in vain, for no explanation was forthcoming.

"I suppose you speak from experience, captain," said I, at length. "Have you seen any ghosts yourself, then?"

"Well, no—I can't say I've ever reg'larly seen a real live ghost with my own eyes," answered the worthy skipper, with the discontented air of an honest man unjustly defrauded of a valuable privilege; "and it ain't for want of trying, neither, for I once kept watch all night by myself in a house that they said was haunted, expecting every moment the *appearance* of an *invisible* spirit.

"I'll tell you what I *have* seen, though," resumed the captain, after a pause—to all appearance quite unconscious of the magnificent "bull" that he had just made. "I've seen"—lowering his voice to an impressive whisper—"how another man looked after *he* had seen a ghost; and, considering who the man was and what he looked like, I can promise you that's quite enough for *me!*"—

A more thoroughly unimaginative man than Captain J— never breathed; and I, naturally supposing him to be absolutely incapable of even picturing to himself such an unpractical thing as a ghost, had regarded his first mention of apparitions as something in the same style as a yarn that he had spun me, a few days before, of a snake so long that it took an hour to crawl across the path in front of him. But as he uttered the last words there was such downright *horror* in his look and tone that it awed me in spite of myself.

Before I could make any reply, however, a clear, fresh, hearty voice suddenly struck in from behind:

"That sounds interesting, Captain J—; and, if you have no objection to tell us the story, I can assure you that I, for one, should be very glad to hear it."

Beside us stood a white-haired old man of tall stature and noble presence, with a face so sweet and pure and kindly that one of our roughest seamen had good cause to say, with a glow of unwonted enthusiasm on his hard, weather-beaten visage,

"Every time as I looks in that old gen'lman's face, I'm blest if I don't feel jist as if I was in church!"

Although the veteran missionary (for such he was) had only been a few days aboard our steamer—being on his way from the Gold Coast port at which we had picked him up to another mission station further east, to which he had just been transferred—he was already a prime favorite with crew and passengers alike; and even our stolid captain had been heard to remark, in a very bold flight of fancy for *him:*

"It's my belief that, if that old gent could only git him alone for half an hour, he'd convert Old Nick himself!"

As Mr. E— appeared on the poop deck the captain turned to him with a rough attempt at a salute, and replied:

"Well, Mr. E—, it's not much of a story, when all's said and done; but if you want to hear it, why, here you are:

"There was an English trader of the name of P— (I dare say you've heard of him, for he's very well known all along this coast) who'd taken a house near Porto Novo, which stands, as you'll remember, on one of the lagoons a little to the west'ard of Lagos. It had been a slave station once upon a time, and the barracoons where the n-----s used to be chained up were all round it still; and it was said that the last chap who owned the place had been a noted slaver, and something of a pirate into the bargain—he was a Portigoose swell, Don Whiskerandos de Pickled Porko, or some such crackjaw name. So, as you may think, there were plenty of queer stories about the place, and most of the folks in the neighborhood were mighty shy of venturing near it after dark.

"But P— was one of them chaps that, saving your presence, care neither for man or devil, as they say; and he said that the house suited *him,* and that, for all he cared, there might be as many ghosts in it as there were cockroaches; and in he went. It was the middle of April when he moved in, and everything went as right as ninepence till toward the latter end of July, and P—

thought he had made a stunning good bargain; but he didn't know what was coming!"

Here Captain J— made a dramatic pause, while the missionary eyed him keenly.

"Well," he resumed, "it was the 24th of July, last summer but one (I shall remember that day as long as I live), that I came ashore at Porto Novo the first thing in the morning, and went to breakfast with my old chum Tom Carter, the shipping agent—who, I should tell you, was the owner of this house that P— had taken.

"Just as we were in the middle of breakfast the door flies open, and in comes P— himself, with such a face that we fairly started at the sight of it. Although the day was roasting hot, he was as white as a sheet; his eyes stared as if they'd jump out of his head, and he was shaking all over like a man in a fever.

"He took no more heed of *me* (though he knew me well enough) than if I hadn't been there at all; but he marched right up to Tom, and said, in a voice that wasn't like his own:

"'Carter, I'll pay you your rent for the full term, or anything else you like; but not another night do I stay in that house of yours, for love or money!'

"'What's up?' cried Tom and I, both at once—for I can tell you the mere look of his face made us feel pretty queer, let alone what he said.

"'Don't ask me!' says P—, forcing out the words as if they choked him. 'I saw *something* last night,' he says, 'that I'll never forget as long as I live; and I don't want to see it again,' says he.

"And he didn't; for out of that house he went that same blessed day, and I've heard since that he's given up his business and left the coast altogether, and gone right away home to England."

Here the narrator made another impressive halt.

"And now, gentlemen," he added, at length, "I've told you what sort o' chap P— was; and if just *seeing* something was enough to frighten a man like him out of house and harbor, *what* could it have been that he saw?"

Having put this difficult question, Captain J— paused, as if for a reply. But Mr. E— and I both remained silent, and the captain, evidently regarding the old clergyman's presence as a fortunate chance of bringing to bear upon this weird mystery the weight of a higher authority than his own, appealed to the latter point-blank.

"Mr. E—, you're a missionary, and a parson to boot, and I s'pose it's your business to know all about such matters as them. Now, will you just tell me, *are* there such things as ghosts, or ain't there?"

"It is not for me, nor for any man," answered the old hero, with a quiet smile, "to presume to pronounce *what* things may or may not be allowed to exist in God's universe; but of this at least we may be certain, that, even if spirits are permitted to appear upon earth, they can have no power over us, except by the will of our heavenly Father. Good night!"

II

My return voyage from the Congo was marked by no special incident, and after several weeks of that monotonous tranquility which is the despair of those lively historians who think nothing worth chronicling but wars, revolutions and murders, I found myself anchored off the West African settlement of Lagos (annexed by England in 1861), where, after more than one narrow escape of being capsized, a light coast steamer brought me safely through the perilous surf that foams and gnashes around the narrow entrance of the wide, shallow, muddy lagoon upon which stands the town itself.

I had thought of making my way up the Ogoon River from Lagos to take a peep at Abbeokuta (Under the Stone), the great city of the Egba tribes, which lies a few days' journey inland; but just after my arrival at Lagos itself one of the local English officials, with whom I had been previously acquainted, told me that he was about to start upon a special mission through that strange amphibious region lying between the mouth of the Ogoon and the Dahoman port of Whydah; and, as I had just then plenty of time on my hands, he suggested that I should accompany him.

Such a chance was too good to be lost. I assented at once, and, a few days later, we found ourselves—after various adventures which would make too long a story to be told here—at a queer little native town in the midst of a perfect maze of small lakes and inlets, which, my companion said, was called "Porto Novo."

Porto Novo! Where *had* I heard that name before?

It sounded familiar to my ear, and it even seemed to me as if I could remember that the association connected with it was one of gloom and terror; but I was still trying in vain to fix and define this vague recollection, when the clew was suddenly furnished by my comrade himself.

"Now, Mr. Ker, you'll have something to write about," said he, as we marched out of the town with our white umbrellas over our heads, attended by half a dozen negroes carrying our baggage, and four more in readiness to carry ourselves over the huge knee-deep pools of black, half-liquid mud which met us every twenty yards or so, giving to the whole country the look of a monster sheet of blotting paper. "I shall have to stay here three or four days, and Harry F—, the fellow who is going to put us up, lives in a haunted house!"

"That's it!" cried I, starting; "I remember all about it now."

And then, as briefly and clearly as I could, I repeated the captain's mysterious tale, to which Mr. Parker listened with visible interest.

"Well, that's curious," said he; "it is the 23d July, then, upon which this business, whatever it may be, always comes off. The last man who had the house before F— was my cousin Dick, who isn't a fellow to be easily scared, I can promise you. Well, on the night of the 23d July last year Dick saw a man prowling

round the courtyard—saw him so plain in the moonlight as to
see that he wore a slouched Spanish hat, an embroidered jacket,
a red silk sash with a silver-hilted dagger in it, and black velvet
trousers stuffed into his boots—just the rig, in fact, of the old
buccaneers. Dick took him for a thief, and let slap at him with
his revolver, and seemed to hit him fair; but just then the figure disappeared, and the ball was found in the tree in front of
which the thing had stood!"

"Now I think of it," cried I, "this is the 21st July; so the day
after to-morrow will be *the* day!"

"So it will!" exclaimed Parker. "Well, then, I'll tell you
what—we'll say nothing to F—

and avoid reminding him of the anniversary in any way until
it comes; and then, if there is any truth in the story at all, we
shall have a good chance to find it out. But see! yonder's the
house itself."

I looked at the "haunted house" with no small interest as
we approached it. It was a long, low building of the true West
African type, with a huge top-heavy thatch coming down within
a few yards of the ground, and giving to the whole structure the
look of a child with its father's hat on. It stood in the midst
of a large courtyard encircled with a strong and high stockade,
across which our host, Mr. F— (a frank, hearty, stalwart young
Englishman, whose bold, handsome face was hidden by a vast
white "sun hat"), came hurrying with outstretched hand to welcome us.

I was at home in a twinkling, and for the next two days
everything went on in the regular "West Coast" style. A light
meal of biscuits, fruit and tea or coffee about 6:30 a.m.; an
early walk or ride, followed by work till eleven; then a bath and
a substantial breakfast; work again till 5 p.m., with perhaps
another cup of tea about three to "keep you going." At five you
start out for a stroll or a canter in the cool of the evening, and
come back to dinner at seven.

At length came the evening of the memorable 23d, and F—, who had been away all afternoon, brought back with him another guest, in whom I at once recognized Mr. E—, my missionary acquaintance of the outward voyage.

Parker, who knew the good old man well by reputation, was delighted to meet him; and a very merry party we were. The missionary's long and varied experience of the Dark Continent, and the wonderful series of adventures through which he had passed, made him a most entertaining companion; and the four of us sat talking till the candles upon our dinner table were beginning to burn low.

"By the by," said Mr. E—, suddenly, "wasn't it on this very day, Mr. Ker, that you were shipwrecked somewhere upon this coast?"

"Yes," said I, "it's just a year to-day since the poor old *Corisco* struck upon that reef at the mouth of Cestos River, and chucked us ashore among the savages. I'll be bound poor King Oko Jumbo of Bonny, who was wrecked along with us, will remember *that* anniversary as long as he lives!"

I saw Parker's face cloud slightly, and guessed at once that he feared that this talk might contravene his plans by recalling to F—'s memory the supernatural associations which had made the same anniversary memorable in connection with his own house.

Nor were his fears groundless, for at that moment F— called out:

"Now I think of it, it was on this very day that old Visagrande de Pico Parco, who owned this house of mine in the old slaving times, was murdered by one of his own men, as he richly deserved; and they say his ghost comes back every now and then to have a look at the old place. Wouldn't it be a joke if he were to pop up among us just now? Anyhow, we'd have fair warning if he did, for I've heard that when he's going to show himself all the lights burn blue, and then go out one by one!"

The careless laugh that accompanied the words was still on his lips, when one of our four candles suddenly *burned blue, and then went out!*

We all looked at each other. Parker (who knew the legend better than anyone present) cast an instinctive glance toward the courtyard. Mr. E— raised himself expectantly in his chair, with an unwontedly grave and almost stern look upon his calm and kindly face. No one spoke a word.

F— himself rose from his seat with a somewhat puzzled air, and, uttering another laugh—which sounded to me slightly forced—relighted the candle; but scarcely had he done so when it went out again as before.

Just at that moment a cloud swept over the moon, and, as if this had been a signal, the second candle went out—then the third—then the fourth!

The cloud passed as quickly as it had come, and in the cold splendor of the full moon—which seemed to shine on that memorable night, as I well remember, with a singular and almost unearthly brightness—we all four saw plainly a human figure moving slowly across the courtyard just inside the palisade, at no very great distance from where we sat.

Notwithstanding the weird portent which had heralded the appearance of this figure, it did not at the moment occur to one of us (as we subsequently learned by comparing notes) to think of it as supernatural. Our first idea was—as that of Parker's cousin had been before us—that the intruder was some prowling rogue on the watch for a chance of plunder, a theory borne out to some extent by the lonely situation of the house. But we were all struck with the strange way in which he moved, more like the gliding of a shadow than the walk of a living man. Then, too—though the soft sand might perhaps account for *that*—his steps, large and strongly built though he seemed to be, made not the slightest sound; and, moreover, at the moment when we first caught sight of him, I had felt (and I afterward discovered that the others felt it too at the very same instant) a sudden chill run through me, like the rush of a blast of cold wind.

By this time the figure—which appeared to be moving in a parallel line to our position—had come right opposite to us, and every detail of its appearance could be plainly seen. Parker and I looked blankly at each other, for the form before us corresponded in every point with the spectre of his legend. The slouched Spanish hat, leaving nothing of the face visible save a thick black beard streaked with gray, the embroidered jacket, the red silk sash, the black velvet trousers thrust into high boots, the long silver-hilted poniard—all were there; and, moreover, the dagger was placed in such a way that it looked just as if, instead of being stuck in the crimson sash, it were buried to the hilt in the wearer's body!

We were still gazing at this strange sight in utter bewilderment, when we saw the mysterious form move straight toward the smaller gate of the courtyard, which was fast shut and barred, being hardly ever used; but at his approach it seemed to fall down flat and let him pass over.

Then we all eyed each other in silence, no one liking to be the first to utter the thought which was in the mind of one and all. But Mr. E— rose suddenly to his feet, with a gleam in those deep, earnest eyes of his such as I had never seen there before—a gleam like that which lights up a soldier's face when the word is given to charge.

"Whatever this may be," he said, "I must go and speak to it."

"Not *alone,* though!" cried F—, springing to his side. "If that fellow yonder's the devil himself, I'll see what he's made of!"

And out we all four sallied together.

The figure had halted at the foot of a large tree just outside the palisade; and here, for the first time, it raised its head, and the moonlight fell full upon its face. Such a face I never saw before or since—gaunt, haggard, ghastly as a corpse risen from the grave, yet less terrific from the hideousness of the features themselves than from the expression of unutterable agony and despair.

It seemed to struggle frantically to speak, as if oppressed by the burden of some horrible secret which it strove in vain to reveal; but though the horror and anguish that glared from its starting eyes was more eloquent than any words, its quivering lips were dumb. It pointed vehemently downward, thrice over, and then, slowly raising its arms and shaking its clinched hands above its head with a gesture of frantic desperation, vanished as if it had never been. For hundreds of yards round nothing living was in sight; not a footprint was visible in the soft sand, and the gate that we had seen fall down flat was standing fast shut as before!

For an instant we all stood spellbound, overpowered by the strong and terrible conviction that what we had seen was no being of this world. The first to recover himself was the brave old missionary, who, seizing a pickax that had been left lying beside the courtyard gate, began digging with all his might and main at the spot to which the apparition had pointed.

This seemed to break the spell, and in a trice the rest of us had seized whatever implements came first to hand, and were helping him with all our strength. It was not long ere we unearthed a perfect skeleton (between the ribs of which was driven *a long silver-hilted dagger!*) and sundry shreds of clothing, which seemed to correspond exactly with the spectre's dress.

Nor was this all. Mr. E—'s last pickax stroke encountered some hard object which gave forth a metallic ring, and we speedily laid bare a small iron case, filled to the brim with gold pieces, jewels, costly ornaments and valuables of every description, including several massive gold and silver crucifixes and sacramental chalices, the appearance of which was an amply sufficient proof that the dead man whose bones lay at our feet had been not merely a slaver, but a pirate as well!

"What's to be done with this money?" asked F—, breaking silence for the first time, for till then none of us had uttered a word. "I, for one, will have nothing to do with it, after what we've seen to-night."

"Nor I," said Parker, with a shudder; "I wouldn't touch it with the end of my little finger!"

"Well, if I may be permitted to offer a suggestion, gentlemen," interposed the mild voice of the old missionary, "I would recommend you to employ it for good, as it was formerly employed for evil; and since this wealth was doubtless acquired by selling men into slavery, the best thing you can do with it is to use it in ransoming as many slaves as possible, and establishing them in the native settlements along the coast of Liberia."

Mr. E—'s counsel was followed out to the letter; and since that time, so far as I have been able to ascertain, neither sight nor sound of any supernatural presence has disturbed the "haunted house." But when I afterward pressed the good old missionary to give a definite opinion as to the real nature of that ghastly vision he looked grave and made no reply; and I must confess myself to be as little able to find any answer to that question as *he* was.

The Haunted Station
Hume Nisbet (1892)

It looked as if a curse rested upon it, even under that glorious southern morn which transformed all that it touched into old oak and silver-bronze.

I use the term silver-bronze, because I can think of no other combination to express that peculiar bronzy tarnish, like silver that has lain covered for a time, which the moonlight in the tropics gives to the near objects upon which it falls—tarnished silver surfaces and deep sepia-tinted shadows.

I felt the weird influence of that curse even as I crawled into the gully that led to it; a shiver ran over me as one feels when they say some stranger is passing over your future grave; a chill gripped at my vitals as I glanced about me apprehensively, expectant of something ghoulish and unnatural to come upon me from the sepulchral gloom and mystery of the overhanging boulders under which I was dragging my wearied limbs. A deathly silence brooded within this rut-like and treeless gully that formed the only passage from the arid desert over which I had struggled, famishing and desperate; where it led to I neither knew nor cared, so that it did not end in a *cul-de-sac*.

At last I came to what I least expected to see in that part, a house of two storeys, with the double gables facing me, as it stood on a mound in front of a water-hole, the mellow full moon behind the shingly roof, and glittering whitely as it repeated itself in the still water against the inky blackness of the reflections cast by the denser masses of the house and vegetation about it.

It seemed to be a wooden erection, such as squatters first raise for their homesteads after they have decided to stay; the intermediate kind of station, which takes the place of the temporary shanty while the proprietor's bank account is rapidly swelling, and his children are being educated in the city boarding schools to know their own social importance. By and bye, when he is out of the mortgagee's hands, he may discard this comfortable house, as he has done his shanty, and go in for stateliness and stone-work, but to the tramp or the bushranger, the present house is the most welcome sight, for it promises to the one shelter, and to the other a prospect of loot.

There was a verandah round the basement that stood clear above the earth on piles, with a broad ladder stair leading down to the garden walk which terminated at the edge of the pool or water hole; under the iron roofing of the verandah I could make out the vague indications of French doors that led to the reception rooms, etc., while above them were bedroom windows, all dark with the exception of one of the upper windows, the second one from the end gable, through which a pale greenish light streamed faintly.

Behind the house, or rather from the centre of it, as I afterwards found out, projected a gigantic and lifeless gum tree, which spread its fantastic limbs and branches wildly over the roof, and behind that again a mass of chaotic and planted greenery, all softened and generalized in the thin silvery mist which emanated from the pool and hovered over the ground.

At the first glance it appeared the abode of a romantic owner, who had fixed upon a picturesque site, and afterwards devoted himself to making it comfortable as well as beautiful. He had planted creepers and trained them over the walls, passion-fruit and vines clung closely to the posts and trellis work and broke the square outlines of windows and angles, a wild tangle of shrubs and flowers covered the mound in front and trailed into the water without much order, so that it looked like the abode of an imaginative poet rather than the station of a practical money-grubbing squatter.

As I quitted the desolate and rock-bound gully and entered upon this romantic domain, I could not help admiring the artful manner in which the owner had left Nature alone where he could do so; the gum trees which he had found there were still left as they must have been for ages, great trees shooting up hundreds of feet into the air, some of them gaunt and bald with time, others with their leafage still in a flourishing condition, while the more youthful trees were springing out of the fertile soil in all directions, giving the approach the appearance of an English park, particularly with the heavy night-dew that glistened over them.

But the chill was still upon me that had gripped me at the entrance of the gully, and the same lifeless silence brooded over the house, garden, pool and forest which had awed me amongst the boulders, so that as I paused at the edge of the water and regarded the house, I again shuddered as if spectres were round me, and murmured to myself, "Yes, it looks like a place upon which has fallen a curse."

Two years before this night, I had been tried and condemned to death for murder, the murder of the one I loved best on earth, but, through the energy of the press and the intercession of a number of influential friends, my sentence had been *mercifully* commuted to transportation for life in Western Australia.

The victim, whom I was proved by circumstantial evidence to have murdered, was my young wife, to whom I had been married only six months before; ours was a love match, and until I saw her lying stark before me, those six months had been an uninterrupted honeymoon, without a cloud to cross it, a brief term of heaven, which accentuated the after misery.

I was a medical practitioner in a small country village which I need not name, as my supposed crime rang through England.

My practice was new but growing, so that, although not too well off, we were fairly comfortable as to position, and, as my wife was modest in her desires, we were more than contented with our lot.

I suppose the evidence was strong enough to place my guilt beyond a doubt to those who could not read my heart and the heart of the woman I loved more than life. She had not been very well of late, yet, as it was nothing serious, I attended her myself; then the end came with appalling suddenness, a post-mortem examination proved that she had been poisoned, and that the drug had been taken from my surgery, by whom or for what reason is still a mystery to me, for I do not think I had an enemy in the world, nor do I think my poor darling had either.

At the time of my sentence, I had only one wish, and that was to join the victim of this mysterious crime, so that I saw the judge put on the fatal black cap with a feeling of pleasure, but when afterwards I heard it was to be transportation in-stead, then I flung myself down in my cell and hurled impreca-tions on those officious friends who had given me slavery and misery instead of release. Where was the mercy in letting me have life, since all had been taken from it which made it worth holding?—the woman who had lain in my arms while together we built up glowing pictures of an impossible future, my good name lost, my place amongst men destroyed; henceforward I would be only recognised by a number, my companions the vilest, my days dragged out in chains until the degradation of my lot encrusted over that previous memory of tenderness and fidelity, and I grew to be like the other numbered felons, a mindless and emotionless animal.

Fortunately, at this point of my sufferings, oblivion came in the form of delirium, so that the weeks passed in a dream, during which my lost wife lived once more with me as we had been in the past, and by the time the ship's doctor pronounced me recovered, we were within a few days of our dreary destin-ation. Then my wife went from me to her own place, and I woke up to find that I had made some friends amongst my fellow-convicts, who had taken care of me during my insanity.

We landed at Fremantle, and began our life, road-making, that is; each morning we were driven out of the prison like cattle chained together in groups, and kept in the open until sundown, when we were once more driven back to sleep.

For fourteen months this dull monotony of eating, working and sleeping went on without variation, and then the chance came that I had been hungering for all along; not that liberty was likely to do me much good, only that the hope of accomplishing it kept me alive.

Three of us made a run for it one afternoon, just before the gun sounded for our recall, while the rest of the gang, being in our confidence, covered our escape until we had got beyond gunshot distance. We had managed to file through the chain which linked us together, and we ran towards the bush with the broken pieces in our hands as weapons of defence.

My two comrades were desperate criminals, who, like myself, had been sentenced for life, and, as they confessed themselves, were ready to commit any atrocity rather than be caught and taken back.

That night and the next day we walked in a straight line about forty miles through the bush, and then, being hungry and tired, and considering ourselves fairly safe, we lay down to sleep without any thought of keeping watch.

But we had reckoned too confidently upon our escape, for about daybreak the next morning we were roused up by the sound of galloping horses, and, springing to our feet and climbing a gum tree, we saw a dozen of mounted police, led by two black trackers, coming straight in our direction. Under the circumstances there were but two things left for us to do, either to wait until they came and caught us, or run for it until we were beaten or shot down.

One of my companions decided to wait and be taken back, in spite of his bravado the night before; an empty stomach demoralizes most men; the other one made up his mind, as I did, to run as long as we could. We started in different directions, leaving our mate sitting under the gum tree, he promising to keep them off our track as long as possible.

The fact of him being there when the police arrived gave us a good start. I put all my speed out, and dashed along until I had covered, I daresay, about a couple of miles, when all at once the scrub came to an end, and before me I saw an open space, with another stretch of bush about half a mile distant, and no shelter between me and it.

As I stood for a few minutes to recover my breath, I heard two or three shots fired to the right, the direction my companion had taken, and on looking that way I saw that he also had gained the open, and was followed by one of the trackers and a couple of the police. He was still running, but I could see that he was wounded from the way he went.

Another shot was sent after him, that went straight to its mark, for all at once he threw up his arms and fell prone upon his face, then, hearing the sounds of pursuit in my direction, I waited no longer, but bounded full into the morning sunlight, hoping, as I ran, that I might be as lucky as he had been, and get a bullet between my shoulders and so end my troubles.

I knew that they had seen me, and were after me almost as soon as I had left the cover, for I could hear them shouting for me to stop, as well as the clatter of their horses' hoofs on the hard soil, but still I kept to my course, waiting upon the shots to sound which would terminate my wretched existence, my back-nerves quivering in anticipation and my teeth meeting in my under-lip.

One!

Two!!

Two reports sounded in my ears; a second after the bullets had whistled past my head; and then, before the third and fourth reports came, something like hot iron touched me above my left elbow, while the other bullet whirred past me with a singing wail, cooling my cheek with the wind it raised, and then I saw it ricochet in front of me on the hill side, for I was going up a slight rise at the time.

I had no pain in my arm, although I knew that my humerus was splintered by that third last shot, but I put on a final spurt in order to tempt them to fire again.

What were they doing? I glanced over my shoulder as I rushed, and saw that they were spreading out, fan-like, and riding like fury, while they hurriedly reloaded. Once more they were taking aim at me, and then I looked again in front.

Before me yawned a gulf, the depth of which I could not estimate, yet in width it was over a hundred feet. My pursuers had seen this impediment also, for they were reining up their horses, while they shouted to me, more frantically than ever, to stop.

Why should I stop? flashed the thought across my mind as I neared the edge. Since their bullets had denied me the death I courted, why should I pause at the death spread out for me so opportunely?

As the question flashed through me, I answered it by making the leap, and as I went down I could hear the reports of the rifles above me.

Down into shadow from the sun-glare I dropped, the outer branches of a tree breaking with me as I fell through them.

Another obstacle caught me a little lower, and gave way under my weight, and then with an awful wrench, that nearly stunned me, I felt myself hanging by the remnant of the chain which was still rivetted to my waist-band, about ten feet from the surface, and with a hundred and fifty feet of a drop below me before I could reach the bottom. The chain had somehow got entangled in a fork of the last tree through which I had broken.

Although that sudden wrench was excruciating, the exigency of my position compelled me to collect my faculties without loss of time. Perhaps my months of serfdom and intercourse with felons had blunted my sensibility, and rendered me more callous to danger and bodily pain than I had been in my former and happier days, or the excitement of that terrible chase was still urging within me, for without more than a second's pause, and almost indifferent glance downwards to those distant boulders, I made a wild clutch with my unwounded arm at the branch which had caught me, and with an effort drew myself up to it, so that the next instant I was astride it, or rather crouching, where my loose chain had caught. Then, once more secure, I looked upwards to where I expected my hunters to appear.

When I think upon it now, it was a marvel how I ever got to be placed where I was, for I was under the shelving ledge from which I had leapt, that is, it spread over me like a roof, so that I must conclude that the first tier of branches must have bent inwards, and so landed me on to the second tree at a slant. At least, this is the only way in which I can account for my position.

The tree on which I sat grew from a crevice on the side of the precipice, and from the top could not be seen by those above, neither could I see them, although they looked down after me, but I could hear them plainly enough and what they said.

"That fellow has gone right enough, Jack, although I don't see his remains below; shall we try to get down and make sure?" I heard one say, while another replied:

"What's the good of wasting time; he's as dead as the other chap, after that drop, and they will both be picked clean enough, so let us get back to Fremantle with the living one, and report the other two as wiped out; we have a long enough journey before us, sergeant."

"Yes, I suppose so," answered the sergeant. "Well, boys, we may say that there are two promising bushrangers the less for this colony to support, so right about, home's the word."

I heard their horses wheel round and go off at a canter after this final speech, and then I was left alone on my airy perch, to plan out how best I was to get down with my broken arm, for it was impossible to get up, and also what I was likely to do with my liberty in that desolate region.

Desperate men are not very particular about the risks they run, and I ran not a few before I finally reached the bottom of that gulch, risky drops from one ledge to another, frantic clutchings at branches and tree roots; sufficient that I did reach the level ground at last more nearly dead than alive, so that I was fain to lie under the shadow of a boulder for hours without making an effort to rise and continue my journey.

Then, as night was approaching, I dragged myself along until I came to some water, where, after drinking and bracing up my broken arm with a few gum-trunk shards, and binding them round with some native grasses, while I made my supper of the young leaves of the eucalyptus bushes, I went on.

On, on, on for weeks, until I had lost all count of time, I wandered, carrying my broken fetters with me, and my broken arm gradually mending of its own accord. Sometimes I killed a snake or an iguana during the day with the branch I used for a stick, or a 'possum or wild cat at night, which I devoured raw. Often I existed for days on grass roots or the leaves of the gum-tree, anything was good enough to fill up the gap.

My convict garb was in tatters and my feet bootless by this time, and my hair and beard hung over my shoulders and chest, while often I went for days in a semi-conscious state, for the fierce sun seemed to wither up my blood and set fire to my brain.

Where I was going I could not tell, and still, with all the privation and misery, the love of life was once again stronger in me than it had been since I had lost my place amongst civilized men, for I was at liberty and alone to indulge in fancy.

And yet it did not seem altogether fancy that my lost wife was with me on that journey. At first she came only when I lay down to sleep, but after a time she walked with me hand in hand during the day as well as in my dreams.

Dora was her name, and soon I forgot that she had been dead, for she was living and beautiful as ever as we went along together, day after day, speaking to each other like lovers as we used to speak, and she did not seem to mind my ragged, degraded costume, or my dirty, tangled beard, but caressed me with the same tenderness as of yore.

Through the bush, down lonely gullies, over bitter deserts and salt marshes, we passed as happy and affectionate as fond lovers could be who are newly married, and whom the world cannot part, my broken chain rattling as I staggered onwards, while she smiled as if pleased with the music, because it was the chain which I was wearing for her dear sake.

Let me think for a moment—was she with me through that last desert before I came to that gloomy gully? I cannot be quite sure of that, but this I do know that she was not with me after the chill shadows of the boulders drew me into them, and I was quite alone when I stood by the water-hole looking upon that strange and silent house.

It was singular that the house should be here at all in this far-off and as yet unnamed portion of Western Australia, for I naturally supposed that I had walked hundreds of miles since leaving the convict settlement, and as I had encountered no one, not even a single tribe of wandering blacks, it seemed impossible to believe that I was not the first white man who had penetrated so far, and yet there it loomed before me, substantial-looking in its masses, with painted weatherboards, shingles, iron-sheeting, carved posts and trellis-work, French windows, and the signs of cultivation about it, although bearing the traces of late neglect.

Was it inhabited? I next asked myself as I looked steadily at that dimly-illumined window; seemingly it was, for as I mentally asked the question, a darkness blotted out the light for a few moments and then moved slowly aside, while the faint pallor once more shone out; it appeared to be from the distance a window with a pale green blind drawn down, behind which a lamp turned low was burning, possibly some invalid who was restlessly walking about, while the rest of the household slept.

Would it be well to rouse them up at this hour of the night? I next queried as I paused, watching the chimney tops from which no wreath of smoke came, for although it did not seem late, judging from the height of the moon, yet it was only natural to suppose that in this isolated place the people would retire early. Perhaps it would be better to wait where I was till morning and see what they were like before I ventured to ask hospitality from them, in my ragged yet unmistakably convict dress. I would rather go on as I was than run the risk of being dragged back to prison.

How chilly the night vapours were which rose from this large pool, for it was more like the moat round some ancient ruin than an ordinary Australian water-hole. How ominous the shadows that gathered over this dwelling, and which even the great and lustrous moon, now clear of the gable end, seemed unable to dissipate, and what a dismal effect that dimly-burning lamp behind the pale green blind gave to it.

I turned my eyes from the window to the pond from which the ghostly vapours were steaming upwards in such strange shapes; they crossed the reflections like grey shadows and floated over the white glitter which the moon cast down, like spectres following each other in a stately procession, curling upwards interlaced, while the gaunt trees behind them altered their shapes and looked demoniac in their fantastic outlines, shadows passing along and sending back doleful sighs, which I tried all my might to think was the night breeze but without succeeding.

Hush! was that a laugh which wafted from the house, a low, but blood-curdling cachinnation such as an exultant devil might utter who had witnessed his fell mischief accomplished, followed by the wail of a woman, intermixed with the cry of a child!

Ah! what a fool I was to forget the cry of the Australian king-fisher; of course that was it, of course, of course, but—

The shapes are thickening over that mirror-like pool, and as I look I see a woman with a chalk-white face and eyes distended in horror, with a child in her hands—a little girl—and beside them the form of a man whose face changes into two different men, one the face of death, and the other like that of a demon with glaring eyeballs, while he points from the woman and child to the sleeping pool.

What is the devil-spectre pointing at, as he laughs once more while the woman and child shrink with affright?

The face that he wore a moment ago, the face of the dead man whom I can see floating amongst that silver lustre.

I must have fainted at the weird visions of the night before, or else I may have fallen asleep and dreamt them, for when I opened my eyes again the morning sun was pouring over the landscape and all appeared changed.

The pool was still there, but it looked like a natural Australian water-hole which had been deepened and lengthened, and artificially arranged by a tasteful proprietor to beautify his estate; water-lilies grew round the edges and spread themselves in graceful patches about; it was only in the centre portion, where the moonlight had glinted and the other reflections cast themselves, that the water was clear of weeds, and there it still lay inky and dangerous-like in its depth.

Over the building itself clustered a perfect tangle of vegetable parasites, Star-of-Bethlehem, Maiden-blush roses, and Gloire-de-Dijon, passion-flowers and convolvulus, intermingling with a large grape-laden vine going to waste, and hanging about in half-wild, neglected festoons; a woman's hand had planted these tendrils, as well as the garden in front, for I could see that flowers predominated.

As for the house itself, it still stood silent and deserted-looking, the weatherboards had shrunk a good deal with the heat of many suns beating upon them, while the paint, once tasteful in its varied tints, was bleached into dry powder; the trellis-work also on the verandah had in many places been torn away by the weight of the clinging vines, and between the window-frames and the windows yawned wide fissures where they had shrunk from each other.

I looked round at the landscape, but could see no trace of sheep or cattle, or humanity; it spread out a sun-lit solitude where Nature, for a little while trained to order, had once more asserted her independent lavishness.

A little of my former awe came upon me as I stood for a few moments hesitating to advance, but at the sight of those luscious-looking bunches of grapes, which seemed to promise some fare more substantial inside, the dormant cravings for food which I had so long subdued came upon me with tenfold force, and, without more than a slight tremor of superstitious dread, I hurriedly crushed my way through the tangle of vegetation, and made for the verandah and open door of the hall.

Delicious grapes they were, as I found when, after tearing off a huge bunch, and eating them greedily, I entered the silent hall and began my exploration.

The dust and fine sand of many *"brick-fielders,"* i.e., sand-storms, lay thickly on every object inside, so that as I walked I left my footprints behind me as plainly as if I had been walking over snow. In the hall I found a handsome stand and carved table with chairs, a hat and riding-whip lay on the table, while on the rack I saw two or three coats and hats hanging, with sticks and umbrellas beneath, all white with dust.

The dining-room door stood ajar, and as I entered I could see that it also had been undisturbed for months, if not for years. It had been handsomely furnished, with artistic hangings and stuffed leather chairs and couches, while on the elaborately carved cheffonier was a plentiful supply of spirit and wine de-canters, with cut glasses standing ready for use. On the table stood a bottle of Three-star brandy, half-emptied, and by its side a water-filter and glass as they had been left by the last user.

I smelt the bottle, and found that the contents were mel-low and good, and when, after dusting the top, I put it to my mouth, I discovered that the bouquet was delicious; then, invigorated by that sip, I continued my voyage of discovery.

The cheffonier was not locked, and inside I discovered rows of sealed bottles, which satisfied me that I was not likely to run short of refreshments in the liquid form at any rate, so, content with this pleasant prospect, I ventured into the other apartments.

The drawing-room was like the room I had left, a picture of comfort and elegance, when once the accumulation of dust and sand had been removed.

The library or study came next, which I found in perfect order, although I left the details for a more leisurely examination.

I next penetrated the kitchen, which I saw was comfortable, roomy and well-provided, although in more disorder than the other rooms; pans stood rusting in the fire-place, dishes lay dirty and in an accumulated pile on the table, as if the servants had left in a hurry and the owners had been forced to make what shifts they could during their absence.

Yet there was no lack of such provisions as an up-country station would be sure to lay in; the pantry I found stored like a provision shop, with flitches of bacon, hams sewn in canvas, tinned meat and soups of all kinds, with barrels and bags and boxes of flour, sugar, tea and other sundries, enough to keep me going for years if I was lucky enough to be in possession.

I next went upstairs to the bedrooms, up a thickly-carpeted staircase, with the white linen overcloth still upon it. In the first room I found the bed with the bed-clothes tumbled about as if the sleeper had lately left it; the master of the house I supposed, as I examined the wardrobe and found it well stocked with male apparel. At last I could cast aside my degrading rags, and fit myself out like a free man, after I had visited the workshop and filed my fetters from me.

Another door attracted me on the opposite side of the lobby, and this I opened with some considerable trepidation because it led into the room which I had seen lighted up the night before.

It seemed untenanted, as I looked in cautiously, and like the other bed-room was in a tumble of confusion, a woman's room, for the dresses and underclothing were lying about, a bed-room which had been occupied by a woman and a child, for a crib stood in one corner, and on a chair lay the frock and other articles belonging to a little girl of about five or six years of age.

I looked at the window, it had Venetian blinds upon it, and they were drawn up, so that my surmise had been wrong about the pale green blind, but on the end side of the room was another window with the blinds also drawn up, and thus satisfied I walked in boldly; what I had thought to be a light, had only been the moonlight streaming from the one window to the other, while the momentary blackening of the light had been caused, doubtless, by the branches of the trees outside, moved forward by the night breeze. Yes, that must have been the cause, so that I had nothing to fear, the house was deserted, and my own property, for the time at least. There was a strange and musty odour in this bed-room, which blended with the perfume which the owner had used, and made me for a moment almost giddy, so the first thing I did was to open both windows and let in the morning air, after which I looked over to the unmade bed, and then I staggered back with a cry of horror.

There amongst the tumble of bed-clothes lay the skeletons of what had been two human beings, clad in embroidered night-dresses. One glance was enough to convince me, with my medical knowledge, that the gleaming bones were those of a woman and a child, the original wearers of those dresses which lay scattered about.

What awful tragedy had taken place in this richly furnished but accursed house? Recovering myself, I examined the remains more particularly, but could find no clue, they were lying reposefully enough, with arms interlacing as if they had died or been done to death in their sleep, while those tiny anatomists,

the ants, had found their way in, and cleaned the bones completely, as they very soon do in this country.

With a sick sensation at my heart, I continued my investigations throughout the other portions of the station. In the
servants' quarters I learnt the cause of the unwashed dishes;
three skeletons lay on the floor in different positions as they
had fallen, while their shattered skulls proved the cause of their
end, even if the empty revolver that I picked up from the floor
had not been evidence enough. Some one must have entered
their rooms and woke them rudely from their sleep in the night
time for they lay also in their blood-stained night-dresses, and
beside them, on the boards, were dried-up markings which were
unmistakable.

The rest of the house was as it had been left by the murderer
or murderers. Three domestics, with their mistress and child,
had been slaughtered, and then the guilty wretches had fled
without disturbing anything else.

It was once again night, and I was still in the house which my
first impulse had been to leave with all haste after the gruesome
discoveries that I had made.

But several potent reasons restrained me from yielding to
that impulse. I had been wandering for months, and living like
a wild beast, while here I had everything to my hand which
I needed to recruit my exhausted system. My curiosity was
roused, so that I wanted to penetrate the strange mystery if I
could, by hunting after and reading all the letters and papers
that I might be able to find, and to do this required leisure;
thirdly, as a medical practitioner who had passed through the
anatomical schools, the presence of five skeletons did not have
much effect upon me, and lastly, before sun-down the weather
had broken, and one of those fierce storms of rain, wind, thunder and lightning had come on, which utterly prevented any
one who had the chance of a roof to shelter him from turning
out to the dangers of the night.

These were some of my reasons for staying where I was, at least the reasons that I explained to myself, but there was another and a more subtle motive which I could not logically explain, and which yet influenced me more than any of the others. *I could not leave the house, now that I had taken possession of it,* or rather, if I may say it, *now that the house had taken possession of me.*

I had lifted the bucket from the kitchen, and found my way to the draw-well in the back-garden, with the uncomfortable feeling that some unseen force was compelling me to stay here. I discovered a large file and freed myself from my fetters, and then, throwing my rags from me with disgust, I clad myself in one of the suits that I found in the wardrobe upstairs, then I set to work dusting and sweeping out the dining-room, after which I lit a fire, retrimmed the lamps, and cooked a substantial meal for myself, then the storm coming on decided me, so that I spent the remainder of the afternoon making the place comfortable, and when darkness did come, I had drawn the blinds down and secured the shutters, and with a lighted lamp, a bottle of good wine, and a box of first-class cigars which I also found in the cheffonier, with a few volumes that I had taken from the book shelves at random, and an album of photographs that I picked up from the drawing-room table, I felt a different man from what I had been the night previous, particularly with that glowing log fire in the grate.

I left the half-emptied bottle of brandy where I had found it, on the table, with the used glass and the water filter untouched, as I did also the chair that had been beside them. I had a repugnance to those articles which I could not overcome; the murderer had used them last, possibly as a reviver after his crimes, for I had reasoned out that one hand only had been at the work, and that man's the owner of the suit which I was then wearing and which fitted me so exactly, otherwise why should the house have been left in the condition that it was?

As I sat at the end of the table and smoked the cigar, I rebuilt the whole tragedy, although as yet the motive was not so clear, and as I thought the matter out, I turned over the leaves of the album and looked at the photographs.

Before me, on the walls, hung three oil portraits, enlargements they were, and as works of art vile things, yet doubtless they were faithful enough likenesses. In the album, I found three cabinet portraits from which the paintings had been enlarged.

They were the portraits of a woman of about twenty-six, a girl of five years, and a man of about thirty-two.

The woman was good-looking, with fresh colour, blue eyes and golden-brown hair. The girl—evidently her daughter—for the likeness was marked between the two, had one of those seraphic expressions which some delicate children have who are marked out for early death, that places them above the plane of grosser humanity. She looked, as she hung between the two portraits, with her glory of golden hair, like the guardian angel of the woman who was smiling so contentedly and unconsciously from her gilded frame.

The man was pallid-faced and dark, clean-shaven, all except the small black moustache, with lips which, except the artist had grossly exaggerated the colour, were excessively and disagreeably vivid. His eyes were deep set, and glowing as if with the glitter of a fever.

"These would be the likenesses of the woman and child whose skeletons lay unburied upstairs, and that pallid-faced, feverish-eyed ghoul, the fiend who had murdered them, his wife and child," I murmured to myself as I watched the last portrait with morbid interest.

"Right and wrong, Doctor, as you medical men mostly are," answered a deep voice from the other end of the table.

I started with amazement, and looked from the painting to the vacant chair beside the brandy bottle, which was now occupied by what appeared to be the original of the picture I had been looking at, face, hair, vivid scarlet lips and deep-set fiery eyes, which were fixed upon me intently and mockingly.

How had he entered without my observing him? By the window? No, for that I had firmly closed and secured myself, and as I glanced at it I saw that it still remained the same. By the door? Perhaps so, although he must have closed it again after he had entered without my hearing him, as he might easily have done during one of the claps of thunder, which were now almost incessant, as were the vivid flashes of wild fire or lightning that darted about, while the rain lashed against the shutters outside.

He was dripping wet, as I could see, so that he must have come from that deluge, bareheaded and dripping, with his hair and moustache draggling over his glistening, ashy cheeks and bluish chin, as if he had been submerged in water, while weeds and slime hung about his saturated garments; a gruesome sight for a man who fancied himself alone to see start up all of a sudden, and no wonder that it paralyzed me and prevented me from finding the words I wanted at the moment. Had he lain hidden somewhere watching me take possession of his premises, and being, as solitary men sometimes are, fond of dramatic effect, slipped in while my back was turned from the door to give me a surprise? If so, he had succeeded, for I never before felt so craven-spirited or horror-stricken, my flesh was creeping and my hair bristling, while my blood grew to ice within me. The very lamp seemed to turn dim, and the fire smouldered down on the hearth, while the air was chill as a charnel vault, as I sat with shivering limbs and chattering teeth before this evil visitor.

Outside, the warring elements raged and fought, shaking the wooden walls, while the forked flames darted between us, lighting up his face with a ghastly effect. He must have seen my horror, for he once more laughed that low, malicious chuckle that I had heard the night before, as he again spoke.

"Make yourself at home, Doctor, and try some of this cognac instead of that washy stuff you are drinking. I am only sorry that I cannot join you in it, but I cannot *just yet.*"

I found words at last and asked him questions, which seemed impertinent in the extreme, considering where I was.

"Who are you? Where do you come from? What do you want?"

Again that hateful chuckle, as he fixed his burning eyes upon me with a regard which fascinated me in spite of myself.

"Who am I, do you ask? Well, before you took possession of this place I was its owner. Where do I come from? From out of there last."

He pointed backwards towards the window, which burst open as he uttered the words, while through the driving rain a flash of lightning seemed to dart from his outstretched finger and disappear into the centre of the lake, then after that hurried glimpse, the shutters clashed together again and we were as before.

"What do I want? You, for lack of a better."

"What do you want with me?" I gasped.

"To make you myself."

"I do not understand you, what are you?"

"At present nothing, yet with your help, I shall be a man once more, while you shall be free and rich, for you shall have more gold than you ever could dream of."

"What can I do for you?"

"Listen to my story and you will see. Ten years ago I was a successful gold finder, the trusting husband of that woman, and the fond father of that girl. I had likewise a friend whom I trusted, and took to live with me as a partner. We lived here together, my friend, myself, my wife and my daughter, for I was romantic and had raised this house to be close to the mine which I had discovered, and which I will show you if you consent to my terms.

"One night my friend murdered me and pitched my body into that water-hole where the bones still lie. He did this because he coveted my wife and my share of the money."

I was calm now, but watchful, for it appeared that I had to deal with a madman.

"In my life-time I had been a trusting and guileless simpleton, but no sooner was my spirit set free than vengeance transformed its nature. I hovered about the place where all my affections had been centred, watching him beguile the woman who had been mine until he won her. She waited three years for me to return, and then she believed his story that I had been killed by the natives, and married him. They travelled to where you came from, to be married, and I followed them closely, for that was the chance I waited upon. The union of those two once accomplished he was in my power for ever, for this had established the link that was needed for me to take forcible possession of him."

"And where was his spirit meantime?" I asked, to humour the maniac.

"In my grasp also, a spirit rendered impotent by murder and ingratitude; a spirit which I could do with as I pleased, so long as the wish I had was evil. I took possession of his body, the mirage of which you see now, and from that moment until the hour that our daughter rescued her from his clutches, he made the life of my former wife a hell on earth. I prompted his murder-embrued spirit to madness, leaving him only long enough to himself after I had braced him up to do the deed of vengeance."

"How did the daughter save the mother?"

"By dying with her, and by her own purity tearing the freed spirit from my clutches. I did not intend the animal to do all that he did, for I wanted the mother only, but once the murder lust was on him, I found that he was beyond my influence. He slew the two by poison, as he had done me, then, frenzied, he murdered the servants, and finally exterminated himself by flinging himself into the pool. That was why I said that I came last from out of there, where both my own remains and his lie together."

"Yes, and what is my share of the business?"

"To look on me passively for a few moments, as you are at present doing, that is all I require."

I did not believe his story about his being only a mirage or spectre, for he looked at the moment corporal enough to do me a considerable amount of bodily harm, and therefore to humour him, until I could plan out a way to overpower him, I fixed my eyes upon his steadfastly, as he desired.

Was I falling asleep, or being mesmerized by this homicidal lunatic? As he glared at me with those fiery orbs and an evil contortion curling the blood-red lips, while the forked lightning played around him, I became helpless. He was creeping slowly towards me as a cat might steal upon a mouse, and I was unable to move, or take my eyes from his eyes which seemed to be charming my life-blood from me, when suddenly I heard the distant sound of music, through a lull of the tempest, the rippling of a piano from the drawing-room with the mingling of a child's silvery voice as it sang its evening hymn, and at the sound his eyes shifted while he fell back a step or two with an agonized spasm crossing his ghastly and dripping wet face.

Then the hurricane broke loose once more, with a resistless fury, while the door and window burst open, and the shutters were dashed into the room.

I leapt to my feet in a paroxysm of horror, and sprang towards the open door with that demon, or maniac, behind me.

Merciful heavens! the drawing-room was brilliantly lighted up, and there, seated at the open piano, was the woman whose bones I had seen bleaching upstairs, with the seraphic-faced child singing her hymn.

Out to the tempest I rushed madly, and heedless of where I went, so that I escaped from that accursed and haunted house, on, past the water-hole and into the glade, where I turned my head back instinctively, as I heard a wilder roar of thunder and the crash as if a tree had been struck.

What a flash that was which lighted up the scene and showed me the house collapsing as an erection of cards. It went down like an avalanche before that zig-zag flame, which seemed to lick round it for a moment, and then disappear into the earth.

Next instant I was thrown off my feet by the earthquake which shook the ground under me, while, as I still looked on where the house had been, I saw that the ruin had caught fire, and was blazing up in spite of the torrents that still poured down, and as it burned, I saw the mound sink slowly out of sight, while the reddened smoke eddied about in the same strange shapes which the vapours had assumed the night before, scarlet ghosts of the demon and his victims.

Two months after this, I woke up to find myself in a Queensland back-country station. They had found me wandering in a delirious condition over one of their distant runs six weeks before my return to consciousness, and as they could not believe that a pedestrian, without provisions, could get over that unknown stretch of country from Fremantle, they paid no attention to my ravings about being an escaped convict, particularly as the rags I had on could never have been prison made. Learning, however, that I had medical knowledge, by the simple method of putting it to the test, my good rescuers set me up in my old profession, where I still remain—a Queensland back-country doctor.

The Dâk Bungalow at Dakor
Bithia Mary Croker (1893)

"When shall these phantoms flicker away,
　Like the smoke of the guns on the wind-swept
　　hill;
　Like the sounds and colours of yesterday,
　And the soul have rest, and the air be still?"

Sir A. Lyall

"And so you two young women are going off on a three days'
journey, all by yourselves, in a bullock tonga, to spend Christmas with your husbands in the jungle?"

The speaker was Mrs. Duff, the wife of our deputy commissioner, and the two enterprising young women were Mrs.
Goodchild, the wife of the police officer of the district, and
myself, wife of the forest officer. We were the only ladies in
Karwassa, a little up-country station, more than a hundred
miles from the line of rail. Karwassa was a pretty place, an oasis
of civilization, amid leagues and leagues of surrounding forest
and jungle; it boasted a post-office, public gardens (with tennis
courts), a tiny church, a few well-kept shady roads, and half a
dozen thatched bungalows, surrounded by luxuriant gardens.
In the hot weather all the community were at home, under the
shelter of their own roof-trees and punkahs, and within reach of
ice—for we actually boasted an ice machine! During these hot

months we had, so to speak, our "season." The deputy commissioner, forest officer, police officer, doctor, and engineer were all "in," and our gaieties took the form of tennis at daybreak, moonlight picnics, whist-parties, little dinners, and now and then a beat for tiger, on which occasions we ladies were safely roosted in trustworthy trees.

It is whispered that in small and isolated stations the fair sex are either mortal enemies or bosom-friends! I am proud to be in a position to state that we ladies of Karwassa came under the latter head. Mrs. Goodchild and I were especially intimate; we were nearly the same age, we were young, we had been married in the same year and tasted our first experiences of India together. We lent each other books, we read each other our home letters, helped to compose one another's dirzee-made costumes, and poured little confidences into one another's ears. We had made numerous joint excursions in the cold season, had been out in the same camp for a month at a time, and when our husbands were in a malarious or uncivilized district, had journeyed on horseback or in a bullock tonga and joined them at some accessible spot, in the regions of dâk bungalows and bazaar fowl.

Mrs. Duff, stout, elderly, and averse to locomotion, contented herself with her comfortable bungalow at Karwassa, her weekly budget of letters from her numerous olive-branches in England, and with adventures and thrilling experiences at secondhand.

"And so you are off to-morrow," she continued, addressing herself to Mrs. Goodchild. "I suppose you know *where* you are going?"

"Yes," returned my companion promptly, unfolding a piece of foolscap as she spoke; "I had a letter from Frank this morning, and he has enclosed a plan copied from the D. P. W. map. We go straight along the trunk road for two days, stopping at Korai bungalow the first night and Kular the second, you see; then we turn off to the left on the Old Jubbulpore Road and make a march of twenty-five miles, halting at a place called Chanda. Frank and Mr. Loyd will meet us there on Christmas Day."

"Chanda—Chanda," repeated Mrs. Duff, with her hand to her head. "Isn't there some queer story about a bungalow near there—that is unhealthy—or haunted—or something?"

Julia Goodchild and I glanced at one another significantly. Mrs. Duff had set her face against our expedition all along; she wanted us to remain in the station and spend Christmas with her, instead of going this wild-goose chase into a part of the district we had never been in before. She assured us that we would be short of bollocks, and would probably have to walk miles; she had harangued us on the subject of fever and cholera and bad water, had warned us solemnly against dacoits, and now she was hinting at ghosts.

"Frank says that the travellers' bungalows after we leave the main road are not in very good repair—the road is so little used now that the new railway line comes within twenty miles; but he says that the one at Chanda is very decent, and we will push on there," returned Julia, firmly. Julia was nothing if not firm; she particularly prided herself on never swerving from any fixed resolution or plan. "We take my bullock tonga, and Mr. Loyd's peon Abdul, who is a treasure, as you know; he can cook, interpret, forage for provisions, and drive bullocks if the worst comes to the worst."

"And what about bullocks for three days' journey—a hundred miles if it's a yard?" inquired Mrs. Duff, sarcastically.

"Oh, the bazaar master has sent on a chuprassie and five natives, and we shall find a pair every five miles at the usual stages. As to food, we are taking tea, bread, plenty of tinned stores, and the plum-pudding. We shall have a capital outing, I assure you, and I only wish we could have persuaded you into coming with us."

"Thank you, my dear," said Mrs. Duff, with a patronizing smile. "I'm too old, and I hope too sensible to take a trip of a hundred miles in a bullock tonga, risking fever and dacoits and dâk bungalows full of bandicoots, just for the sentimental pleasure of eating a pudding with my husband. However, you are both young and hardy and full of spirits, and I wish you a happy Christmas, a speedy journey and safe return. Mind you take plenty of quinine—and a revolver;" and, with this cheerful parting suggestion, she conducted us into the front verandah and dismissed us each with a kiss, that was at once a remonstrance and a valediction.

Behold us the next morning, at sunrise, jogging off, behind a pair of big white bullocks, in the highest spirits. In the front seat of the tonga we had stowed a well-filled tiffin basket, two Gladstone bags, our blankets and pillows, a hamper of provisions, and last, not least, Abdul. Julia and I and Julia's dog "Boss" occupied the back seat, and as we rumbled past Mrs. Duff's bungalow, with its still silent compound and closed Venetians, we mutually agreed that she was "a silly old thing," that she would have far more enjoyment of life if she was as enterprising as we were.

Our first day's journey went off without a hitch. Fresh and well-behaved cattle punctually awaited us at every stage. The country we passed through was picturesque and well wooded; doves, peacocks, and squirrels enlivened the roads; big black-faced monkeys peered at us from amid the crops that they were ravaging within a stone's throw of our route. The haunt of a well-known man-eating tiger was impressively pointed out to us by our cicerone Abdul—this beast resided in some dense jungle, that was unpleasantly close to human traffic. Morning and afternoon wore away speedily, and at sundown we found ourselves in front of the very neat travellers' bungalow at Korai. The interior was scrupulously clean, and contained the usual furniture: two beds, two tables, four chairs, lamps, baths, a motley collection of teacups and plates, and last, not least, the framed rules of the establishment and visitors' book. The khansamah cooked us an excellent dinner (for a travellers' bungalow), and, tired out, we soon went to bed and slept the sleep of the just. The second day was the same as the first—highly successful in every respect.

On the third morning we left the great highway and turned to the left, on to what was called the Old Jubbulpore Road, and here our troubles commenced! Bullocks were bad, lame, small, or unbroken; one of Mrs. Duff's dismal prophecies came to pass, for after enduring bullocks who lay down, who kicked and ran off the road into their owners' houses, or rushed violently down steep places, we arrived at one stage where there were no bullocks *at all!* It was four o'clock, and we were still six-teen miles from Chanda. After a short consultation, Julia and I agreed to walk on to the next stage or village, leaving Abdul to draw the neighbourhood for a pair of cattle and then to over-take us at express speed.

"No one coming much this road now, mem sahib," he ex-plained apologetically; "village people never keeping tonga bullocks—only plough bullocks, and plenty bobbery."

"Bobbery or not, get them," said Julia with much decision; "no matter if you pay four times the usual fare. We shall expect you to overtake us in half an hour." And having issued this edict we walked on, leaving Abdul, a bullock-man, and two villagers all talking together and yelling at one another at the top of their voices.

Our road was dry and sandy, and lay through a perfectly flat country. It was lined here and there by rows of graceful trees, covered with wreaths of yellow flowers; now and then it was bordered by a rude thorn hedge, inside of which waved a golden field of ripe jawarri; in distant dips in the landscape we beheld noble topes of forest trees and a few red-roofed dwellings—the abodes of the tillers of the soil; but, on the whole, the country was silent and lonely; the few people we encountered driving their primitive little carts stared hard at us in utter stupefac-tion, as well they might—two mem sahibs trudging along, with no escort except a panting white dog. The insolent crows and lazy blue buffaloes all gazed at us in undisguised amazement as we wended our way through this monotonous and melancholy scene. One milestone was passed and then another, and yet another, and still no sign of Abdul, much less the tonga. At length we came in sight of a large village that stretched in a ragged way at either side of the road. There were the usual little mud hovels, shops displaying, say, two bunches of plantains and a few handfuls of grain, the usual collection of gaunt red pariah dogs, naked children, and unearthly-looking cats and poultry.

Julia and I halted afar off under a tree, preferring to wait for Abdul to chaperon us, ere we ran the gauntlet of the village streets. Time was getting on, the sun was setting; men were returning from the fields, driving bony bullocks before them; women were returning from the well, with water and the last bit of scandal; at last, to our great relief, we beheld Abdul approaching with the tonga, and our spirits rose, for we had begun to ask one another if we were to spend the night sitting on a stone under a tamarind tree without the village.

"No bullocks," was Abdul's explanation. The same tired pair had come on most reluctantly, and in this village of cats and cocks and hens it was the same story—"no bullocks." Abdul brought us this heavy and unexpected intelligence after a long and animated interview with the head man of the place.

"What is to be done?" we demanded in a breath.

"Stop here all night; going on to-morrow."

"Stop where?" we almost screamed.

"Over there," rejoined Abdul, pointing to a grove of trees at some little distance. "There is a travellers' bungalow; Chanda is twelve miles off."

A travellers' bungalow! Sure enough there was a building of some kind beyond the bamboos, and we lost no time in getting into the tonga and having ourselves driven in that direction. As we passed the village street, many came out and stared, and one old woman shook her hand in a warning manner, and called out something in a shrill cracked voice.

An avenue of feathery bamboos led to our destination, which proved to be the usual travellers' rest-house, with white walls, red roof, and roomy verandah; but when we came closer, we discovered that the drive was as grass-grown as a field; jungle grew up to the back of the house, heavy wooden shutters closed all the windows, and the door was locked. There was a forlorn, desolate, dismal appearance about the place; it looked as if it had not been visited for years. In answer to our shouts and calls no one appeared; but, as we were fully resolved to spend the night there, we had the tonga unloaded and our effects placed in the verandah, the bullocks untackled and turned out among the long rank grass. At length an old man in dirty ragged clothes, and with a villainous expression of countenance, appeared from some back cook-house, and seemed anything but pleased to see us. When Abdul told him of our intention of occupying the house, he would not hear of it. "The bungalow was out of repair; it had not been opened for years; it was full of rats; it was unhealthy; plenty fever coming. We must go on to Chanda."

Naturally we declined his hospitable suggestion. "Was he the khansamah—caretaker of the place?" we inquired imperiously.

"Yees," he admitted with a grunt.

"Drawing government pay, and refusing to open a government travellers' bungalow!" screamed Julia. "Let us have no more of this nonsense; open the house at once and get it ready for us, or I shall report you to the commissioner sahib."

The khansamah gave her an evil look, said "Missus please," shrugged his shoulders and hobbled away—as we hoped, to get the *key;* but after waiting ten minutes we sent Abdul to search for him, and found that he had departed—his lair was empty. There was nothing for it but to break the padlock on the door, which Abdul effected with a stone, and as soon as the door moved slowly back on its hinges Julia and I hurried in. What a dark, damp place! What a smell of earth, and what numbers of bats; they flew right in our faces as we stood in the doorway and tried to make out the interior. Abdul and the bullock-man

quickly removed the shutters and let in the light, and then
we beheld the usual dâk sitting-room—a table, chairs, and two
charpoys (native beds), and an old pair of candlesticks; the table
and chairs were covered with mould; cobwebs hung from the
ceiling in dreadful festoons, and the walls were streaked with
dreary green stains. I could not restrain an involuntary shudder
as I looked about me rather blankly.

"I should think this *was* an unhealthy place!" I remarked to
Julia. "It looks feverish; and see—the jungle comes right up to
the back verandah; fever plants, castor-oil plants, young bamboos, all growing up to the very walls."

"It will do very well for to-night," she returned. "Come
out and walk down the road whilst Abdul and the bullock-man
clean out the rooms and get dinner. Abdul is a wonderful man—
and we won't know the place in an hour's time; it's just the same
as any other travellers' bungalow, only it has been neglected for
years. I shall certainly report that old wretch! The *idea* of a dâk
bungalow caretaker refusing admittance and running away with
the key! What is the name of this place?" she asked, deliberately
taking out her pocket-book; "did you hear?"

"Yes; I believe it is called Dakor."

"Ah, well! I shall not forget to tell Frank about the way we
were treated at Dakor bungalow."

The red, red sun had set at last—gone down, as it were,
abruptly behind the flat horizon; the air began to feel chilly,
and the owl and the jackal were commencing to make themselves heard, so we sauntered back to the bungalow, and found it
indeed transformed: swept and garnished, and clean. The table
was neatly laid for dinner, and one of our own fine hurricane
lamps blazed upon it; our beds had been made up with our rugs
and blankets, one at either end of the room; hot water and towels were prepared in a bath-room, and we saw a roaring fire in
the cook-house in the jungle. Dinner, consisting of a sudden-
death fowl, curry, bread, and *pâté de foie gras,* was, to our
unjaded palates, an excellent meal. Our spirits rose to normal,

the result of food and light, and we declared to one another that this old bungalow was a capital find, and that it was really both comfortable and cheerful, despite a slight *arrière pensée* of earth in the atmosphere!

Before going to bed we explored the next room, a smaller one than that we occupied, and empty save for a rickety camp table, which held some dilapidated crockery and a press. Need you ask if we opened this press? The press smelt strongly of mushrooms, and contained a man's topee, inch-deep with mould, a tiffin basket, and the bungalow visitors' book. We carried this away with us to read at leisure, for the visitors' book in dâk bungalows occasionally contains some rather amusing observations. There was nothing funny in this musty old volume! Merely a statement of who came, and how long they stayed, and what they paid, with a few remarks, not by any means complimentary to the khansamah: "A dirty, lazy rascal," said one; "A murderous-looking ruffian," said another; "An insolent, drunken hound," said a third—the last entry was dated seven years previously!

"Let us write our names," said Julia, taking out her pencil; "'Mrs. Goodchild and Mrs. Loyd, December 23rd. Bungalow deserted, and very dirty khansamah.' What shall we say?" she asked, glancing at me interrogatively.

"Why, there he is!" I returned with a little jump; and there he was sure enough, gazing in through the window. It was the face of some malicious animal, more than the face of a man, that glowered out beneath his filthy red turban. His eyes glared and rolled as if they would leave their sockets; his teeth were fangs, like dogs' teeth, and stood out almost perpendicularly from his hideous mouth. He surveyed us for a few seconds in savage silence, and then melted away into the surrounding darkness as suddenly as he appeared.

"He reminds me of the Cheshire cat in 'Alice in Wonderland,'" said Julia with would-be facetiousness, but I noticed that she looked rather pale.

"Let us have the shutters up at once," I replied, "and have them well barred and the doors bolted. That man looked as if he could cut our throats."

In a very short time the house was made last. Abdul and the bullock-man spread their mats in the front verandah, and Julia and I retired for the night. Before going to bed we had a controversy about the lamp. I wished to keep it burning all night (I am a coward at heart), but Julia would not hear of this—impossible for her to sleep with a light in the room—and in the end I was compelled to be content with a candle and matches on a chair beside me. I fell asleep very soon. I fancy I must have slept long and soundly, when I was awoke by a bright light shining in my eyes. So, after the ridiculous fuss she had made, Julia *had* lit the candle after all! This was my first thought, but when I was fully awake I found I was mistaken, or dreaming. No, I was not dreaming, for I pinched my arm and rubbed my eyes. There was a man in the room, apparently another traveller, who appeared to be totally unaware of our vicinity, and to have made himself completely at home. A gun-case, a tiffin basket, a bundle of pillows and rugs—the usual Indian traveller's belongings—lay carelessly scattered about on the chairs and the floor. I leant up on my elbow and gazed at the intruder in profound amazement. He did not notice me, no more than if I had no existence; true, my charpoy was in a corner of the room and rather in the shade, so was Julia's. Julia was sound asleep and (low be it spoken) snoring. The stranger was writing a letter at the table facing me. Both candles were drawn up close to him, and threw a searching light upon his features. He was young and good-looking, but very, very pale; possibly he had just recovered from some long illness. I could not see his eyes, they were bent upon the paper before him; his hands, I noticed, were well shaped, white, and very thin. He wore a signet-ring on the third finger of the left hand, and was dressed with a care and finish not often met with in the jungle. He wore some kind of light Norfolk jacket and a blue bird's-eye tie. In front of him stood an open despatch-box, very shabby and scratched, and I could see that the upper tray contained a stout roundabout bag, presumably full of rupees, a thick roll of notes, and a gold watch. When I had deliberately taken in every item, the unutterable calmness of this stranger, thus establishing himself in our room, came home to me most forcibly, and clearing my throat I coughed—a clear decided cough of expostulation, to draw his attention to the enormity of the situation. It had no effect—he must be stone-deaf! He went on writing as indefatigably as ever. What he was writing was evidently a pleasant theme, possibly a love-letter, for he smiled as he scribbled. All at once I observed that the door was ajar. Two faces were peering in—a strange servant in a yellow turban, with cruel, greedy eyes, and the *khansamah!* Their gaze was riveted on the open despatch-box, the money, the roll of notes, and the watch. Presently the traveller's servant stole up behind his master noiselessly, and seemed to hold his breath; he drew a long knife from his sleeve. At this moment the stranger raised his eyes and looked at me. Oh, what a sad, strange look! a look of appeal. The next instant I saw the flash of the knife— it was buried in his back; he fell forward over his letter with a crash and a groan, and all was darkness. I tried to scream, but I could not. My tongue seemed paralyzed. I covered my head up in the clothes, and oh, how my heart beat! thump, thump, thump—surely *they* must hear it, and discover me. Half suffocated, at length I ventured to peer out for a second. All was still, black darkness. There was nothing to be seen, but much to be heard—the dragging of a heavy body, a *dead* body, across the room; then, after an appreciable pause, the sounds of digging outside the bungalow. Finally, the splashing of water—*some one washing the floor.* When I awoke the next morning, or came to myself—for I believe I had fainted—daylight was demanding admittance at every crevice in the shutters; night, its dark hours and its horrors, was past. The torture, the agony of fear, that had held me captive, had now released me, and, worn out, I fell fast asleep. It was actually nine o'clock when I opened my eyes.

Julia was standing over me and shaking me vigorously, and saying, "Nellie, Nellie, wake; I've been up and out this two hours; I've seen the head man of the village."

"Have you?" I assented sleepily.

"Yes, and he says there are no bullocks to be had until tomorrow; we must pass another night here."

"Never!" I almost shrieked. "Never! Oh, Julia, I've had such a night. I've seen a murder!" And straightway I commenced, and told her of my awful experiences. "That khansamah murdered him. He is buried just outside the front step," I concluded tearfully. "Sooner than stay here another night I'll walk to Chanda."

"Ghosts! murders! walk to Chanda!" she echoed scornfully. "Why, you silly girl, did *I* not sleep here in this very room, and sleep as sound as a top? It was all the *pâté de foie gras*. You know it never agrees with you."

"I know nothing about *pâté de foie gras*," I answered angrily; "but I know what I saw. Sooner than sleep another night in this room I'd *die*. I might as well—for such another night would kill me!"

Bath, breakfast, and Julia brought me round to a certain extent. I thought better of tearing off to Chanda alone and on foot, especially as we heard (per coolie) that our respective husbands would be with us the next morning—Christmas Day. We spent the day cooking, exploring the country, and writing for the English mail. As night fell, I became more and more nervous, and less amenable to Julia and Julia's jokes. I would sleep in the verandah; either there, or in the compound. In the bungalow again—never. An old witch of a native woman, who was helping Abdul to cook, agreed to place her mat in the same locality as my mattress, and Julia Goodchild valiantly occupied the big room within, alone. In the middle of the night I and my protector were awoke by the most piercing, frightful shrieks. We lit a candle and ran into the bungalow, and found Julia lying on the floor in a dead faint. She did not come round for more than an hour, and when she opened her eyes she gazed about her with a shudder and displayed symptoms of going off again, so I instantly hunted up our flask and administered some raw brandy, and presently she found her tongue and attacked the old native woman quite viciously.

"Tell the truth about this place!" she said fiercely. "What is it that is here, in this room?"

"Devils," was the prompt and laconic reply.

"Nonsense! Murder has been done here; tell the truth."

"How I knowing?" she whined. "I only poor native woman."

"An English sahib was murdered here seven years ago; stabbed and dragged out, and buried under the steps."

"Ah, bah! ah, bah! How I telling? this not my country," she wailed most piteously.

"Tell all you know," persisted Julia. "You do know! My husband is coming to-day; he is a police officer. You had better tell me than him."

After much whimpering and hand-wringing, we extracted the following information in jerks and quavers:—

The bungalow had a bad name, no one ever entered it, and in spite of the wooden shutters there were *lights* in the windows every night up to twelve o'clock. One day (so the villagers said), many years ago, a young sahib came to this bungalow and stayed three days. He was alone. He was in the Forest Department. The last evening he sent his horses and servants on to Chanda, and said he would follow in the morning after having some shooting, he and his "boy;" but though his people waited two weeks, he never appeared—was never seen again. The khansamah declared that he and his servant had left in the early morning, but no one met them. The khansamah became suddenly very rich; said he had found a treasure; also, he sold a fine gold watch in Jubbulpore, and took to drink. He had a bad name, and the bungalow had a bad name. No one would stay there more than one night, and no one had stayed there for many years till we came. The khansamah lived in the cook-house; he was *always* drunk. People said there were devils in the house, and no one would go near it after sundown. This was all she knew.

"Poor fellow, he was so good-looking!" sighed Julia when we were alone. "Poor fellow, and he was murdered and buried here!"

"So I told you," I replied, "and you would not believe me, but insisted on staying to see for yourself."

"I wish I had not—oh, I wish I had not! I shall never, never forget last night as long as I live."

"That must have been *his* topee and tiffin basket that we saw in the press," I exclaimed. "As soon as your husband comes, we will tell him everything, and set him on the track of the murderers."

Breakfast on Christmas morning was a very doleful meal; our nerves were completely shattered by our recent experiences, and we could only rouse ourselves up to offer a very melancholy sort of welcome to our two husbands, when they cantered briskly into the compound. In reply to their eager questions as to the cause of our lugubrious appearance, pale faces, and general air of mourning, we favoured them with a vivid description of our two nights in the bungalow. Of course, they were loudly, rudely incredulous, and, of course, we were very angry; vainly we re-stated our case, and displayed the old topee and tiffin basket; they merely laughed still more heartily and talked of "nightmare," and gave themselves such airs of offensive superiority, that Julia's soul flew to arms.

"Look here," she cried passionately, "*I* laughed at Nellie as you laugh at us. We will go out of this compound, whilst you two dig, or get people to dig, below the front verandah and in front of the steps, and if you don't find the skeleton of a murdered man, then you may laugh at us for ever."

With Julia impulse meant action, and before I could say three words I was out of the compound, with my arm wedged under hers; we went and sat on a little stone bridge within a stone's throw of the bungalow, glum and silent enough. What a Christmas Day! Half an hour's delay was as much as Julia's patience could brook. We then retraced our steps and discovered what seemed to be the whole village in the dâk bungalow compound. Frank came hurrying towards us, waving us frantically away. No need for questions; his face was enough. They had found it.

Frank Goodchild had known him—he was in his own department, a promising and most popular young fellow; his name was Gordon Forbes; he had been missed but never traced, and there was a report that he had been gored and killed in the jungle by a wild buffalo. In the same grave was found the battered despatch-box, by which the skeleton was identified. Mr. Goodchild and my husband re-interred the body under a tree, and read the Burial Service over it, Nellie and I and all the village patriarchs attending as mourners. The khansamah was eagerly searched for—alas! in vain. He disappeared from that part of the country, and was said to have been devoured by a tiger in the Jhanas jungles; but this is too good to be true. We left the hateful bungalow with all speed that same afternoon, and spent the remainder of the Christmas Day at Chanda; it was the least merry Christmas we ever remembered. The Goodchilds and ourselves have subscribed and placed a granite cross, with his name and the date of his death, over Gordon Forbes's lonely grave, and the news of the discovery of the skeleton was duly forwarded to the proper authorities, and also to the unfortunate young man's relations, and to these were sent the despatch-box, letters, and ring.

Mrs. Duff was full of curiosity concerning our trip. We informed her that we spent Christmas at Chanda, as we had originally intended, with our husbands, that they had provided an excellent dinner of black buck and jungle fowl, that the plum-pudding surpassed all expectations; but we never told her a word about our two nights' halt at Dakor bungalow.

"To Let"
Bithia Mary Croker (1893)

"List, list, O list!"—*Hamlet,* Act I

Some years ago, when I was a slim young spin, I came out to India to live with my brother Tom: he and I were members of a large and somewhat impecunious family, and I do not think my mother was sorry to have one of her four grown-up daughters thus taken off her hands. Tom's wife, Aggie, had been at school with my eldest sister; we had known and liked her all our lives, and regarded her as one of ourselves; and as she and the children were at home when Tom's letter was received, and his offer accepted, she helped me to choose my slender outfit, with judgment, zeal, and taste; endowed me with several pretty additions to my wardrobe; superintended the fitting of my gowns and the trying on of my hats, with most sympathetic interest, and finally escorted me out to Lucknow, under her own wing, and installed me in the only spare room in her comfortable bungalow in Dilkousha.

My sister-in-law is a pretty little brunette, rather pale, with dark hair, brilliant black eyes, a resolute mouth, and a bright, intelligent expression. She is orderly, trim, feverishly energetic, and seems to live every moment of her life. Her children, her wardrobe, her house, her servants, and last, not least, her husband, are all models in their way; and yet she has plenty of time for tennis, and dancing, and talking and walking. She is,

undoubtedly, a remarkably talented little creature, and especially prides herself on her nerve, and her power of will, or will
power. I suppose they are the same thing? and I am sure they
are all the same to Tom, who worships the sole of her small slip-
per. Strictly between ourselves, she is the ruling member of the
family, and turns her lord and master round her little finger.
Tom is big and fair (of course), the opposite to his wife, quiet,
rather easy-going and inclined to be indolent; but Aggie rouses
him up, and pushes him to the front, and keeps him there. She
knows all about his department, his prospects of promotion,
his prospects of furlough, of getting acting appointments, and
so on, even better than he does himself. The chief of Tom's
department—have I said that Tom is in the Irritation Office?—
has placed it solemnly on record that he considers little Mrs.
Shandon a surprisingly clever woman. The two children, Bob
and Tor, are merry, oppressively active monkeys, aged three and
five years respectively. As for myself, I am tall, fair—and I wish
I could add pretty! but this is a true story. My eyes are blue, my
teeth are white, my hair is red—alas, a blazing red; and I was, at
this period, nineteen years of age; and now I think I have given
a sufficient outline of the whole family.

We arrived at Lucknow in November, when the cold weather
is delightful, and everything was delightful to me. The bustle
and life of a great Indian station, the novelty of my surroundings, the early morning rides, picnics down the river, and dances
at the "Chutter Munzil," made me look upon Lucknow as a
paradise on earth; and in this light I still regarded it, until
a great change came over the temperature, and the month of
April introduced me to red-hot winds, sleepless nights, and the
intolerable "brain fever" bird. Aggie had made up her mind
definitely on one subject: we were not to go away to the hills
until the rains. Tom could only get two months' leave (July
and August), and she did not intend to leave him to grill on
the plains alone. As for herself and the children—not to speak
of me—we had all come out from home so recently that we did

not require a change. The trip to Europe had made a vast hole in the family stocking, and she wished to economize; and who can economize with two establishments in full swing? Tell me this, ye Anglo-Indian matrons? With a large, cool bungalow, plenty of punkhas, khuskhus tatties, ice, and a thermantidote, surely we could manage to brave May and June—at any rate the attempt was made. Gradually the hills drained Lucknow week by week; family after family packed up, warned us of our folly in remaining on the plains, offered to look for houses for us, and left by the night mail. By the middle of May, the place was figuratively empty. Nothing can be more dreary than a large station in the hot weather—unless it is an equally forsaken hill station in the depths of winter, when the mountains are covered with snow, the mall no longer resounds with gay voices and the tramp of Jampanies, but is visited by bears and panthers, and the houses are closed, and, as it were, put to bed in straw! As for Lucknow in the summer, it was a melancholy spot; the public gardens were deserted, the chairs at the Chutter Munzil stood empty, the very bands had gone to the hills! the shops were shut, the baked-white roads, no longer thronged with carriages and bamboo carts, gave ample room to the humble ekka, or a Dhobie's meagre donkey, shuffling along in the dust.

Of course we were not the *only* people remaining in the place, grumbling at the heat and dust and life in general; but there can be no sociability with the thermometer above 100° in the shade. Through the long, long Indian day we sat and gasped, in darkened rooms, and consumed quantities of "Nimbo pegs," *i.e.* limes and soda water, and listened to the fierce hot wind roaring along the road and driving the roasted leaves before it; and in the evening, when the sun had set, we went for a melancholy drive through the Wingfield Park, or round by Martiniere College, and met our friends at the library, and compared sensations and thermometers. The season was exceptionally bad (but people say that every year), and presently Bobby and Tor began to fade: their little white faces and listless eyes appealed to Aggie as Tom's anxious expostulations had never done. "Yes, they must go to the hills with *me.*" But this idea I repudiated at once; I refused to undertake the responsibility—I, who could scarcely speak a word to the servants—who had no experience! Then Bobbie had a bad go of fever—intermittent fever; the beginning of the end to his alarmed mother; the end being represented by a large gravestone! She now became as firmly determined to go, as she had previously been resolved to stay; but it was so late in the season to take a house. Alas, alas, for the beautiful tempting advertisements in the *Pioneer,* which we had seen and scorned! Aggie wrote to a friend in a certain hill station, called (for this occasion only) "Kantia," and Tom wired to a house agent, who triumphantly replied by letter, that there was not one unlet bungalow on his books. This missive threw us into the depths of despair; there seemed no alternative but a hill hotel, and the usual quarters that await the last comers, and the proverbial welcome for children and dogs (we had only four); but the next day brought us good news from Aggie's friend Mrs. Chalmers.

"Dear Mrs. Shandon (she said),
"I received your letter, and went at once to Cursit-jee, the agent. Every hole and corner up here seems full, and he had not a single house to let. To-day I had a note from him, saying that Briar-wood is vacant; the people who took it are not coming up, they have gone to Naini Tal. You *are* in luck. I have just been out to see the house, and have secured it for you. It is a mile and a half from the club, but I know that you and your sister are capital walkers. I envy you. Such a charming place—two sitting-rooms, four bedrooms, four bath-rooms, a hall, servants' go-downs, stabling, and a splendid view from a very pretty garden, and only Rs. 800 for the season! Why, I am paying

Rs. 1000 for a *very* inferior house, with scarcely a stick of furniture and no view. I feel so proud of myself, and I am longing to show you my trea-sure-trove. Telegraph when you start, and I shall have a milkman in waiting and fires in all the rooms.

    "Yours sincerely,
      "Edith Chalmers."

We now looked upon Mrs. Chalmers as our best and dearest friend, and began to get under way at once. A long journey in India is a serious business, when the party comprises two ladies, two children, two ayahs, and five other servants, three fox ter-riers, a mongoose, and a Persian cat—all these animals going to the hills for the benefit of their health—not to speak of a ton of luggage, including crockery and lamps, a cottage piano, a goat, and a pony. Aggie and I, the children, one ayah, two terriers, the cat and mongoose, our bedding and pillows, the tiffin bas-ket and ice basket, were all stowed into one compartment, and I must confess that the journey was truly miserable. The heat was stifling, despite the water tatties. One of the terriers had a violent dispute with the cat, and the cat had a difference with the mongoose, and Bob and Tor had a pitched battle; more than once I actually wished myself back in Lucknow. I was most truly thankful to wake one morning, to find myself under the shadow of the Himalayas—not a mighty, snow-clad range of everlasting hills, but merely the spurs—the moderate slopes, covered with scrub, loose shale, and jungle, and de-ceitful little trickling watercourses. We sent the servants on ahead, whilst we rested at the Dak bungalow near the railway station, and then followed them at our leisure. We accomplished the ascent in dandies—open kind of boxes, half box, half chair, carried on the shoulders of four men. This was an entirely novel sensation to me, and at first an agreeable one, so long as the slopes were moderate, and the paths wide; but the higher we

went, the narrower became the path, the steeper the naked precipice; and as my coolies would walk at the extreme edge, with
the utmost indifference to my frantic appeals to "Beetor! Beetor!"—and would change poles at the most agonizing corners—
my feelings were very mixed, especially when droves of loose
pack ponies came thundering downhill, with no respect for the
rights of the road. Late at night we passed through Kantia, and
arrived at Briarwood, far too weary to be critical. Fires were
blazing, supper was prepared, and we despatched it in haste,
and most thankfully went to bed and slept soundly, as any one
would do who had spent thirty-six hours in a crowded compartment, and ten in a cramped wooden case.

The next morning, rested and invigorated, we set out on a
tour of inspection; and it is almost worth while to undergo a
certain amount of baking in the sweltering heat of the lower
regions, in order to enjoy those deep first draughts of cool hill
air, instead of a stifling, dust-laden atmosphere; and to appreciate the green valleys and blue hills, by force of contrast to the
far-stretching, eye-smarting, white glaring roads, that intersect
the burnt-up plains—roads and plains, that even the pariah
abandons, salamander though he be!

To our delight and surprise, Mrs. Chalmers had by no means
overdrawn the advantages of our new abode. The bungalow was
solidly built of stone, two storied, and ample in size. It stood on
a kind of shelf, cut out of the hillside, and was surrounded by a
pretty flower garden, full of roses, fuchsias, and carnations. The
high road passed the gate, from which the avenue descended,
direct to the entrance door, at the end of the house, and from
whence ran a long passage. Off this passage three rooms opened
to the right, all looking south, and all looking into a deep,
delightful, flagged verandah. The stairs were very steep. At the
head of them, the passage and rooms were repeated. There were
small nooks, and dressing-rooms, and convenient outhouses,
and plenty of good water; but the glory of Briarwood was undoubtedly its verandah: it was fully twelve feet wide, roofed

with zinc, and overhung a precipice, of a thousand feet—not a startlingly sheer khud, but a tolerably straight descent of grey-blue shale, rocks, and low jungle. From it there was a glorious view, across a valley, far away, to the snowy range. It opened at one end into the avenue, and was not inclosed; but at the side next the precipice, there was a stout wooden railing, with netting at the bottom, for the safety of too enterprising dogs or children. A charming spot, despite its rather bold situation; and as Aggie and I sat in it, surveying the scenery and inhaling the pure hill air, and watching Bob and Tor tearing up and down, playing horses, we said to one another that "the verandah alone was worth half the rent."

"It's absurdly cheap," exclaimed my sister-in-law complacently. "I wish you saw the hovel *I* had, at Simla, for the same rent. I wonder if it is feverish, or badly drained, or what?"

"Perhaps it has a ghost," I suggested facetiously; and at such an absurd idea we both went into peals of laughter.

At this moment Mrs. Chalmers appeared, brisk, rosy, and breathlessly benevolent, having walked over from Kantia.

"So you have found it," she said as we shook hands. "I said nothing about this delicious verandah! I thought I would keep it as a surprise. I did not say a word too much for Briarwood, did I?"

"Not half enough," we returned rapturously; and presently we went in a body, armed with a list from the agent, and proceeded to go over the house and take stock of its contents.

"It's not a bit like a *hill* furnished house," boasted Mrs. Chalmers, with a glow of pride, as she looked round the drawing-room; "carpets, curtains, solid, *very* solid chairs, and Berlin wool-worked screens, a card-table, and any quantity of pictures."

"Yes, don't they look like family portraits?" I suggested, as we gazed at them. There was one of an officer in faded water colours, another of his wife, two of a previous generation in oils and amply gilded frames, two sketches of an English country house, and some framed photographs—groups of grinning cricketers, or wedding guests. All the rooms were well, almost handsomely, furnished in an old-fashioned style. There was no scarcity of wardrobes, looking-glasses, or even armchairs, in the bedrooms, and the pantry was fitted out—a most singular circumstance—with a large supply of handsome glass and china, lamps, old moderators, coffee and teapots, plated side dishes, and candlesticks, cooking utensils and spoons and forks, wine coasters and a cake-basket. These articles were all let with the house (much to our amazement), provided we were responsible for the same. The china was spode, the plate old family heirlooms, with a crest—a winged horse—on everything, down to the very mustard spoons.

"The people who own this house must be lunatics," remarked Aggie, as she peered round the pantry; "fancy hiring out one's best family plate, and good old china! And I saw some ancient music-books in the drawing-room, and there is a side saddle in the bottle khana."

"My dear, the people who owned this house are dead," explained Mrs. Chalmers. "I heard all about them last evening from Mrs. Starkey."

"Oh, is *she* up there?" exclaimed Aggie, somewhat fretfully.

"Yes, her husband is cantonment magistrate. This house belonged to an old retired colonel and his wife. They and his niece lived here. These were all their belongings. They died within a short time of one another, and the old man left a queer will, to say that the house was to remain precisely as they left it for twenty years, and at the end of that time, it was to be sold and all the property. Mrs. Starkey says she is sure that he never intended it to be let, but the heir-at-law insists on that, and is furious at the terms of the will."

"Well, it is a very good thing for us," remarked Aggie; "we are as comfortable here, as if we were in our own house: there is a stove in the kitchen, there are nice boxes for firewood in every room, clocks, real hair mattresses—in short, it is as you said, a treasure trove."

We set to work to modernize the drawing-room with phool-karies, Madras muslin curtains, photograph screens and frames, and such-like portable articles. We placed the piano across a corner, arranged flowers in some handsome Dresden china vases, and entirely altered and improved the character of the room. When Aggie had despatched a most glowing description of our new quarters to Tom, and when we had had tiffin, we set off to walk into Kantia to put our names down at the library, and to inquire for letters at the post-office. Aggie met a good many acquaintances—who does not, who has lived five years in India in the same district?

Among them Mrs. Starkey, an elderly lady with a prominent nose and goggle eyes, who greeted her loudly across the reading-room table, in this agreeable fashion:

"And so you have come up after *all*, Mrs. Shandon. Some one told me that you meant to remain below, but I knew you never could be so wicked as to keep your poor little children in that heat." Then coming round and dropping into a chair beside her, she said, "And I suppose this young lady is your sister-in-law?"

Mrs. Starkey eyed me critically, evidently appraising my chances in the great marriage market. She herself had settled her own two daughters most satisfactorily, and had now nothing to do, but interest herself in other people's affairs.

"Yes," acquiesced Aggie; "Miss Shandon—Mrs. Starkey."

"And so you have taken Briarwood?"

"Yes, we have been most lucky to get it."

"I hope you will think so, at the end of three months," observed Mrs. Starkey, with a significant pursing of her lips. "Mrs. Chalmers is a stranger up here, or she would not have been in such a hurry to jump at it."

"Why, what is the matter with it?" inquired Aggie. "It is well built, well furnished, well situated, and very cheap."

"That's just it—*suspiciously* cheap. Why, my dear Mrs. Shandon, if there was not something against it, it would let for two hundred rupees a month. Common sense would tell you that!"

"And what is against it?"

"It's haunted! There you have the reason in two words."

"Is that all? I was afraid it was the drains. I don't believe in ghosts and haunted houses. What are we supposed to see?"

"Nothing," retorted Mrs. Starkey, who seemed a good deal nettled at our smiling incredulity.

"Nothing!" with an exasperating laugh.

"No, but you will make up for it in hearing. Not now—you are all right for the next six weeks—but after the monsoon breaks, I give you a week at Briarwood. No one would stand it longer, and indeed you might as well bespeak your rooms at Cooper's Hotel *now*. There is always a rush up here in July, by the two months' leave people, and you will be poked into some wretched go-down."

Aggie laughed, rather a careless ironical little laugh, and said, "Thank you, Mrs. Starkey; but I think we will stay on where we are—at any rate for the present."

"Of course it will be as *you* please. What do you think of the verandah?" she inquired, with a curious smile.

"I think, as I was saying to Susan, that it is worth half the rent of the house."

"And in *my* opinion the house is worth double rent without it;" and with this enigmatic remark, she rose, and sailed away.

"Horrid old frump!" exclaimed Aggie, as we walked home in the starlight. "She is jealous and angry that she did not get Briarwood *herself*—I know her so well. She is always hinting, and repeating stories about the nicest people—always decrying your prettiest dress, or your best servant."

We soon forgot all about Mrs. Starkey, and her dismal prophecy, being too gay, and too busy, to give her, or it, a thought. We had so many engagements—tennis-parties and tournaments, picnics, concerts, dances, and little dinners. We ourselves gave occasional afternoon teas in the verandah—using the best spode cups and saucers, and the old silver cake-basket—and were warmly complimented on our good fortune in securing such a charming house and garden. One day the children discovered, to their great joy, that the old chowkidar belonging to the bungalow possessed an African grey parrot—a rare bird indeed in India; he had a battered Europe cage, doubtless a remnant of better days, and swung on his ring, looking up at us inquiringly, out of his impudent little black eyes.

The parrot had been the property of the former inmates of Briarwood, and as it was a long-lived creature, had survived its master and mistress, and was boarded out with the chowkidar, at one rupee per month.

The chowkidar willingly carried the cage into the verandah, where the bird seemed perfectly at home.

We got a little table for its cage, and the children were delighted with him, as he swung to and fro, with a bit of cake in his wrinkled claw.

Presently he startled us all by suddenly calling "Lucy," in a voice that was as distinct as if it had come from a human throat. "Pretty Lucy—Lu—cy."

"That must have been the niece," said Aggie. "I expect she was the original of that picture over the chimney-piece in your room; she looks like a Lucy."

It was a large, framed, half-length photograph of a very pretty girl, in a white dress, with gigantic open sleeves. The ancient parrot talked incessantly now that he had been restored to society; he whistled for the dogs, and brought them flying to his summons—to his great satisfaction, and their equally great indignation. He called "Qui hye" so naturally, in a lady's shrill soprano, or a gruff male bellow, that I have no doubt our servants would have liked to have wrung his neck. He coughed and expectorated like an old gentleman, and whined like a puppy, and mewed like a cat, and, I am sorry to add, sometimes swore like a trooper; but his most constant cry was, "Lucy, where are you, pretty Lucy—Lucy—Lu—cy?"

Aggie and I went to various picnics, but to that given by the
Chalmers (in honour of Mr. Chalmers' brother Charlie, a captain in a Ghoorka regiment, just come up to Kantia on leave)
Aggie was unavoidably absent. Tor had a little touch of fever,
and she did not like to leave him; but I went under my hostess's
care, and expected to enjoy myself immensely. Alas! on that
selfsame afternoon, the long-expected monsoon broke, and we
were nearly drowned! We rode to the selected spot, five miles
from Kantia, laughing and chattering, indifferent to the big
blue-black clouds that came slowly, but surely, sailing up from
below; it was a way they had had for days, and nothing had
come of it! We spread the table-cloth, boiled the kettle, unpacked the hampers, in spite of sharp gusts of wind and warning rumbling thunder. Just as we had commenced to reap the
reward of our exertions, there fell a few huge drops, followed
by a vivid flash, and then a tremendous crash of thunder, like a
whole park of artillery, that seemed to shake the mountains—
and after this the deluge. In less than a minute we were soaked
through; we hastily gathered up the table-cloth by its four ends,
gave it to the coolies, and fled. It was all I could do to stand
against the wind; only for Captain Chalmers I believe I would
have been blown away; as it was, I lost my hat, it was whirled
into space. Mrs. Chalmers lost her boa, and Mrs. Starkey, not
merely her bonnet, but some portion of her hair. We were truly
in a wretched plight, the water streaming down our faces, and
squelching in our boots; the little trickling mountain rivulets
were now like racing seas of turbid water; the lightning was
almost blinding; the trees rocked dangerously, and lashed one
another with their quivering branches. I had never been out in
such a storm before, and sincerely hope I never may again. We
reached Kantia more dead than alive, and Mrs. Chalmers sent
an express to Aggie, and kept me till the next day. After raining as it only can rain in the Himalayas, the weather cleared,
the sun shone, and I rode home in borrowed plumes, full of
my adventures, and in the highest spirits. I found Aggie sitting

over the fire in the drawing-room, looking ghastly white: that was nothing uncommon; but terribly depressed, which was most unusual.

"I am afraid you have neuralgia?" I said, as I kissed her.

She nodded, and made no reply.

"How is Tor?" I inquired, as I drew a chair up to the fire.

"Better—quite well."

"Any news—any letter?"

"Not a word—not a line."

"Has anything happened to Pip"—Pip was a fox-terrier, renowned for having the shortest tail and being the most impertinent dog in Lucknow—"or the mongoose?"

"No, you silly girl! Why do you ask such ridiculous questions?"

"I was afraid something was amiss; you seem rather down on your luck."

Aggie shrugged her shoulders, and then said, "Pray, what put such an absurd idea into your head? Tell me all about the picnic," and she began to talk rapidly, and to ask me various questions; but I observed that once she had set me going—no difficult task—her attention flagged, her eyes wandered from my face to the fire. She was not listening to half I said, and my most thrilling descriptions were utterly lost on this indifferent, abstracted little creature! I noticed from this time, that she had become strangely nervous (for her). She invited herself to the share of half my bed; she was restless, *distrait,* and even irritable; and when I was asked out to spend the day, dispensed with my company with an alacrity that was by no means flattering. Formerly, of an evening she used to herd the children home at sundown, and tear me away from the delights of the reading-room at seven o'clock; now she hung about the library, until almost the last moment, until it was time to put out the lamps, and kept the children with her, making transparent pretexts for their company. Often we did not arrive at home till half-past eight o'clock. I made no objections to these late hours, neither did Charlie Chalmers, who often walked back with us and remained to dinner. I was amazed to notice that Aggie seemed delighted to have his company, for she had always expressed a rooted aversion to what she called "tame young men," and here was this new acquaintance dining with us, at least twice a week!

About a month after the picnic we had a spell of dreadful weather—thunderstorms accompanied by torrents. One pouring afternoon, Aggie and I were cowering over the drawing-room fire, whilst the rain came fizzing down among the logs, and ran in rivers off the roof, and out of the spouts. There had been no going out that day, and we were feeling rather flat and dull, as we sat in a kind of ghostly twilight, with all outdoor objects swallowed up in mist, listening to the violent battering of the rain on the zinc verandah, and the storm which was growling round the hills. "Oh, for a visitor!" I exclaimed; "but no one but a fish, or a lunatic, would be out on such an evening."

"No one, indeed," echoed Aggie, in a melancholy tone. "We may as well draw the curtains, and have in the lamp and tea to cheer us up."

She had scarcely finished speaking, when I heard the brisk trot of a horse along the road.

It stopped at the gate, and came rapidly down our avenue. I heard the wet gravel crunching under his hoofs, and—yes, a man's cheery whistle. My heart jumped, and I half rose from my chair. It must be Charlie Chalmers braving the elements to see *me!*—such, I must confess, was my incredible vanity! He did not stop at the front door as usual, but rode straight into the verandah, which afforded ample room, and shelter for half a dozen mounted men.

"Aggie," I said eagerly, "do you hear? It must be—"

I paused, my tongue silenced, by the awful pallor of her face, and the expression of her eyes, as she sat with her little hands clutching the arms of her chair, and her whole figure bent forward in an attitude of listening—an attitude of rigid tenor.

"What is it, Aggie?" I said. "Are you ill?"

As I spoke, the horse's hoofs made a loud clattering noise on the stone-paved verandah outside, and a man's voice—a young man's eager voice—called, "Lucy."

Instantly a chair near the writing-table was pushed back, and some one went quickly to the window—a French one—and bungled for a moment with the fastening. I always had a difficulty with that window *myself*. Aggie and I were within the bright circle of the firelight, but the rest of the room was dim, and outside the streaming grey sky was spasmodically illuminated by occasional vivid flashes, that lit up the surrounding hills as if it were daylight. The trampling of impatient hoofs, and the rattling of a door-handle, were the only sounds that were audible for a few breathless seconds; but during those seconds Pip, bristling like a porcupine, and trembling violently in every joint, had sprung off my lap and crawled abjectly under Aggie's chair, seemingly in a transport of fear. The door was opened audibly, and a cold, icy blast swept in, that seemed to freeze my very heart, and made me shiver from head to foot. At this moment there came, with a sinister blue glare, the most vivid flash of lightning I ever saw. It lit up the whole room, which was empty save for ourselves, and was instantly followed by a clap of thunder, that caused my knees to knock together, and that terrified me and filled me with horror. It evidently terrified the horse too; there was a violent plunge, a clattering of hoofs on the stones, a sudden loud crash of smashing timber, a woman's long, loud, piercing shriek, which stopped the very beating of my heart, and then a frenzied struggle in the cruel, crumbling, treacherous shale, the rattle of loose stones, and the hollow roar of something sliding down the precipice.

I rushed to the door and tore it open, with that awful despairing cry still ringing in my ears. The verandah was empty; there was not a soul to be seen, or a sound to be heard, save the rain on the roof.

"Aggie," I screamed, "come here! Some one has gone over the verandah, and down the khud! You heard him."

"Yes," she said, following me out; "but come in—come in."

"I believe it was Charlie Chalmers"—shaking her violently as I spoke. "He has been killed—killed—killed! And you stand, and do nothing. Send people! Let us go ourselves! Bearer! Ayah! Khidmatgar!" I cried, raising my voice.

"Hush! It was *not* Charlie Chalmers," she said, vainly endeavouring to draw me into the drawing-room. "Come in—come in."

"No, no!" pushing her away, and wringing my hands. "How cruel you are! How inhuman! There is a path. Let us go at once—at once!"

"You need not trouble yourself, Susan," she interrupted; "and you need not cry and tremble;—they will bring him up. What you heard was supernatural; it was not real."

"No—no—no! It was all real. Oh! that scream is in my ears still."

"I will convince you," said Aggie, taking my hand as she spoke. "Feel all along the verandah. Are the railings broken?"

I did as she bade me. No, though very wet, and clammy, the railing was intact!

"Where is the broken place?" she asked, imperatively.

Where, indeed?

"Now," she continued, "since you will not come in, look over, and you will see something more presently."

Shivering with fear, and the cold, drifting rain, I gazed down as she bade me, and there, far below, I saw lights moving rapidly to and fro, evidently in search of something. After a little delay they congregated in one place. There was a low, buzzing murmur—they had found him—and presently they commenced to ascend the hill, with the "hum-hum" of coolies carrying a burden. Nearer and nearer the lights and sounds came; up to the very brink of the khud, past the end of the verandah. Many steps and many torches—faint blue torches held by invisible hands—invisible but heavy-footed bearers carried their burden slowly upstairs, and along the passage, and deposited it with a dump in Aggie's bedroom! As we stood clasped in one another's arms, and shaking all over, the steps descended, the ghostly lights passed up the avenue, and gradually disappeared in the gathering darkness. The repetition of the tragedy was over for that day.

"Have you heard it before?" I asked with chattering teeth, as I bolted the drawing-room window.

"Yes, the evening of the picnic, and twice since. That is the reason I have always tried to stay out till late, and to keep you out. I was hoping and praying you might never hear it. It always happens just before dark: I am afraid you have thought me very queer of late. I have told no end of stories to keep you and the children from harm. I have—"

"I think you have been very kind," I interrupted. "Oh, Aggie, shall you ever get that crash, and that awful cry out of your head?"

"Never!" hastily lighting the candles as she spoke.

"Is there anything more?" I inquired tremulously.

"Yes; sometimes at night, the most terrible weeping and sobbing in my bedroom;" and she shuddered at the mere recollection.

"Do the servants know?" I asked anxiously.

"The ayah Mumà has heard it, and the khánsámáh says his mother is sick, and he must go, and the bearer wants to attend his brother's wedding. They will *all* leave."

"I suppose most people know too?" I suggested dejectedly.

"Yes; don't you remember Mrs. Starkey's warnings, and her saying that without the verandah the house was worth double rent? We understand that dark speech of hers *now,* and we have not come to Cooper's Hotel yet."

"No, not yet. I wish we *had.* I wonder what Tom will say? He will be here in another fortnight. Oh, I wish he was here now!"

In spite of our heart-shaking experience, we managed to eat, and drink, and sleep, yea, to play tennis—somewhat solemnly, it is true—and go to the club, where we remained to the very *last* moment; needless to mention, that I now entered into Aggie's manoeuvre *con amore*. Mrs. Starkey evidently divined the reason of our loitering in Kantia, and said in her most truculent manner, as she squared up to us—

"You keep your children out very late, Mrs. Shandon."

"Yes, but we like to have them with us," rejoined Aggie, in a meek apologetic voice.

"Then why don't you go home earlier?"

"Because it is so stupid, and lonely," was the mendacious answer.

"Lonely is not the word I should use. I wonder if you are as wise as your neighbours now? Come now, Mrs. Shandon."

"About what?" said Aggie, with ill-feigned innocence.

"About Briarwood. Haven't you heard it yet? The ghastly precipice and horse affair?"

"Yes, I suppose we may as well confess that we *have.*"

"Humph! you are a brave couple to stay on. The Tombs tried it last year for three weeks. The Paxtons took it the year before, and then sub-let it; not that *they* believed in ghosts—oh, dear no!" and she laughed ironically.

"And what is the story?" I inquired eagerly.

"Well, the story is this. An old retired officer and his wife, and their pretty niece, lived at Briarwood a good many years ago. The girl was engaged to be married to a fine young fellow in the Guides. The day before the wedding, what you know of happened, and has happened every monsoon ever since. The poor girl went out of her mind, and destroyed herself, and the old colonel and his wife did not long survive her. The house is uninhabitable in the monsoon, and there seems nothing for it but to auction off the furniture, and pull it down; it will always be the same as long as it stands. Take *my* advice, and come into Cooper's Hotel. I believe you can have that small set of rooms at the back. The sitting-room smokes—but beggars can't be choosers."

"That will only be our very last resource," said Aggie, hotly.

"It's not very grand, I grant you; but any port in a storm."

Tom arrived, was doubly welcome, and was charmed with Briarwood, chaffed us unmercifully, and derided our fears until he himself had a similar experience, and heard the phantom horse plunging in the verandah, and that wild, unearthly and utterly appalling shriek. No, he could not laugh that away; and seeing that we had now a mortal abhorrence of the place, that the children had to be kept abroad in the damp till long after dark, that Aggie was a mere hollow-eyed spectre, and that we had scarcely a servant left, that—in short, one day, we packed up precipitately and fled in a body to Cooper's Hotel. But we did not basely endeavour to sub-let, nor advertise Briarwood as "a delightfully situated pucka built house, containing all the requirements of a gentleman's family." No, no. Tom bore the loss of the rent, and—a more difficult feat—Aggie bore Mrs. Starkey's insufferable "I told you so."

Aggie was at Kantia again last season. She walked out early one morning to see our former abode. The chowkidar and parrot are still in possession, and are likely to remain the sole tenants on the premises. The parrot suns and dusts his ancient feathers in the empty verandah, which re-echoes with his cry of "Lucy, where are you—pretty Lucy?" The chowkidar inhabits a secluded go-down at the back, where he passes most of the day in sleeping, or smoking the soothing "huka." The place has a forlorn, uncared-for appearance now; the flowers are nearly all gone; the paint has peeled off the doors and windows; the avenue is grass-grown. Briarwood appears to have resigned itself to emptiness, neglect, and decay, although outside the gate there still hangs a battered board, on which, if you look very closely, you can decipher the words *"To Let."*

A Malagasy Ghost-Story
C. P. Cory (1893)

One evening I was sitting beneath the verandah of a house on the borders of the upper forest in Madagascar. It was one of those glorious evenings only to be found in the tropics, when the afterglow of sunset enriches and enhances the beauty of everything before darkness hides them for another night, when red flowers look like flame, and yellow like burnished gold. As the sun sank deeper below the horizon the colours slowly changed, one blending with another till all grew sombre. Over to the east, behind the forest, shot up the great white beams of the rising moon, distinct and regular. The trees stood out in bold relief; the very leaves seemed to separate and let the moonbeams through.

Grand as was the scene, my thoughts, I must confess, were hardly in keeping with it; I was thinking of pigs. I had been told by some natives that some wild-pigs had been devastating their crops, and I was wondering how I could get a shot at them that night.

As I sat puffing at my cigar, and wondering if it were possible to secure the services of an old native who was said to be exceptionally skilled in the matter of pigs, I saw a shadowy form coming towards me; and presently the dusky figure of a native stepped out of the shadow into the moonlight, his white *làmba* (a long cloth worn by natives) shining brightly as he threw it farther over his shoulder.

"Why!" I exclaimed, "it is Rainikòto himself—the very man I wanted. Hi! Rainikòto, will you go pig-hunting with me to-night?"

"How do you do, sir?" he said, with native politeness, before he answered the question. "What did you ask, sir?"

"Come with me to-night to look for that old boar that is eating up all your manioc, will you?"

"Where?"

"Oh, anywhere; I don't mind. At that little open glade in the forest about a rice-cooking* off, away to the east."

"At the clearing to the east?"

"Yes."

"I can't go; I have business to do."

"Nonsense, man! What business can you have to do?"

"I can't go, sir," he said again, squatting down on his hams beside me, and arranging his *làmba* so as to cover his mouth.

"But why?"

"I am an old man and don't care for sitting up all night, as I used to do. I like sleeping better than shooting. But what made you choose that place?"

"I thought it looked a likely spot, so many paths meet there."

"Go about midnight; you are certain to see a pig," he said, looking up with a curious expression.

I was surprised by the man's manner, it was so totally different from anything I had been accustomed to see in a native.

"Funny you should pick that place," he added after a time.

"You seem to know it well and say it is good; then why 'funny,' my relation?"

"Oh, I know it very well."

"I'll give you a dollar to come with me!"

The old man laughed. "It is a big sum," he said, "a week's pay. But not for fifteen weeks' pay would I come to that place at night, my master."

---

* A native way of measuring distance, equal to about a mile and a quarter.

"Oh, all right!" I said, pretending not to be curious, "I'll go myself."

I watched for some sign; but he sat looking out straight before him and evidently disinclined to talk. "Is there a ghost there, Rainikòto?"

"Yes, perhaps," he said, readjusting his *làmba*.

"Will you tell me about it?"

The old man sat perfectly still, as if in deep thought. No European could sit so long without moving. Not a limb moved, not the quiver of an eyelid. I waited for an answer, but none came. After a time, he took out his small polished bamboo to-bacco-box. Shaking out a large pinch of the snuff-like preparation into the palm of his hand, he opened his mouth, and with a peculiar jerk, tipped it in below his tongue, a decided hint for me that he meant to keep his story to himself, whatever it might be. I knew it was no good pressing him then, so I lit another cigar and took no apparent notice. Presently, native fashion, he spat out his tobacco, and seemingly addressing himself as much as me, he began:

"White men don't believe in ghosts and witchcraft and *Vazimba;** they laugh at them and at those who do."

"Witchcraft, perhaps, my friend, and *Vazimba* and *sikidy* [divination]; but we like to hear of ghosts. I do not feel at all like laughing, indeed, I very much wish to hear about it."

"It was a long time ago" (he began so suddenly it made me start), "it was a long time ago; two kings and queens have turned their backs upon us since then.† I was but a little lad, but I remember it quite distinctly. I am old; but I remember it well, as well as if it were only yesterday. My father was going

---

* The Vazimba are the supposed aboriginal inhabitants, whose graves and spirits are held in great awe and respect.

† The native idiom in speaking of the decease of a Sovereign. These do not *die,* they 'turn their backs' on their subjects.

into the forest to get wood, only a short distance, so he took me with him. We had not gone far when we heard the long low whine of a lost dog. 'The boar-hunters are out early,' said my father, evidently surprised, 'they must have slept in the forest. Ho! è, è, è, è!' he shouted; but there was no answer except from several dogs, which joined in one long howl. 'Ah! they are all lost,' he said, 'and no one shouting to let them hear. Ho! è, è, è, è! Ho! è, è, è, è!'

"Again the loud chorus came ringing and echoing through the wood. We turned aside and made our way in the direction of the dogs. Cry upon cry now arose. I remember it well. Am I likely to forget it? It was early morning, and there had been a heavy dew; my feet were cold and wet, and the dogs frightened me. I felt chilled and scared. My father had girded himself, and his brown skin glistened in the morning sun. How fast he went! pushing his way through the tangled growth. I could scarcely keep up with him, for the thorny creepers caught my legs, although my father helped to clear the way, striking with his axe at the great lianas that stopped our path. I think in the excitement he almost forgot me, for he guessed that something was wrong, and he held his spear ready shortened in his right hand. It seemed a long, long time before we reached the dogs. They were all together in the clearing to the east. It has not grown up as others do; it is just the same. There they sat, some howling, some licking the wounds received from a tussle with the boar. 'Look, father; what is that?' I cried. 'Adrè! adrè! it is a corpse. There are two: Rainimànga and Rainizàfy both killed by one pig,' he said, turning them over. Ah! I remember them well, sir, those gashed bodies. It was a horrible sight for any one, much more for a little lad. The shaft of a broken spear lay near; and still grasped in the hand of one lay the second spear. A look of surprise spread over my father's face as he gazed upon the man who held the spear. 'This wound would not have killed, and he never threw his spear. The other is nearly torn to bits! His spear has gone,' he said. 'I do not understand. And what is this?

Money! fifteen dollars! How came that money here? Seven in
one purse, and eight in the other?' He looked at me, and then,
as if thinking aloud, he added: 'No! I will not take it. It has bad
luck in it. I'll give it to their wives. Besides, if I kept it they
would say I had killed these men. I wish I knew how they got
it, though!'

"We soon raised the whole neighbourhood. The two men
had come from the village over yonder, he said, pointing with
his lips to a village about three miles away, and their friends
went and brought the bodies in. What wailing and mourning
there was! what beating of tom-toms! But the money my father
gave up was much more talked about than the deaths. Never had
any one but the chief—nay not even he—had so much before.
The funeral was very grand: several oxen were killed, and there
was a lot of *tòaka* [native rum] in *sìny* [earthen water-pots].
The money was a great comfort to their wives. We heard soon
afterwards that a trader from the coast had dropped his purse,
and he offered a reward; but then the reward was less than the
money in the purse, so of course he never got it.

"I soon ceased to think of that day, though the shock lasted
long. As I grew up, I too became a hunter and forester. Malagasy, as you know, are not fond of hunting like you white men;
the Bezánozàno tribe are the most so; but even only a few of
us care for it. I liked it and soon became proficient. One day a
white man came to our village and stayed there. He was looking
for birds, which he skinned; he never ate them, which surprised
us. He taught me to skin and shoot; and when he went away
he gave me the gun. I was very proud of it; and soon I found
I could get wild-pig much easier by waiting for them at nights
and shooting than by hunting them with dogs. So I used to go
to the bush where you wish to go to to-night."

He looked up at me with a sharp, keen, sidelong glance, as if
to read my thoughts, and then proceeded: "I nearly always got
some, though you white men don't, for you have no patience;
you sit and wait for one hour, perhaps, and then you get up and

walk a little, or think another place better, or go home; but we Malagasy will sit without moving for hours. Whenever pigs came this way, I was sure to be waiting for them, and the glade you mentioned was a favourite place. You'll see some to-night, sir, when you go, for I know their habits well. The herd that were in the sweet-potatoes and manioc last night will come that way; they will be there about midnight and return about second cock-crow."

H is wrinkled old face broke into a sort of satirical smile, as he paused. Without knowing quite why, I began to feel creepy but I answered with apparent unconcern: "Well, I hope so, Rainikòto. But you have not yet told me about the ghost, you know."

"Oh, I shall, I am coming to it. But you had better go, and it will save me the trouble of telling you. You will see it all then for yourself."

"I should like to hear it first, you know, to see if it agrees with what you saw."

"Well, master, you are my father and mother, and I should like to please you, but it is a long story."

"Go on, my relation," I said, answering his politeness in the orthodox way. He got up, readjusted his *làmba*, and squatting down a little more in front of me, began:

"It was on the 15th day of the moon Alàhasàty"—

"Why! that's to-day!" I said.

"Is it?" he said. "Let me think. Yes: so it is. That is funny.—Well, it was on this very day, about ten years ago, I went to watch for pigs at yonder glade. It was just such another night as this. The day had been very hot, and these little whirlwinds had been raising their dusty columns on the road—the spirits of our forefathers visiting the earth or returning to heaven, we Malagasy say. There had been a good many that day, I remember well. But they have not much to do with the story, nothing at least in your eyes. A herd of pigs had been among the village crops the night before. I had tracked them and found out the way they had come. I noticed the slot of a huge boar, and I meant to have him. They passed right through the clearing. That glade has never altered, as the others do; it is the same now as then; and it was the same then as when I was a little boy; but it never struck me till after that night, and then I noticed it. The grass grows just the same, and the trees do not seem to change."

The old man, I noticed, was dropping into the native style of rhetoric, a form not unseldom heard in British pulpits, a certain reckless way of wandering up and down the keys of thought, and then the persistent striking of a single chord, with an emphasis varying directly as the number of repetitions.

"Ay, it was just such another night as this, just the same; the same little fleecy clouds rushed across the full moon. The children were dancing in its rays, as they are now down yonder, and their song came rising and falling on the wind as now you hear it. The night was just the same; the crickets chirped and whistled in the grass; the great cicada rang his rattle as loudly as he now is doing—just the same. The dew was sparkling on the broad leaves, like tears on the cheeks of a young wife who has lost her child, her first-born. The frogs croaked in the marshes —a sign of rain, I've heard you say; we call it the women's parliament, for it is no sign of rain. Croak they will, as frogs and women always must. They could not live without it; aye master, the night was just—"

"The same, my dear relation. Let us agree that the night was just the same," I said, breaking in rather rudely, perhaps. "The very birds, beasts, fishes, insects, you know, they always are the same except when it is raining."

"I said you would laugh at me. If you laugh already, what will you do before the end?"

"I laugh! My dearest father and mother, I am so anxious to hear the end that I have even been rude. Pray excuse my haste; my eagerness out-stepped my manners." Malagasy are not easily offended, and he soon went on again.

"It was a short time before midnight that I started. I took my gun and spear and the usual little hatchet we all carry. No one went with me—I was quite alone. I soon reached the place and sat down, hiding behind a large clump of *sèvabe** through the broad leaves of which I could watch the whole glade from end to end, It is about thirty *rèfy* (fathoms) long. The moon shone brightly; not a cloud obscured its rays; not a breath of wind could be felt inside the forest; but the tops of the taller trees rustled gently, and the twisting leaves showed their white linings with every little puff. The tree-frogs alone seemed to break the silence, for they alone were near me.

"I had sat about two hours and had seen nothing. I began to think the pigs must have passed out, or gone another way; and I had made up my mind to alter my position, so as to see them better when they came back in the early morning; but still I sat on, not caring to own myself at fault. I was just opening my tobacco-box, and had put my gun down by my side; my spear was sticking upright in the ground before me, and my axe on my knees, when I became conscious that something was going to happen, but I knew not what. I felt my head, to see if I were faint or dreaming. I never felt any feeling like it before, or since—a sort of trembling, cold, indescribable feeling, as if one's spirit were fighting with one's body. I was afraid, and thought I was ill—perhaps dying, perhaps bewitched, and I rose to go home. So disturbed was I, that I forgot to pick up my gun. Just at that moment a huge boar rushed past, his bristles all up, and his little eyes flaming from under his grizzled brows. He was covered with mud from head to tail; his jaws were set as if for fighting; he looked distressed and evidently hunted, being hard put to it. He was the largest and oldest boar I had ever seen, for his horns† were very long and large, and his tusks gleamed long

* [A shrub, *Solanum auriculatum,* Ait.—Eds.]

† The Malagasy wild-boar has a large horn-like growth above each tusk.

and sharp in the moonlight. I could easily have shot him, had I had my gun; but I was startled and surprised, and he was past before I regained my presence of mind. I held my axe, though, and without knowing what I did, I hurled it after him. Round and round it flew and lit a foot in front. I thought it must have grazed him, but he never stopped. I was astonished, for nothing followed; and a thing that did not strike me at once, but which I vividly recalled afterwards, was that there was no sound, yet he had run right through some dry fern."

The old man stopped and altered his position. It evidently made him nervous to recall that night's adventures, even when sitting inside a verandah and near one of the all-powerful white men. Glancing timidly over his shoulder, be began again:

"I got up, master, and picked up the axe. For a time the funny feeling had left me, owing, I suppose, to the excitement; but as I touched the axe, my hand shook like a rush in the wind and became as cold as the dead. I looked at it to see if there was blood on it, and I ran my finger along the edge. It was the finger of the other hand, and it shivered like the hand that held the axe. I was horribly afraid now, and knew not what to think. I wished to go home; but I wished still more to know what had become of the boar, and what had chased it. I remembered his enormous size, and I thought my eyes, being ill, might have magnified it, or that I had even seen a vision. I stooped down to examine the slot in the wet clay, but there was not a mark. I could not believe it. I knelt down and peered into the clay; not a sign. I was on the point of rising—oh, sir, I shall never forget it, no! not to my dying day. There he was!—the boar! right on me, not ten yards off, and coming hard down on me—looking death in every line. I gasped, I shuddered; but I was still a man, and all my trembling ceased as I jumped up for one last effort. There was no room to move, for I had followed him out of the glade to that narrow passage between the high clay banks; for there, if anywhere, I knew his marks would show. Five feet perpendicular banks on either hand, and an immense boar in full

charge. He had come without noise, or I must have heard him
yards away. I had just time to get on my feet and strike at his
head with the axe with all my force; I meant, as soon as I felt
the axe bite, to jump high and so miss the rush and tusks. It was
no use to jump and not strike, for he would have turned on me
again. I just saw his great red carcass as it loomed before me;
there was time for much thought, but for little action. Down
came my axe on his head; but there was no resistance! I lost my
balance, for I had thrown all my weight on to the blow, and fell
right on to the top of him!

"I shut my eyes and breathed a prayer to the Great Spirit to
receive my soul. I knew I was a dead man, unless a miracle was
wrought, for I should never be able to get up before he would be
on me again, even if he missed me then. How long I lay I knew
not; but at last I found I was lying unhurt in the path, and no
sign of the boar. I looked cautiously round without rising, in
case he was there, waiting for me. How I ever missed his head
I could not then imagine, for I was an expert axeman, and saw
the blade fairly on him. Some sudden twist had saved him, I
thought. But what was he doing? I thought him mad. For there
he stood at bay against a tree near the glade; but not a sound,
not a grunt, rushing as if at dogs with all his bristles set. Look,
master, I see him now!" The old man had got up; his eyes glared
as his excitement increased, and I confess to having felt very
uncomfortable myself.

"Look! there he stands! No, no! you can't see him, but I do!
Yes! I see it all over again. I see him rushing madly at those
phantom dogs, biting, goring, trampling, shaking them off; and
then with one wild rush he broke his bay and run right up
to me—spirit of my forefathers!—right through me, and only
a shudder, a dull, trembling, cold, clammy shudder, as on he
went. My hair stood on end; my tongue clave to the roof of
my mouth, a horrid taste filled it; my knees shook; my heart
leaped and bounded against my ribs, and I could not move. On
he rushed. I watched him—aye, how I watched him! the great

boar's ghost, for now I knew. Back again he came. He kept about the place. In desperation and half crazy myself, I gained strength to strike another blow. My axe passed through him, leaving a large gap, that closed again. My dread increased, and I thought I should have died. Fifteen dollars, you say! Nay! not for all the money you have would I pass that night again. It would mean death now, for I am older, and my heart could not bear the strain, even if that were all.

"But there is worse, worse! I wonder I ever lived to tell the tale. The boar had broken by twice, and was standing for the third time, when I saw two men run into the glade. They were girded tight, and had on the little straw skull-caps we foresters wear. They each had his spear raised, and rushed together to-wards the boar. I saw their mouths work, but heard no sound. They were both fine tall men, almost of the same height, and very like each other—for were they not brothers! I was then almost in a stupor from long-continued fear. I could neither move nor speak, only look. I wished to cry out, but could not, for I knew they must be the two men, Rainimànga and Rain-izàfy, whose bodies we had found dead years ago, when I was but a little boy. I knew I should see how it all happened now. I was close to where they passed, but they took no notice of me. As they did so, the same chill ran through me once more, as it had done when the boar passed by. As they ran on, an evil look came over the face of the hindermost. I never saw so fiendish an expression; all the evil passions man is prone to seemed stamped upon that face. Handsome as he was, he looked like a *kinòly*.*

"I could see all plainly, for an artificial light lit upon both the men and the boar. The hideousness of the man's expression increased till he got within a few yards of the boar; then he leaped upon his brother from behind and seized his throat. Ah!

* A kind of ghostly demon, the half-decomposed body of a man come to life again.

what a fearful struggle that was! I shrieked and shrieked; but my mouth was parched, and the scream ended only in an uncertain sound. I tried to shut my eyes, but I could not. Over and over the two rolled, but the vice-like grip never relaxed. The eyes seemed to start from the head of the one that was held; his face blackened, blood began to trickle from his mouth. It was horrible, horrible! A few moments more and all was over.

"The murderer arose, gave one look at the corpse, picked up his spear and rushed at the boar, which still stood at bay. High above his head he raised his spear, poised it, gave it the twisting motion, and then, quick as lightning, threw it. It struck well, just behind the shoulder. With one savage bite, the boar severed the shaft and charged the man. In the murder of his brother he had forgotten his axe. The boar was upon him. One great shock, and his leg was ripped up as he turned to flee. Back again, another rush before he had recovered himself, and the tusks ran into the bone and severed the sinews. The man staggered and fell. He dragged himself slowly, but another rush of the huge animal, and his side was open. Then the boar, with bloodshot eyes and staggering gait, ran away to die. I fainted, and when I recovered, it was dawn. For a year I was ill, and I have never sat for pig in that glade since."

"That day was the 15th day of the moon Alàhasàty?" I asked. He nodded. "I think, my dearest father and mother," I said, "you must have been asleep." Whereupon he shook his head, rose slowly and departed.

The North Devonshire Ghost Story
A. Louis Paul (1894)

Of all the regiments which had been quartered in Calcutta for a generation, the North Devonshire was the most popular. And the inhabitants of the viceregal city were careful that no officer of the North Devonshire, from the oldest to the youngest, should be without an invitation to dinner on Christmas Day. The acceptance of these invitations was a matter of some debate. For some years previously the North Devonshire had been at an up-country station with few civilian inhabitants, and the regiment's Christmas Day guest nights had been a feature of the mess, and an occasion for gathering many of its old friends together.

The ladies of Calcutta were, however, not to be denied, and some other night had to be selected. Engagements were many, and it was difficult to fix on a suitable evening, but finally Christmas Eve was chosen, not without some searchings of heart. It was, as I have indicated, chiefly a regimental gathering, but as a cousin of the Major I was honoured with an invitation, and I was the only outsider so privileged.

The dinner went off brilliantly. We moved on to the billiard-room, and began a game of pool, which was cheery enough, but I was looking forward to midnight, when, according to custom, the cardroom would be thrown open, and we should set forth upon whist until any hour of the morning. The North Devonshire was famous in love, more famous in battle, but perhaps most famous of all for its whist. The night was cold, and, like the immortal Mrs. Battle, I was looking forward to "a clean hearth, a clear fire, and the rigour of the game."

To my intense astonishment, shortly before twelve o'clock struck the numerous guests prepared to depart. A peep round the corner was sufficient for me to see that the card-room was in pitch darkness, and I was offered drinks with the effusiveness which men adopt towards a guest of whom they are only anxious to be rid. Now I had ordered my dogcart for 2.30 a.m., and although my *syce* was, for a native, a fairly punctual man, I knew well that it would be fully 4 a.m. before that worthy would turn up. My cousin-host saw my little difficulty, and suggested an adjournment to his quarters, where, over the pegs and cheroots, I heard the strange story which explained why the North Devonshire never played whist on Christmas Eve. Thus spoke the Major:

Towards the end of the year 1858 the North Devonshire, then known as the 150th Foot, was ordered to a small station called Bhilpore, some thirty or more miles north-west of Lucknow. The country was still in a disturbed state, and the Bheels, a tribe of disaffected aborigines, were supposed to be in force in the neighbourhood. The Anglo- Indian of to-day knows the Bheels as useful shikaries. They have been taken in hand by a paternal government, and are tamed. In those times the popular definition was:

> A Bheel is a hairy man:
> He will scrag you, and leave you in a ditch.
> By this you may know a Bheel.

Like other aboriginal tribes, the Bheels had got somewhat out of hand during the Mutiny. They had laid waste some Mohammedan villages, were more than suspected of some recent dacoities, and, generally speaking, wanted watching. Colonel

Faulkner, the C.O. of the 150th, had orders to that effect. The Bheels knew him of old, for at the outset of the Mutiny, when only a captain, he had been at Bhilpore with a detachment of the 150th, and he had severely chastised them for an incipient insurrection. They knew him as "Falcon Sahib" (and the name was not ill-chosen); and when they heard that Falcon Sahib had become a commanding officer by the rapid promotion of those days, and was again in the district with what was to them an army, it was with feelings of terror and thoughts of revenge.

Rumours reached the Colonel that the Bheels meant mischief to him personally, but beyond warning the police at the *thana* on the road to Lucknow, a mile from the cantonment, to challenge all nocturnal passers-by, no special precautions were taken. The Colonel was a man of tried and conspicuous courage, but the most remarkable trait in his character was his punctilious observance of all that he undertook, however trifling, even in cases when the non-observance would have caused no annoyance nor inconvenience. This had not always been the case. Until he was about twenty-five years of age, Faulkner had been the most unreliable of men. He broke engagements with the utmost callousness. If he undertook a matter of no great importance, it was nearly certain that the undertaking would not be fulfilled. If he accepted an invitation, he was sure to be late.

Some years before the period of my story his habits were rudely changed by a tragic occurrence which cannot here be related at length. It is enough to say that, owing to some carelessness on his part, a shock was given to the mind of a favourite sister, which eventually resulted in her early death. The effect upon Faulkner was immediate. When his grief had subsided, his friends observed that his mode of life had completely changed. No longer careless, he had become scrupulous, and, to use a somewhat vulgar expression, Faulkner's word was as good as any other man's oath.

On Christmas Eve Colonel Faulkner was seated at whist with Fraser, Collier, and Morley, all officers of the 150th. They were playing chick points and a gold mohur on the rubber, as men did more often in days when the rupee was a rupee. The Colonel and Morley were partners, and had won a fairly large sum. A rubber was just over, when the Colonel, at about half past twelve, remembered that he must write a note to the General commanding at Lucknow, and send it off by the mail-cart, which started from the post-office, nearly a mile from the cantonments, at one o'clock. It was a small matter, a Christmas greeting to an old chum, which Faulkner had not omitted to send for the last five years, and Fraser tried to persuade the Colonel not to break up the party.

"No," said Faulkner, "I cannot stay, I must write the note. I will slip across to the bungalow to do it, and my orderly can take it to the mail-cart. But I will come back, if you like, to finish the night."

"Yes, do," said Fraser. "Collier wants his revenge, and so do I."

"All right," said the Colonel; "I will be back by a quarter past one. I feel as if my luck had deserted me, and that we shall be quits on Christmas Day. I am sorry for Morley, who is just having a run."

"Don't mind me," said Morley; "ruin rather than bed at this time of night."

Off went Faulkner to his bungalow, and the note was soon written. On calling his orderly, however, there was no answer; since no messenger was forthcoming, the Colonel decided to take the note himself, and he put on his cloak and started instantly. The night was very dark; the road was lonely.

The trio in the mess-room sat over brandy pawnee by the fire, and the hands of the clock crept slowly round. They grew drowsy towards one o'clock, for Morley, despite his boast, was in reality a fat, sleepy soul, and Fraser and Collier had been out all day together after snipe. When the clock struck they woke up, and, half unconsciously, all three gave a slight shiver.

"Did you feel anything, Fraser?" said Collier, looking at his companion. "I fancy that it turned very cold all of a sudden."

"A passing draught, I suppose," said Fraser, turning towards Morley. "You look quite pale too. Try some more brandy and water."

"The Colonel takes a long time to write that note," said Morley in a sleepy voice. "I don't see why he should have broken up our party for a thing he might have done just as well to-morrow. Still, what he promises he will perform to the minute. But I say," he added, looking at the clock, "it will be a joke if he has fallen asleep at his bungalow, and forgets to come back to give you fellows your revenge."

The hand was close upon the quarter, and Morley turned round towards the door. The other men did the same, and as they turned they observed the Colonel seated at the table, quietly shuffling the cards. He was very pale, very stern, and his military cloak was fastened close to the throat.

"Hulloa, Colonel," said Collier, "we were afraid you were going to fail us for once, and were just going off to bed."

"Never," said Faulkner, and he pushed the cards towards Fraser, who cut for deal.

The same shiver which the three men had felt at one o'clock passed through them again. There was a look in the Colonel's face and a tone in his voice which they had never observed before, but he was a reserved man, they were all a little in awe of him, and no one asked for an explanation. While he was dealing, Faulkner named his bets with Fraser and Collier, to which they agreed. If he and Morley lost the rubber, they would be square upon the evening's play.

They were not long about it. Faulkner and Morley held execrable cards, and in ten minutes a bumper had been lost and won. Not a word had been spoken round the table, but as the last card was played Faulkner exclaimed, in a voice which seemed to come from the shades themselves: "Now we are quits."

Again a cold shiver seemed to freeze the very marrow in the bones of the other three men. Morley lit a cheroot, the others turned to their tumblers, and when they looked up again Colonel Faulkner had vanished.

"Upon my word," said Fraser, "the Colonel looked as if he had seen a ghost."

"And you look much the same," said Morley.

The words were scarcely out of his mouth when a native policeman rushed breathlessly into the room, followed by the sentry, and fell at Morley's feet, crying out, "The Colonel Sahib! The Colonel Sahib!"

"Son of an owl," said Morley, "what do you want? The Colonel has just gone to bed. Are the Bheels rising? or what are you afraid of?"

"Sahib," said the man, recovering himself with dignity, "I fear nothing if I have your honour's favour, but the Colonel is lying dead at the *thana,* his throat cut by the Bheels. As the clock was striking one, we heard a cry down the road, near the place where the mail-cart is loaded. We hurried out, and found the Colonel with this letter in his hand. He had been shot from behind with an arrow, and his throat was then cut. He was quite dead, and it is my misfortune to bring you the news. His body is in the *thana,* Sahib. Will you come and see it?"

Colonel Faulkner had kept his word, even in death.

"And now," concluded my cousin, "you understand why the North Devonshire never play whist upon Christmas Eve. It has been a long story. There is your dogcart, so I will say good-bye, and a merry Christmas to you and yours."

Pollock and the Porroh Man
H. G. Wells (1895)

It was in a swampy village on the lagoon river behind the Turner Peninsula that Pollock's first encounter with the Porroh man occurred. The women of that country are famous for their good looks—they are Gallinas with a dash of European blood that dates from the days of Vasco de Gama and the English slave-traders, and the Porroh man too, was possibly inspired by a faint Caucasian taint in his composition. (It's a curious thing to think that some of us may have distant cousins eating men on Sherboro Island or raiding with the Sofas.) At anyrate, the Porroh man stabbed the woman to the heart as though he had been a mere low-class Italian, and very narrowly missed Pollock. But Pollock, using his revolver to parry the lightning stab which was aimed at his deltoid muscle, sent the iron dagger flying, and firing, hit the man in the hand.

He fired again and missed, knocking a sudden window out of the wall of the hut. The Porroh man stooped in the doorway, glancing under his arm at Pollock. Pollock caught a glimpse of his inverted face in the sunlight, and then the Englishman was alone, sick and trembling with the excitement of the affair, in the twilight of the place. It had all happened in less time than it takes to read about it.

The woman was quite dead, and having ascertained this, Pollock went to the entrance of the hut and looked out. Things outside were dazzling bright. Half a dozen of the porters of the expedition were standing up in a group near the green huts they occupied, and staring towards him, wondering what the shots might signify. Behind the little group of men was the broad stretch of black fetid mud by the river, a green carpet of rafts of papyrus and water-grass, and then the leaden water. The mangroves beyond the stream loomed indistinctly through the blue haze. There were no signs of excitement in the squat village, whose fence was just visible above the cane-grass.

Pollock came out of the hut cautiously and walked towards the river, looking over his shoulder at intervals. But the Porroh man had vanished. Pollock clutched his revolver nervously in his hand.

One of his men came to meet him, and as he came, pointed to the bushes behind the hut in which the Porroh man had disappeared. Pollock had an irritating persuasion of having made an absolute fool of himself; he felt bitter, savage, at the turn things had taken. At the same time, he would have to tell Waterhouse—the moral, exemplary, cautious Waterhouse—who would inevitably take the matter seriously. Pollock cursed bitterly at his luck, at Waterhouse, and especially at the West Coast of Africa. He felt consummately sick of the expedition. And in the back of his mind all the time was a speculative doubt where precisely within the visible horizon the Porroh man might be.

It is perhaps rather shocking, but he was not at all upset by the murder that had just happened. He had seen so much brutality during the last three months, so many dead women, burnt huts, drying skeletons, up the Kittam River in the wake of the Sofa cavalry, that his senses were blunted. What disturbed him was the persuasion that this business was only beginning.

He swore savagely at the black, who ventured to ask a question, and went on into the tent under the orange-trees where Waterhouse was lying, feeling exasperatingly like a boy going into the headmaster's study.

Waterhouse was still sleeping off the effects of his last dose of chlorodyne, and Pollock sat down on a packing-case beside him, and lighting his pipe, waited for him to awake. About him were scattered the pots and weapons Waterhouse had collected from the Mendi people, and which he had been repacking for the canoe voyage to Sulyma.

Presently Waterhouse woke up, and after judicial stretching, decided he was all right again. Pollock got him some tea. Over the tea, the incidents of the afternoon were described by Pollock, after some preliminary beating about the bush. Waterhouse took the matter even more seriously than Pollock had anticipated. He did not simply disapprove, he scolded, he insulted.

"You're one of those infernal fools who think a black man isn't a human being," he said. "I can't be ill a day without you must get into some dirty scrape or other. This is the third time in a month that you have come crossways-on with a native, and this time you're in for it with a vengeance. Porroh, too! They're down upon you enough as it is, about that idol you wrote your silly name on. And they're the most vindictive devils on earth! You make a man ashamed of civilisation. To think you come of a decent family! If ever I cumber myself up with a vicious, stupid young lout like you again—"

"Steady on, now," snarled Pollock, in the tone that always exasperated Waterhouse; "steady on."

At that Waterhouse became speechless. He jumped to his feet.

"Look here, Pollock," he said, after a struggle to control his breath. "You must go home. I won't have you any longer. I'm ill enough as it is, through you—"

"Keep your hair on," said Pollock, staring in front of him. "I'm ready enough to go."

Waterhouse became calmer again. He sat down on the campstool. "Very well," he said. "I don't want a row, Pollock you know, but it's confoundedly annoying to have one's plans put out by this kind of thing. I'll come to Sulyma with you, and see you safe aboard—"

"You needn't," said Pollock. "I can go alone. From here."

"Not far," said Waterhouse. "You don't understand this Porroh business."

"How should *I* know she belonged to a Porroh man?" said Pollock bitterly.

"Well, she did," said Waterhouse; "and you can't undo the thing. Go alone, indeed! I wonder what they'd do to you. You don't seem to understand that this Porroh hokey-pokey rules this country, is its law, religion, constitution, medicine, magic . . . They appoint the chiefs. The Inquisition, at its best, couldn't hold a candle to these chaps. He will probably set Awajale, the chief here, on to us. It's lucky our porters are Mendis. We shall have to shift this little settlement of ours . . . Confound you, Pollock! And, of course, you must go and miss him."

He thought, and his thoughts seemed disagreeable. Presently he stood up and took his rifle. "I'd keep close for a bit, if I were you," he said, over his shoulder, as he went out. "I'm going out to see what I can find out about it."

Pollock remained sitting in the tent, meditating. "I was meant for a civilised life," he said to himself, regretfully, as he filled his pipe. "The sooner I get back to London or Paris the better for me."

His eye fell on the sealed case in which Waterhouse had put the featherless poisoned arrows they had bought in the Mendi country. "I wish I had hit the beggar somewhere vital," said Pollock viciously.

Waterhouse came back after a long interval. He was not communicative, though Pollock asked him questions enough. The Porroh man, it seems was a prominent member of that mystical society. The village was interested, but not threatening. No doubt the witch-doctor had gone into the bush. He was a great witch-doctor. "Of course, he's up to something," said Waterhouse, and became silent.

"But what can he do?" asked Pollock, unheeded.

"I must get you out of this. There's something brewing, or things would not be so quiet," said Waterhouse, after a gap of silence. Pollock wanted to know what the brew might be. "Dancing in a circle of skulls", said Waterhouse; "brewing a stink in a copper pot." Pollock wanted particulars. Waterhouse was vague, Pollock pressing. At last Waterhouse lost his temper. "How the devil should *I* know?" he said to Pollock's twentieth inquiry what the Porroh man would do. "He tried to kill you off-hand in the hut. *Now,* I fancy he will try something more elaborate. But you'll see fast enough. I don't want to help unnerve you. It's probably all nonsense."

That night, as they were sitting at their fire, Pollock again tried to draw Waterhouse out on the subject of Porroh methods. "Better get to sleep," said Waterhouse, when Pollock's bent became apparent; "we start early to-morrow. You may want all your nerve about you."

"But what line will he take?"

"Can't say. They're versatile people. They know a lot of rum dodges. You'd better get that copper-devil, Shakespear, to talk."

There was a flash and a heavy bang, out of the darkness behind the huts, and a clay bullet came whistling close to Pollock's head. This, at least, was crude enough. The blacks and half-breeds sitting and yarning round their own fire jumped up, and someone fired into the dark.

"Better go into one of the huts," said Waterhouse quietly, still sitting unmoved.

Pollock stood up by the fire and drew his revolver. Fighting, at least, he was not afraid of. But a man in the dark is in the best of armour. Realising the wisdom of Waterhouse's advice, Pollock went into the tent and lay down there.

What little sleep he had was disturbed by dreams, variegated dreams, but chiefly of the Porroh man's face, upside down, as he went out of the hut, and looked up under his arm. It was odd that this transitory impression should have stuck so firmly in Pollock's memory. Moreover, he was troubled by queer pains in his limbs.

In the white haze of the early morning, as they were loading the canoes, a barbed arrow suddenly appeared quivering in the ground close to Pollock's foot. The boys made a perfunctory effort to clear out the thicket, but it led to no capture.

After these two occurrences, there was a disposition on the part of the expedition to leave Pollock to himself, and Pollock became, for the first time in his life, anxious to mingle with blacks. Waterhouse took one canoe, and Pollock, in spite of a friendly desire to chat with Waterhouse, had to take the other. He was left all alone in the front part of the canoe, and he had the greatest trouble to make the men—who did not love him— keep to the middle of the river, a clear hundred yards or more from either shore. However, he made Shakespear, the Freetown half-breed, come up to his own end of the canoe and tell him about Porroh, which Shakespear, failing in his attempts to leave Pollock alone, presently did with considerable freedom and gusto.

The day passed. The canoe glided swiftly along the ribbon of lagoon water, between the drift of water-figs, fallen trees, papyrus, and palm-wine palms, and with the dark mangrove swamp to the left, through which one could hear now and then the roar of the Atlantic surf. Shakespear told in his soft, blurred English of how the Porroh could cast spells; how men withered up under their malice; how they could send dreams and devils; how they tormented and killed the sons of Ijibu; how they kidnapped a white trader from Sulyma who had maltreated one of the sect, and how his body looked when it was found. And Pollock after each narrative cursed under his breath at the want of missionary enterprise that allowed such things to be, and at the inert British Government that ruled over this dark heathendom of Sierra Leone. In the evening they came to the Kasi Lake, and sent a score of crocodiles lumbering off the island on which the expedition camped for the night.

The next day they reached Sulyma, and smelt the sea breeze, but Pollock had to put up there for five days before he could get on to Freetown. Waterhouse, considering him to be comparatively safe here, and within the pale of Freetown influence, left him and went back with the expedition to Gbemma, and Pollock became very friendly with Perera, the only resident white trader at Sulyma—so friendly, indeed, that he went about with him everywhere. Perera was a little Portuguese Jew, who had lived in England, and he appreciated the Englishman's friendliness as a great compliment.

For two days nothing happened out of the ordinary; for the most part Pollock and Perera played Nap—the only game they had in common—and Pollock got into debt. Then, on the second evening, Pollock had a disagreeable intimation of the arrival of the Porroh man in Sulyma by getting a flesh-wound in the shoulder from a lump of filed iron. It was a long shot, and the missile had nearly spent its force when it hit him. Still it conveyed its message plainly enough. Pollock sat up in his hammock, revolver in hand, all that night, and next morning confided, to some extent, in the Anglo-Portuguese.

Perera took the matter seriously. He knew the local customs pretty thoroughly. "It is a personal question, you must know. It is revenge. And of course he is hurried by your leaving de country. None of de natives or half-breeds will interfere wid him very much—unless you make it wort deir while. If you come upon him suddenly, you might shoot him. But den he might shoot you."

"Den dere's dis—infernal magic," said Perera. "Of course, I don't believe in it—superstition—but still it's not nice to tink dat wherever you are, dere is a black man, who spends a moonlight night now and den a-dancing about a fire to send you bad dreams . . . Had any bad dreams?"

"Rather," said Pollock. "I keep on seeing the beggar's head upside down grinning at me and showing all his teeth as he did in the hut, and coming close up to me, and then going ever so far off, and coming back. It's nothing to be afraid of, but somehow it simply paralyses me with terror in my sleep. Queer things—dreams. I know it's a dream all the time, and I can't wake up from it."

"It's probably only fancy," said Perera. "Den my n------s say Porroh men can send snakes. Seen any snakes lately?"

"Only one. I killed him this morning, on the floor near my hammock. Almost trod on him as I got up."

"Ah!" said Perera, and then, reassuringly, "Of course it is a— coincidence. Still I would keep my eyes open. Den dere's pains in de bones."

"I thought they were due to miasma," said Pollock.

"Probably dey are. When did dey begin?"

Then Pollock remembered that he first noticed them the night after the fight in the hut. "It's my opinion he don't want to kill you," said Perera—"at least not yet. I've heard deir idea is to scare and worry a man wid deir spells, and narrow misses, and rheumatic pains, and bad dreams, and all dat, until he's sick of life. Of course, it's all talk, you know. You mustn't worry about it . . . But I wonder what he'll be up to next."

"I shall have to be up to something first," said Pollock, staring gloomily at the greasy cards that Perera was putting on the table. "It don't suit my dignity to be followed about, and shot at, and blighted in this way. I wonder if Porroh hokey-pokey upsets your luck at cards."

He looked at Perera suspiciously.

"Very likely it does," said Perera warmly, shuffling. "Dey are wonderful people."

That afternoon Pollock killed two snakes in his hammock, and there was also an extraordinary increase in the number of red ants that swarmed over the place; and these annoyances put him in a fit temper to talk over business with a certain Mendi rough he had interviewed before. The Mendi rough showed Pollock a little iron dagger, and demonstrated where one struck in the neck, in a way that made Pollock shiver, and in return for certain considerations Pollock promised him a double-barrelled gun with an ornamental lock.

In the evening, as Pollock and Perera were playing cards, the Mendi rough came in through the doorway, carrying something in a blood-soaked piece of native cloth.

"Not here!" said Pollock very hurriedly. "Not here!"

But he was not quick enough to prevent the man, who was anxious to get to Pollock's side of the bargain, from opening the cloth and throwing the head of the Porroh man upon the table. It bounded from there on to the floor, leaving a red trail on the cards, and rolled into the corner, where it came to rest upside down, but glaring hard at Pollock.

Perera jumped up as the thing fell among the cards, and began in his excitement to gabble in Portuguese. The Mendi was bowing, with the red cloth in his hand. "De gun!" he cried. Pollock stared back at the head in the corner. It bore exactly the expression it had in his dreams. Something seemed to snap in his own brain as he looked at it.

Then Perera found his English again.

"You got him killed?" he said. "You did not kill him yourself?"

"Why should I?" said Pollock.

"But he will not be able to take it off now!"

"Take *what* off?" said Pollock.

"And all dese cards are spoiled!"

"*What* do you mean by taking off?" said Pollock.

"You must send me a new pack from Freetown. You can buy dem dere."

"But—'take it off'?"

"It is only superstition. I forgot. De n-----s say dat if de witches—he was a witch— But it is rubbish . . . You must make de Porroh man take it off, or kill him yourself . . . It is very silly."

Pollock swore under his breath, still staring hard at the head in the corner.

"I can't stand that glare," he said. Then suddenly he rushed at the thing and kicked it. It rolled some yards or so, and came to rest in the same position as before, upside down, and looking at him.

"He is ugly," said the Anglo-Portuguese. "Very ugly. Dey do it on deir faces with little knives."

Pollock would have kicked the head again, but the Mendi man touched him on the arm. "De gun?" he said, looking nervously at the head.

"Two—if you will take that beastly thing away," said Pollock.

The Mendi shook his head, and intimated that he only wanted one gun now due to him, and for which he would be obliged. Pollock found neither cajolery nor bullying any good with him. Perera had a gun to sell (at a profit of three hundred per cent), and with that the man presently departed. Then Pollock's eyes, against his will, were recalled to the thing on the floor.

"It is funny dat his head keeps upside down," said Perera, with an uneasy laugh. "His brains must be heavy, like de weight in de little images one sees dat keep always upright wid lead in dem. You will take him wiv you when you go presently. You might take him now. De cards are all spoilt. Dere is a man sell dem in Freetown. De room is in a filthy mess as it is. You should have killed him yourself."

Pollock pulled himself together, and went and picked up the head. He would hang it up by the lamp-hook in the middle of the ceiling of his room, and dig a grave for it at once. He was under the impression that he hung it up by the hair, but that must have been wrong, for when he returned for it, it was hanging by the neck upside down.

He buried it before sunset on the north side of the shed he occupied, so that he should not have to pass the grave after dark when he was returning from Perera's. He killed two snakes before he went to sleep. In the darkest part of the night he awoke with a start, and heard a pattering sound and something scraping on the floor. He sat up noiselessly, and felt under his pillow for his revolver. A mumbling growl followed, and Pollock fired at the sound. There was a yelp, and something dark passed for a moment across the hazy blue of the doorway. "A dog!" said Pollock, lying down again.

In the early dawn he awoke again with a peculiar sense of unrest. The vague pain in his bones had returned. For some time he lay watching the red ants that were swarming over the ceiling, and then, as the light grew brighter, he looked over the edge of his hammock and saw something dark on the floor. He gave such a violent start that the hammock overset and flung him out.

He found himself lying, perhaps, a yard away from the head of the Porroh man. It had been disinterred by the dog, and the nose was grievously battered. Ants and flies swarmed over it. By an odd coincidence, it was still upside down, and with the same diabolical expression in the inverted eyes.

Pollock sat paralysed, and stared at the horror for some time. Then he got up and walked round it—giving it a wide berth—and out of the shed. The clear light of the sunrise, the living stir of vegetation before the breath of the dying land-breeze, and the empty grave with the marks of the dog's paws, lightened the weight upon his mind a little.

He told Perera of the business as though it was a jest—a jest to be told with white lips. "You should not have frighten de dog," said Perera, with poorly simulated hilarity.

The next two days, until the steamer came, were spent by Pollock in making a more effectual disposition of his possession. Overcoming his aversion to handling the thing, he went down to the river mouth and threw it into the sea-water, but by some miracle it escaped the crocodiles, and was cast up by the tide on the mud a little way up the river, to be found by an intelligent Arab half-breed, and offered for sale to Pollock and Perera as a curiosity, just on the edge of night. The native hung about in the brief twilight, making lower and lower offers, and at last, getting scared in some way by the evident dread these wise white men had for the thing, went off, and passing Pollock's shed, threw his burden in there for Pollock to discover in the morning.

At this Pollock got into a kind of frenzy. He would burn the thing. He went out straightway into the dawn, and had constructed a big pyre of brushwood before the heat of the day.

He was interrupted by the hooter of the little paddle steamer from Monrovia to Bathurst, which was coming through the gap in the bar. "Thank Heaven!" said Pollock, with infinite piety, when the meaning of the sound dawned upon him. With trembling hands he lit his pile of wood hastily, threw the head upon it, and went away to pack his portmanteau and make his adieux to Perera.

That afternoon, with a sense of infinite relief, Pollock watched the flat swampy foreshore of Sulyma grow small in the distance. The gap in the long line of white surge became narrower and narrower. It seemed to be closing in and cutting him off from his trouble. The feeling of dread and worry began to slip from him bit by bit. At Sulyma belief in Porroh malignity and Porroh magic had been in the air, his sense of Porroh had been vast, pervading, threatening, dreadful. Now manifestly the domain of Porroh was only a little place, a little black band between the sea and the blue cloudy Mendi uplands.

"Good-bye, Porroh!" said Pollock. "Good-bye—certainly not *au revoir*."

The captain of the steamer came and leant over the rail beside him, and wished him good-evening, and spat at the froth of the wake in token of friendly ease.

"I picked up a rummy curio on the beach this go," said the captain. "It's a thing I never saw done this side of Indy before."

"What might that be?" said Pollock.

"Pickled 'ed," said the captain.

"*What!*" said Pollock.

"'Ed—smoked. 'Ed of one of those Porroh chaps, all ornamented with knife-cuts. Why! What's up? Nothing? I shouldn't have took you for a nervous chap. Green in the face. By gosh! You're a bad sailor. All right, eh? Lord, how funny you went . . . ! Well, this 'ed I was telling you of is a bit rum in a way. I've got it, along with some snakes, in a jar of spirit in my cabin what I keeps for such curios, and I'm hanged if it don't float upsy down. Hullo!"

Pollock had given an incoherent cry, and had his hands in his hair. He ran towards the paddle-boxes with a half-formed idea of jumping into the sea, and then he realised his position and turned back towards the captain.

"Here!" said the captain. "Jack Philips, just keep him off me! Stand off! No nearer, mister! What's the matter with you? Are you mad?"

Pollock put his hand to his head. It was no good explaining. "I believe I am pretty nearly mad at times," he said. "It's a pain I have here. Comes suddenly. You'll excuse me, I hope."

He was white and in a perspiration. He saw suddenly very clearly all the danger he ran of having his sanity doubted. He forced himself to restore the captain's confidence, by answering his sympathetic inquiries, noting his suggestions, even trying a spoonful of neat brandy in his cheek, and that matter settled, asking a number of questions about the captain's private trade in curiosities. The captain described the head in detail. All the while Pollock was struggling to keep under a preposterous persuasion that the ship was as transparent as glass, and that he could distinctly see the inverted face looking at him from the cabin beneath his feet.

Pollock had a worse time almost on the steamer than he had at Sulyma. All day he had to control himself in spite of his intense perception of the imminent presence of that horrible head that was overshadowing his mind. At night his old nightmare returned, until, with a violent effort, he would force himself awake, rigid with the horror of it, and with the ghost of a hoarse scream in his throat.

He left the actual head behind at Bathurst, where he changed ship for Teneriffe, but not his dreams nor the dull ache in his bones. At Teneriffe, Pollock transferred to a Cape liner, but the head followed him. He gambled, he tried chess, he even read books, but he knew the danger of drink. Yet whenever a round black shadow, a round black object came into his range, there he looked for the head, and—saw it. He knew clearly enough that his imagination was growing traitor to him, and yet at times it seemed the ship he sailed in, his fellow-passengers, the sailors, the wide sea, was all part of a filmy phantasmagoria that hung, scarcely veiling it, between him and a horrible real world. Then the Porroh man, thrusting his diabolical face through that curtain, was the one real and undeniable thing. At that he would get up and touch things, taste something, gnaw something, burn his hand with a match, or run a needle into himself.

So, struggling grimly and silently with his excited imagination, Pollock reached England. He landed at Southampton, and went on straight from Waterloo to his banker's in Cornhill in a cab. There he transacted some business with the manager in a private room, and all the while the head hung like an ornament under the black marble mantel and dripped upon the fender. He could hear the drops fall, and see the red on the fender.

"A pretty fern," said the manager, following his eyes. "But it makes the fender rusty."

"Very," said Pollock; "a *very* pretty fern. And that reminds me. Can you recommend me a physician for mind troubles? I've got a little—what is it—? Hallucination."

The head laughed savagely, wildly. Pollock was surprised the manager did not notice it. But the manager only stared at his face.

With the address of a doctor, Pollock presently emerged in Cornhill. There was no cab in sight, and so he went on down to the western end of the street, and essayed the crossing opposite the Mansion House. The crossing is hardly easy even for the expert Londoner; cabs, vans, carriages, mail-carts, omnibuses go by in one incessant stream; to anyone fresh from the malarious solitudes of Sierra Leone it is a boiling, maddening confusion. But when an inverted head suddenly comes bouncing, like an india-rubber ball, between your legs, leaving distinct smears of blood every time it touches the ground, you can scarcely hope to avoid an accident. Pollock lifted his feet convulsively to avoid it, and then kicked at the thing furiously. Then something hit him violently in the back, and a hot pain ran up his arm.

He had been hit by the pole of an omnibus, and three of the fingers of his left hand smashed by the hoof of one of the horses—the very fingers, as it happened, that he shot from the Porroh man. They pulled him out from between the horse's legs, and found the address of the physician, in his crushed hand.

For a couple of days Pollock's sensations were full of the sweet, pungent smell of chloroform, of painful operations that caused him no pain, of lying still and being given food and drink. Then he had a slight fever, and was very thirsty, and his old nightmare came back. It was only when it returned that he noticed it had left him for a day.

"If my skull had been smashed instead of my fingers, it might have gone altogether," said Pollock, staring thoughtfully at the dark cushion that had taken on for the time the shape of the head.

Pollock at the first opportunity told the physician of his mind trouble. He knew clearly that he must go mad unless something should intervene to save him. He explained that he had witnessed a decapitation in Dahomey, and was haunted by one of the heads. Naturally, he did not care to state the actual facts. The physician looked grave.

Presently he spoke hesitatingly. "As a child, did you get very much religious training?"

"Very little," said Pollock.

A shade passed over the physician's face. "I don't know if you have heard of the miraculous cures—it may be, of course, they are not miraculous—at Lourdes."

"Faith-healing will hardly suit me, I am afraid," said Pollock, with his eye on the dark cushion.

The head distorted its scarred features in an abominable grimace. The physician went upon a new track. "It's all imagination," he said, speaking with sudden briskness. "A fair case for faith-healing, anyhow. Your nervous system has run down, you're in that twilight state of health when the bogles come easiest. The strong impression was too much for you. I must make you up a little mixture that will strengthen your nervous system—especially your brain. And you must take exercise."

"I'm no good for faith-healing," said Pollock.

"And therefore we must restore tone. Go in search of stimulating air—Scotland, Norway, the Alps—"

"Jericho, if you like," said Pollock—"where Naaman went."

However, so soon as his fingers would let him, Pollock made a gallant attempt to follow out the doctor's suggestion. It was now November. He tried football, but to Pollock the game consisted in kicking a furious inverted head about a field. He was no good at the game. He kicked blindly, with a kind of horror, and when they put him back into goal, and the ball came swooping down upon him, he suddenly yelled and got out of its way. The discreditable stories that had driven him from England to wander in the tropics shut him off from any but men's society, and now his increasingly strange behaviour made even his man friends avoid him. The thing was no longer a thing of the eye merely; it gibbered at him, spoke to him. A horrible fear came upon him that presently, when he took hold of the apparition, it would no longer become some mere article of furniture, but would feel like a real dissevered head. Alone, he would curse at the thing, defy it, entreat it; once or twice, in spite of his grim self-control, he addressed it in the presence of others. He felt the growing suspicion in the eyes of the people that watched him—his landlady, the servant, his man.

One day early in December his cousin Arnold—his next of kin—came to see him and draw him out, and watch his sunken yellow face with narrow eager eyes. And it seemed to Pollock that the hat his cousin carried in his hand was no hat at all, but a Gorgon head that glared at him upside down, and fought with its eyes against his reason. However, he was still resolute to see the matter out. He got a bicycle, and, riding over the frosty road from Wandsworth to Kingston, found the thing rolling along at his side, and leaving a dark trail behind it. He set his teeth and rode faster. Then suddenly, as he came down the hill towards Richmond Park, the apparition rolled in front of him and under his wheel, so quickly that he had no time for thought, and, turning quickly to avoid it, was flung violently against a heap of stones and broke his left wrist.

The end came on Christmas morning. All night he had been in a fever, the bandages encircling his wrist like a band of fire, his dreams more vivid and terrible than ever. In the cold, colourless, uncertain light that came before the sunrise, he sat up in his bed, and saw the head upon the bracket in the place of the bronze jar that had stood there overnight.

"I know that is a bronze jar," he said, with a chill doubt at his heart. Presently the doubt was irresistible. He got out of bed slowly, shivering, and advanced to the jar with his hand raised. Surely he would see now his imagination had deceived him, recognise the distinctive sheen of bronze. At last, after an age of hesitation, his fingers came down on the patterned cheek of the head. He withdrew them spasmodically. The last stage was reached. His sense of touch had betrayed him.

Trembling, stumbling against the bed, kicking against his shoes with his bare feet, a dark confusion eddying round him, he groped his way to the dressing-table, took his razor from the drawer, and sat down on the bed with this in his hand. In the looking-glass he saw his own face, colourless, haggard, full of the ultimate bitterness of despair.

He beheld in swift succession the incidents in the brief tale of his experience. His wretched home, his still more wretched schooldays, the years of vicious life he had led since then, one act of selfish dishonour leading to another; it was all clear and pitiless now, all its squalid folly, in the cold light of the dawn. He came to the hut, to the fight with the Porroh man, to the retreat down the river to Sulyma, to the Mendi assassin and his red parcel, to his frantic endeavours to destroy the head, to the growth of his hallucination. It was a hallucination! He *knew* it was. A hallucination merely. For a moment he snatched at hope. He looked away from the glass, and on the bracket, the inverted head grinned and grimaced at him . . . With the stiff fingers of his bandaged hand he felt at his neck for the throb of his arteries. The morning was very cold, the steel blade felt like ice.

The Square Diamond
Clinton Ross (1896)

The *Britannia* pitched in the Biscayan swell, and the crowd in the smoking-room had lessened until five men were left, exchanging yarns, as men will who go to and fro in slops. Captain Willoughby had been silent through most, and only the subject of Indian trickery seemed to arouse him. Now and then the screw gave its dismal whir, the men drew closer, and the steward hurried with the Scotch, almost tumbling in a quick lurch.

"You know that old trick, when the fakir takes a boy, cuts him into pieces, and then puts him together again?" said the short, fat, dark man.

"Yes, but I never knew a man who could swear positively he had seen it."

"I have seen it," said the short, fat, dark man, swigging his Scotch.

"And I," said Captain Willoughby, beating a tattoo with his boot.

"But while we stood at first in horror, in amazement, a boy climbed down a tree, saying he had seen the fakir cut up a squash—that was all," said the short, fat, dark man.

"You mean that the boy was outside the mesmeric circle? Do you believe that bosh?" said one.

"I do," said the short, fat, dark man.

"I do," said Captain Willoughby, decidedly.

"Oh, you do?"

"Yes, for I know," said the bronzed captain, who bore his fifty years as lightly as a coquette her second affair. He paused, looking about. Still the screw whirred its chorus to the now beating storm. Willoughby suddenly reached into his waistcoat, taking from a little leathern case a ring, in a curious setting—a single, square diamond. Holding it up, he asked, "Do you notice that ring?"

"It's beautiful," said the short, fat, dark man; "and the setting an antique, too. But it's hard to sell a square stone, the dealers say."

"Yes," said Willoughby. "But the setting is new—an imitation; I had it made for the stone."

"Yes, but what has this to do with occultism and our fakir? Is it the old tale of the Rajah's diamond?" said the sceptic.

"Yes, the old tale," said Willoughby, soberly. He put the ring back into its case and looked about. He was not given to story-telling, and yet to-night the whirring screw, the beating storm—some strange impulse—led him on.

"I will tell you how it was," he said, stretching his long legs. "That stone cost me the best servant, and, indeed, the best friend a man ever had—an Irish boy who was brought up with me. You may say what you will about theosophy, or occultism, or fakirism. I only know what I have experienced, and there are twenty men in the Sixtieth Bengal who will bear me out. I am too old a man, gentlemen, to sneer at the unknown. I have not lived in India, and spent my youth and some health, without having reached the knowledge that the unknown sits in the lap of the known, and that there is some curious relation between matter and mind which doubtless will be made known some day. Only the day before our sailing you heard of the Roentgen discovery of the cathodic rays. Why may there not be some light that one mind may shed on another, creating an illusion? That is mesmerism, you may say. Why may there not be a material object, like my square diamond, which may be able, in connection with some particular personality, to produce certain illusions?"

"Can you do it with your diamond?" asked the sceptic.

"Listen," Willoughby continued, almost sternly, "and I will tell you why I always carry that stone with me, a circumstance which may appear strange. I don't know why I tell the story now. But I have begun, and something seems to make me.

"Two years ago I had been down in the old place in Devon, and there developed a sentimentality—you know how it may be with a very old bachelor—requiring a ring. Passing a shop in Regent Street, I saw in a tiara—a new one, made in an old fashion—this stone. I have a fancy for unusual things, you know. The man agreed to take the stone from the tiara."

"'Your taste is excellent, sir,' he was pleased to comment, in their way. 'The stone is very old; five thousand years, maybe; an Indian stone from an old tiara.'

"'The present setting is modern.'

"'Yes, I tried to imitate the idea of the old piece—that is all. I came by the stone very curiously.'

"'How curiously?'

"He moved uneasily.

"'I can't tell you, sir.'

"I looked at him narrowly; yet it was one of the best shops in London, and why should I ask questions. We bargained a bit, and securing the stone at a remarkably low price—it seemed to me, considering its intrinsic value and Regent Street—I drew myself a design for a fitting setting to carry an unique gem. But when my ring was ready, my sentimental affair was over, like many another in my life; and I simply had the ring, instead of its once probable wearer. On my return to India, and in my duties, which came over me with all the force of habit to a man long in the service, I almost forgot it.

"Well, a year ago, if you may remember, came the little trouble with the little Rajah of Renaub. You may not even remember it, or know that Renaub is on the northern border among the Himalayas. The affair did not amount to much, and I, with some twenty men of the Sixtieth Bengal, had reason to curse it—and particularly my servant, Teddy Burns, had his reason, poor devil!

"In the first place, we were stationed in a narrow, barren, gray valley, a pass perhaps a quarter of a mile broad, with a sheer rise of the gray mountains five thousand feet each side. The valley is about fifteen miles wide, opening at the north on the plateau of Renaub. We were at a wretched village, some five miles from the northern opening, a station with an official. The official had a wife, a pale little London woman, worn out by Indian life. I pitied the pair from the bottom of my heart in that God-for-saken spot—not the only dismal spot in India, as I know. We played cards, and talked, and drank, until we were tired of ourselves; and the man's sad-eyed pale little wife would chatter of London, and tell how she longed to see just Trafalgar Square.

"One afternoon, going back to my quarters, I had occasion to look for something in a box, when out tumbled a case with some pins and trinkets which Teddy had put in, probably thinking that Renaub was a gay spot and that I might wish to dress up. I opened it, throwing out among other things the ring, which I had forgotten. What I wanted was a little painting on porcelain—very decently done—of our place in Devon, which I wished to show to the homesick woman. As I looked at it, leaving the other things on the table, I heard a rustling behind, and saw a tall, thin native peering over my shoulder. His ascetic face was illuminated by great eyes, with a reddish glow as of rubies—greedy, covetous.

"'What the devil?' I began.

"'Did the Sahib call?' he said, bending. I thought he might be a servant I had not seen.

"'Get out!' I said, simply; for such a place leaves you irritable; when he turned, and, with all the dignity of a personage, stalked through the door.

"'Teddy,' I called, thinking Teddy could not be far away. And sure enough Teddy appeared.

"'What are you coming to in your old age, that you need an assistant to help you now?' I asked.

"'What d'yez mean, sor?' said Teddy, most respectfully, although the words may not so sound.

"'Who was the man in here just now?'

"'I saw no one, sor.'

"'Didn't you pass him, coming in?'

"'Who, sor?'

"The matter seemed strange. I knew Teddy wouldn't lie; and I concluded it had been some familiar servant who had the run of the house, whom, in a short stay, neither Teddy nor I had noticed.

"'Put those things up then,' I said, knowing Teddy was incorruptible, and starting to take the porcelain to our official's wife. I hardly was at the outer door when I heard a scuffle and a muffled cry. With a sudden fear I rushed back, and at the threshold, for a moment, stood horrified. Teddy was stretched speechless in a pool of blood, a knife with a strangely carved handle sticking in his side; and a stealthy figure—the same that had faced me so shortly before—stood over him. For a moment we looked at each other; for a moment I could not move; and then, with a snarl, the creature sprang toward me. I was ready for him, but he slipped through my hands, and passed me—through the door.

"Raising a dreadful cry, I was after. At the outside door I saw him; a lithe figure, that had dropped the loin-cloth from his naked legs, running up the valley, past three of my men, who were on ponies.

"'Stop him!' I cried. But he slipped past; and before they had recovered from their astonishment I was by them.

"'Go in! Look to Teddy,' I called, dragging one from his pony and taking his seat.

"'After him!' I said, kicking my brute. 'Shoot him, if you can bring him down.' I hadn't my pistols.

"And we chased up that brown valley under the glaring North Indian sun. He seemed to run as fast as our ponies; but at last we gained a little. He looked about, showing white, grinning teeth. Two of the men answered with pistol-shots. I bent well onto the pony's neck.

"'Where is he?' asked one of the men.

"'Where—?' began the other.

"For before our eyes the runner had vanished, faded; what you will; and where he should have been was a lean wolf, turning now and then hungry eyes, and snarling lips, and grinning teeth.

"The thing was so uncanny that I pulled up my pony; and then was charging up to the spot where the man had disappeared and the wolf appeared—believing he had found a hole in the earth. But there the short, yellow furze was unbroken. There was another click and report—a long, horrid, brutish howl—and the wolf was over a low slope, too, out of view, and the men after. After a moment I followed, to find them dismounted by the man we had been chasing—without a wolf in sight; the man on his back.

"'Damn it, sir, where's the wolf?' one of my bewildered fellows asked.

"The great eyes stared brutishly up to mine. One fist was clinched. With sudden expectation I leaned over, and opened the sinewy fist, when from it fell the ring. I put it into my pocket, leaving the men with the dead thing, and rode back to Teddy, only to be met by my friend the official. Teddy was dead, like his murderer, who proved to be unknown at the station, and probably some wandering thief.

"I told the eager listener of our hallucination."

"'The men will swear to it, and I.'

"He looked at me a moment, curiously.

"'I have lived too long in India to doubt it,' said he, slowly. 'Tell me how did you come by the stone?' When I had finished he asked, strangely:

"'Have you not heard that a certain mind associated with a certain talisman can produce such an illusion?'

"'I have seen it,' said I.

"As I said at the beginning of this story, 'I have seen it.' That square diamond at any rate cost me the best servant a man ever had—more than servant, a friend. Whether it were ordinary cupidity, or some desire for that particular stone, I cannot say. But I saw the wolf where the man was, and the dead man where the dead wolf should have been. Some persons would have given the diamond away, or have sold it, but I have kept it."

"There was no boy up a tree outside the mesmeric influence," said the sceptic. "May I see that stone again?"

"Yes, certainly," said Captain Willoughby, taking the diamond from the case. "That thing happened a year ago to-day."

They passed it from hand to hand; and above the storm roared.

"Will you mind if I look at it, sir?" asked a low, distant voice. They looked up startled, for no one had seen this last enter; they saw a tall, dark person, modishly dressed—with all the western affectations of some East Indians.

"You were listening," said Willoughby. "I didn't hear or see you. I must have been so absorbed in my story. Certainly, sir. I should like to have one of your race look at that stone."

A lean, sinewy hand stretched out, grasping the stone. Willoughby shivered and looked up.

"Where the devil?" he began; for hand, and ring, and man, were not there. They rubbed their eyes, ran into the passage.

The steward was called. He knew no one on the ship answering the description; nor did the thorough search the next morning show the thief; perhaps he had been some strange stowaway—perhaps he had been washed from the deck.

The *Britannia* then was tossing and groaning in the arms of the roaring storm, and, as far as that ship's company was concerned, the dark-visaged unknown seemed to have gone back into the tempest whence he had come.

The Tiger-Charm
Alice Perrin (1901)

The sun, the sky, the burning dusty atmosphere, and the waving sea of tall yellow grass seemed molten into one blinding blaze of pitiless heat to the aching vision of little Mrs. Wingate. In spite of blue goggles, pith sun-hat, and enormous umbrella, she felt as though she were being slowly roasted alive, for the month was May, and she and her husband were perched on the back of an elephant, traversing a large tract of jungle at the foot of the Himalayas.

Colonel Wingate was one of the keenest sportsmen in India, and every day for the past week had he and his wife, and their friend Captain Bastable, sallied forth from the camp with a line of elephants to beat through forests of grass that reached to the animals' ears; to squelch over swamps, disturbing herds of antelope and wild pig; to pierce thick tangles of jungle, from which rose pea-fowl, black partridge, and birds of gorgeous plumage; to cross stony beds of dry rivers—ever on the watch for the tigers that had hitherto baffled all their efforts.

As each 'likely' spot was drawn a blank, Netta Wingate heaved a sigh of relief, for she hated sport, was afraid of the elephants, and lived in hourly terror of seeing a tiger. She longed for the fortnight in camp to be over, and secretly hoped that the latter week of it might prove as unsuccessful as the first. Her skin was burnt to the hue of a berry, her head ached perpetually from the heat and glare, the motion of the elephant made her feel sick, and if she ventured to speak her husband only impatiently bade her be quiet.

This afternoon, as they ploughed and rocked over the hard uneven ground, she could scarcely keep awake, dazzled as she was by the vista of scorched yellow country and the gleam of her husband's rifle barrels in the melting sunshine. She swayed drowsily from side to side in the howdah, her head drooped, her eyelids closed. . . .

She was roused by a torrent of angry exclamations. Her umbrella had hitched itself obstinately into the collar of Colonel Wingate's coat, and he was making infuriated efforts to free himself. Jim Bastable, approaching on his elephant, caught a mixed vision of the refractory umbrella and two agitated sun-hats, the red face and fierce blue eyes of the Colonel and the anxious, apologetic, sleepy countenance of Mrs. Wingate, as she hurriedly strove to release her irate lord and master. The whole party came to an involuntary halt, the natives listening with interest as the sahib stormed at the memsahib and the umbrella in the same breath.

"That howdah is not big enough for two people," shouted Captain Bastable, coming to the rescue. "Let Mrs. Wingate change to mine. It's bigger, and my elephant has easier paces."

Hot, irritated, angry, Colonel Wingate commanded his wife to betake herself to Bastable's elephant, and to keep her infernal umbrella closed for the rest of the day, adding that women had no business out tiger-shooting; and why the devil had she come at all?—oblivious of the fact that Mrs. Wingate had begged to be allowed to stay in the station, and that he himself had insisted on her coming.

She well knew that argument or contradiction would only make matters worse, for he had swallowed three stiff whiskies and sodas at luncheon in the broiling sun, and since the severe sunstroke that had so nearly killed him two years ago, the smallest quantity of spirits was enough to change him from an exceedingly bad-tempered man into something little short of a maniac. She had heedlessly married him when she was barely nineteen, turning a deaf ear to warnings of his violence, and now, at twenty-three, her existence was one long fear. He never allowed her out of his sight, he never believed a word she said; he watched her, suspected her, bullied her unmercifully, and was insanely jealous. Unfortunately, she was one of those nervous, timid women, who often rather provoke ill-treatment than otherwise.

This afternoon she marvelled at being permitted to change to Captain Bastable's howdah, and with a feeling of relief scrambled off the elephant, though trembling, as she always did, lest the great beast should seize her with his trunk or lash her with his tail, that was like a jointed iron rod. Then, once safely perched up behind Captain Bastable, she settled herself with a delightful sense of security. He understood her nervousness, he did not laugh or grumble at her little involuntary cries of fear; he was not impatient when she was convinced the elephant was running away or sinking in a quicksand, or that the howdah was slipping off. He also understood the Colonel, and had several times helped her through a trying situation; and now the sympathy in his kind eyes made her tender heart throb with gratitude.

"All right?" he asked.

She nodded, smiling, and they started again ploughing and lurching through the coarse grass, great wisps of which the elephant uprooted with his trunk, and beat against his chest to get rid of the soil before putting them in his mouth. Half an hour later, as they drew near the edge of the forest, one of the elephants suddenly stopped short, with a jerky, backward movement, and trumpeted shrilly. There was an expectant halt all along the line, and a cry from a native of "Tiger! Tiger!" Then an enormous striped beast bounded out of the grass and stood for a moment in a small open space, lashing its tail and snarling defiance. Colonel Wingate fired. The tiger, badly wounded, charged, and sprang at the head of Captain Bastable's elephant. There was a confusion of noise; savage roars from the tiger; shrieks from the excited elephants, shouts from the natives; banging of rifles. Mrs. Wingate covered her face with her hands. She heard a thud, as of a heavy body falling to the ground, and then she found herself being flung from side to side of the howdah, as the elephant bolted madly towards the forest, one huge ear torn to ribbons by the tiger's claws.

She heard Captain Bastable telling her to hold on tight, and shouting desperate warnings to the mahout to keep the elephant as clear of the forest as possible. Like many nervous people in the face of real danger, she suddenly became absolutely calm, and uttered no sound as the pace increased and they tore along the forest edge, escaping overhanging boughs by a miracle. To her it seemed that the ponderous flight lasted for hours. She was bruised, shaken, giddy, and the crash that came at last was a relief rather than otherwise. A huge branch combed the howdah off the elephant's back, sweeping the mahout with it, while the still terrified animal sped on trumpeting and crashing through the forest.

Mrs. Wingate was thrown clear of the howdah. Captain Bastable had saved himself by jumping, and only the old mahout lay doubled up and unconscious amongst the debris of shattered wood, torn leather, and broken ropes. Netta could hardly believe she was not hurt, and she and Captain Bastable stared at one another with dazed faces for some moments before they could collect their senses. Far away in the distance they could hear the elephant still running. Between them they extricated the mahout, and, seating herself on the ground, Netta took the old man's unconscious head on to her lap, while Captain Bastable anxiously examined the wizened shrunken body.

"Is he dead?" she asked.

"I can't be sure. I'm afraid he is. I wonder if I could find some water. I haven't an idea where we are, for I lost all count of time and distance. I hope Wingate is following us. Should you be afraid to stay here while I have a look round and see if we are anywhere near a village?"

"Oh no, I shan't be frightened," she said steadily. Her delicate, clear-cut face looked up at him fearlessly from the tangled background of mighty trees and dense creepers; and her companion could scarcely believe she was the same trembling, nervous little coward of an hour ago.

He left her, and the stillness of the jungle was very oppressive when the sound of his footsteps died away. She was alone with a dead, or dying, man, on the threshold of the vast, mysterious forest, with its possible horrors of wild elephants, tigers, leopards, snakes! She tried to turn her thoughts from such things, but the scream of a peacock made her start as it rent the silence, and then the undergrowth began to rustle ominously. It was only a porcupine that came out, rattling his quills, and, on seeing her, ran into further shelter out of sight. It seemed to be growing darker, and she fancied the evening must be drawing in. She wondered if her husband would overtake them. If not, how were she and Jim Bastable to get back to the camp? Then she heard voices and footsteps, and presently a little party of natives came in sight, led by Jim and bearing a string bedstead.

"I found a village not far off," he explained, "and thought we'd better take the poor old chap there. Then, if the Colonel doesn't turn up by the time we've seen him comfortably settled, we must find our way back to the camp as best we can."

The natives chattered and exclaimed as they lifted the unconscious body on to the bedstead, and then the little procession started. Netta was so bruised and stiff she could hardly walk; but, with the help of Bastable's arm, she hobbled along till the village was gained. The headman conducted them to his house, which consisted of a mud hovel shared by himself and his family, with several relations, besides a cow, and a goat with two kids. He gave Netta a wicker stool to sit on and some smoky buffalo's milk to drink, while the village physician was summoned, who at last succeeded in restoring the mahout to consciousness and pouring a potion down his throat.

"I die," whispered the patient feebly.

Netta went to his side, and he recognised her.

"A—ree! memsahib!" he quavered. "So Allah has guarded thee. But the anger of the Colonel sahib will be great against me for permitting the elephant to run away, and it is better that I die. Where is that daughter of a pig? She was a rascal from her youth up; but to-day was the first time she ever really disobeyed my voice."

He tried to raise himself, but fell back groaning, for his injuries were internal and past hope.

"It is growing dark." He put forth his trembling hand blindly. "Where is the little white lady who so feared the sahib, and the elephants, and the jungle? Do not be afraid, memsahib. Those who fear should never go into the jungle. So if thou seest a tiger be bold, be bold; call him 'uncle' and show him the tiger-charm. Then will he turn away and harm thee not—" He wandered on incoherently, his fingers fumbling with something at his throat, and presently he drew out a small silver amulet attached to a piece of cord. As he held it towards Netta, it flashed in the light of the miserable native oil lamp that some one had just brought in and placed on the floor.

"Take it, memsahib, and feel no fear while thou hast it, for no tiger would touch thee. It was my father's and his father's before him, and there is that written on it which has ever protected us from the tiger's tooth. I myself shall need it no longer, for I am going, whereat my nephew will rejoice; for he has long coveted my seat. Thou shalt have the charm, memsahib, for thou hast stayed by an old man, and not left him to die alone in a Hindu village and a strange place. Some day, in the hour of danger, thy little fingers may touch the charm, and then thou wilt recall old Mahomed Bux, mahout, with gratitude."

He groped for Netta's hand, and pushed the amulet into her palm. She took it, and laid her cool fingers on the old man's burning forehead.

"Salaam, Mahomed Bux,' she said softly. "Bahut, bahut sa-laam." Which is the nearest Hindustani equivalent for "Thank you."

But he did not hear her. He was wandering again, and for half an hour he babbled of elephants, of tigers, of camps and jungles, until his voice became faint and died away in hoarse gasps.

Then he sighed heavily and lay still, and Jim Bastable took Mrs. Wingate out into the air, and told her that the old mahout was dead. She gave way and sobbed, for she was aching all over and tired to death, and she dreaded the return to the camp.

"Oh! my dear girl, please don't cry!" said Jim distressfully. "Though really I can't wonder at it, after all you've gone through to-day; and you've been so awfully plucky, too."

Netta gulped down her tears. It was delicious to be praised for courage, when she was only accustomed to abuse for cowardice.

"How are we to get back to the camp?" she asked dolefully. "It's so late."

And, indeed, darkness had come swiftly on, and the light of the village fires was all that enabled them to see each other.

"The moon will be up presently; we must wait for that. They say the village near our camp lies about six miles off, and that there is a cart-track of sorts towards it. I told them they must let us have a bullock-cart, and we shall have to make the best of that."

They sat down side by side on a couple of large stones, and listened in silence to the lowing of the tethered cattle, the ceaseless, irritating cry of the brain-fever bird, and the subdued conversation of a group of children and village idlers, who had assembled at a respectful distance to watch them with inquisitive interest. Once a shrill trumpeting in the distance told of a herd of wild elephants out for a night's raid on the crops, and at intervals packs of jackals swept howling across the fields, while the moon rose gradually over the collection of squalid huts and

flooded the vast country with a light that made the forest black
and fearful.

Then a clumsy little cart, drawn by two small, frightened
white bullocks, rattled into view. Jim and Netta climbed into
the vehicle, and were politely escorted off the premises by the
headman and the concourse of interested villagers and excited
women and children.

They bumped and shook over the rough, uneven track. The
bullocks raced or crawled alternately, while the driver twisted their tails and abused them hoarsely. The moonlight grew
brighter and more glorious. The air, now soft and cool, was
filled with strong scents and the hum of insects released from
the heat of the day.

At last they caught the gleam of white tents against the dark
background of a mango-grove.

"The camp," said Captain Bastable shortly. Netta made a
nervous exclamation.

"Do you think there will be a row?" he asked with some
hesitation. They had never discussed Mrs. Wingate's domestic
troubles together.

"Perhaps he is still out looking for us," she said evasively.

"If he had followed us at all, he must have found us. I believe he went on shooting, or back to the camp." There was an
angry impatience in his voice. "Don't be nervous," he added
hastily. "Try not to mind anything he may say. Don't listen. He
can't always help it, you know. I wish you could persuade him
to retire; the sun out here makes him half off his head."

"I wish I could," she sighed. "But he will never do anything
I ask him, and the big game shooting keeps him in India."

Jim nodded, and there was a comprehending silence between
them till they reached the edge of the camp, got out of the cart,
and made their way to the principal tent. There they discovered Colonel Wingate still in his shooting clothes, sitting by
the table, on which stood an almost empty bottle of whisky.
He rose as they entered, and delivered himself of a torrent of

bad language. He accused the pair of going off together on purpose, declaring he would divorce his wife and kill Bastable. He
stormed, raved, and threatened, giving them no opportunity of
speaking, until at last Jim broke in and insisted on being heard.

"For Heaven's sake be quiet," he said firmly, "or you'll have a
fit. You saw the elephant run away, and apparently you made no
effort to follow us and come to our help. We were swept off by a
tree, and the mahout was mortally hurt. It was a perfect miracle
that neither your wife nor I was killed. The mahout died in a
village, and we had to get here in a bullock-cart." Then, seeing
Wingate preparing for another onslaught, Bastable took him by
the shoulders. "My dear chap, you're not yourself. Go to bed,
and we'll talk it over to-morrow if you still wish to."

Colonel Wingate laughed harshly. His mood had changed
suddenly.

"Go to bed?" he shouted boisterously. "Why, I was just going out when you arrived. There was a kill last night, only a
mile off, and I'm going to get the tiger." He stared wildly at
Jim, who saw that he was not responsible for his words and
actions. The brain, already touched by sunstroke, had given way
at last under the power of whisky. Jim's first impulse was to prevent his carrying out his intention of going after the tiger. Then
he reflected that it was not safe for Netta to be alone with the
man, and that, if Wingate were allowed his own way, it would
at least take him out of the camp.

"Very well," said Jim quietly, "and I will come with you."

"Do," answered the Colonel pleasantly, and then, as Bastable turned for a moment, Mrs. Wingate saw her husband make
a diabolical grimace at the other's unconscious back. Her heart
beat rapidly with fear. Did he mean to murder Jim? She felt
convinced he contemplated mischief; but the question was how
to warn Captain Bastable without her husband's knowledge.
The opportunity came more easily than she had expected, for
presently the Colonel went outside to call for his rifle and give
some orders. She flew to Bastable's side.

"Be careful," she panted; "he wants to kill you, I know he does. He's mad! Oh, don't go with him—don't go—"

"It will be all right," he said reassuringly. "I'll look out for myself, but I can't let him go alone in this state. We shall only sit up in a tree for an hour or two, for the tiger must have come and gone long ago. Don't be frightened. Go to bed and rest."

She drew from her pocket the little polished amulet the mahout had given her.

"At any rate take this," she said hysterically. "It may save you from a tiger, if it doesn't from my husband. I know I am silly, but do take it. There may be luck in it, you can never tell; and old Mahomed Bux said it had saved him and his father and his grandfather—and that you ought to call a tiger 'uncle'—" she broke off half laughing, half crying, utterly unstrung.

To please her he put the little charm into his pocket, and after a hasty drink went out and joined Wingate, who insisted that they should proceed on foot and by themselves. Bastable knew it would be useless to make any opposition, and they started, their rifles in their hands; but, when they had gone some distance and the tainted air told them they were nearing their destination, Jim discovered he had no cartridges.

"Never mind," whispered the Colonel. "I have plenty, and our rifles have the same bore. We can't go back now; we've no time to lose."

Jim submitted, and he and Wingate tip-toed to the foot of a tree, the low branches and thick leaves of which afforded an excellent hiding place, down-wind from the half-eaten carcass of the cow. They climbed carefully up, making scarcely any noise, and then Jim held out his hand to the other for some cartridges. The Colonel nodded.

"Presently," he whispered, and Jim waited, thinking it extremely unlikely that cartridges would be wanted at all.

The moonlight came feebly through the foliage of the surrounding trees on to the little glade before them, in which lay the remains of the carcass pulled under a bush to shield it from the carrion birds. A deer pattered by towards the river, casting startled glances on every side; insects beat against the faces of the two men; and a jackal ran out with his brush hanging down, looked round, and retired again, with a melancholy howl. Then there arose a commotion in the branches of the neighbouring trees, and a troop of monkeys fought and crashed and chattered, as they leapt from bough to bough. Jim knew that this often portended the approach of a tiger, and the moment afterwards a long, hoarse call from the river told him that the warning was correct. He made a silent sign for the cartridges; but Wingate took no notice: his face was hard and set, and the whites of his eyes gleamed.

A few seconds later a large tiger crept slowly out of the grass, his stomach on the ground, his huge head held low.

Jim remembered the native superstition that the head of a man-eating tiger is weighed down by the souls of its victims. With a run and a spring the creature attacked its meal, and began growling and munching contentedly, purring like a cat, and stopping every now and then to tear up the earth with its claws.

A report rang out. Wingate had fired at and hit the tiger. The great beast gave a terrific roar and sprang at the tree. Jim lifted his rifle, only to remember that it was unloaded.

"Shoot again!" he cried excitedly, as the tiger fell back and prepared for another spring. To his horror, Wingate deliberately fired the second barrel into the air, and throwing away the rifle, grasped him by the arms. The man's teeth were bared, his face distorted and hideous, his purpose unmistakable—he was trying to throw Bastable to the tiger. Wingate was strong with the diabolical strength of madness, and they swayed till the branches of the tree crackled ominously. Again the tiger roared and sprang, and again fell back, only to gather itself together for another effort. The two men rocked and panted, the branches cracked louder with a dry splitting sound, then broke off altogether, and, locked in each other's arms, they fell heavily to the ground.

Jim Bastable went undermost, and was half stunned by the shock. He heard a snarl in his ear, followed by a dreadful cry. He felt the weight of Wingate's body lifted from him with a jerk, and he scrambled blindly to his feet. As in a nightmare, he saw the tiger bounding away, carrying something that hung limply from the great jaws, just as a cat carries a dead mouse.

He seized the Colonel's rifle that lay near him; but he knew it was empty, and that the cartridges were in the Colonel's pocket. He ran after the tiger, shouting, yelling, brandishing the rifle, in hopes of frightening the brute into dropping its prey; but, after one swift glance back, it bounded into the thick jungle with the speed of a deer, and Bastable was left standing alone.

Faint and sick, he began running madly towards the camp for help, though he knew well that nothing in this world could ever help Wingate again. His forehead was bleeding profusely, either hurt in the fall or touched by the tiger's claw, and the blood trickling into his eyes nearly blinded him. He pulled his handkerchief from his pocket as he ran, and something came with it that glittered in the moonlight and fell to the ground with a metallic ring.

It was the little silver amulet. The tiger-charm.

The Grove of Ashtaroth
John Buchan (1910)

I

We were sitting around the camp fire, some thirty miles north
of a place called Taqui, when Lawson announced his intention
of finding a home. He had spoken little the last day or two, and
I had guessed that he had struck a vein of private reflection. I
thought it might be a new mine or irrigation scheme, and I was
surprised to find that it was a country house.

"I don't think I shall go back to England," he said, kicking
a sputtering log into place. "I don't see why I should. For business purposes I am far more useful to the firm in South Africa
than in Throgmorton Street. I have no relations left except a
third cousin, and I have never cared a rush for living in town.
That beastly house of mine in Hill Street will fetch what I gave
for it,—Isaacson cabled about it the other day, offering for furniture and all. I don't want to go into Parliament, and I hate
shooting little birds and tame deer. I am one of those fellows
who are born Colonial at heart, and I don't see why I shouldn't
arrange my life as I please. Besides, for ten years I have been
falling in love with this country, and now I am up to the neck."

He flung himself back in the camp-chair till the canvas
creaked, and looked at me below his eyelids. I remember glancing at the lines of him. and thinking what a fine make of a man
he was. In his untanned field-boots, breeches, and grey shirt he
looked the born wilderness-hunter, though less than two months

before he had been driving down to the City every morning in the sombre regimentals of his class. Being a fair man, he was gloriously tanned, and there was a clear line at his shirt-collar to mark the limits of his sunburn. I had first known him years ago, when he was a broker's clerk working on half commission. Then he had gone to South Africa, and soon I heard he was a partner in a mining house which was doing wonders with some gold areas in the North. The next step was his return to London as the new millionaire,—young, good-looking, wholesome in mind and body, and much sought after by the mothers of marriageable girls. We played polo together, and hunted a little in the season, but there were signs that he did not propose to become the conventional English gentleman. He refused to buy a place in the country, though half the Homes of England were at his disposal. He was a very busy man, he declared, and had not time to be a squire. Besides, every few months he used to rush out to South Africa. I saw that he was restless, for he was always badgering me to go big-game hunting with him in some remote part of the earth. There was that in his eyes, too, which marked him out from the ordinary blonde type of our countrymen. They were large and brown and mysterious, and the light of another race was in their odd depths.

To hint such a thing would have meant a breach of friendship, for Lawson was very proud of his birth. When he first made his fortune he had gone to the Heralds to discover his family, and those obliging gentlemen had provided a pedigree. It appeared that he was a scion of the house of Lowson or Lowieson, an ancient and rather disreputable clan on the Scottish side of the Border. He took a shooting in Teviotdale on the strength of it, and used to commit lengthy Border ballads to memory. But I had known his father, a financial journalist who never quite succeeded, and I had heard of a grandfather who sold antiques in a back street at Brighton. The latter, I think, had not changed his name, and still frequented the synagogue. The father was a progressive Christian, and the mother had been a blonde Saxon from the Midlands. In my mind there was no doubt, as I caught Lawson's heavy-lidded eyes fixed on me. My friend was of a more ancient race than the Lowsons of the Border.

"Where are you thinking of looking for your house?" I asked. "In Natal or in the Cape Peninsula? You might get the Fishers' place if you paid a price."

"The Fishers' place be hanged!" he said crossly. "I don't want any stuccoed overgrown Dutch farm. I might as well be at Roehampton as in the Cape."

He got up and walked to the far side of the fire, where a lane ran down through thornscrub to a gully of the hills. The moon was silvering the bush of the plains, forty miles off and three thousand feet below us.

"I am going to live somewhere hereabouts," he answered at last.

I whistled. "Then you've got to put your hand in your pocket, old man. You'll have to make everything, including a map of the countryside."

"I know," he said; "that's where the fun comes in. Hang it all, why shouldn't I indulge my fancy? I'm uncommonly well off, and I haven't chick or child to leave it to. Supposing I'm a hundred miles from railhead, what about it? I'll make a motor-road and fix up a telephone. I'll grow most of my supplies, and start a colony to provide labour. When you come and stay with me, you'll get the best food and drink on earth, and sport that will make your mouth water. I'll put Lochleven trout in these streams,—at 6000 feet you can do anything. We'll have a pack of hounds, too, and we can drive pig in the woods, and if we want big game there are the Mangwe flats at our feet. I tell you I'll make such a country-house as nobody ever dreamed of. A man will come plumb out of stark savagery into lawns and rose-gardens." Lawson flung himself into his chair again and smiled dreamily at the fire.

"But why here, of all places?" I persisted. I was not feeling very well and did not care for the country.

"I can't quite explain. I think it's the sort of land I have always been looking for. I always fancied a house on a green plateau in a decent climate looking down on the tropics. 1 like heat and colour, you know, but I like hills too, and greenery, and the things that bring back Scotland. Give me a cross between Teviotdale and the Orinoco, and, by Gad! I think I've got it here."

I watched my friend curiously, as with bright eyes and eager voice he talked of his new fad. The two races were very clear in him—the one desiring gorgeousness, the other athirst for the soothing spaces of the North. He began to plan out the house. He would get Adamson to design it, and it was to grow out of the landscape like a stone on the hillside. There would be wide verandahs and cool halls, but great fireplaces against winter time. It would all be very simple and fresh—"clean as morning" was his odd phrase; but then another idea supervened, and he talked of bringing the Tintorets from Hill Street. "I want it to be a civilised house, you know. No silly luxury, but the best pictures and china and books. . . . I'll have all the furniture made after the old plain English models out of native woods. I don't want second-hand sticks in a new country. Yes, by Jove, the Tintorets are a great idea, and all those Ming pots I bought. I had meant to sell them, but I'll have them out here."

He talked for a good hour of what he would do, and his dream grew richer as he talked, till by the time we went to bed he had sketched something liker a palace than a country-house. Lawson was by no means a luxurious man. At present he was well content with a Wolseley valise, and shaved cheerfully out of a tin mug. It struck me as odd that a man so simple in his habits should have so sumptuous a taste in bric-à-brac. I told myself, as I turned in, that the Saxon mother from the Midlands had done little to dilute the strong wine of the East.

It drizzled next morning when we inspanned, and I mounted my horse in a bad temper. I had some fever on me, I think, and I hated this lush yet frigid table-land, where all the winds on earth lay in wait for one's marrow. Lawson was, as usual, in great spirits. We were not hunting, but shifting our hunt-ing-ground, so all morning we travelled fast to the north along the rim of the uplands.

At midday it cleared, and the afternoon was a pageant of pure colour. The wind sank to a low breeze; the sun lit the infinite green spaces, and kindled the wet forest to a jewelled coronal. Lawson gaspingly admired it all, as he cantered bare-headed up a bracken-clad slope. "God's country," he said twenty times. "I've found it." Take a piece of Saxon downland; put a stream in every hollow and a patch of wood; and at the edge, where the cliffs at home would fall to the sea, put a cloak of forest muffling the scarp and dropping thousands of feet to the blue plains. Take the diamond air of the Görnergrat, and the riot of colour which you get by a West Highland lochside in late September. Put flowers everywhere, the things we grow in hothouses, geraniums like sun-shades and arums like trumpets. That will give you a notion of the countryside we were in. I began to see that after all it was out of the common.

And just before sunset we came over a ridge and found something better. It was a shallow glen, half a mile wide, down which ran a blue-grey stream in linns like the Spean, till at the edge of the plateau it leaped into the dim forest in a snowy cascade. The opposite side ran up in gentle slopes to a rocky knoll, from which the eye had a noble prospect of the plains. All down the glen were little copses, half moons of green edging some silvery shore of the burn, or delicate clusters of tall trees nodding on the hill brow. The place so satisfied the eye that for the sheer wonder of its perfection we stopped and stared in silence for many minutes.

Then "The House," I said, and Lawson replied softly, "The House!"

We rode slowly into the glen in the mulberry gloaming. Our transport waggons were half an hour behind, so we had time to explore. Lawson dismounted and plucked handfuls of flowers from the water-meadows. He was singing to himself all the time—an old French catch about *Cadet Rousselle* and his *trois maisons*.

"Who owns it?" I asked.

"My firm, as like as not. We have miles of land about here. But whoever the man is, he has got to sell. Here I build my tabernacle, old man. Here, and nowhere else!"

In the very centre of the glen, in a loop of the stream, was one copse which even in that half light struck me as different from the others. It was of tall, slim, fairy-like trees, the kind of wood the monks painted in old missals. No, I rejected the thought. It was no Christian wood. It was not a copse, but a "grove,"—one such as Diana may have flitted through in the moonlight. It was small, forty or fifty yards in diameter, and there was a dark something at the heart of it which for a second I thought was a house.

We turned between the slender trees, and—was it fancy?—an odd tremor went through me. I felt as if I were penetrating the *temenos* of some strange and lovely divinity, the goddess of this pleasant vale. There was a spell in the air, it seemed, and an odd dead silence.

Suddenly my horse started at a flutter of light wings. A flock of doves rose from the branches, and I saw the burnished green of their plumes against the opal sky. Lawson did not seem to notice them. I saw his keen eyes staring at the centre of the grove and what stood there.

It was a little conical tower, ancient and lichened, but, so far as I could judge, quite flawless. You know the famous Conical Temple at Zimbabwe, of which prints are in every guide-book. This was of the same type, but a thousandfold more perfect. It stood about thirty feet high, of solid masonry, without door or window or cranny, as shapely as when it first came from the hands of the old builders. Again I had the sense of breaking in on a sanctuary. What right had I, a common vulgar modern, to be looking at this fair thing, among these delicate trees, which some white goddess had once taken for her shrine?

Lawson broke in on my absorption. "Let's get out of this," he said hoarsely, and he took my horse's bridle (he had left his own beast at the edge) and led him back to the open.

But I noticed that his eyes were always turning back, and that his hand trembled.

"That settles it," I said after supper. "What do you want with your mediaeval Venetians and your Chinese pots now? You will have the finest antique in the world in your garden—a temple as old as time, and in a land which they say has no history. You had the right inspiration this time."

I think I have said that Lawson had hungry eyes. In his enthusiasm they used to glow and brighten; but now, as he sat looking down at the olive shades of the glen, they seemed ravenous in their fire. He had hardly spoken a word since we left the wood.

"Where can I read about those things?" he asked, and I gave him the names of books.

Then, an hour later, he asked me who were the builders. I told him the little I knew about Phoenician and Sabaean wanderings, and the ritual of Sidon and Tyre. He repeated some names to himself and went soon to bed.

As I turned in, I had one last look over the glen, which lay ivory and black in the moon. I seemed to hear a faint echo of wings, and to see over the little grove a cloud of light visitants. "The Doves of Ashtaroth have come back," I said to myself. "It is a good omen. They accept the new tenant." But as I fell asleep I had a sudden thought that I was saying something rather terrible.

II

Three years later, pretty nearly to a day, I came back to see what Lawson had made of his hobby. He had bidden me often to Welgevonden, as he chose to call it—though I do not know why he should have fixed a Dutch name to a countryside where Boer never trod. At the last there had been some confusion about dates, and I wired the time of my arrival, and set off without an answer. A motor met me at the queer little wayside station of Taqui, and after many miles on a doubtful highway I came to the gates of the park, and a road on which it was a delight to move. Three years had wrought little difference in the landscape. Lawson had done some planting,—conifers and flowering shrubs and such-like,—but wisely he had resolved that Nature had for the most part forestalled him. All the same, he must have spent a mint of money. The drive could not have been beaten in England, and fringes of mown turf on either hand had been pared out of the lush meadows. When we came over the edge of the hill and looked down on the secret glen, I could not repress a cry of pleasure. The house stood on the farther ridge, the view-point of the whole neighbourhood; and its brown timbers and white rough-cast walls melted into the hillside as if it had been there from the beginning of things. The vale below was ordered in lawns and gardens. A blue lake received the rapids of the stream, and its banks were a maze of green shades and glorious masses of blossom. I noticed, too, that the little grove we had explored on our first visit stood alone in a big stretch of lawn, so that its perfection might be clearly seen. Lawson had excellent taste, or he had had the best advice.

The butler told me that his master was expected home shortly, and took me into the library for tea. Lawson had left his Tintorets and Ming pots at home after all. It was a long, low room, panelled in teak half-way up the walls, and the shelves held a multitude of fine bindings. There were good rugs on the parquet floor, but no ornaments anywhere, save three. On the carved mantelpiece stood two of the old soapstone birds which they used to find at Zimbabwe, and between, on an ebony stand, a half moon of alabaster, curiously carved with zodiacal figures. My host had altered his scheme of furnishing, but I approved the change.

He came in about half-past six, after I had consumed two cigars and all but fallen asleep. Three years make a difference in most men, but I was not prepared for the change in Lawson. For one thing, he had grown fat. In place of the lean young man I had known, I saw a heavy, flaccid being, who shuffled in his gait, and seemed tired and listless. His sunburn had gone, and his face was as pasty as a city clerk's. He had been walking, and wore shapeless flannel clothes, which hung loose even on his enlarged figure. And the worst of it was, that he did not seem over-pleased to see me. He murmured something about my journey, and then flung himself into an arm-chair and looked out of the window.

I asked him if he had been ill.

"Ill! No!" he said crossly. "Nothing of the kind. I'm perfectly well."

"You don't look as fit as this place should make you. What do you do with yourself? Is the shooting as good as you hoped?"

He did not answer, but I thought I heard him mutter something like "shooting be damned."

Then I tried the subject of the house. I praised it extravagantly, but with conviction. "There can be no place like it in the world," I said.

He turned his eyes on me at last, and I saw that they were as deep and restless as ever. With his pallid face they made him look curiously Semitic. I had been right in my theory about his ancestry.

"Yes," he said slowly, "there is no place like it—in the world."

Then he pulled himself to his feet. "I'm going to change," he said. "Dinner is at eight. Ring for Travers, and he'll show you your room."

I dressed in a noble bedroom, with an outlook over the garden-vale and the escarpment to the far line of the plains, now blue and saffron in the sunset. I dressed in an ill temper, for I was seriously offended with Lawson, and also seriously alarmed. He was either very unwell or going out of his mind, and it was clear, too, that he would resent any anxiety on his account. I ransacked my memory for rumours, but found none. I had heard nothing of him except that he had been extraordinarily successful in his speculations, and that from his hill-top he directed his firm's operations with uncommon skill. If Lawson was sick or mad, nobody knew of it.

Dinner was a trying ceremony. Lawson, who used to be rather particular in his dress, appeared in a kind of smoking suit with a flannel collar. He spoke scarcely a word to me, but cursed the servants with a brutality which left me aghast. A wretched footman in his nervousness spilt some sauce over his sleeve. Lawson dashed the dish from his hand, and volleyed abuse with a sort of epileptic fury. Also he, who had been the most abstemious of men, swallowed disgusting quantities of champagne and old brandy.

He had given up smoking, and half an hour after we left the dining-room he announced his intention of going to bed. I watched him as he waddled upstairs with a feeling of angry bewilderment. Then I went to the library and lit a pipe. I would leave first thing

in the morning—on that I was determined. But as I sat gazing at the moon of alabaster and the soapstone birds my anger evaporated, and concern took its place. I remembered what a fine fellow Lawson had been, what good times we had had together. I remembered especially that evening when we had found this valley and given rein to our fancies. What horrid alchemy in the place had turned a gentleman into a brute? I thought of drink and drugs and madness and insomnia, but I could fit none of them into my conception of my friend. I did not consciously rescind my resolve to depart, but I had a notion that I would not act on it.

The sleepy butler met me as I went to bed. "Mr. Lawson's room is at the end of your corridor, sir," he said. "He don't sleep over well, so you may hear him stirring in the night. At what hour would you like breakfast, sir? Mr. Lawson mostly has his in bed."

My room opened from the great corridor, which ran the full length of the front of the house. So far as I could make out, Lawson was three rooms off, a vacant bedroom and his servant's room being between us. I felt tired and cross, and tumbled into bed as fast as possible. Usually I sleep well, but now I was soon conscious that my drowsiness was wearing off and that I was in for a restless night. I got up and laved my face, turned the pillows, thought of sheep coming over a hill and clouds crossing the sky; but none of the old devices were any use. After about an hour of make-believe I surrendered myself to facts, and, lying on my back, stared at the white ceiling and the patches of moonshine on the walls.

It certainly was an amazing night. I got up, put on a dressing-gown, and drew a chair to the window. The moon was almost at its full, and the whole plateau swam in a radiance of ivory and silver. The banks of the stream were black, but the lake had a great belt of light athwart it, which made it seem like a horizon, and the rim of land beyond it like a contorted cloud. Far to the right I saw the delicate outlines of the little wood which I had come to think of as the Grove of Ashtaroth. I listened. There was not a sound in the air. The land seemed to sleep peacefully beneath the moon, and yet I had a sense that the peace was an illusion. The place was feverishly restless.

I could have given no reason for my impression, but there it was. Something was stirring in the wide moonlit landscape under its deep mask of silence. I felt as I had felt on the evening three years ago when I had ridden into the grove. I did not think that the influence, whatever it was, was maleficent. I only knew that it was very strange, and kept me wakeful.

By-and-by I bethought me of a book. There was no lamp in the corridor save the moon, but the whole house was bright as I slipped down the great staircase and over the hall to the library. I switched on the lights and then switched them off. They seemed a profanation, and I did not need them.

I found a French novel, but the place held me and I stayed. I sat down in an armchair before the fireplace and the stone birds. Very odd those gawky things, like prehistoric Great Auks, looked in the moonlight. I remember that the alabaster moon shimmered like translucent pearl, and I fell to wondering about its history. Had the old Sabaeans used such a jewel in their rites in the Grove of Ashtaroth?

Then I heard footsteps pass the window. A great house like this would have a watchman, but these quick shuffling footsteps were surely not the dull plod of a servant. They passed on to the grass and died away. I began to think of getting back to my room.

In the corridor I noticed that Lawson's door was ajar, and that a light had been left burning. I had the unpardonable curiosity to peep in. The room was empty, and the bed had not been slept in. Now I knew whose were the footsteps outside the library window.

I lit a reading-lamp and tried to interest myself in 'La Cruelle Enigme.' But my wits were restless, and I could not keep my eyes on the page. I flung the book aside and sat down again by the window. The feeling came over me that I was sitting in a box at some play. The glen was a huge stage, and at any moment the players might appear on it. My attention was strung as high as if I had been waiting for the advent of some world-famous actress. But nothing came. Only the shadows shifted and lengthened as the moon moved across the sky.

Then quite suddenly the restlessness left me, and at the same moment the silence was broken by the crow of a cock and the rustling of trees in a light wind. I felt very sleepy, and was turning to bed when again I heard footsteps without. From the window I could see a figure moving across the garden towards the house. It was Lawson, got up in the sort of towel dressing-gown that one wears on board ship. He was walking slowly and painfully, as if very weary. I did not see his face, but the man's whole air was that of extreme fatigue and dejection.

I tumbled into bed and slept profoundly till long after day-light.

III

The man who valeted me was Lawson's own servant. As he was laying out my clothes I asked after the health of his master, and was told that he had slept ill and would not rise till late. Then the man, an anxious-faced Englishman, gave me some informa-tion on his own account. Mr. Lawson was having one of his bad turns. It would pass away in a day or two, but till it had gone he was fit for nothing. He advised me to see Mr. Jobson, the factor, who would look to my entertainment in his master's absence.

Jobson arrived before luncheon, and the sight of him was the first satisfactory thing about Welgevonden. He was a big, gruff Scot from Roxburghshire, engaged, no doubt, by Lawson as a duty to his Border ancestry. He had short grizzled whiskers, a weatherworn face, and a shrewd, calm blue eye. I knew now why the place was in such perfect order.

We began with sport, and Jobson explained what I could have in the way of fishing and shooting. His exposition was brief and business-like, and all the while I could see his eye searching me. It was dear that he had much to say on other matters than sport.

I told him that I had come here with Lawson three years before, when he chose the site. Jobson continued to regard me curiously. "I've heard tell of ye from Mr. Lawson. Ye're an old friend of his, I understand."

"The oldest," I said. "And I am sorry to find that the place does not agree with him. Why it doesn't I cannot imagine, for you look fit enough. Has he been seedy for long?"

"It comes and goes," said Mr. Jobson. "Maybe once a month he has a bad turn. But on the whole it agrees with him badly. He's no' the man he was when I first came here."

Jobson was looking at me very seriously and frankly. I risked a question.

"What do you suppose is the matter?"

He did not reply at once, but leaned forward and tapped my knee.

"I think it's something that doctors canna cure. Look at me, sir. I've always been counted a sensible man, but if I told you what was in my head you would think me daft. But I have one word for you. Bide till to-night is past and then speir your question. Maybe you and me will be agreed."

The factor rose to go. As he left the room he flung me back a remark over his shoulder—"Read the eleventh chapter of the First Book of Kings."

After luncheon I went for a walk. First I mounted to the crown of the hill and feasted my eyes on the unequalled loveliness of the view. I saw the far hills in Portuguese territory, a hundred miles away, lifting up thin blue fingers into the sky. The wind blew light and fresh, and the place was fragrant with a thousand delicate scents. Then I descended to the vale, and followed the stream up through the garden. Poinsettias and oleanders were blazing in coverts, and there was a paradise of tinted waterlilies in the slacker reaches. I saw good trout rise at the fly, but I did not think about fishing. I was searching my memory for a recollection which would not come. By-and-by I found myself beyond the garden, where the lawns ran to the fringe of Ashtaroth's Grove.

It was like something I remembered in an old Italian picture. Only, as my memory drew it, it should have been peopled with strange figures—nymphs dancing on the sward, and a prick-eared faun peeping from the covert. In the warm afternoon sunlight it stood, ineffably gracious and beautiful, tantalising with a sense of some deep hidden loveliness. Very reverently I walked between the slim trees, to where the little conical tower stood half in sun and half in shadow. Then I noticed something new. Round the tower ran a narrow path, worn in the grass by human feet. There had been no such path on my first visit, for I remembered the grass growing tall to the edge of the stone. Had the Kaffirs made a shrine of it, or were there other and stranger votaries?

When I returned to the house I found Travers with a message for me. Mr. Lawson was still in bed, but he would like me to go to him. I found my friend sitting up and drinking strong tea,—a bad thing, I should have thought, for a man in his condition. I remember that I looked over the room for some sign of the pernicious habit of which I believed him a victim. But the place was fresh and clean, with the windows wide open, and, though I could not have given my reasons, I was convinced that drugs or drink had nothing to do with the sickness.

He received me more civilly, but I was shocked by his looks. There were great bags below his eyes, and his skin had the wrinkled puffy appearance of a man in dropsy. His voice, too, was reedy and thin. Only his great eyes burned with some feverish life.

"I am a shocking bad host," he said, "but I'm going to be still more inhospitable. I want you to go away. I hate anybody here when I'm off colour."

"Nonsense," I said; "you want looking after. I want to know about this sickness. Have you had a doctor?"

He smiled wearily. "Doctors are no earthly use to me. There's nothing much the matter, I tell you. I'll be all right in a day or two, and then you can come back. I want you to go off with Jobson and hunt in the plains till the end of the week. It will be better fun for you, and I'll feel less guilty."

Of course I pooh-poohed the idea, and Lawson got angry. "Damn it, man," he cried, "why do you force yourself on me when I don't want you? I tell you your presence here makes me worse. In a week I'll be as right as the mail, and then I'll be thankful for you. But get away now; get away, I tell you."

I saw that he was fretting himself into a passion. "All right," I said soothingly; "Jobson and I will go off hunting. But I am horribly anxious about you, old man."

He lay back on his pillows. "You needn't trouble. I only want a little rest. Jobson will

make all arrangements, and Travers will get you anything you want. Good-bye."

I saw it was useless to stay longer, so I left the room. Outside I found the anxious-faced servant. "Look here," I said, "Mr. Lawson thinks I ought to go, but I mean to stay. Tell him I'm gone if he asks you. And for Heaven's sake keep him in bed."

The man promised, and I thought I saw some relief in his face.

I went to the library, and on the way remembered Jobson's remark about 1st Kings. With some searching I found a Bible and turned up the passage. It was a long screed about the misdeeds of Solomon, and I read it through without enlightenment. I began to reread it, and a word suddenly caught my attention—

"For Solomon went after Ashtaroth, the goddess of the Zidonians."

That was all, but it was like a key to a cipher. Instantly there flashed over my mind all that I had heard or read of that strange ritual which seduced Israel to sin. I saw a sunburnt land and a people vowed to the stern service of Jehovah. But I saw, too, eyes turning from the austere sacrifice to lonely hill-top groves and towers and images, where dwelt some subtle and evil mystery. I saw the fierce prophets, scourging the votaries with rods, and a nation penitent before the Lord; but always the backsliding again, and the hankering after forbidden joys. Ashtaroth was the old goddess of the East. Was it not possible that in all Semitic blood there remained, transmitted through the dim generations, some craving for her spell? I thought of the grandfather in the back street at Brighton and of those burning eyes upstairs.

As I sat and mused my glance fell on the inscrutable stone birds. They knew all those old secrets of joy and terror. And that moon of alabaster! Some dark priest had worn it on his forehead when he worshipped, like Ahab, "all the host of Heaven." And then I honestly began to be afraid. I, a prosaic, modern Christian gentleman, a half-believer in casual faiths, was in the presence of some hoary mystery of sin far older than creeds or Christendom. There was fear in my heart,—a kind of uneasy disgust, and above all a nervous eerie disquiet. Now I wanted to go away, and yet I was ashamed of the cowardly thought. I pictured Ashtaroth's Grove with sheer horror. What tragedy was in the air? what secret awaited twilight? For the night was coming, the night of the Full Moon, the season of ecstasy and sacrifice.

I do not know how I got through that evening. I was disinclined for dinner, so I had a outlet in the library and sat smoking till my tongue ached. But as the hours passed a more manly resolution grew up in my mind. I owed it to old friendship to stand by Lawson in this extremity. I could not interfere,—God knows, his reason seemed already rocking,—but I could be at hand in case my chance came. I determined not to undress, but to watch through the night. I had a bath, and changed into light flannels and slippers. Then I took up my position in a corner of the library close to the window, so that I could not fail to hear Lawson's footsteps if he passed.

Fortunately I left the lights unlit, for as I waited I grew drowsy, and fell asleep. When I woke the moon had risen, and I knew from the feel of the air that the hour was late. I sat very still, straining my ears, and as I listened I caught the sound of steps. They were crossing the hall stealthily, and nearing the library door. I huddled into my corner as Lawson entered.

He wore the same towel dressing-gown, and he moved swiftly and silently as if in a trance. I watched him take the alabaster moon from the mantelpiece and drop it in his pocket. A glimpse of white skin showed that the gown was his only clothing. Then he moved past me to the window, opened it, and went out.

Without any conscious purpose I rose and followed, kicking off my slippers that I might go quietly. He was running, running fast, across the lawns in the direction of the grove—an odd shapeless antic in the moonlight. I stopped, for there was no cover, and I feared for his reason if he saw me. When I looked again he had disappeared among the trees.

I saw nothing for it but to crawl, so on my belly I wormed my way over the dripping sward. There was a ridiculous suggestion of deer-stalking about the game which tickled me and dispelled my uneasiness. Almost I persuaded myself I was tracking an ordinary sleepwalker. The lawns were broader than I imagined, and it seemed an age before I reached the edge of the grove. The world was so still that I appeared to be making a most ghastly amount of noise. I remember that once I heard a rustling in the air, and looked up to see the green doves circling about the treetops.

There was no sign of Lawson. On the edge of the grove I think that all my assurance vanished. I could see between the trunks to the little tower, but it was quiet as the grave, save for the wings above. Once more there came over me the unbearable sense of anticipation I had felt the night before. My nerves tingled with mingled expectation and dread. I did not think that any harm would come to me, for the powers of the air seemed not malignant. But I knew them for powers, and felt awed and abased. I was in the presence of the "host of Heaven," and I was no stern Israelitish prophet to prevail against them.

I must have lain for hours waiting in that spectral place, my eyes riveted on the tower and its golden cap of moonshine. I remember that my head felt void and light, as if my spirit were becoming disembodied and leaving its dew-drenched sheath far below. But the most curious sensation was of something drawing me to the tower, something mild and kindly and rather feeble, for there was some other and stronger force keeping me back. I yearned to move nearer, but I could not drag my limbs an inch. There was a spell somewhere which I could not break. I do not think I was in any way frightened now. The starry influence was playing tricks with me, but my mind was half asleep. Only I never took my eyes from the little tower. I think I could not, if I had wanted to.

Then suddenly from the shadows came Lawson. He was stark-naked, and he wore, bound across his brow, the halfmoon of alabaster. He had something, too, in his hand,—something which glittered.

He ran round the tower, crooning to himself, and flinging wild arms to the skies. Sometimes the crooning changed to a shrill cry of passion, such as a maenad may have uttered in the train of Bacchus. I could make out no words, but the sound told its own tale. He was absorbed in some infernal ecstasy. And as he ran, he drew his right hand across his breast and arms, and I saw that it held a knife.

I grew sick with disgust,—not terror, but honest physical loathing. Lawson, gashing his fat body, affected me with an overpowering repugnance. I wanted to go forward and stop him, and I wanted, too, to be a hundred miles away. And the result was that I stayed still. I believe my own will held me there, but I doubt if in any case I could have moved my legs.

The dance grew swifter and fiercer. I saw the blood dripping from Lawson's body, and his face ghastly white above his scarred breast. And then suddenly the horror left me; my head swam; and for one second—one brief second—I seemed to peer into a new world. A strange passion surged up in my heart. I seemed to see the earth peopled with forms—not human, scarcely divine, but more desirable than man or god. The calm face of Nature broke up for me into wrinkles of wild knowledge. I saw the things which brush against the soul in dreams, and found them lovely. There seemed no cruelty in the knife or the blood. It was a delicate mystery of worship, as wholesome as the morning song of birds. I do not know how the Semites found Ashtaroth's ritual; to them it may well have been more rapt and passionate than it seemed to me. For I saw in it only the sweet simplicity of Nature, and all riddles of lust and terror soothed away as a child's nightmares are calmed by a mother. I found my legs able to move, and I think I took two steps through the dusk towards the tower.

And then it all ended. A cock crew, and the homely noises of earth were renewed. While I stood dazed and shivering, Lawson plunged through the Grove towards me. The impetus carried him to the edge, and he fell fainting just outside the shade.

My wits and common-sense came back to me with my bodily strength. I got my friend on my back, and staggered with him towards the house. I was afraid in real earnest now, and what frightened me most was the thought that I had not been afraid sooner. I had come very near the "abomination of the Zidonians."

At the door I found the scared valet waiting. He had apparently done this sort of thing before.

"Your master has been sleepwalking. and has had a fall," I said. "We must get him to bed at once."

We bathed the wounds as he lay in a deep stupor, and I dressed them as well as I could. The only danger lay in his utter exhaustion, for happily the gashes were not serious, and no artery had been touched. Sleep and rest would make him well, for he had the constitution of a strong man. I was leaving the room when he opened his eyes and spoke. He did not recognise me, but I noticed that his face had lost its strangeness, and was once more that of the friend I had known. Then I suddenly bethought me of an old hunting remedy which he and I always carried on our expeditions. It is a pill made up from an ancient Portuguese prescription. One is an excellent specific for fever. Two are invaluable if you are lost in the bush, for they send a man for many hours into a deep sleep, which prevents suffering and madness, till help comes. Three give a painless death. I went to my room and found the little box in my jewel-case. Lawson swallowed two, and turned wearily on his side. I bade his man let him sleep till he woke, and went off in search of food.

IV

I had business on hand which would not wait. By seven, Jobson, who had been sent for, was waiting for me in the library. I knew by his grim face that here I had a very good substitute for a prophet of the Lord.

"You were right," I said. "I have read the 11th chapter of 1st Kings, and I have spent such a night as I pray God I shall never spend again."

"I thought you would," he replied. "I've had the same experience myself."

"The Grove?" I said.

"Ay, the wud," was the answer in broad Scots.

I wanted to see how much he understood.

"Mr. Lawson's family is from the Scotch Border?"

"Ay. I understand they come off Borthwick Water side," he replied, but I saw by his eyes that he knew what I meant.

"Mr. Lawson is my oldest friend," I went on, "and I am going to take measures to cure him. For what I am going to do I take the sole responsibility. I will make that plain to your master. But if I am to succeed I want your help. Will you give it me? It sounds like madness, and you are a sensible man and may like to keep out of it. I leave it to your discretion."

Jobson looked me straight in the face. "Have no fear for me," he said; "there is an unholy thing in that place, and if I have the strength in me I will destroy it. He has been a good master to me, and, for-bye, I am a believing Christian. So say on, sir."

There was no mistaking the air. I had found my Tishbite.

"I want men," I said,—"as many as we can get."

Jobson mused. "The Kaffirs will no' gang near the place, but there's some thirty white men on the tobacco farm. They'll do your will, if you give them an indemnity in writing."

"Good," said I. "Then we will take our instructions from the only authority which meets the case. We will follow the example of King Josiah." I turned up the 23rd chapter of 2nd Kings, and read:—

"And the high places that were before Jerusalem, which were on the right hand of the Mount of Corruption, which Solomon the king of Israel had builded for Ashtaroth the abomination of the Zidonians . . . did the king defile.

"And he brake in pieces the images, and cut down the groves, and filled their places with the bones of men.

"Moreover the altar that was at Beth-el, and the high place which Jeroboam the son of Nebat, who made Israel to sin, had made, both that altar and the high place he brake down, and burned the high place, and stamped it small to powder, and burned the grove."

Jobson nodded. "It'll need dinnymite. But I've plenty of yon down at the workshops. I'll be off to collect the lads."

Before nine the men had assembled at Jobson's house. They were a hardy lot of young farmers from home, who took their instructions docilely from the masterful factor. On my orders they had brought their shot-guns. We armed them with spades and woodmen's axes, and one man wheeled some coils of rope in a handcart.

In the clear, windless air of morning the Grove, set amid its lawns, looked too innocent and exquisite for ill. I had a pang of regret that a thing so fair should suffer; nay, if I had come alone, I think I might have repented. But the men were there, and the grim-faced Jobson was waiting for orders. I placed the guns, and sent beaters to the far side. I told them that every dove must be shot.

It was only a small flock, and we killed fifteen at the first drive. The poor birds flew over the glen to another spinney, but we brought them back over the guns and seven fell. Four more were got in the trees, and the last I killed myself with a long shot. In half an hour there was a pile of little green bodies on the sward.

Then we went to work to cut down the trees. The slim stems were an easy task to a good woodman, and one after another they toppled to the ground. And meantime, as I watched, I became conscious of a strange emotion.

It was as if someone were pleading with me. A gentle voice, not threatening, but pleading—something too fine for the sensual ear, but touching inner chords of the spirit. So tenuous it was and distant that I could think of no personality behind it. Rather it was the viewless, bodiless grace of this delectable vale, some old exquisite divinity of the groves. There was the heart of all sorrow in it, and the soul of all loveliness. It seemed a woman's voice, some lost lady who had brought nothing but goodness unrepaid to the world. And what the voice told me was that I was destroying her last shelter.

That was the pathos of it—the voice was homeless. As the axes flashed in the sunlight and the wood grew thin, that gentle spirit was pleading with me for mercy and a brief respite. It seemed to be telling of a world for centuries grown coarse and pitiless, of long sad wanderings, of hardly won shelter, and a peace which was the little all she sought from men. There was nothing terrible in it, no thought of wrongdoing. The spell which to Semitic blood held the mystery of evil, was to me, of the Northern race, only delicate and rare and beautiful. Jobson and the rest did not feel it, I with my finer senses caught nothing but the hopeless sadness of it. That which had stirred the passion in Lawson was only wringing my heart. It was almost too pitiful to bear. As the trees crashed down and the men wiped the sweat from their brows, I seemed to myself like the murderer of fair women and innocent children. I remember that the tears were running over my cheeks. More than once I opened my mouth to countermand the work, but the face of

Jobson, that grim Tishbite, held me back. I knew now what gave the Prophets of the Lord their mastery, and I knew also why the people sometimes stoned them.

The last tree fell, and the little tower stood like a ravished shrine, stripped of all defence against the world. I heard Jobson's voice speaking. "We'd better blast that stane thing now. We'll trench on four sides and lay the dinnymite. Ye're no' looking weel, sir. Ye'd better go and sit down on the brae-face."

I went up the hillside and lay down. Below me, in the waste of shorn trunks, men were running about, and I saw the mining begin. It all seemed like an aimless dream in which I had no part. The voice of that homeless goddess was still pleading. It was the innocence of it that tortured me. Even so must a merciful Inquisitor have suffered from the plea of some fair girl with the aureole of death on her hair. I knew I was killing rare and unrecoverable beauty. As I sat dazed and heartsick, the whole loveliness of Nature seemed to plead for its divinity. The sun in the heavens, the mellow lines of upland, the blue mystery of the far plains, were all part of that soft voice. I felt bitter scorn for myself. I was guilty of blood; nay, I was guilty of the sin against light which knows no forgiveness. I was murdering innocent gentleness, and there would be no peace on earth for me. Yet I sat helpless. The power of a sterner will constrained me. And all the while the voice was growing fainter and dying away into unutterable sorrow.

Suddenly a great flame sprang to heaven, and a pall of smoke. I heard men crying out, and fragments of stone fell around the ruins of the grove. When the air cleared, the little tower had gone out of sight.

The voice had ceased and there seemed to me to be a bereaved silence in the world. The shock moved me to my feet, and I ran down the slope to where Jobson stood rubbing his eyes.

"That's done the job. Now we maun get up the tree-roots. We've no time to howk. We'll just dinnymite the feck o' them."

The work of destruction went on, but I was coming back to my senses. I forced myself to be practical and reasonable. I thought of the night's experience and Lawson's haggard eyes, and I screwed myself into a determination to see the thing through. I had done the deed; it was my business to make it complete. A text in Jeremiah came into my head: *"Their children remember their altars and their groves by the green trees upon the high hills."* I would see to it that this grove should be utterly forgotten.

We blasted the tree roots, and, yoking oxen, dragged the debris into a great heap. Then the men set to work with their spades, and roughly levelled the ground. I was getting back to my old self, and Jobson's spirit was becoming mine.

"There is one thing more," I told him. "Get ready a couple of ploughs. We will improve upon King Josiah." My brain was a medley of Scripture precedents, and I was determined that no safeguard should be wanting.

We yoked the oxen again and drove the ploughs over the site of the grove. It was rough ploughing, for the place was thick with bits of stone from the tower, but the slow Afrikander oxen plodded on, and sometime in the afternoon the work was finished. Then I sent down to the farm for bags of rock-salt, such as they use for cattle. Jobson and I took a sack apiece, and walked up and down the furrows, sowing them with salt.

The last act was to set fire to the pile of tree-trunks. They burned well, and on the top we flung the bodies of the green doves. The birds of Ashtaroth had an honourable pyre.

Then I dismissed the much-perplexed men, and gravely shook hands with Jobson. Black with dust and smoke I went back to the house, where I bade Travers pack my bags and order the motor. I found Lawson's servant, and heard from him that his master was sleeping peacefully. I gave him some directions, and then went to wash and change.

Before I left I wrote a line to Lawson. I began by transcribing the verses from the 23rd chapter of 2nd Kings. I told him what I had done, and my reason. "I take the whole responsibility upon myself," I wrote. "No man in the place had anything to do with it but me. I acted as I did for the sake of our old friendship, and you will believe it was no easy task for me. I hope you will understand. Whenever you are able to see me send me word, and I will come back and settle with you. But I think you will realise that I have saved your soul."

The afternoon was merging into twilight as I left the house on the road to Taqui. The great fire, where the grove had been, was still blazing fiercely, and the smoke made a cloud over the upper glen, and filled all the air with a soft violet haze. I knew that I had done well for my friend, and that he would come to his senses and be grateful. My mind was at ease on that score, and in something like comfort I faced the future. But as the car reached the ridge I looked back to the vale I had outraged. The moon was rising and silvering the smoke, and through the gaps I could see the tongues of fire. Somehow, I know not why, the lake, the stream, the garden-coverts, even the green slopes of hill, wore an air of loneliness and desecration.

And then my heartache returned, and I knew that I had driven something lovely and adorable from its last refuge on earth.

The Red Bungalow
Bithia Mary Croker (1919)

It is a considerable time since my husband's regiment ("The Snapshots") was stationed in Kulu, yet it seems as if it were but yesterday, when I look back on the days we spent in India. As I sit by the fire, or in the sunny corner of the garden, sometimes when my eyes are dim with reading I close them upon the outer world, and see, with vivid distinctness, events which happened years ago. Among various mental pictures, there is not one which stands forth with the same weird and lurid effect as the episode of "The Red Bungalow."

Robert was commanding his regiment, and we were established in a pretty spacious house at Kulu, and liked the station. It was a little off the beaten track, healthy and sociable. Memories of John Company and traces of ancient Empires still clung to the neighbourhood. Pig-sticking and rose-growing, badminton and polo, helped the resident of the place to dispose of the long, long Indian day—never too long for me!

One morning I experienced an agreeable surprise, when, in reading the *Gazette,* I saw that my cousin, Tom Fellowes, had been appointed Quartermaster-General of the district, and was to take up the billet at once.

Tom had a wife and two dear little children (our nursery was empty), and as soon as I had put down the paper I wired to Netta to congratulate and beg them to come to us immediately. Indian moves are rapid. Within a week our small party had increased to six, Tom, Netta, little Guy, aged four, and Baba, a dark-eyed coquette of nearly two. They also brought with them an invaluable ayah—a Madrassi. She spoke English with a pretty foreign accent, and was entirely devoted to the children.

Netta was a slight young woman with brilliant eyes, jet-black hair, and a firm mouth. She was lively, clever, and a capital helpmate for an army man, with marvellous energy, and enviable taste.

Tom, an easy-going individual in private life, was a red-hot soldier. All financial and domestic affairs were left in the hands of his wife, and she managed him and them with conspicuous success.

Before Netta had been with us three days she began, in spite of my protestations, to clamour about "getting a house."

"Why, you have only just arrived," I remonstrated. "You are not even half unpacked. Wait here a few weeks, and make acquaintance with the place and people. It is such a pleasure to me to have you and the children."

"You spoil them—especially Guy!" she answered with a laugh. "The sooner they are removed the better, and, seriously, I want to settle in. I am longing to do up my new house, and make it pretty, and have a garden—a humble imitation of yours—a badminton court, and a couple of ponies. I'm like a child looking forward to a new toy, for, cooped up in Fort William in Calcutta, I never felt that I had a real home."

"Even so," I answered, "there is plenty of time, and I think you might remain here till after Christmas."

"Christmas!" she screamed. "I shall be having Christmas parties myself, and a tree for the kids; and you, dear Liz, shall come and help me. I want to get into a house next week."

"Then pray don't look to me for any assistance. If you make such a hasty exit the station will think we have quarrelled."

"The station could not be so detestable, and no one could quarrel with *you*, you dear old thing," and as she stooped down and patted my cheek, I realised that she was fully resolved to have her own way.

"I have yards and yards of the most lovely cretonne for cushions, and chairs, and curtains," she continued, "brought out from home, and never yet made up. Your Dirzee is bringing me two men to-morrow. When I was out riding this morning, I went to an auction-room—John Mahomed, they call the man—and inspected some sofas and chairs. Do let us drive there this afternoon on our way to the club, and I also wish to have a look round. I hear that nearly all the good bungalows are occupied."

"Yes, they are," I answered triumphantly. "At present there is not *one* in the place to suit you! I have been running over them with my mind's eye, and either they are near the river, or too small, or—not healthy. After Christmas the Watsons are going home; there will be their bungalow—it is nice and large, and has a capital office, which would suit Tom."

We drove down to John Mahomed's that afternoon, and selected some furniture—Netta exhibiting her usual taste and business capacity. On our way to the club I pointed out several vacant houses, and, among them, the Watsons' charming abode—with its celebrated gardens, beds of brilliant green lucerne, and verandah curtained in yellow roses.

"Oh yes," she admitted, "it is a fine, roomy sort of abode, but I hate a thatched roof—I want one with tiles—red tiles. They make such a nice bit of colour among trees."

"I'm afraid you won't find many tiled roofs in Kulu," I answered; "this will limit you a good deal."

For several mornings, together, we explored bungalows—and I was by no means sorry to find that, in the eyes of Netta, they were all more or less found wanting—too small, too damp, too near the river, too stuffy—and I had made up my mind that the Watsons' residence (despite its thatch) was to be Netta's fate, when one afternoon she hurried in, a little breathless and dusty, and announced, with a wild wave of her sunshade, "I've found it!"

"Where? Do you mean a house?" I exclaimed.

"Yes. What moles we've been! At the back of this, down the next turn, at the cross roads! Most central and suitable. They call it the Red Bungalow."

"The Red Bungalow," I repeated reflectively. I had never cast a thought to it—what is always before one is frequently unnoticed. Also it had been unoccupied ever since we had come to the station, and as entirely overlooked as if it had no existence! I had a sort of recollection that there was some drawback—it was either too large, or too expensive, or too out of repair.

"It is strange that I never mentioned it," I said. "But it has had no tenant for years."

"Unless I am greatly mistaken, it will have one before long," rejoined Netta, with her most definite air. "It looks as if it were just waiting for us—and had been marked 'reserved.'"

"Then you have been over it?"

"No, I could not get in, the doors are all bolted, and there seems to be no chokedar. I wandered round the verandahs, and took stock of the size and proportions—it stands in an imposing compound. There are the ruins at the back, mixed up with the remains of a garden—old guava trees, lemon trees, a vine, and a well. There is a capital place at one side for two badminton courts, and I have mentally laid out a rose-garden in front of the portico."

"How quickly your mind travels!"

"Everything *must* travel quickly in these days," she retorted. "We all have to put on the pace. Just as I was leaving, I met a venerable coolie person, who informed me that John Mahomed had the keys, so I despatched him to bring them at once, and promised a rupee for his trouble. Now do, like a good soul, let us have tea, and start off immediately after to inspect my treasure-trove!"

"I can promise you a cup of tea in five minutes," I replied, "but I am not so certain of your treasure-trove."

"I am. I generally can tell what suits me at first sight. The only thing I am afraid of is the rent. Still, in Tommy's position one must not consider that. He is obliged to live in a suitable style."

"The Watsons' house has often had a staff-tenant. I believe it would answer all your requirements."

"Too near the road, and too near the *General*," she objected, with a gesture of impatience. "Ah, here comes tea at last!"

It came, but before I had time to swallow my second cup, I found myself hustled out of the house by my energetic cousin and *en route* to her wonderful discovery—the Red Bungalow.

We had but a short distance to walk, and, often as I had passed the house, I now gazed at it for the first time with an air of critical interest. In Kulu, for some unexplained reason, this particular bungalow had never counted; it was boycotted—no, that is not the word—*ignored*, as if, like some undesirable character, it had no place in the station's thoughts. Nevertheless, its position was sufficiently prominent—it stood at a point where four ways met. Two gateless entrances opened into different roads, as if determined to obtrude upon public attention. Standing aloof between the approaches was the house—large, red-tiled, and built back in the shape of the letter "T" from an enormous pillared porch, which, with some tall adjacent trees, gave it an air of reserve and dignity.

"The coolie with the keys has not arrived," said Netta, "so I will just take you round and show you its capabilities myself. Here"—as we stumbled over some rough grass—"is where I should make a couple of badminton courts, and this"—as we came to the back of the bungalow—"is the garden."

Yes, here were old choked-up stone water-channels, the traces of walks, hoary guava and apricot trees, a stone pergola and a dead vine, also a well, with elaborate tracery, and odd, shapeless mounds of ancient masonry. As we stood we faced the back verandah of the house. To our right hand lay tall cork trees,

a wide expanse of compound, and the road; to our left, at a
distance, more trees, a high wall, and clustered beneath it the
servants' quarters, the cook-house, and a long range of stables.

It was a fine, important-looking residence, although the
stables were almost roofless and the garden and compound a
wilderness, given over to stray goats and tame lizards.

"Yes, there is only one thing I am afraid of," exclaimed Netta.

"Snakes?" I suggested. "It looks rather snaky."

"No, the rent; and here comes the key at last," and as she
spoke a fat young clerk, on a small yellow pony, trotted quickly
under the porch—a voluble person, who wore spotless white
garments, and spoke English with much fluency.

"I am abject. Please excuse being so tardy. I could not exca-
vate the key; but at last I got it, and now I will hasten to exhibit
premises. First of all, I go and open doors and windows, and
call in the atmosphere—ladies kindly excuse." Leaving his tame
steed on its honour, the baboo hurried to the back, and presently we heard the grinding of locks, banging of shutters, and
grating of bolts. Then the door was flung open and we entered,
walked (as is usual) straight into the drawing-room, a fine,
lofty, half-circular room, twice as large and well-proportioned
as mine. The drawing-room led into an equally excellent dining-
room. I saw Netta measuring it with her eye, and she said,
"One could easily seat thirty people here, and what a place for
a Christmas-tree!"

The dining-room opened into an immense bedroom which
gave directly on the back verandah, with a flight of shallow
steps leading into the garden.

"The nursery," she whispered; "capital!"

At either side were two other rooms, with bath and dressing-rooms complete. Undoubtedly it was an exceedingly com-
modious and well-planned house.

As we stood once more in the nursery—all the wide doors
being open—we could see directly through the bungalow out
into the porch, as the three large apartments were *en suite*.

"A draught right through, you see!" she said. "So cool in the hot weather."

Then we returned to the drawing-room, where I noticed that Netta was already arranging the furniture with her mental eye. At last she turned to the baboo and said, "And what is the rent?"

After a moment's palpable hesitation he replied, "Ninety rupees a month. If you take it for some time it will be all put in repair and done up."

"Ninety!" I mentally echoed—and we paid one hundred and forty!

"Does it belong to John Mahomed?" I asked.

"No—to a client."

"Does he live here?"

"No—he lives far away, in another region; we have never seen him."

"How long is it since this was occupied?"

"Oh, a good while—"

"Some years?"

"Perhaps," with a wag of his head.

"Why has it stood empty? Is it unhealthy?" asked Netta.

"Oh no, no. I think it is too majestic, too gigantic for insignificant people. They like something more altogether and *cosy*; it is not cosy—it is suitable to persons like a lady on the General's staff," and he bowed himself to Netta.

I believe she was secretly of his opinion, for already she had assumed the air of the mistress of the house, and said briskly, "Now I wish to see the kitchen, and servants' quarters," and, picking up her dainty skirts, she led the way thither through loose stones and hard yellow grass. As I have a rooted antipathy to dark and uninhabited places, possibly the haunt of snakes and scorpions, I failed to attend her, but, leaving the baboo to continue his duty, turned back into the house alone.

I paced the drawing-room, dining-room, the nursery, and as I stood surveying the long vista of apartments, with the sun pouring into the porch on one hand, and on the green foliage and baked yellow earth of the garden on the other, I confessed to myself that Netta was a miracle!

She, a new arrival, had hit upon this excellent and suitable residence; and a bargain. But, then, she always found bargains; their discovery was her *métier!*

As I stood reflecting thus, gazing absently into the outer glare, a dark and mysterious cloud seemed to fall upon the place, the sun was suddenly obscured, and from the portico came a sharp little gust of wind that gradually increased into a long-drawn wailing cry—surely the cry of some lost soul! What could have put such a hideous idea in my head? But the cry rang in my ears with such piercing distinctness that I felt myself trembling from head to foot; in a second the voice had, as it were, passed forth into the garden and was stifled among the tamarind trees in an agonised wail. I roused myself from a condition of frightful obsession, and endeavoured to summon my common sense and self-command. Here was I, a middle-aged Scotchwoman, standing in this empty bungalow, clutching my garden umbrella, and imagining horrors!

Such thoughts I must keep exclusively to myself, lest I become the laughing-stock of a station with a keen sense of the ridiculous.

Yes, I was an imaginative old goose, but I walked rather quickly back into the porch, and stepped into the open air, with a secret but invincible prejudice against the Red Bungalow. This antipathy was not shared by Netta, who had returned from her quest all animation and satisfaction.

"The stables require repair, and some of the go-downs," she said, "and the whole house must be recoloured inside, and matted. I will bring my husband round to-morrow morning," she announced, dismissing the baboo. "We will be here at eight o'clock sharp."

By this I knew—and so did the baboo—that the Red Bungalow was let at last!

"Well, what do you think of it?" asked Netta triumphantly, as we were walking home together.

"It is a roomy house," I admitted, "but there is no office for Tom."

"Oh, he has the Brigade Office.—Any more objections?"

"A bungalow so long vacant, so entirely overlooked, must have *something* against it—and it is not the rent—"

"Nor is it unhealthy," she argued. "It is quite high, higher than your bungalow—no water near it, and the trees not too close. I can see that you don't like it. Can you give me a good reason?"

"I really wish I could. No, I do not like it—there is something about it that repels me. You know I'm a Highlander, and am sensitive to impressions."

"My dear Liz," and here she came to a dead halt, "you don't mean me to suppose that you think it is haunted? Why, this is the twentieth century!"

"I did not say it was haunted"—(I dared not voice my fears)—"but I declare that I do not like it, and I wish you'd wait; wait only a couple of days, and I'll take you to see the Watsons' bungalow—so sunny, so lived in—always so cheerful, with a lovely garden, and an office for Tom."

"I'm not sure that *that* is an advantage!" she exclaimed with a smile. "It is not always agreeable to have a man on the premises for twenty-four hours out of the twenty-four hours!"

"But the Watsons—"

"My dear Liz, if you say another word about the Watsons' bungalow I shall have a bad attack of the sulks, and go straight to bed!"

It is needless to mention that Tom was delighted with the bungalow selected by his ever-clever little wife, and for the next week our own abode was the resort of tailors, hawkers, butchers, milkmen, furniture-makers, ponies and cows on sale, and troops of servants in quest of places.

Every day Netta went over to the house to inspect, and to give directions, to see how the mallees were laying out the garden and Badminton courts, and the matting people and white-washers were progressing indoors.

Many hands make light work, and within a week the transformation of the Red Bungalow was astonishing. Within a fortnight it was complete; the stables were again occupied—also the new spick-and-span servants' quarters; badminton courts were ready to be played upon; the verandah and porch were gay with palms and plants and parrots, and the drawing-room was the admiration of all Kulu. Netta introduced plants in pots—pots actually dressed up in pongee silk!—to the station ladies; her sofa cushions were frilled, she had quantities of pretty pictures and photos, silver knick-knacks, and gay rugs.

But before Netta had had the usual name-board—"Major Fellowes, A.Q.M.G."—attached to the gate piers of the Red Bungalow, there had been some demur and remonstrance. My ayah, an old Madrasi, long in my service, had ventured one day, as she held my hair in her hand, "That new missus never taking the old Red Bungalow?"

"Yes."

"My missus then telling her, *please*, that plenty bad place—oh, so bad! No one living there this many years."

"Why—what is it?"

"I not never knowing, only the one word—*bad*. Oh, my missus! you speak, never letting these pretty little children go there—"

"But other people have lived there, Mary—"

"Never long—so people telling—the house man paint bungalow all so nice—same like now—they make great bargain—so pleased. One day they go away, away, away, never coming back. Please, please," and she stooped and kissed my hand, "speak that master, tell him—*bad* bungalow."

Of course I pooh-poohed the subject to Mary, who actually wept, good kind creature, and as she did my hair had constantly to dry her eyes on her saree.

And, knowing how futile a word to Tom would prove, I once more attacked Netta. I said, "Netta, I'm sure you think I'm an ignorant, superstitious imbecile, but I believe in presentiments. I have a presentiment, dear, about that Bungalow—*do* give it up to please and, yes, comfort me—"

"What! my beautiful find—the best house in Kulu—my *bargain*?"

"You may find it a dear bargain!"

"Not even to oblige you, dear Liz, can I break off my agreement, and I have really set my heart on your *bête noire*. I am so, so sorry," and she came over and caressed me.

I wonder if Netta in her secret heart suspected that I, the Colonel's wife, might be a little jealous that the new arrival had secured a far more impressive looking abode than her own, and for this mean reason I endeavoured to persuade her to "move on."

However, her mind must have been entirely disabused of this by a lady on whom we were calling, who said:

"Oh, Mrs. Fellowes, have you got a house yet, or will you wait for the Watsons'? Such a—"

"I am already suited," interrupted Netta. "We have found just the thing—not far from my cousin's, too—a fine, roomy, cheerful place, with a huge compound; we are already making the garden."

"Roomy—large compound; near Mrs. Drummond," she repeated with knitted brow. "No—oh, surely you do not mean the Red Bungalow?"

"Yes, that is its name; I am charmed with it, and so lucky to find it."

"No difficulty in finding it, dear Mrs. Fellowes, but I believe the difficulty is in remaining there."

"Do you mean that it's haunted?" enquired Netta with a rather superior air.

"Something of that sort—the natives call it 'the devil's house.' A terrible tragedy happened there long ago—so long

ago that it is forgotten; but you will find it almost impossible
to keep servants!"

"You are certainly most discouraging, but I hope some day you
will come and dine with us, and see how comfortable we are!"

There was a note of challenge in this invitation, and I could
see with the traditional "half-eye" that Mrs. Dodd and Mrs.
Fellowes would scarcely be bosom friends.

Nor was this the sole warning.

At the club a very old resident, wife of a Government em-
ployé, who had spent twenty years in Kulu, came and seated
herself by me one morning with the air of a person who desired
to fulfil a disagreeable duty.

"I am afraid you will think me presuming, Mrs. Drummond,
but I feel that I *ought* to speak. Do you know that the house
your cousin has taken is said to be unlucky? The last people only
remained a month, though they got it for next to nothing—a
mere song."

"Yes, I've heard of these places, and read of them, too," I
replied, "but it generally turns out that someone has an interest
in keeping it empty; possibly natives live there."

"*Any*where but there!" she exclaimed. "Not a soul will go
near it after night-fall—there is not even the usual chokedar—"

"What is it? What is the tale?"

"Something connected with those old mounds of brickwork,
and the well. I think a palace or a temple stood on the spot
thousands of years ago, when Kulu was a great native city.

"Do try and dissuade your cousin from going there; she will
find her mistake sooner or later. I hope you won't think me very
officious, but she is young and happy, and has two such dear
children, especially the little boy."

Yes, especially the little boy! I was devoted to Guy—my
husband, too. We had bought him a pony and a tiny monkey,
and were only too glad to keep him and Baba for a few days
when their parents took the great step and moved into the Red
Bungalow.

In a short time all was in readiness; the big end room made a delightful nursery; the children had also the run of the back verandah and the garden, and were soon completely and happily at home.

An inhabited house seems so different to the same when it stands silent, with closed doors—afar from the sound of voices and footsteps. I could scarcely recognise Netta's new home. It was the centre of half the station gaieties—badminton parties twice a week, dinners, "Chotah Hazra" gatherings on the great verandah, and rehearsals for a forthcoming play; the pattering of little feet, servants, horses, cows, goats, dogs, parrots, all contributed their share to the general life and stir. I went over to the Bungalow almost daily: I dined, I breakfasted, I had tea, and I never saw anything but the expected and the commonplace, yet I failed to eradicate my first instinct, my secret apprehension and aversion. Christmas was over, the parties, dinners and teas were among memories of the past; we were well advanced in the month of February, when Netta, the triumphant, breathed her first complaint. The servants—excellent servants, with long and *bonâ fide* characters—arrived, stayed one week, or perhaps two, and then came and said, "Please I go!"

None of them remained in the compound at night, except the horsekeepers and an orderly; they retired to more congenial quarters in an adjoining bazaar, and the maddening part was that they would give no definite name or shape to their fears— they spoke of "It" and a "Thing"—a fearsome object, that dwelt within and around the Bungalow.

The children's ayah, a Madras woman, remained loyal and staunch; she laughed at the Bazaar tales and their reciters; and, as her husband was the cook, Netta was fairly independent of the cowardly crew who nightly fled to the Bazaar.

Suddenly the ayah, the treasure, fell ill of fever—the really virulent fever that occasionally seizes on natives of the country, and seems to lick up their very life. As my servants' quarters were more comfortable—and I am something of a nurse—I took the invalid home, and Netta promoted her understudy (a local woman) temporarily into her place. She was a chattering, gay, gaudy creature, that I had never approved, but Netta would not listen to any advice, whether with respect to medicines, servants, or bungalows. Her choice in the latter had undoubtedly turned out well, and she was not a little exultant, and bragged to me that *she* never left it in anyone's power to say, "There—I told you so!"

It was Baba's birthday—she was two—a pretty, healthy child, but for her age backward: beyond "Dadda," "Mamma," and "Ayah," she could not say one word. However, as Tom cynically remarked, "she was bound to make up for it by and by!"

It was twelve o'clock on this very warm morning when I took my umbrella and topee and started off to help Netta with her preparations for the afternoon. The chief feature of the entertainment was to be a bran pie.

I found my cousin hard at work when I arrived. In the verandah a great bath-tub full of bran had been placed on a table, and she was draping the said tub with elegant festoons of pink glazed calico—her implement a hammer and tacks—whilst I burrowed into the bran, and there interred the bodies of dolls and cats and horses, and all manner of pleasant surprises. We were making a dreadful litter, and a considerable noise, when suddenly above the hammering I heard a single sharp cry.

"Listen!" I said.

"Oh, Baba is awake—naughty child—and she will disturb her brother," replied the mother, selecting a fresh tack. "The ayah is there. Don't go."

"But it had such an odd, uncanny sound," I protested.

"Dear old Liz! how nervous you are! Baba's scream is something between a whistle of an express and a fog-horn. She has abnormal lung power—and to-day she is restless and upset by her birthday—and her teeth. Your fears—"

Then she stopped abruptly, for a loud, frantic shriek, the shriek of extreme mortal terror, now rose high above her voice, and, throwing the hammer from her, Netta fled into the draw-ing-room, overturning chairs in her route, dashed across the drawing-room, and burst into the nursery, from whence came these most appalling cries. There, huddled together, we discov-ered the two children on the table which stood in the middle of the apartment. Guy had evidently climbed up by a chair, and dragged his sister along with him. It was a beautiful afternoon, the sun streamed in upon them, and the room, as far as we could see, was empty. Yes, but not empty to the trembling little creatures on the table, for with wide, mad eyes they seemed to follow the motion of a something that was creeping round the room close to the wall, and I noticed that their gaze went up and down, as they accompanied its progress with starting pupils and gasping breaths.

"Oh! *what* is it, my darling?" cried Netta, seizing Guy, whilst I snatched at Baba.

He stretched himself stiffly in her arms, and, pointing with a trembling finger to a certain spot, gasped, "Oh, Mummy! look, look, *look!*" and with the last word, which was a shriek of horror, he fell into violent convulsions.

But look as we might, we could see nothing, save the bare matting and the bare wall. What frightful object had made it-self visible to these innocent children has never been discovered to the present day.

Little Guy, in spite of superhuman efforts to save him, died of brain fever, unintelligible to the last; the only words we could distinguish among his ravings were, "Look, look, look! Oh, Mummy! look, look, look!" and as for Baba, whatever was seen by her is locked within her lips, for she remains dumb to the present day.

The ayah had nothing to disclose; she could only beat her head upon the ground and scream, and declare that she had just left the children for a moment to speak to the milkman.

But other servants confessed that the ayah had been gos-siping in the cook-house for more than half an hour. The sole living creature that had been with the children when "It" had appeared to them, was Guy's little pet monkey, which was subsequently found under the table quite dead.

At first I was afraid that after the shock of Guy's death poor Netta would lose her reason. Of course they all came to us, that same dreadful afternoon, leaving the birthday feast already spread, the bran pie in the verandah, the music on the piano; never had there been such a hasty flight, such a domestic earthquake. We endeavoured to keep the mysterious tragedy to ourselves. Little Guy had brain fever; surely it was natural that relations should be together in their trouble, and I declared that I, being a noted nurse, had bodily carried off the child, who was followed by the whole family.

People talked of "A stroke of the sun," but I believe something of the truth filtered into the Bazaar—where all things are known. Shortly after little Guy's death Netta took Baba home, declaring she would never, never return to India, and Tom applied for and obtained a transfer to another station. He sold off the household furniture, the pretty knick-knacks, the pictures, all that had gone to make Netta's house so attractive, for she could not endure to look on them again. They had been in *that* house. As for the Red Bungalow, it is once more closed, and silent. The squirrels and hoo-poos share the garden, the stables are given over to scorpions, the house to white ants. On application to John Mahomed, anyone desirous of becoming a tenant will certainly find that it is still to be had for a mere song!

The Nameless City
H. P. Lovecraft (1921)

When I drew nigh the nameless city I knew it was accursed. I was travelling in a parched and terrible valley under the moon, and afar I saw it protruding uncannily above the sands as parts of a corpse may protrude from an ill-made grave. Fear spoke from the age-worn stones of this hoary survivor of the deluge, this great-grandmother of the eldest pyramid; and a viewless aura repelled me and bade me retreat from antique and sinister secrets that no man should see, and no man else had ever dared to see.

Remote in the desert of Araby lies the nameless city, crumbling and inarticulate, its low walls nearly hidden by the sands of uncounted ages. It must have been thus before the first stones of Memphis were laid, and while the bricks of Babylon were yet unbaked. There is no legend so old as to give it a name, or to recall that it was ever alive; but it is told of in whispers around campfires and muttered about by grandams in the tents of sheiks, so that all the tribes shun it without wholly knowing why. It was of this place that Abdul Alhazred the mad poet dreamed on the night before he sang his unexplainable couplet:

"That is not dead which can eternal lie,
And with strange aeons even death may die."

I should have known that the Arabs had good reason for shunning the nameless city, the city told of in strange tales but seen by no living man, yet I defied them and went into the untrodden waste with my camel. I alone have seen it, and that is why no other face bears such hideous lines of fear as mine; why no other man shivers so horribly when the night-wind rattles the windows. When I came upon it in the ghastly stillness of unending sleep it looked at me, chilly from the rays of a cold moon amidst the desert's heat. And as I returned its look I forgot my triumph at finding it, and stopped still with my camel to wait for the dawn.

For hours I waited, till the east grew grey and the stars faded, and the grey turned to roseate light edged with gold. I heard a moaning and saw a storm of sand stirring among the antique stones though the sky was clear and the vast reaches of the desert still. Then suddenly above the desert's far rim came the blazing edge of the sun, seen through the tiny sandstorm which was passing away, and in my fevered state I fancied that from some remote depth there came a crash of musical metal to hail the fiery disc as Memnon hails it from the banks of the Nile. My ears rang and my imagination seethed as I led my camel slowly across the sand to that unvocal stone place; that place too old for Egypt and Meroë to remember; that place which I alone of living men had seen.

In and out amongst the shapeless foundations of houses and palaces I wandered, finding never a carving or inscription to tell of those men, if men they were, who built the city and dwelt therein so long ago. The antiquity of the spot was unwholesome, and I longed to encounter some sign or device to prove that the city was indeed fashioned by mankind. There were certain proportions and dimensions in the ruins which I did not like. I had with me many tools, and dug much within the walls of the obliterated edifices; but progress was slow, and nothing significant was revealed. When night and the moon returned I felt a chill wind which brought new fear, so that I did not dare to remain in the city. And as I went outside the antique walls to sleep, a small sighing sandstorm gathered behind me, blowing over the grey stones though the moon was bright and most of the desert still.

I awaked just at dawn from a pageant of horrible dreams, my ears ringing as from some metallic peal. I saw the sun peering redly through the last gusts of a little sandstorm that hovered over the nameless city, and marked the quietness of the rest of the landscape. Once more I ventured within those brooding ruins that swelled beneath the sand like an ogre under a coverlet, and again dug vainly for relics of the forgotten race. At noon I rested, and in the afternoon I spent much time tracing the walls, and the bygone streets, and the outlines of the nearly vanished buildings. I saw that the city had been mighty indeed, and wondered at the sources of its greatness. To myself I pictured all the splendours of an age so distant that Chaldaea could not recall it, and thought of Sarnath the Doomed, that stood in the land of Mnar when mankind was young, and of Ib, that was carven of grey stone before mankind existed.

All at once I came upon a place where the bed-rock rose stark through the sand and formed a low cliff; and here I saw with joy what seemed to promise further traces of the antediluvian people. Hewn rudely on the face of the cliff were the unmistakable facades of several small, squat rock houses or temples; whose interiors might preserve many secrets of ages too remote for calculation, though sandstorms had long since effaced any carvings which may have been outside.

Very low and sand-choked were all of the dark apertures near me, but I cleared one with my spade and crawled through it, carrying a torch to reveal whatever mysteries it might hold. When I was inside I saw that the cavern was indeed a temple, and beheld plain signs of the race that had lived and worshipped before the desert was a desert. Primitive altars, pillars, and niches, all curiously low, were not absent; and though I saw no sculptures nor frescoes, there were many singular stones clearly shaped into symbols by artificial means. The lowness of the chiselled chamber was very strange, for I could hardly more than kneel upright; but the area was so great that my torch shewed only part at a time. I shuddered oddly in some of the far corners; for certain altars and stones suggested forgotten rites of terrible, revolting, and inexplicable nature, and made me wonder what manner of men could have made and frequented such a temple. When I had seen all that the place contained, I crawled out again, avid to find what the other temples might yield.

Night had now approached, yet the tangible things I had seen made curiosity stronger than fear, so that I did not flee from the long moon-cast shadows that had daunted me when first I saw the nameless city. In the twilight I cleared another aperture and with a new torch crawled into it, finding more vague stones and symbols, though nothing more definite than the other temple had contained. The room was just as low, but much less broad, ending in a very narrow passage crowded with obscure and cryptical shrines. About these shrines I was prying when the noise of a wind and of my camel outside broke through the stillness and drew me forth to see what could have frightened the beast.

The moon was gleaming vividly over the primeval ruins, lighting a dense cloud of sand that seemed blown by a strong but decreasing wind from some point along the cliff ahead of me. I knew it was this chilly, sandy wind which had disturbed the camel, and was about to lead him to a place of better shelter when I chanced to glance up and saw that there was no wind atop the cliff. This astonished me and made me fearful again, but I immediately recalled the sudden local winds I had seen and heard before at sunrise and sunset, and judged it was a normal thing. I decided that it came from some rock fissure leading to a cave, and watched the troubled sand to trace it to

its source; soon perceiving that it came from the black orifice
of a temple a long distance south of me, almost out of sight.
Against the choking sand-cloud I plodded toward this temple,
which as I neared it loomed larger than the rest, and shewed a
doorway far less clogged with caked sand. I would have entered
had not the terrific force of the icy wind almost quenched my
torch. It poured madly out of the dark door, sighing uncannily
as it ruffled the sand and spread about the weird ruins. Soon it
grew fainter and the sand grew more and more still, till finally
all was at rest again; but a presence seemed stalking among the
spectral stones of the city, and when I glanced at the moon
it seemed to quiver as though mirrored in unquiet waters. I
was more afraid than I could explain, but not enough to dull
my thirst for wonder; so as soon as the wind was quite gone I
crossed into the dark chamber from which it had come.

This temple, as I had fancied from the outside, was larger than
either of those I had visited before; and was presumably a natural cavern, since it bore winds from some region beyond. Here
I could stand quite upright, but saw that the stones and altars
were as low as those in the other temples. On the walls and roof
I beheld for the first time some traces of the pictorial art of the
ancient race, curious curling streaks of paint that had almost
faded or crumbled away; and on two of the altars I saw with
rising excitement a maze of well-fashioned curvilinear carvings.
As I held my torch aloft it seemed to me that the shape of the
roof was too regular to be natural, and I wondered what the
prehistoric cutters of stone had first worked upon. Their engi-
neering skill must have been vast.

Then a brighter flare of the fantastic flame shewed me that
for which I had been seeking, the opening to those remoter
abysses whence the sudden wind had blown; and I grew faint
when I saw that it was a small and plainly artificial door chiselled in the solid rock. I thrust my torch within, beholding a
black tunnel with the roof arching low over a rough flight of

very small, numerous, and steeply descending steps. I shall always see those steps in my dreams, for I came to learn what they
meant. At the time I hardly knew whether to call them steps or
mere foot-holds in a precipitous descent. My mind was whirl-
ing with mad thoughts, and the words and warnings of Arab
prophets seemed to float across the desert from the lands that
men know to the nameless city that men dare not know. Yet I
hesitated only a moment before advancing through the portal
and commencing to climb cautiously down the steep passage,
feet first, as though on a ladder.

It is only in the terrible phantasms of drugs or delirium
that any other man can have had such a descent as mine. The
narrow passage led infinitely down like some hideous haunted
well, and the torch I held above my head could not light the
unknown depths toward which I was crawling. I lost track of
the hours and forgot to consult my watch, though I was frightened when I thought of the distance I must be traversing. There
were changes of direction and of steepness, and once I came to
a long, low, level passage where I had to wriggle feet first along
the rocky floor, holding my torch at arm's length beyond my
head. The place was not high enough for kneeling. After that
were more of the steep steps, and I was still scrambling down
interminably when my failing torch died out. I do not think I
noticed it at the time, for when I did notice it I was still holding it high above me as if it were ablaze. I was quite unbalanced
with that instinct for the strange and the unknown which has
made me a wanderer upon earth and a haunter of far, ancient,
and forbidden places.

In the darkness there flashed before my mind fragments of
my cherished treasury of daemoniac lore; sentences from Alhazred the mad Arab, paragraphs from the apocryphal nightmares
of Damascius, and infamous lines from the delirious *Image du
Monde* of Gauthier de Metz. I repeated queer extracts, and muttered of Afrasiab and the daemons that floated with him down
the Oxus; later chanting over and over again a phrase from one

of Lord Dunsany's tales—"the unreverberate blackness of the
abyss". Once when the descent grew amazingly steep I recited
something in sing-song from Thomas Moore until I feared to
recite more:

> "A reservoir of darkness, black
>   As witches' cauldrons are, when fill'd
> With moon-drugs in th' eclipse distill'd.
>   Leaning to look if foot might pass
> Down thro' that chasm, I saw, beneath,
>   As far as vision could explore,
> The jetty sides as smooth as glass,
>   Looking as if just varnish'd o'er
> With that dark pitch the Sea of Death
>   Throws out upon its slimy shore."

Time had quite ceased to exist when my feet again felt a level
floor, and I found myself in a place slightly higher than the
rooms in the two smaller temples now so incalculably far above
my head. I could not quite stand, but could kneel upright, and
in the dark I shuffled and crept hither and thither at random.
I soon knew that I was in a narrow passage whose walls were
lined with cases of wood having glass fronts. As in that Palae-
ozoic and abysmal place I felt of such things as polished wood
and glass I shuddered at the possible implications. The cases
were apparently ranged along each side of the passage at regular
intervals, and were oblong and horizontal, hideously like cof-
fins in shape and size. When I tried to move two or three for
further examination, I found they were firmly fastened.

I saw that the passage was a long one, so floundered ahead
rapidly in a creeping run that would have seemed horrible had
any eye watched me in the blackness; crossing from side to side
occasionally to feel of my surroundings and be sure the walls
and rows of cases still stretched on. Man is so used to thinking

visually that I almost forgot the darkness and pictured the endless corridor of wood and glass in its low-studded monotony as
though I saw it. And then in a moment of indescribable emotion I did see it.

Just when my fancy merged into real sight I cannot tell; but
there came a gradual glow ahead, and all at once I knew that
I saw the dim outlines of the corridor and the cases, revealed
by some unknown subterranean phosphorescence. For a little
while all was exactly as I had imagined it, since the glow was
very faint; but as I mechanically kept on stumbling ahead into
the stronger light I realised that my fancy had been but feeble.
This hall was no relic of crudity like the temples in the city
above, but a monument of the most magnificent and exotic art.
Rich, vivid, and daringly fantastic designs and pictures formed
a continuous scheme of mural painting whose lines and colours
were beyond description. The cases were of a strange golden
wood, with fronts of exquisite glass, and contained the mummified forms of creatures outreaching in grotesqueness the most
chaotic dreams of man.

To convey any idea of these monstrosities is impossible.
They were of the reptile kind, with body lines suggesting sometimes the crocodile, sometimes the seal, but more often nothing
of which either the naturalist or the palaeontologist ever heard.
In size they approximated a small man, and their fore legs bore
delicate and evidently flexible feet curiously like human hands
and fingers. But strangest of all were their heads, which presented a contour violating all known biological principles. To nothing can such things be well compared—in one flash I thought of
comparisons as varied as the cat, the bulldog, the mythic Satyr,
and the human being. Not Jove himself had so colossal and
protuberant a forehead, yet the horns and the noselessness and
the alligator-like jaw placed the things outside all established
categories. I debated for a time on the reality of the mummies,
half suspecting they were artificial idols; but soon decided they
were indeed some palaeogean species which had lived when the

nameless city was alive. To crown their grotesqueness, most of them were gorgeously enrobed in the costliest of fabrics, and lavishly laden with ornaments of gold, jewels, and unknown shining metals.

The importance of these crawling creatures must have been vast, for they held first place among the wild designs on the frescoed walls and ceiling. With matchless skill had the artist drawn them in a world of their own, wherein they had cities and gardens fashioned to suit their dimensions; and I could not but think that their pictured history was allegorical, perhaps shewing the progress of the race that worshipped them. These creatures, I said to myself, were to the men of the nameless city what the she-wolf was to Rome, or some totem-beast is to a tribe of Indians.

Holding this view, I thought I could trace roughly a wonderful epic of the nameless city; the tale of a mighty sea-coast metropolis that ruled the world before Africa rose out of the waves, and of its struggles as the sea shrank away, and the desert crept into the fertile valley that held it. I saw its wars and triumphs, its troubles and defeats, and afterward its terrible fight against the desert when thousands of its people—here represented in allegory by the grotesque reptiles—were driven to chisel their way down through the rocks in some marvellous manner to another world whereof their prophets had told them. It was all vividly weird and realistic, and its connexion with the awesome descent I had made was unmistakable. I even recognised the passages.

As I crept along the corridor toward the brighter light I saw later stages of the painted epic—the leave-taking of the race that had dwelt in the nameless city and the valley around for ten million years; the race whose souls shrank from quitting scenes their bodies had known so long, where they had settled as nomads in the earth's youth, hewing in the virgin rock those primal shrines at which they never ceased to worship. Now that the light was better I studied the pictures more closely, and, remembering that the strange reptiles must represent the unknown men, pondered upon the customs of the nameless city. Many things were peculiar and inexplicable. The civilisation, which included a written alphabet, had seemingly risen to a higher order than those immeasurably later civilisations of Egypt and Chaldaea, yet there were curious omissions. I could, for example, find no pictures to represent deaths or funeral customs, save such as were related to wars, violence, and plagues; and I wondered at the reticence shewn concerning natural death. It was as though an ideal of earthly immortality had been fostered as a cheering illusion.

Still nearer the end of the passage were painted scenes of the utmost picturesqueness and extravagance; contrasted views of the nameless city in its desertion and growing ruin, and of the strange new realm or paradise to which the race had hewed its way through the stone. In these views the city and the desert valley were shewn always by moonlight, a golden nimbus hovering over the fallen walls and half revealing the splendid perfection of former times, shewn spectrally and elusively by the artist. The paradisal scenes were almost too extravagant to be believed; portraying a hidden world of eternal day filled with glorious cities and ethereal hills and valleys. At the very last I thought I saw signs of an artistic anti-climax. The paintings were less skilful, and much more bizarre than even the wildest of the earlier scenes. They seemed to record a slow decadence of the ancient stock, coupled with a growing ferocity toward the outside world from which it was driven by the desert. The forms of the people—always represented by the sacred reptiles—appeared to be gradually wasting away, though their spirit as shewn hovering about the ruins by moonlight gained in proportion. Emaciated priests, displayed as reptiles in ornate robes, cursed the upper air and all who breathed it; and one terrible final scene shewed a primitive-looking man, perhaps a pioneer of ancient Irem, the City of Pillars, torn to pieces by members of the elder race. I remembered how the Arabs fear the nameless city, and was glad that beyond this place the grey walls and ceiling were bare.

As I viewed the pageant of mural history I had approached very closely the end of the low-ceiled hall, and was aware of a great gate through which came all of the illuminating phosphorescence. Creeping up to it, I cried aloud in transcendent amazement at what lay beyond; for instead of other and brighter chambers there was only an illimitable void of uniform radiance, such as one might fancy when gazing down from the peak of Mount Everest upon a sea of sunlit mist. Behind me was a passage so cramped that I could not stand upright in it; before me was an infinity of subterranean effulgence.

Reaching down from the passage into the abyss was the head of a steep flight of steps—small numerous steps like those of the black passages I had traversed—but after a few feet the glowing vapours concealed everything. Swung back open against the left-hand wall of the passage was a massive door of brass, incredibly thick and decorated with fantastic bas-reliefs, which could if closed shut the whole inner world of light away from the vaults and passages of rock. I looked at the steps, and for the nonce dared not try them. I touched the open brass door, and could not move it. Then I sank prone to the stone floor, my mind aflame with prodigious reflections which not even a death-like exhaustion could banish.

As I lay still with closed eyes, free to ponder, many things I had lightly noted in the frescoes came back to me with new and terrible significance—scenes representing the nameless city in its heyday, the vegetation of the valley around it, and the distant lands with which its merchants traded. The allegory of the crawling creatures puzzled me by its universal prominence, and I wondered that it should be so closely followed in a pictured history of such importance. In the frescoes the nameless city had been shewn in proportions fitted to the reptiles. I wondered what its real proportions and magnificence had been, and reflected a moment on certain oddities I had noticed in the ruins. I thought curiously of the lowness of the primal temples and of the underground corridor, which were doubtless hewn thus out of deference to the reptile deities there honoured; though it perforce reduced the worshippers to crawling. Perhaps the very rites had involved a crawling in imitation of the creatures. No religious theory, however, could easily explain why the level passage in that awesome descent should be as low as the temples—or lower, since one could not even kneel in it. As I thought of the crawling creatures, whose hideous mummified forms were so close to me, I felt a new throb of fear. Mental associations are curious, and I shrank from the idea that except for the poor primitive man torn to pieces in the last painting, mine was the only human form amidst the many relics and symbols of primordial life.

But as always in my strange and roving existence, wonder soon drove out fear; for the luminous abyss and what it might contain presented a problem worthy of the greatest explorer. That a weird world of mystery lay far down that flight of peculiarly small steps I could not doubt, and I hoped to find there those human memorials which the painted corridor had failed to give. The frescoes had pictured unbelievable cities, hills, and valleys in this lower realm, and my fancy dwelt on the rich and colossal ruins that awaited me.

My fears, indeed, concerned the past rather than the future. Not even the physical horror of my position in that cramped corridor of dead reptiles and antediluvian frescoes, miles below the world I knew and faced by another world of eerie light and mist, could match the lethal dread I felt at the abysmal antiquity of the scene and its soul. An ancientness so vast that measurement is feeble seemed to leer down from the primal stones and rock-hewn temples in the nameless city, while the very latest of the astounding maps in the frescoes shewed oceans and continents that man has forgotten, with only here and there some vaguely familiar outline. Of what could have happened in the geological aeons since the paintings ceased and the death-hating race resentfully succumbed to decay, no man might say. Life had once teemed in these caverns and in the luminous realm beyond; now I was alone with vivid relics, and I trembled to think of the countless ages through which these relics had kept a silent and deserted vigil.

Suddenly there came another burst of that acute fear which had intermittently seized me ever since I first saw the terrible valley and the nameless city under a cold moon, and despite my exhaustion I found myself starting frantically to a sitting posture and gazing back along the black corridor toward the tunnels that rose to the outer world. My sensations were much like those which had made me shun the nameless city at night, and were as inexplicable as they were poignant. In another moment, however, I received a still greater shock in the form of a definite sound—the first which had broken the utter silence of these tomb-like depths. It was a deep, low moaning, as of a distant throng of condemned spirits, and came from the direction in which I was staring. Its volume rapidly grew, till soon it reverberated frightfully through the low passage, and at the same time I became conscious of an increasing draught of cold air, likewise flowing from the tunnels and the city above.

The touch of this air seemed to restore my balance, for I instantly recalled the sudden gusts which had risen around the mouth of the abyss each sunset and sunrise, one of which had indeed served to reveal the hidden tunnels to me. I looked at my watch and saw that sunrise was near, so braced myself to resist the gale which was sweeping down to its cavern home as it had swept forth at evening. My fear again waned low, since a natural phenomenon tends to dispel broodings over the unknown.

More and more madly poured the shrieking, moaning night-wind into that gulf of the inner earth. I dropped prone again and clutched vainly at the floor for fear of being swept bodily

through the open gate into the phosphorescent abyss. Such fury
I had not expected, and as I grew aware of an actual slipping of
my form toward the abyss I was beset by a thousand new terrors
of apprehension and imagination.

The malignancy of the blast awakened incredible fancies;
once more I compared myself shudderingly to the only other
human image in that frightful corridor, the man who was torn
to pieces by the nameless race, for in the fiendish clawing of the
swirling currents there seemed to abide a vindictive rage all the
stronger because it was largely impotent.

I think I screamed frantically near the last—I was almost
mad—but if I did so my cries were lost in the hell-born babel
of the howling wind-wraiths. I tried to crawl against the murderous invisible torrent, but I could not even hold my own as I
was pushed slowly and inexorably toward the unknown world.
Finally reason must have wholly snapped, for I fell to bab-
bling over and over that unexplainable couplet of the mad Arab
Alhazred, who dreamed of the nameless city:

> "That is not dead which can eternal lie,
>   And with strange aeons even death may die."

Only the grim brooding desert gods know what really took
place—what indescribable struggles and scrambles in the dark I
endured or what Abaddon guided me back to life, where I must
always remember and shiver in the night-wind till oblivion—
or worse—claims me. Monstrous, unnatural, colossal, was the
thing—too far beyond all the ideas of man to be believed except
in the silent damnable small hours when one cannot sleep.

I have said that the fury of the rushing blast was infernal—
cacodaemoniacal—and that its voices were hideous with the
pent-up viciousness of desolate eternities. Presently those voices, while still chaotic before me, seemed to my beating brain
to take articulate form behind me; and down there in the grave

of unnumbered aeon-dead antiquities, leagues below the dawn-lit world of men, I heard the ghastly cursing and snarling of strange-tongued fiends. Turning, I saw outlined against the luminous aether of the abyss what could not be seen against the dusk of the corridor—a nightmare horde of rushing devils; hate-distorted, grotesquely panoplied, half-transparent; devils of a race no man might mistake—the crawling reptiles of the nameless city.

And as the wind died away I was plunged into the ghoul-peopled blackness of earth's bowels; for behind the last of the creatures the great brazen door clanged shut with a deafening peal of metallic music whose reverberations swelled out to the distant world to hail the rising sun as Memnon hails it from the banks of the Nile.

The Horn
Hilton Brown (1922)

I

The rare and occasional traveller who crosses the long jungle uplands westward of the Mohnds comes in time to the step-like drop of three thousand feet into the Gamsatri plain and the little zamindari township of Khankota. As you look back from this plain country the bulwark of the higher levels rises like a wall, a forbidding battlement of black sheet rock, picked out here and there with the feathery bamboo, which clings where nothing else can find a roothold.

Seen thus, it looks impassable; and indeed there is but the one ghat, or passage, down it in a distance of many miles—one only, that is to say, which is possible for pack-bullock, pony, or elephant. Down this ghat the traveller will have come, and he may pick it out from the plains below by a roundish black knob at its summit—the grim rock of Hoondi. So, looking back from the pleasance of these open and cultivated lands, he may think, perhaps with a shudder, of that gloomy and sable place; for that which from below looks like a mere turret or mound is at close quarters a semi-isolated hill, buttressed on to the main mountain on the side away from the pass, but hanging over the ghat path in a sheer and dreadful rock.

The rock swells out convexly; it is black as coal, and no plant can find a holding on its shining face; and over its surface in the old days men—and not only men—have rolled and hurtled down to destruction. Coming from the uplands you see it blocking the pass ahead like the rounded back of some monstrous crouching beast; and on the crest of it are the sad-coloured ruins of the old fort and watch-tower. As you come fairly into the jaws of the pass the rock seems to swell and tower above you with an extraordinary effect of menacing life; the descent goes in fear and trembling along the valley of a torrent, on whose cruel stones human beings have time and again smashed and broken like eggs. From the ghat the place looks inaccessible, but it is not really so, because a path of sorts, much cut and destroyed by rains, twists away round the mountain, and carries the venturesome by a flight of battered steps into the fort itself. Once there, you may see the reason of its building, for it looks out thirty miles over the upland plateau and sixty over the Gamsatri plain. Khankota you cannot see, because it lies too close to the foot of the hills, and that is doubtless the reason why the horn came into being.

The horn is there to this day at the inner door of the squat temple that lurks in one corner of the fort; it and the carven deities crudely designed, eloquently evil of face, are the sole remains of the ancient glory. Those who have opportunity and are prepared to buy themselves illicit admission to the holy ground may see and even handle it, may finger the great iron chains that hold it to the wall, and run a timorous hand along its smooth side. It seems to be fashioned of the horn of a wild buffalo—such a buffalo as is unknown to the annals of Rowland Ward; such a buffalo, indeed, as never existed upon earth, for the thing is a deception. In reality it is made of brass, covered cunningly with leather, with that strange pervert genius of the Hindu for giving a thing the semblance of something else. It is undatably old—though the leather must, of course, have been periodically renewed. The imitation is excellent— Macfadyen, indeed, whose story we shall presently consider, was deceived, and thought it really a gigantic buffalo horn.

No human agency has blown or sounded that horn for forty years; there was a trick in it, and the trick is lost. Upwards of forty years ago there lived in Khankota a very old man called Bodi, and if the day and hour were propitious, and authority could be brought to bear, Bodi could be induced to climb the ghat and sound the horn—though never with a very good grace, and always in the extremity of fear. So much the curious may learn from the old Administration Reports of these parts; may learn, too, the melancholy and disheartening sound that was produced, "utterly unmistakable and like no cry of animals or movement of earth or any elemental noise." "The sound rose in a minor sweep which made one's flesh shudder, then dropped to a sustained booming howl somewhere about D flat of the middle octave. But whether from the associations of the place or from some trick of echoes"—thus a lucid account of the 'seventies—"there was something in that sound that no note humanly devised and played upon a human instrument should contain."

Long before such records came into being, the fort of Hoondi was abandoned and the mysteries of its squat, repulsive temple were enacted no more. Bodi had been the sounder of the horn for sixty years, and must have known the place in the last days of its horrible fame; but in such times as we have sober and authentic record of he sounded only for show or demonstration, to please the visiting Agent. He had no descendants and no connections, and one thing seems positively and absolutely assured—that the secret of the sounding perished with him these forty years back. Several men of Khankota, tempted by enormous backsheesh, have tried, and failed to produce any sound whatsoever.

Bodi being dead, the horn should never again have been heard: but it has been heard. Always, and at all periods—so runs the credited tradition of Khankota—that dreadful sound has on odd occasion been heard, by night as well as by day, when there was no man there to blow. No priest, or guard, or *pujari* lived at Hoondi latterly—it was too terrible a place even for that; it lay a stark and tenantless ruin, save for those beings who kept upon that evil rock. Yet the horn sounded.

Clearly the horn was first instituted as a warning, and was sounded originally when bands of hill marauders were sighted approaching across the plateau. Any concerted attack on Khankota must pass down the Hoondi ghat, and however rapidly and stealthily these wild people might manoeuvre, the blast of the horn would outrun them. The garrison of the fort of Hoondi had, of course, nothing to fear; there are great tanks of water in the summit of the rock, and they could have supported themselves indefinitely. Later, however, this function of the horn disappeared, the civilisation of the uplands died out, and Khankota became a metropolis. Then, it would seem, Hoondi became a sort of observatory and a place of great sacredness; it was there that the priests made their observations, and probably the horn was blown to announce to those in Khankota that the moment for action in whatever they had in hand had arrived. From Macfadyen's account this seems absolutely beyond doubt, and from his narrative it will be seen also why it was advisable to have the business of augury done at Hoondi and not in Khankota itself.

At some risk of tedium it has been necessary to set forth this as introduction. One could gladly go on to describe the buildings of Hoondi itself—the uncommunicative remnants of that fort which must in its day have witnessed violence and cruelty unparalleled, for it was to Hoondi that the prisoners and those fallen in favour came for lingering and ghastly despatch. One would fain tarry to think of the hideous days and nights that place has made and witnessed; to reflect on the frightful fates of offspring undesired, of wives become encumbrances, of viziers discredited and dismissed. One could enumerate the sad victims of that grim deity who was worshipped upon the rock; could enter into the lurid and bloody history of Khankota, and of the long and diabolical line of petty potentates who held evil sway in that unnoticed corner. Perhaps without this the dreadfulness of Hoondi, with its black rock and mouldering ruins, cannot be appreciated; only to those saturated with the full abomination of its traditions would the terror of the horn be attainable. And to read this narrative aright you should have seen Hoondi—should have seen it in all weathers, in the glare of the steely March sunshine, in the crashing thunder-storms of May, in the wet mists of the monsoon, or in the false lights of some hour when the sun and the moon are struggling together. At such times Hoondi was no rock, but a black, crouching beast, full of sluggish, sinister life. Make all allowances for the curious twists that loneliness and wild places give men's minds, and still it was an unnaturally dreadful place.

Inevitably one asks—what followed these soundings of the horn: disasters, changes, upheavals? No such things occurred. If the sounding of the horn had aught to do with affairs, it was with the affairs of others than mere men. It sounded without human motive and without human consequence, just as it sounded without human agency. The most we can say is that it came at oppressive times, when the spirits of men were low—at times, one would have said, when the powers of evil seemed abroad. Those who have studied such matters assure us that evil deeds leave behind them traces of evil which may at times be manifest in inexplicable forms. So it may have been with the Horn of Hoondi. But whose coming did it herald? What manner of creatures assembled at its call?

II

There is no even tolerably authentic notice of the horn prior to that of Josiah Macfadyen, and none subsequent for many long years. Macfadyen was one of those remarkable men who fill the Anglo-Indian records of the early nineteenth century, and who died out with the period that begat them. He was an unofficial pioneer, a man who had deliberately deserted his own country and immersed himself in India. He does not appear to have been attached to the East India Company; rather he worked in his own interests, wandering over immense areas of country, trading and making notes of what he saw. He lived and throve in circumstances which would have killed the weaker generation of to-day a score of times over. Principally he worked along the northern seaboard of Madras, but he made several expeditions into the wild upland jungles—then practically unexplored and deadly dangerous—and the garrulous records he kept of his journeyings have time and again been of value.

The precise date of his visit to Khankota is not ascertainable, but it was probably not far off the year of Waterloo. He had some idea, it seems, of finding precious stones among the Mohnds, but went on to investigate the possibilities of the Gamsatri plain, and so came down by Hoondi to Khankota. With the great gift for sociability that characterised his class, he at once struck up a friendship with Bhupati Deo, the reigning zemindar; and the zemindar being about to celebrate the marriage of his son, Macfadyen was invited to attend the astrological ceremonies at Hoondi.

"It is the practice of this family," says Macfadyen—extracts only must suffice us, as his account is voluminous—"when any event of domestic import is impending to ascend the mountains to this rock of Hoondi; there the priests busy themselves with the auguries until the auspicious moment has arrived. On this at a given signal an immense buffalo horn is blown. The noise of this is easily heard at Khankota, seven miles off, and the business to be done is then instantly set in hand. On this occasion the bridal ceremonies were to commence on the signal of the horn, and the zemindar gave himself so many pains on the subject that he came himself to Hoondi for the ceremonies, and carried me and my servants with him."

Macfadyen describes the ascent of the ghat by this imposing cavalcade, and then tells how they waited in the fort of Hoondi for nearly eight days. The monsoon was about to break, and appalling thunder-storms burst about them day and night. The weather was gloomy and menacing in the extreme; "and this," says Macfadyen, "together with the dismalness of the spot, of which I have never encountered the like, served to cast me into a great depression of spirit. I was unable to suppress a dreadful boding of horror." He elaborates this idea, and it is evident that the place preyed upon him a good deal. He was not, of course, allowed to enter the temple itself, but was so situated in the fort that he could command a view of all that went on outside it. There was a great and constant uproar of gongs and bells within, but little sign of life until the eighth evening, when, he says, he observed some new and singular proceedings.

"I was seated at my window looking out towards the gate of the temple when I beheld a procession approaching. It was composed mainly of the *jangams,* or priests, and of members of the zemindar's retinue, and they seemed to be conveying into the temple two women of a different caste, whose attitude was one of very extreme depression and fear, and who wailed loudly as they went. These women were garlanded with flowers and decorated with superior cloths, and they carried some objects in their hands which I was not able to distinguish. They all entered the temple, and the gate was immediately shut fast."

Macfadyen, who seems to have been utterly devoid of fear, now got out of his window, finding himself unwatched, and, making his way round the outside edge of the fort—a hideous feat in itself on a dark and gusty night, with that huge cliff yawning beneath him—climbed on to the temple wall. Lying flat there, he saw all that went on. His description of what he witnessed is detailed, but too distressing and even revolting for quotation; but there is no conceivable doubt that he looked on at a *Meriah* sacrifice—that cruel and bloodthirsty form of human slaughter that persisted in these remote tracts up to an astonishingly recent date. "I was so horrified," says he, "that I thought to fall from the wall, in which case I should have gone down a thousand feet." He controlled himself, however, and presently was able to witness the first historical blowing of the

horn. The horrors had terminated, "and now on a sudden there
burst forth a bright light, and by this I saw on a high pinnacle
or pulpit a man holding in his hands the great buffalo horn of
which I have spoken. This he instantly blew, producing a noise
at once so violent, detestable, and horrifying, that I all but lost
my senses. I cannot in any way describe the dreadfulness of the
sound. I conceived, however, that this was the desired signal
that would terminate the proceedings, and so made haste to get
back to the fort, though I was so much upset and sickened that
I was put to it to keep my footing on the rock."

Macfadyen then describes the descent of the ghat, which was
instantly made; and now comes the portion of his annals which
is of present interest.

"We were now perhaps a mile from the bottom," says he,
"and it was not far off day, the moon struggling with the rack
and with the effulgence of the East, so that, between this and
the flares we carried, a most ghastly light beat upon us all, ren-
dering even well-known faces horrid, ghoulish, and unfamiliar.
I was near the zemindar, who was carried in an open *palkee,*
when suddenly without warning I heard the blast of the horn
ring out above us. I was about to inquire the reason of this of
the zemindar, when I saw he was struck with a most pitiable and
fearsome horror. His face became gray, his eyes stood out in his
head, and in a despairing voice he cried out to the bearers to
hasten. The retinue, in the most abandoned confusion, dashed
past us and fled recklessly downwards; several ponies fell; there
was a terrific panic; and in the middle of all the zemindar, who
was a huge fat man, leapt out of his *palkee* and began plunging
down over the stony ground, crying out terribly in fear. I ran
after him, though I felt no great terror. 'Who is at the fort?' I
said. 'There is no one at the fort,' said he.

"Now this, had he not spoken, was my own impression; for
before we started every one had been got out of the premises
and off the rock altogether, and all locked, bolted, and made
fast. I assuredly thought no human being had been left behind.

Yet, although the rumour among these people has it that the horn is at times blown by some dreadful and supernatural agency, I cannot but think that there must have been some trick to it, and that some one out of wantonness or sheer malice did remain behind, and blew the horn. For how else, in the name of all Christian things, could it have sounded?"

How indeed? Macfadyen is honest in his account; he had no call to invent, for his narrative of the doings at Hoondi carried horror enough to the reader to satisfy the most ambitious. His own explanation of a practical joker at work may seem to suit the incidents of this single case, but not for long. A strange and sorry jester would that have been—and a wonderfully bold; such a jester as never lived, then or now, within the bounds of southern India.

III

Stephen Bannerman, in the late 'nineties Superintendent of Police in the place of which I write, was one of those men destined seemingly by nature to drift into backwaters and there make anchorage. A bleak, dark, inhuman fellow, he was fitted into these outlandish districts less from inability to perform his duties than from a total social uselessness. He spoke little, neither smoked nor drank, played no games, loathed all women, and was possessed of an untiring physical endurance that made him a little contemptuous of most men. He was a man ceaselessly on the move, ranging continually over the big area at his command, an interminable walker, and a *shikari* of long experience and skill. Withal he was an officer of distinction, no less dreaded by the cut-throats and forgers of Khankota than by the flying dacoits of the uplands. He was no sort of mystic, held an entirely practical outlook, possessed not a grain of imagination, and was the last of men to give way to any affection of the nerves. As a final item in this category, he told on all occasions the strict and sober truth, and where another might amplify or embellish, Bannerman would only prune and minimise.

In the late autumn of 1898 Bannerman was returning from a long tour in the upland country, and had reached the last camping-place before Khankota—to wit, Hoondi. Servants and coolies were ever loath to lie overclose to that accursed rock, and as a result the camp was actually made at a village called Kirridi, a short mile from the dip of the pass, the black rock glooming on the skyline like a monster. It was weary weather; the first burst of the monsoon over, there remained a chronic dampness of atmosphere, mist and thin rain billowing cease-lessly round the crest of the ghats, giving way occasionally to a delusive glimpse of a watery and ineffective sun. There had been a good deal of sickness on the tour. The cruel, indigenous malaria of these parts had struck them badly; an orderly had died of it at Gudra, and Bannerman himself, case-hardened as he was, had had a worse time than usual. They came into Kirridi on a menacing afternoon of black and scurrying cloud, a down-pour threatening, the ghat roads churned into mud, the thatch of the miserable rest-shed dripping and leaking everywhere, a rising wind sweeping the God-forsaken street of the village; and they had not been there half-an-hour when word was brought to Bannerman that a tiger had killed four miles away to the north.

There was still good time to shift the camp and make the new place before night, but Bannerman, looking round on his sodden and wretched retinue, could not find it in his heart to give the order. He ate some *tiffin* therefore—it was four in the afternoon, but in these wild places men eat when they can—strapped a wallet to his pony's saddle, slung his rifle, and set out by himself. As he turned away from Kirridi into the jungle, there came another momentary split in the clouds, and there burst out suddenly such a sunset as he had never seen. I have said Bannerman was an unimaginative man, but he drew rein to look at it, and as he looked he felt the flesh creep on his back. Under the flying rack there poured a level crimson light, terrifying in its intensity; Kirridi stood like a village in a fire; the harsh, cruel country round about him sprang into flaming life. Fair in the mid-line of it, round, black, crouching, like the last thing between earth and hell, stood the dreadful rock of Hoondi.

Bannerman gazed at it for a little with a curious and, for him, a novel feeling. He even put this feeling into words, speaking half aloud, as men do who have been much in lonely places. "If ever there was a setting for a Witches' Sabbath, this is it;" and some phrase came into his mind about "the powers of darkness riding on the monsoon." These were unusual thoughts for Bannerman, and still more unusual phrases. As he stared the light shifted and lowered to a deeper scarlet, and for a long moment Bannerman felt that curious expectant terror which, according to the old Greeks, heralded the coming of Pan. For an interval everything seemed terrifying and dreadful, the solid earth alive with horror, the air pregnant with something that was to come. Then it passed, and Bannerman went on through the baleful light to the place of the tiger's kill. He sat there unsuccessfully till it was too dark to see, satisfied himself that the moon, which should have been nearly full, was hopelessly obscured for the night, and then set out on his return journey to his camp at Kirridi.

The night was now impenetrably dark, and by the moisture on his face Bannerman knew that the flying mist-clouds were still driving past. Now and then a gust of wind shook a cataract of heavy drops from the trees, but for the most it was still. It felt to Bannerman unusually hot and close, but this he put down as a forerunning symptom of a fresh attack of malaria. To this also he attributed his growing depression and gloom, and a sort of fear like a child's on a dark staircase, that kept him glancing quickly this way and that. That strange sense of expectant waiting seemed again to be all round him; sombre thoughts came and went in his mind; odd faces, unimaginable pictures, appeared to spring out momentarily on the background of darkness against which he strove. He told himself again and again that it was fever; but presently he was fighting with panic. The hot darkness, wild with expectation, seemed to press upon him like a living thing; he could not keep unbearable images from his mind. He reached the ridge above Kirridi about ten, and as he came to the place where he had halted to watch the sunset over Hoondi the clouds broke yet again, and a yellow and sickly moon rode suddenly into a patch of velvet sky. In its light, a curiously dun and eclipse-like glow, Bannerman saw the tents of his camp, the streaming hovels of Kirridi, the black, murderous bulk of the Hoondi rock. He went hurrying down.

He had intended to leave a message about the tiger with the head-man of the village, but the whole place was deserted, and the silence of death itself hung over it. "I had been depressed and wretched so far," says Bannerman in one of his letters, "but now for the first time I tasted real terror. 'My God!' I thought, 'I'm here—and all alone.'" He ran about the village street like a madman, banging at doors, shouting names. No living thing appeared, except a village dog, which danced in front of him yelping in an ecstasy of excitement. Here and there he could hear cattle stirring in their sheds, and once or twice he was convinced that there were movements, as of human beings, in the houses, but not a soul came out. He went through the village and on, half-walking, half-running, to his camp.

At his camp he had left two servants and an orderly, and he ran from tent to tent calling the names of these three. Nothing answered him. The moon still mocked him with its unnatural glow. The sense of an expectant earth gathered round him again. He called frantically; not a sound came back to him in answer. Then suddenly, at the east side of the camp, and well away from the tents, he saw a white figure sprawled on the ground, as if fallen prone in running. With a beating heart he went up to it. It was his body-servant. The other servant lay a little farther on, and the orderly, in his uniform, farther still, all in the same attitude as of men running rapidly who had been struck down from behind, and had pitched heavily on their faces. All three were unquestionably dead.

Bannerman sat down on a stone and stared at his dead servants. And to him, sitting there, in that yellow and unearthly moonlight, there came, clear as the day, loud as the last trump, utterly unmistakable, the blast of the Horn of Hoondi. He heard the long, minor, upward sweep of it, that curdled the air and made the earth shudder all round; then, when it seemed that one could endure no more, it burst into the full-toned blast of the signal. It was too loud for any delusion—Kirridi, a mile away, roared and rang and shook with it, too ineffably appalling for any imagination. The horn blew at Hoondi in that autumn midnight, and Bannerman, smitten to the heart with horror, sat in his dead camp and heard it.

When it had done, he rose to his feet and went quickly, if unsteadily, towards the head of the ghat. He knew he would have to pass the rock of Hoondi very close and alone; and he knew that was a thing to be done at once or not at all.

IV

It was about two years later that Duchesne, the then Agent, had his experience, he also being encamped at Kirridi for Hoondi. It is to be taken for what it is worth. Duchesne drank heavily, and was thought to take opium; he was eventually retired—though a good many years after this—for what was charitably called ill-health. Duchesne wrote home about what happened, and in his letter he says that it was a hottish night of April, with a very fine clear moon, nearly full, and that he was sleeping outside his tent. He started up about one in the morning with the almost ludicrous conviction that he had just heard the trumpet sound on the Day of Judgment, and that it had a peculiarly horrible sound. He was quite clear that what had wakened him was the blast of a monstrous horn; but at first he was conscious of nothing except an unusually oppressive and deathly stillness. Then, as he lay listening, the night remaining clear, bright, and airless, he heard in the direction of the ghat a roaring sound, as of a heavy wind in the trees. As this approached and grew louder, he became seized with overmastering terror; he threw himself about in his bed and sweated profusely. "I was convinced," says he, "that I was about to witness a manifestation of the devil and all his ministers." The thing, whatever it was, swept upon him in a few minutes, and passed over him with the effect of a terrific blast of wind; yet it was not a wind either, for the tent-flaps hung quite motionless, nothing fell over, and some papers he had been studying in bed before he went to sleep did not blow away. It lasted for about ninety seconds, and disturbed no one but himself. The night then continued close, brilliant, and serene.

That is Duchesne's story. He says further that the horn was heard in Khankota that night, but we have nothing for this beyond his own statement. There let it stand.

V

The narrative of Godfrey Moray has the advantage of being told by a prince of *shikaris,* whose books have carried the Indian jungles and their peoples over half the seas of the world. Moray calls the story "The Man-eater of Hoondi," that being the aspect which interested him most; it is only in manuscript, and you will not find it in any of his charming books on *shikar,* for reasons which he gives himself in the story. These are "partly because I have been at some pains to build up a reputation for strict veracity, which this yarn would most certainly annul; and partly because there are times when I myself begin to doubt if it ever could have happened."

Moray knew nothing of the history or tradition of Hoondi— it was a chance he ever learned its name; he had never heard of Josiah Macfadyen and the *Meriah* sacrifices; he had not read the Administration Reports; and in spite of what occurred to him, he never investigated the more or less authenticated instances of the horn's activities. He tells his story quite naively as an individual experience, and one can see that all along he is half-doubtful as to whether he did not dream it. This and his own special style—the matter-of-fact narrative with an occasional telling or picturesque phrase—make the story peculiarly interesting. There seems no doubt whatever that Moray neither dreamed nor imagined the happenings he records, and if he had realised or had taken the trouble to ascertain how much the sounding of the horn had been written of and discussed, he would not have shrunk from publishing his own contribution.

To cut out the unessentials, Moray was really looking for the record spotted stag up and down the Gamsatri River, in which valley if that creature is not to be found, it does not exist within the bounds of British India. It was when he was laid up for a day or two with fever at Khankota that he heard of a particularly bad man-eater that haunted the ghat-head at Hoondi, and had taken heavy toll of all coiners for the past two or three years. All this, mark you, was as recent as 1906, and Bodi and his secret with him had been in the grave for a quarter of a century.

Moray, having shot the best part of a score of man-eaters, was little interested, but he seems to have had a garrulous bearer, who regaled him through his convalescence—as no local would ever have done—with all the bazaar stories of this monstrous creature and its prowess. It was then Moray heard of the horn, which was now said to sound without human agency every time the man-eater claimed a victim. The general opinion was that the black god of Hoondi was god still, that the old days of human sacrifice were coming back, with the difference that, as the Government now forbade human agency to assist, the god claimed his victims by the stroke of this demoniac tiger. As of yore, the horn sounded to mark the consummation of the rite. But most striking of all were the accounts of the tiger. Some said it was black, some that it was fiery; some made it out of monstrous size or parts; some said it was not a tiger at all.

Moray was fired. He determined to look into the matter for himself, and from the moment he sets foot on the first steep of the Hoondi ghat, his story is worth following verbatim.

"We got up the ghat," he says, "in a few hours, the gradient being easy and the path for these parts good. It was very much the usual sort of place, thick bamboo on the lower slopes, *yegisi* and *nallamadi* and such trees higher up, with a good deal of Bauhinia creeper all over. I heard a jungle sheep coughing away, and now and then the screech of a Malabar squirrel, but saw no tracks. There was one striking place about a mile below the summit, where we came slap out into a clearing, and there, right in front of us, was a huge, round black rock, two or three hundred feet high, with a trace of ruins on the top of it. From these last the demon horn was wont to sound. It came so suddenly it was almost like coming out on to the top of some huge, dangerous beast. Rock scenery is always rather terrifying, I think, but this place—whether from all I had heard about it or not—produced a feeling I can't very well explain.

"At the top of the ghat was more trouble. There used to be a village called Kirridi hereabouts, where one could camp, but the scare of the man-eater—and other things—had driven every soul away. As no one would consent to pitch camp at the ghat-head itself, and as no supplies would have been forthcoming if we had, we were forced to trek on a very unnecessary three miles or so to another village. Here I could get very little done. I have often, of course, come across stories of demon tigers and so forth at some distance from the spot, but I have usually found that when one gets to his haunts the beast is a beast and nothing more, and the local *shikaris* are only too keen to come out on his trail. This wasn't so at Hoondi. I could not get a *shikari* of any sort to undertake the business; not one of the villagers would have anything to do with it. Even Ameer" (Ameer was the garrulous bearer already mentioned), "whom I had credited with more sense, began to suggest that I should leave the place alone; he had some long-winded tale about a policeman who had gone after a tiger hereabouts and had been caught by a devil, so that he himself went mad and all his following died. I am bound to admit that it was a most depressing bit of country;

one was never out of sight of that great black rock, and it tended to get upon one's nerves. I fancy it was feverish—more so, I mean, than ordinary.

"The only creature who did me any obligement was the man-eater himself. I had not been in camp a day when a squat-faced Gobhari came running in to say the man-eater had killed a fellow who had gone out looking for a lost bullock. The kill was just at the foot of the Hoondi rock on the ghat side. I have usually found some difficulty in such cases in persuading the relatives to let the body lie for me to sit up by: not so here. To begin with, no one would admit to being any sib to the deceased at all, and when at length a family was identified as being his, they were only too happy to let me do anything I liked, provided they were not asked to go near. I said I would sit up all that afternoon and night—the moon served splendidly—and at that they gazed at me in a kind of horror—and bolted!

"It ended, as I had expected, in my having everything to do myself. Fortunately the ground was easy, and if I had placed the kill with my own hand I could not have got a better situation. I rigged up a small *machan* with a screen of branches, and began to promise myself the Hoondi man-eater's skin.

"As I am now coming to decidedly queer occurrences, it seems right here to say a word or two as to the kill. It was perfectly normal: the man had got a smash on the back of the head, and only a very little had been eaten so far. I found a good many pug-marks, and from them I concluded that, as is often the case, the man-eater was a smallish beast. The man had come up to a little high ground to look about for his bullock; the brute had crept up alongside through a belt of bamboo and sprung out on him from behind. Let me say here and now that, if my experience as a *shikari* is worth anything at all, that unfortunate man was killed by an ordinary man-eating tiger, just as surely as any of the other thousand or so who appeared in that year's Government returns. Of that I have no doubt whatsoever.

What else could it have been? That is just the question I shall
be left asking at the end of this yarn.

"I had a very tedious sederunt. I was in my *machan* by two
in the afternoon, and by the fall of dusk nothing whatever had
happened. Considering that the beast had evidently killed deliberately and had eaten little or nothing, I was surprised at
this, and began to fear he must have winded me. I had expected
him by five at the latest. There was a bad interval, just after
dusk fell, before the moon would rise, when it was very dark
indeed, and the row of the crickets and the frogs in a little
swamp at the ghat-head made it difficult to catch any sound;
but at last the moon came sailing up from the direction of my
camp and climbed up the heavens, getting steadily brighter and
brighter. As I have said, I could not have placed the kill to
better advantage; the horrid object lay full in the broadest ray
of the moon, and would lie so for hours to come. About eight
I had a sandwich and a cigarette, and a little whisky and soda
from my flask. I believe strongly in these amenities on vigils of
this sort, and have always held that, if you make no noise over
it, a smoke does no harm; if the beast doesn't smell you yourself, the smoke won't worry him. I felt very happy and contented, and quite sure of the man-eater.

"I come now to happenings I find difficult to describe and
quite impossible to explain.

"From the time I took the refreshment, or perhaps I should
say from nine o'clock onwards, I began to feel less and less comfortable, not in my body but in my mind. Normally, I am never
so happy as when sitting up over a kill; I like the quiet sounds
and scents of the night, and the pleasant expectation. Now I
began to feel sensations that were quite new to me. All kinds
of gruesome ideas began to fill my mind. I began to think how
dreadful it would be if the corpse were to sit up and talk to me;
I began to picture myself dragged down and mauled by the tiger
—a thing I had never done in my life before; in fact, all sorts

of grisly and horrible ideas, most of which I cannot now recall, raced through my mind. I tried to put it down to fever, but I knew I had no fever. As the night went on it grew worse, and I think I may say that between the hours of nine and eleven that night I tasted to the very full the sensation of fear. It is a thing I had not known before. I am not boasting; I have many a time been thoroughly scared or frightened; but this crawling, deadly, sickening feeling of nameless terror was something utterly new. I could not wish my bitterest enemy anything worse.

"The thing—it is not for me to say what it was—came just before midnight. It conveyed itself to me first as a distant, rushing sound, then as a sudden darkening of the moon and a gust of wind. I saw no cloud and I felt no rush of air, yet the moon darkened and the wind seemed to blow. And then it was as if something—God or the devil knows what—swept roaring through the place and was gone. Time and again I have tried to reconstruct these moments and what I saw—or rather, for I don't think I actually saw anything, what I felt. Sometimes I think I saw a great black beast: sometimes a dark cloud: sometimes a shapeless body; I doubt if any of these impressions is worth a straw. All I can definitely say is that I had an impression of some immense rushing thing that swept past me; and I can further say that that thing swept up with it the body—which was that of a well-grown man—and carried it away, and I never saw it again. And I am further prepared to swear that whatever on earth or out of it it was, it was no tiger, man-eating or otherwise, that ever lived.

"I sat on in the *machan,* sweating and shivering like a horse. The moon seemed bright and clear again, and as I looked for the kill and saw it gone, the terror came on me afresh. I took out my flask, and as I unscrewed the top of it there burst out upon me the most dreadful sound I ever heard. The first of it was a long, sweeping howl running upwards till it seemed one's nerves must break; then it gave way to one long, indescribable note more fearful than any. It was just such a noise as might be made by a gigantic horn, and, unless I am a madman, it came from above me—from the summit of the rock of Hoondi."

I follow Moray no further; indeed, except for Hamlet's re-mark to Horatio anent things in heaven and earth, there seems nothing more to be said. We are left with a hundred questions all unanswerable. What happened to Bannerman's servants? From what were they running? What passed through Duchesne's tent in the semblance of a rushing wind? What took the man-eater's kill? Think of the age-old horror of Hoondi; figure to yourself, if you can, what things may have lurked about that fort and temple; suggest, if you dare, what manner of creature crept into these evil ruins and blew that monstrous horn. Thereafter, put yourself in the place of those forsaken men at Hoondi who heard that horn to sound, knowing well that it was never mortal man that blew.

The Abu Laheeb
Lord Dunsany (1926)

When I met my friend Murcote in London he talked much of his club. I had seldom heard of it, and the name of the street in which Murcote told me it stood was quite unknown to me, though I think I had driven through it in a taxi, and remembered the houses as being mean and small. And Murcote admitted that it was not very large, and had no billiard-table and very few rooms; and yet there seemed something about the place that entirely filled his mind and made that trivial street for him the centre of London. And when he wanted me to come and see it, I suggested the following day; but he put me off, and again when I suggested the next one. There was evidently nothing much to see, no pictures, no particular wines, nothing that other clubs boast of; but one heard tales there, he said—very odd ones sometimes; and if I cared to come and see the club, it would be a good thing to come some evening when old Jorkens was there. I asked who Jorkens was; and he said he had seen a lot of the world. And then we parted, and I forgot about Jorkens, and saw nothing more of Murcote for some days. And then one day Murcote rang me up, and asked me if I'd come to the club that evening.

I had agreed to come; but before I left my house Murcote surprised me by coming round to see me. There was something he wanted to tell me about Jorkens. He sat and talked to me for some time about Jorkens before we started, though all he said of him might be expressed by the one word 'liar.' Jorkens was a good-hearted fellow, he said, and would always tell a story in the evening to anyone who offered him a small drink;— whiskey and soda was what he preferred;—and he really had seen a good deal of the world, and the club relied on stories in the evening;—they were quite a feature of it;—and the club wouldn't be the club without them, and it helped the evening to pass, anyway; but one thing he must warn me, and that was never to believe a word Jorkens said. It wasn't Jorkens' fault; he didn't mean to be inaccurate; he merely wished to interest his fellow members and to make the evening pass pleasantly. He had nothing to gain by any inaccuracies, and had no intention to deceive; he just did his best to entertain the club, and all the members were grateful to him. But once more Murcote warned me never to believe one of his tales, or any part of them, not even the smallest detail of local color.

"I see," I said, "a bit of a liar."

"Oh, poor old Jorkens," said Murcote, "that's rather hard. But still, I've warned you, haven't I?"

And, with that quite clearly understood, we went down and hailed a taxi.

It was after dinner that we arrived at the club; and we went straight up into a small room, in which a group of members was sitting about near the fire, and I was introduced to Jorkens, who was sitting gazing into the glow, with a small table at his right hand. And then he turned to Murcote to pour out what he had probably already said to all the other members.

"A most unpleasant episode occurred here last evening," he said, "a thing I have never known before, and shouldn't have thought possible in any decent club—shouldn't have thought possible."

"Oh, really," said Murcote. "What happened?"

"A young fellow came in yesterday," said Jorkens. "They tell me he's called Carter. He came in here after dinner, and I hap-pened to be speaking about a curious experience I had once had in Africa, over the watershed of the Congo, somewhere about latitude six, a long time ago. Well, never mind the experience, but I had no sooner finished speaking about it when the young fellow—Carter or whatever he is—said simply he didn't believe me, simply and unmistakably that he disbelieved my story; claimed to know something of geography or zoology which did not tally in his impudent mind with the actual experience that I had had on the Congo side of the watershed. Now, what are you to do when a young fellow has the effrontery, the brazen-faced audacity—"

"Oh, but we must have him turned out," said Murcote. "A case like that should come before the Committee at once. Don't you think so?"

And his eye turned to the other members, roving till it fell on a weary and weak individual who was evidently one of the Committee.

"Oh—er—yes," said he unconvincingly.

"Well, Mr. Jorkens," said Murcote, "we'll get that done at once."

And one or two more members muttered "Yes," and Jorkens' indignation sank now to minor mutterings, and to occasional ejaculations that shot out petulantly, but in an undertone. The waters of his imagination were troubled still, though the storm was partly abated.

"It seems to me outrageous," I said, but hardly liked to say any more, being a guest in the club.

"Outrageous!" the old man replied, and we seemed no nearer to getting any story.

"I wonder if I might ask for a whiskey and soda?" I said to Murcote, for a silence had fallen; and at the same time I nodded sideways towards Jorkens to suggest the destination of the whiskey. I had waited for Murcote to do this without being asked, and now he ordered three whiskies and sodas listlessly, as though he thought there weren't much good in it. And when

the whiskey drew near the lonely table that waited desolate at
Jorkens' right hand, Jorkens said, "Not for me."

I thought I saw surprise for a moment pass like a ghost
through that room, although no one said anything.

"No," said old Jorkens, "I never drink whiskey. Now and
then I use it in order to stimulate my memory. It has a wonderful effect on the memory. But as a drink I never touch it. I
dislike the taste of it."

So his whiskey went away. We seemed no nearer that story.

I took my glass with very little soda, sitting in a chair near
Jorkens. I had nowhere to put it down.

"Might I put my glass on your table?" I said to Jorkens.

"Certainly," he said, with the utmost indifference in his
voice, but not entirely in his eye, which caught the deep yellow
flavor as I put it close to his elbow.

We sat for a long time in silence; everyone wanted to hear
him talk. And at last his right hand opened wide enough to take
a glass, and then closed again. And a while later it opened once
more, and moved a little along the table and then drew back,
as though for a moment he had thought the drink was his and
then had realized his mistake. It was a mere movement of the
hand, and yet it showed that here was a man who would not
consciously take another man's drink. And, that being clearly established, a dreamy look came over his face as though he
thought of far-off things, and his hand moved very absently. It
reached the glass unguided by his eye and brought it to his lips,
and he drained it, thinking of far other things.

"Dear me," he said suddenly, "I hope I haven't drunk your
whiskey."

"Not at all," I said.

"I was thinking of a very curious thing," he said, "and hardly
noticed what I was doing."

"Might I ask what it was you were thinking of?" I said.

"I really hardly like to tell you," he said, "to tell anyone,
after the most unpleasant incident that occurred yesterday."

As I looked at Murcote he seemed to divine my thoughts, and ordered three more whiskies.

It was wonderful how the whiskey did brighten old Jorkens' memory, for he spoke with a vividness of little details that could only have been memory; imagination could not have done it. I leave out the details and give the main points of his story for its zoological interest; for it touches upon a gap in zoology which I believe is probably there, and if the story is true it bridges it.

Here then is the story: "One that you won't often hear in London," said Jorkens, "but in towns at the Empire's edge it's told of often. There's probably not a mess out there in which it's not been discussed, scarcely a bungalow where it's not been talked of, and always with derision. In places like Malakal there's not a white man that hasn't heard of it, and not one that believes it. But the last white man that you meet on lonely journeys, the last white man that there is before the swamps begin and you see nothing for weeks but papyrus—he believes in it.

"I have noticed that more than once. Where a lot of men get together, all knowing equally little, and this subject comes up, one will laugh, and they will all laugh at it, and none will trust his imagination to study the rumor, and it remains a rumor, no more. But when a man gets all alone by himself, somewhere on the fringe of that country out of which the rumor arises, and there's no silly laughter to scare his imagination—why, then he can study the thing and develop it, and get much nearer to facts than mere incredulity will ever get him. I find a touch of fever helps in working out problems like that.

"Well, the problem is a very simple one; it is simply the question whether man with his wisdom and curiosity has discovered all the animals that there are in the world, or whether there's one, and a very curious one too, hidden amongst the papyrus, that white men have never seen. And that's not quite what I mean, for there are white men that have seen things that not every young whipper-snapper will believe. I should rather have said an animal that our civilization has not yet taken cognizance of. At Kosti, more than twenty years ago, I first heard two men definitely speak of it,—the *abu laheeb* they called it,—and I think they both believed in it too; but Khartoum was only a hundred and fifty miles off, and they had evening clothes with them, and used to wear them at dinner, and they had china plates and silver forks, and ornaments on their mantelpiece, and one thing and another; and all these things seemed to appall their imagination, and they wouldn't honestly let themselves believe it. 'Had three or four fires round his tent,' said one of them, telling of someone, 'and says that the abu laheeb came down about two a.m., and he saw it clear in the firelight.' 'Did it get what it wanted?' said the other. 'Yes— went away hugging it.'

"And one of them said in a rather wandering tone: 'The only animal that uses—' He was lowering his voice, and looking round, and he saw me, and said no more. They turned it all away at once with a laugh or two, as Columbus might have turned away from the long low line of land and refused to believe a new continent. I questioned them, but got no information that could be of any use; they seemed to like laughter more than imagination, so I got jokes instead of truth.

"It was weeks later and far southwards that I found a man who was ready to approach this most interesting point of zoology in the proper spirit of a scientist, a white man all alone in a hut that he had near the mouth of the Bahr-el-Zeraf. There are things in Africa that you couldn't believe, and the Bahr-el-Zeraf is one of them. It rises out of the marshes of the White Nile, and flows forty or fifty miles, and into the White Nile again. And one can't easily believe in a white man living all alone in such a place as that, but somebody has to be the last white man you see as you go through the final fringes of civilization, and it was him. He had had full opportunities of studying the whole question of the abu laheeb, he had had years of leisure to compare all the stories the natives brought him, which they shyly told when he had won their confidence, though what he won it with he never told. He had sifted the evidence and knew all that was told about it; and in long malarial nights, with no one and nothing to care for him but quinine, he had pictured the beast so clearly that he could make me a very good drawing of it. I have that drawing to this very day—a beast on his hind legs something like a South American sloth that I once saw, stuffed, in a museum; built rather on the lines of a kangaroo, but much stouter and bigger, and with nothing pointed about his face; it was square and blunt, with great teeth. He had hand-like paws on shortish arms or forelegs.

"I must tell you that I was in a small dahabeeyah, going up those great rivers, any great rivers I might meet, leaving civilization because I was tired of it, and looking for wonders in Africa. And I came to this lonely man.—Lindon his name was,—full of curiosity aroused by those words that I had heard in Malakal. And talking to Lindon like two old friends that have spent all their schooldays together, as white men will who meet in that part of Africa, I soon came to the abu laheeb, thinking he would know more of it than they knew in Malakal. And I found a man grown sensitive, as you only can grow in loneliness: he feared I would disbelieve him, and would scarcely say a word. Yes, the natives believed in some such animal, but his own opinion he would not expose to the possibility of my ridicule. The more questions I asked, the shorter the answers became. And then I drew him by saying, 'Well, there's one thing he uses that no other animal ever did,' the one mysterious thing about this beast that had haunted my mind for weeks, though I did not know what on earth the mystery was. And that got him talking. He saw that I was committed to belief in the beast, and was no longer shy of his own.

"He told me that the upper reaches of the Bahr-el-Zeraf were a god-forsaken place: 'And if God forsook the Zeraf,' he said, 'He certainly didn't go to the Jebel,' for the Bahr-el-Jebel was worse. And somewhere between those two rivers in the desolation of papyrus the abu laheeb certainly lived. He very reasonably said that there were beasts in the plains, beasts in the forests, and beasts in the sea; why not in the huge area of the papyrus into which no man had ever penetrated? If I chose to go to these god-forsaken places I could see the abu laheeb, he said. 'But, of course,' he added, 'you must never go up wind on him.' 'Down wind?' I said. 'No, nor down wind either,' he answered. 'He can smell as well as a rhino. That's the difficulty; you have to go just between up wind and down wind; and you always find the north wind blowing there.'

"It was some while before I discovered why one can't go up wind on him. I didn't like to over-question Lindon, for questions are akin to criticism, and you cannot apply criticism and cross-examination to the patient work of imagination upon rumor; it is liable to destroy the whole fabric, and one loses valuable scientific data. Nor was Lindon in the mood for the superior disbelief of a traveler only just come from civilization; he had had malaria too recently to put up with that sort of thing. It was as he was giving me various clear proofs of the existence of some such animal that I suddenly realized what it all meant. He was telling me how more than once he had seen fires in the reeds, not only earlier in the year than the Dinkas light their fires, but in marshes where no Dinka would ever come, nor a Shilluk either, or any kind of man—marshes utterly desolate and for ever shut to humanity. It was then that the truth flashed on me—truth, sir, that I have since verified with my own eyes: that the abu laheeb plays with fire.

"Well, I needn't tell you how the idea flared up in my mind to be the first white man that had ever seen the abu laheeb, and to shoot him and bring his huge skin home, and have something to show for all that lonely wandering. It was a fascinating idea. I asked Lindon if he thought my rifle was big enough,—I only had a .350,—and whether to use soft-nosed or solid bullets. 'Soft,' he said. I sat up late and asked him many questions. And he warned me about those marshes. I needn't tell you of all the things he warned me against, because you see me alive before you; but they were there all right, they were there. And I went down the little path he'd made from his house to the bank of the river, and went on board my sailing boat under huge white bands of stars, and lay down on board and looked up at them from under my blankets until I fell asleep, while the Arabs cast off and the north wind held good. And when the sun blazed on me at dawn I woke to the Bahr-el-Zeraf. Scarlet trees with green foliage at first; we were not yet come to those marshes.

"Well, for days we went up the Zeraf, past the white fish-eagles, haughty and silent and watchful on queer trees, with birds sailing over us that I daren't describe to you for fear you should think I exaggerate the brilliancy of their colors. And so we came to those marshes where anything might hide, and be utterly hidden by those miles of rushes, and be well enough protected from explorers by a region of monotony more dismal than any other desolate land I've seen. And all the while the sailors were talking a language I did not know, till my imagination, brooding in that monotony, seemed to hear clear English phrases now and then starting suddenly out of their talk, commonest phrases of our daily affairs, on the other side of the earth. I would swear that I heard one of them say one evening, 'Stop the bus a moment.' But it couldn't have been, for they were talking Dinka talk, and not one of them knew a single word of English; I used to talk Arabic of a sort to the reis.

"Well, at last we came on fires in the reeds, burning at different points. Who lit them I couldn't say; there were no men there, black, white, or grey (the Dinkas are grey, you know). But I wanted absolute proof; and then one day I found his tracks in the rushes. He bounds through the rushes, you know, often breaking several of them where he takes off, and sometimes scattering mud on the tips of them as he springs through; then alighting and taking off again, leaving another huge mark.

"I examined the rushes carefully, till I was sure that I had his tracks. And then I followed them, always watching the wind.

It was a dreadful walk. I went alone so as to make less noise.
I wanted to get quite close and make sure of my shot. I had a
haversack tied close round my neck, and my cartridges were in
that. Even then it got wet sometimes. The water was always up
to my waist, and often it came higher. I had to hold up my rifle
in one hand all the time. The reeds were far over my head.

"Sometimes one came to open spaces of water, with huge
blue water-lilies floating on them. And it was always deeper
there. Sometimes one walked upon the roots of the rushes, and
all the rushes trembled round one for yards, and sometimes one
found a bottom of good hard clay and knew one could sink no
further. And all the while I was tracking the abu laheeb.

"The north wind blew as usual. I was too old a shikari to be
walking down wind, but I was not always able to act strictly on
Lindon's advice about never going up wind on the abu laheeb,
because his tracks sometimes led that way. At any rate, that was
better than the other direction, for he would have been off at
once. You wouldn't believe how tired one can be of blue water-
lilies. At any rate the water was not cold, but the weariness of
lifting each foot was terrible. Each foot, as one lifted it for
every step, one would rather have left just where it was for ever.
I don't know how many hours I tracked that beast, I don't know
what time was doing while I walked in those marshes. But in
all that weariness of spirit and utter fatigue of limb I suddenly
saw a scrap of quite fresh mud on the tip of one of the reeds,
and knew that I was getting near him at last. I put the safety
catch of my rifle over, and suddenly saw in my mind what I
was so nearly doing for Science. Of all the steps Science had
taken from out of the early darkness toward that distant point
of which we cannot guess, which shall be full of revelations to
man, one of her footsteps would be due to me. I could, as it
were, write my name on that one footprint, and no one would
question my right to.

"I got nearer and nearer. I was no longer weary now; and
suddenly, closer than I had dared to hope, was a little puff of

smoke above the rushes. I stopped for one moment to steady my breath, and got my rifle ready. In that moment I named him—yes, I called him *Prometheus Jorkensi*. There was a patch of dry land ahead, and the rushes still protected me. I moved with ten-inch paces so as to make no ripple, but I couldn't keep the rushes quiet; perhaps the north wind blew stronger than I thought, for he never seemed to hear me. And then, oh so close that it couldn't have been ten yards, I saw the little fire on a patch of earth; and the rushes still hid me completely. I saw a patch of brown fur and a huge body crouching. I could only guess what part of the body I saw, but a vital part I thought, and I raised my rifle. Still it had no idea I was anywhere near it. And then I saw its hands stretched out to the fire, warming themselves by the edge of those bleak marshes. I don't cut much ice, you know; I didn't then; no one had ever heard my name, or, if they had, it meant nothing; and here was I on the verge of this discovery, with the proof of it ten yards away just waiting for a rifle bullet. I'd shoot a monkey, I'd shoot an ape, I'd shoot a poor old hippo; I wouldn't mind shooting a horse if it had to be killed, though lots of men can't bear that; but those black hands stretched out over the fire were the one thing I couldn't destroy.

"The idea that flashed on me standing amongst those reeds I have been turning over in my mind for years, and it always seemed sound to me, and it does even now. You see, of all the links in the world that there are between us, and of all the barriers against those that are not as us, it seems to me that there is one link, one barrier, more outstanding than any other you could possibly name. We talk of our human reason, that may or may not be superior to the dream of the dog or the elephant: we say it is—that is all. We say that we alone have belief in an after-life, and that the lion has not: we say so—that's all. Some of them are stronger, some live longer than us, many may be more cunning. But there is one thing, gentlemen, one thing they haven't got, and that is the knowledge of fire. That seems

to me the great link, the great bond between all who have it and
the barrier against all who have not. Look what we've done with
it: look at those fire-irons, that fender, the bricks of which this
house is made, and the steel structure of it; look at this whole
city. That's our one great possession—knowledge of fire. And,
when I saw those dark hands stretched out to that fire on the
edge of the marshes, that is what I thought of all at once, not at
such length as I have told you of course,—it flashed all through
my mind in a moment,—but during that moment I hesitated,
and the abu laheeb saw the sun on the tip of my rifle or heard
me breathing there, for he suddenly craned his great neck over
the rushes, then stooped again and scattered the fire with his
forepaws with one swift jerk into the reeds all round me. They
were alight at once, and through the flame and smoke I only
dimly caught sight of him leaping away, but, above the crackle
of the burning reeds and the thump of his hind legs leaping, I
heard him uttering gusts of human-like laughter."

He paused a moment. We were all quite silent, thinking what
he had lost. He had lost a famous name. He shook his head, and
seemed full of the same thoughts as the rest of us.

"I never went after him again," he said. "I had seen him, but
who'll believe that? I have never quite been able to bring myself
any more to try to shoot a creature that shared that great secret
with us."

There was silence again; we were wondering, I think, whether his scruples should have prevented him from doing so much
for Science. I suppose that the too-sensitive and over-scrupu-
lous seldom make famous names. A man leaning forward, and
smoking a pipe, took his pipe out of his mouth and broke the
silence at last.

"Mightn't you have photographed him?" he said.

"Photographed him!" said Mr. Jorkens, straightening himself up in his chair. "Photographed him! Aren't half the photographs fakes? Here, look at the *Evening Picture*. Look at that,

now. There's a child handing a bouquet to someone with its left hand, so that both of them may expose as much of their surface as possible to the camera. And here's a man welcoming his brother from abroad. Welcoming indeed! They are both of them being photographed, and that's obviously all that they're doing."

We looked at the paper and it was so; they were almost turning their backs on one another in order to be photographed.

"No," he said, and he looked me straight in the eyes, and flashed that glance of his from face to face. "If Truth cannot stand alone, she scorns the cheap aid of photography."

So dominant was his voice as he said these words, so flashed his eyes in the dim light of the room, that none of us spoke any more. I think we felt that our voices would shock the silence. And we all went quietly away.

The Tree-Man
Henry S. Whitehead (1931)

My first sight of Fabricius, the tree-man, was within a week of my first arrival on the island of Santa Cruz not long after the United States had purchased the Danish West Indies and officially re-named its new colony the Virgin Islands of the United States.

My ship came into Frederiksted harbour on the west coast of the island just at dusk and I saw for the first time a half-moon of white sand beach with the charming little town in its middle. In the midst of the bustle incident to anchoring in the roadstead, there came over the side an upstanding gentleman in a glistening white drill uniform who came up to me, bowed in a manner to commend itself to kings, and said:

"I am honoured to welcome you to Santa Cruz, Mr. Canevin. I am Director Despard of the Police Department. The police boat is at your disposal when you are ready to go ashore. May I see to your luggage?"

This was a welcome indeed. I was nearly knocked off my feet by such an unexpected reception. I thanked Director Despard and before many minutes my trunks were overside, my luggage bestowed in the police boat waiting at the foot of the ladder-gangway, and I was seated beside him in the boat's stern-sheets, he holding the tiller-ropes while four coal-black convicts rowed us ashore with lusty pulls at their long sweeps.

Through the lowering dusk as we approached the landing I observed that the wharf was crowded with black people. Behind these stood half a dozen knots of white people, conversing together. A long row of cars stood against the background of waterfront buildings. I remarked to the Police Director:

"Isn't it unusual for so many persons to be on the docks for the arrival of a vessel, Mr. Director?"

"It is not usual," replied the dignified gentleman beside me. "It is for you, Mr. Canevin."

"For me?" said I. "Extraordinary! What—for me? Certainly,—my dear sir,—certainly not for me. Why, it's . . ."

Mr. Despard turned about and smiled at me.

"You are Captain McMillin's great-nephew, you know, Mr. Canevin."

So that was it. My great-uncle, one of my Scots kinsfolk, my great-uncle who had died many years before I had seen the light of day, my grandfather's oldest brother, the one who had been in the British Army and later a planter here on Santa Cruz. He had been the very last person I should have thought of, and now—

The police boat landed smartly at the concrete jetty. Mr. Despard and I landed, and in the lowering dusk I could not help noticing the quietly-expressed but very genuine interest of the thousand or more negroes who thronged the wharf as they courteously parted a way for us while we proceeded towards the groups of white people, thronging forward now with an unanimous and unmistakable greeting shining from dozens of kindly faces.

I will pass over the rest of that first evening ashore. At the end of it and all its lavish hospitality I found myself comfortably installed in a small private hotel pending the final preparations to my own hired residence. I found every estate-house on Santa Cruz open to me. Hospitalities were showered upon me to the point of embarrassment, kindnesses galore, considerate and timely bits of information, help of every imaginable kind. I learned in this process much about my late great-uncle, all of which information was new to me, and it was not long after my arrival when it was arranged for me to visit his estate, Great Fountain.

I went with Hans Grumbach, in his Ford car, a bumpy journey of more than three hours up hills and through ravines and along precipitous trails on old roads incredibly roundabout and primitive.

All the way Hans Grumbach talked about this section of the island, now rarely visited. Here, up to ten years before, Grumbach had lived as the last of a long line of estate-managers which the old place had had in residence since the day, in 1879, when my Scottish relatives had sold their Santa Crucian holdings. It was now the property of the largest of the local sugar-growing corporations, known as the Copenhagen Concern. Because of its inaccessibility cultivation on it had finally been abandoned and Hans Grumbach had come to live in Frederiksted, married the daughter of a respectable *creole* family, and settled down to keeping store on one of the town's side streets.

But, it came out, Grumbach had wanted for all those ten years, to go back to the northern hills. This trip to the old place stimulated his loquacity. He sang its praises: the beauty of its configuration, its magnificent views and vistas, the amazing fertility of its soil.

We arrived at last. All about us the vegetation had grown to be ideally tropical, the "tropical" of old-fashioned pictures on calendars! The soil appeared to be rich, blackish "bottomland."

The old estate was in a sad state of rack and ruin. We walked over a good part of it under the convoy of the courteous black caretaker, and looked out over its rolling domain from various angles and coigns of vantage. The Negro village was half tumbled-down. The cabins remaining were all out of repair. The characteristic quick tropical inroads upon land "turned out" of active cultivation were everywhere apparent. The ancient Great House was entirely gone. The farm buildings, though built of sound stone and mortar, were terribly dilapidated.

On that visit to Great Fountain I had my first experience of the "grapevine" method of communication among Africans. I had been perhaps four days on the island, and it is reasonably certain that none of these people had ever so much as heard of me before; these obscure village negroes cut off here in the hills from others the nearest of whom lived miles away. Yet, we had hardly come within a stone's throw of the remains of the village before we were surrounded by the total population, of perhaps twenty adults, and at least as many children of all ages.

As one would expect, these blacks were of very crude appearance; not only "country negroes" but that in an exaggerated form. Negroes in the West Indies have some tendency to live on the land where they originated, and as it happened most of these negroes had been born up here and several generations of their forebears before them.

We had brought our lunch along, and this Hans Grumbach and I ate sitting in the Ford under the shade of a grove of magnificent old mahogany trees, and afterwards Grumbach took me up along a ravine to see the "fountain" from which the old estate had originally derived its title.

The "fountain" itself was a delicate natural waterfall, streaming thinly over the edge of a high rock. It was when we were coming back, by a slightly different route, for Grumbach wanted me to take in everything possible, that I saw the tree-man.

He stood, a youngish, coal-black Negro, of about twenty-five years, scantily dressed in a tattered shirt and a sketchy pair of trousers, about ten yards away from the field-path we were following and from which a clear view of a portion of the estate was obtained, and beside him, towering over him, was a magnificent coconut-palm. The Negro stood motionless. I thought, in fact, that he had gone asleep standing there, both arms clasped about the tree's smooth, elegant trunk, the right side of his face pressed against it.

He was not, however, asleep, because I looked back at him and his eyes—rather intelligent eyes, they seemed to me—were wide open, although to my surprise he had not changed his position, nor even the direction of his gaze, to glance at us; and, I was quite sure, he had not been in that village group when we had stood among them just before our lunch.

Grumbach did not speak to him, as he had done to every other Negro we had seen. Indeed, I observed that his face looked a trifle—well, apprehensive; and I thought he very slightly quickened his pace. I stepped nearer to him as we walked past the man and the tree, and then I noticed that his lips were moving, and when I came closer I observed that he was muttering to himself. I said, very quietly, almost in his ear:

"What's the matter with that fellow, Grumbach?"

Grumbach glanced at me out of the corner of his eye, and my impression that he was disturbed grew upon me.

"He's listening!" was all that I got out of Grumbach. I supposed, of course, that there was something odd about the fellow; perhaps he was slightly demented and might be an annoyance; and I supposed that Grumbach meant to convey that the young fellow was "listening" for our possible comment upon him and his strange behaviour. Later, after we had said good-bye to the courteous caretaker and he had seen us off down the first hillside road, with its many ruts, I brought up the subject of the young black fellow at the tree.

"You mentioned that he was listening," said I, "so I dropped the matter, but, why does he do that, Grumbach— I mean, why does he stand against the tree in that unusual manner? Why, he didn't even gee his eyes to look at us, and that surprised me. They don't have visitors up here every day, I understand."

"He was listening—to *his* tree!" said Hans Grumbach, as though reluctantly. "*That* was what I meant, Mr. Canevin." And

he drew my attention to an extraordinarily picturesque ruined
windmill, the kind once used for the grinding of cane in the
old days of "muscovado" sugar, which dominated a cone-like
hillside off to our left as we bumped over the road. It was not
until months later, when I had gained the confidence of Hans
Grumbach, that that individual gave me any further enlightenment on the subject of the man and his tree.

Then I learned that, along with his nostalgia for the life of
an agriculturist—an incurable matter with some persons I have
found—there was mixed in with his feelings about the Great
Fountain estate a kind of inconsistent thankfulness that he was
no longer stationed there! This inconsistency, this being dragged sentimentally in two opposite directions, rather intrigued
me. I saw something of Grumbach and got rather well acquainted
with him as the months passed that first year of my residence.
Bit by bit, in his reluctant manner of speech, it came out.

To put the whole picture of his mind on this subject together, I got the idea that Grumbach, while always suffering
from a faint nostalgia for his deep-country residence and the
joys of tilling the soil, felt, somehow, safe here in the town. If
he chafed, mildly, at the restrictions of town life and his store-
keeping, there was yet the certainty that "something"—a vague
matter at first, as it came out—was not always hanging over
him; something connected with a lingering fear.

The negroes, it appeared—this came to me very gradually,
of course—up there at Great Fountain, were not, quite, like the
rest of the island's black population; in the two towns; out on
the many sugar-estates; even those residues of village commu-
nities which continued to live, in that mild, beneficent climate,
on "turned-out" estate land because there was no one sufficiently interested to eject these squatters. No—the Great Fountain
village was, somehow, at least in Hans Grumbach's dark hints,
different; *sui generis;* a peculiar people.

They were, to begin with, almost purely of Dahomeyan
stock. These Dahomeyans had drifted "down the islands" from

Hayti, beginning soon after the revolt against France in the early Nineteenth Century. They were tall, very black, extremely clannish blacks. And just as the Loromantyn slaves in British Jamaica had brought to the West Indies their *Obay-i-,* or herb-magic, so, it seemed, had the Dahomeyans carried with them from Guinea their *vodu,* which properly defined, means the practices accompanying the worship of "the Snake."

This worship, grown into a vast localised *cultus* in unfettered Hayti and in the Guiana hinterlands down in South America, is very imperfectly understood. But its accompaniments, all the charms, *ouangas,* philtres, potions, talismans, amulets, "doctoring" and whatnot, have spread all through the West India islands, and these are thoroughly established in highly developed and widely variant forms. Hayti is its West Indian home, of course. But down in French Martinique its extent and intensity is a fair rival to the Haytian supremacy. It is rife on Dominica, Guadeloupe, even on British Montserrat. Indeed, one might name every island from Cuba to Trinidad, and, allowing for the variations, the local preferences, and all such matters, one might say, and truly, that the *vodu,* generically described by the blacks themselves as "obi," is very thoroughly established.

According to Grumbach, the handful of villagers at Great Fountain was very deeply involved in this sort of thing. Left to themselves as they had been for many years, forming a little, self-sustaining community of nearly pure-blooded Dahomeyans, they had, it seemed, reverted very nearly to their African type; and this, Grumbach alleged, was the fact despite their easy kindliness, their use of "English," and the various other outward appearances which caused them to seem not greatly different from other "country negroes" on this island of Santa Cruz.

Grumbach had known Silvio Fabricius since he had been a pick'ny on the estate. He knew, so far as his limited understanding of black people's magic extended, all about Silvio. He had been estate-manager at the time the boy had begun his attentions to the great coconut palm. He had heard and seen what he called the "stupidness" which had attended the setting apart of this neophyte. There had been three days—and nights; particularly the nights—when not a single plantation-hand would do a piece of work for any consideration. It was, as Grumbach bitterly remembered it all, "the crop season." His employers, not sensing, businessmen as they were, any underlying reason for no work done when they needed the cane from Great Fountain for their grinding-mill, had been hard on him. They had, in Santa Crucian phraseology, "pressed him" for cane deliveries. And there, in his village, quite utterly ignoring his authority as estate-manager, those blacks had danced and pounded drums, and burned flares, and weaved back and forth in their interminable ceremonies—"stupidness"—for three strategic days and nights, over something which had Silvio Fabricius, then a rising pick'ny of twelve or thirteen, as its apparent centre and underlying cause. It was no wonder that Hans Grumbach raved and probably swore mightily and threatened the estate-hands.

But his anger and annoyance, the threats and cajolings, the offers of "snaps" of rum, and pay for piece-work; all these efforts to get his ripe cane cut and delivered; had come to nothing. The carts stood empty. The mules gravely ate the long guinea-grass. The cane-tops waved in the soft breath of the North-East Trade Wind, while those three days stretched themselves out to their conclusion.

This conclusion, which was ceremonial, took place in the daytime, about ten o'clock in the morning of the fourth day. After that, which was a very brief and apparently meaningless matter indeed, the hands sheepishly resumed the driving of their mule-carts and the swinging of their cane-bills, and once more the Fountain cane travelled slowly down the rutted hill road towards the factory below. On that morning, before resuming their work, the whole village had accompanied young Silvio Fabricius in silence as he walked ahead of them up towards the source of the perennial stream, stepped out into the field, and

clasped his arms about a young, but tall and promising coconut
palm which stood there as though accidentally in solitary towering grandeur. There the villagers had left the little black boy
when they turned away and filed slowly and silently back to the
village and to their interrupted labour.

And there, beside his tree, Grumbach said, Silvio Fabricius
had stood ever since, only occasionally coming in to the village
and then at any hour of the day or night, apparently "reporting"
something to the oldest inhabitant, a gnarled, ancient grandfather with pure white wool. After such a brief visit Fabricius
would at once, and with an unshaken gravity, return to his
tree. Food, said Grumbach, was always carried out to him from
the village. He toiled not, neither spun! There, day and night,
under the blazing sun, through showers and drenching down-
pours, erect, apparently unsleeping—unless he slept standing
up against his tree as Grumbach suspected—stood Silvio Fabricius, and there he had stood, except when he climbed the tree
to trim out the "cloth" or chase out a rat intent on nesting up
there, or to gather the coconuts, for eleven years.

The coconuts, it seemed, were his perquisite. They were,
Grumbach said, absolutely *tabu* to anybody else. It was over the
question of some green coconuts from this superior tree that
Grumbach himself, with all his authority as estate-manager behind his demand, had come to grips with Silvio Fabricius; or,
to be more precise, with the entire estate-village.

I never succeeded in getting this story in detail from Grumbach, who was plainly reluctant to tell it. It reflected, you see,
upon him; his authority as estate-manager, his pride, were here
heavily involved. But, as I gathered it, his houseman, sent to
that particular tree for a basket of green coconuts—Grumbach
was entertaining some friends and wanted the coconut-water
and jelly to put in a Danish concoction based on Holland gin—
had returned half an hour late, delivered the coconuts, and
later, it came out that he had gone *down* the hill to a neighbouring estate for the nuts. Taken to task for this duplicity, the

house-man had balked, "gone stupid" over the affair, and upon the dispute which followed the village itself had joined in. The conclusion, as Grumbach gathered it, to his great mystification, was that the coconut tree "belonged to" young Silvio Fabricius, was *tabu,* and that the village was solid against him on the issue. He, the manager, with control of everything, could not get coconuts from the best tree on the estate! This, attributed to the usual black "stupidness" had rankled. It also more or less accounted for Grumbach's attitude towards Silvio Fabricius, an attitude which I myself had witnessed. That his "fear" of this young negro went deeper than that, I sensed, however. I was, later, to see that suspicion justified.

For a long time I had no occasion to revisit Great Fountain. But six years later, while in the States during the summer, I made the acquaintance of a man named Carrington who wanted to know "all about the Virgin Islands" with a view to investing some money there in a proposal to grow pineapples on a large scale. I talked with Mr. Carrington at some length, and in the course of our discussions it occurred to me that Great Fountain estate would be virtually ideal for his purpose. Here was a very considerable acreage of rich land: the Copenhagen Company would probably rent it out for a period of ten years for a very reasonable price since it was bringing them in nothing. I spread before Carrington these advantages, and he travelled down on the ship with me that autumn to make an investigation in person.

Carrington, a trained fruit-grower, spent a day with me on the estate, and thereafter with characteristic American energy started in to put his plan into practice. A lease was easily secured, the village was repaired and the fallen stone cabins rebuilt, and within a few weeks cultivating machinery of the most modern type began to arrive on the Frederiksted wharf.

After a considerable consultation with Hans Grumbach, to whose lamentations over the restrictions of town-life I had been listening for years, I recommended him to Mr. Carrington as manager of the labourers, and Hans, after going over the matter with his good wife and coming to an amicable understanding, went back to Great Fountain where a manager's house had been thrown up for him on the foundation of one of the ruined buildings. At Carrington's direction, Grumbach set the estate labourers at work on the job of repairing the roads; and, as the village cabins went up, one after another, labourers, enticed by the prospect of good wages, filled them up and ancient Great Fountain became once more a busy scene of industry.

During these preparatory works I spent a good deal of time on the estate because I was naturally interested in Joseph Carrington's venture being a success. I had, indeed, put several thousand dollars into it myself, not solely because it looked like a good investment, but in part for sentimental reasons connected with my great-uncle. Being by then thoroughly familiar with the odd native speech, I made it a point to visit the village and talk at length with the "people." They were courteous to me, markedly so; deferential would be a better word to describe their attitude. This, of course, was wholly due to the family connection. Only a very few of them, and those the oldest, had any personal recollection of Captain McMillin, but his memory was decidedly green among them. The old gentleman had been greatly beloved by the negroes of the island.

In the course of my reading I had run across the peculiar affair of a "tree-man." I understood, therefore, the status of Silvio Fabricius in that queer little black community; why he had been "devoted" to the tree; what were the underlying reasons for that strange sacrifice.

It was, on the part of that handful of nearly pure-blooded Dahomeyan villagers there at my great-uncle's old place, a revival of a custom probably as old as African civilisation. For— the African *has* a civilisation. He is at a vast disadvantage when among Caucasians, competing, as he necessarily must, with Caucasian "cultures." His native problems are entirely different, utterly diverse, from the white man's. The African's whole history among us Caucasians is a history of more or less successful adaptation. Place an average American businessman in the heart of "uncivilised" Africa, in the Liberian hinterland, for example, and what will he do—how survive? The answer is simple. He will perish miserably, confronted with the black jungle night, the venomous reptilian and insect-life, the attacks of wild beasts, the basic problems of how to feed and warm himself—for even this last is an African problem. I know. I have been on *safari* in Uganda, in British East Africa, in Somaliland. I speak from experience.

Africans, supposedly static in cultural matters, have solved all these problems. And, very prominent among these, especially as it concerns the agricultural peoples; for there are, perhaps, as many black nations, kindreds, peoples, tongues, as there are Caucasian; is, of course, the question of weather.

Hence, the "tree-man."

Set apart with ceremonies which were ancient when Hammurabi sat on his throne in Babylon, a young boy is dedicated to a forest tree. Thereafter he spends his life beside that tree, cares for it, tends it, listens to it; becomes "the-brother-of-the-tree" in time. He is truly "set apart." To the tree he devotes his entire life, dying at last beside it, in its shade. And—this is African "culture" if you will; a culture of which we Caucasians get, perhaps, the faint reactions in the (to us) meaningless jumble of negro superstition which we sense all about us; the "stupidness" of the West Indies; faint, incomprehensible reflections of a system as practical, as dogmatic, as utilitarian, as the now well-nigh universal system of synthetic exercise for the tired businessman which goes by the name of golf!

These negroes at Great Fountain were, primarily, agriculturists. They had the use of the soil bred deeply in their blood and bones. That, indeed, is why the canny French brought their Hispaniola slaves from Dahomey. Left to themselves at the old estate in the north central hills of Santa Cruz the little community rapidly reverted to their African ways. They tilled the soil, sporadically, it is true, yet they tilled it. They needed a weather prognosticator. There are sudden storms in summer throughout the vast sweep of the West India Islands, devastating storms, hurricanes indeed; long, wasting periods of drought. They needed a tree-man up there. They set apart Silvio Fabricius.

That fact made the young fellow what a white man would call "scared." Not for nothing had they danced and performed their "stupid" rites those three long days and nights to the detriment of Hans Grumbach's deliveries. No. Silvio Fabricius, from the moment he had clasped his arms about that growing coconut-palm, was as much a person "set apart," dedicated, as any white man's pundit, priest, or yogi. Hence the various *tabus* which, like the case of the green coconuts, had puzzled Hans Grumbach. He must never take his attention away from the tree. There, beside it, he was consecrated to live and to die. When he departed from his "brother" the tree, it was only for the purpose of reporting something which the tribe should know; something, that is, which his brother the tree had told him! There would be drenching rain the second day following. A plague of small green flies would, the third day later, come to annoy the animals. The banana grove must be propped forthwith. Otherwise, a high wind, two days hence, would nullify all the work of its planting and care.

Such were the messages that Silvio Fabricius, austere, introspective, unnoticing, his mind fully preoccupied with his brotherhood to the tree, brought to his tribe; proceeding, the message delivered, austerely back to his station beside the magnificent palm.

All this, because of my status as the great-nephew of an old Bukra whom he remembered with love and reverence, and because he discovered that I knew about tree-men and many other matters usually sealed books to Bukras, the old fellow who was the village patriarch, who, by right of his seniority, received and passed on from Silvio the messages from Silvio's brother the tree, amply substantiated. There was nothing secretive about him, once he knew my interest in these things. Such procedure

as securing the possession of a tree-man for his tribe seemed to
the old man entirely reasonable; there was no necessary secret
about it, certainly not from sympathetic me, the "yoong marster" of Great Fountain Estate.

And Hans Grumbach, once he had finished with his roadwork, not being aware of all this, but sensing something out of
the ordinary and hence to be feared about Silvio Fabricius and
his palm tree, decided to end the stupidness out there. Grumbach decided to cut down the tree.

If I had had any inkling of this intention I could have saved
Grumbach. It would have been a comparatively simple matter
for me to have said enough to Carrington to have him forbid it;
or, indeed, as a partner in the control of the estate, to forbid it
myself. But I knew nothing about it, and have in my statement
of his intention to destroy the tree supplied my own conception
of his motives.

Grumbach, although virtually Caucasian in appearance,
was of mixed blood, and quite without the Caucasian background of superior quality which makes the educated West
Indian mestizo the splendid citizen he is in so many notable
instances. His white ancestry was derived from a grandfather,
a Schleswig-Holsteiner, who had been a sergeant of the Danish
troops stationed on Santa Cruz and who, after the term of his
enlistment had expired, had married into a respectable coloured
family, and remained on the island. Grumbach was without
the Caucasian aristocrat's tolerance for the preoccupations of
the blacks. To him such affairs were "stupidness," merely. Like
others of his kind he held the black people in a kind of contempt;
was wholly, I imagine, without sympathy for them, though a
worthy fellow enough in his limited way. And, perhaps, he had
not enough Negro in him to understand instinctively even so
much as what Silvio Fabricius, the tree-man, stood for in his
community.

I had, too, you will remember, known something in those
six years, of his viewpoints, his reactions to the "stupidness,"

and, specifically, some knowledge at least of his direct reaction, his pique and resentment, as these arose from his contacts with the tree-man. As I have indicated, the element of fear coloured this attitude.

He chose, cannily, one of the periods when Fabricius was away from his tree, reporting to the village. It was early in the afternoon, and Grumbach, having finished his roadwork several days before, was directing a group of labourers who were grubbing ancient "bush"—heavy undergrowth, brush, rank weeds, small trees—from along the winding trail which led from the village to the fountain or waterfall. This was now feeding a tumbling stream which Carrington intended to dam, lower down, for a central reserve reservoir.

The majority, if not all, of these labourers under his eye at the moment were new to the village; members of the increasing group which were coming into the restored stone cabins as fast as these became habitable. They were cutting out the brush with machetes, canebills, and knives; and, for the small trees, a couple of axes were being used from time to time. This work was being done quite near the great tree, and from his position in the roadway overlooking his gang, Grumbach must have seen the tree-man leave his station and start towards the village with one of his "messages."

This opportunity—he had, unquestionably, made up his mind about it all—was too good to be lost. As I learned from the two men whom he detached from his grubbing-gang and took with him, Silvio Fabricius was hardly out of sight over the sweep of the lower portion of the great field near the upper edge of which the coconut-palm towered, when Grumbach called to the two axe-men to follow him, and, with a word to the rest of the gang, led the way across the field's edge to the tree.

About this time Carrington and I were returning from one of our inspections of the fountain. We had been up there several times of late, since the scheme for the dam had been working in our minds. We were returning towards the village and the construction work progressing there along that same pathway through the big field from which, years before, I had had my first sight of the tree-man.

As we came in sight of the tree, towards which I invariably looked when I was near it, I saw, of course, that Fabricius was not there. Grumbach and his two labourers stood under it, Grumbach talking to the men. One of them as we approached— we were still perhaps a hundred yards distant—shook his head emphatically. He told me later that Grumbach had led them straight to the tree and commanded them to chop it down.

Both men had demurred. They were not of the village, it is true, not, certainly, Dahomeyans. But—they had some idea, even after generations away from "Guinea," that here was something strange; something over which the suitable course was to "go stupid." Both men, therefore, "went stupid" forthwith.

Grumbach, as was usual with him, poor fellow, was vastly annoyed by this process. I could hear him barge out at the labourers; see him gesticulate. Then from the nearest, he seized the axe and attacked the tree himself. He struck a savage blow at it, then, gathering himself together, for he was stout like the middle-aged of all his class, and unused to such work, he struck again, somewhat above the place where the first axe-blow had landed on the tree.

"You'd better stop him, Carrington," said I, "and I will explain my reasons to you afterwards."

Carrington cupped his hands and shouted, and both negroes looked towards us. But Grumbach, apparently, had not heard, or, if he had, supposed that the words were directed to somebody other than himself. Thus, everybody within view was occupied, you will note—Carrington looking at Grumbach; the two labourers looking towards us; Grumbach intent upon making an impression on the tough coconut wood. I alone, for some instinctive reason, thought suddenly of Silvio Fabricius, and directed my gaze towards the point, down the long field, over which horizon he would appear when returning.

Perhaps it was the sound of the axe's impact against his brother the tree apprehended by a set of senses for seventeen years attuned to the tree's moods and rustlings, to the "messages" which his brother the tree imparted to him; perhaps some uncanny instinct merely, that arrested him in his course towards the village down there, carrying the current "message" from the tree about tomorrow's weather.

As I looked, Silvio Fabricius, running lightly, erect, came over the distant horizon of the lower field's bosomed slope. He stopped there, a distant figure, but clearly within my view. Without taking my eyes off him I spoke again to Carrington:

"You must stop Grumbach, Carrington—there's more in this than you know. Stop him—at once!"

And, as Carrington shouted a second time, Grumbach raised the axe for the third blow at the tree, the blow which did not land.

As the axe came up, Silvio Fabricius, a distant figure down there, reached for the small sharp canebill which hung beside him from his trouser-belt, a cutting tool with which he smoothed the bark of his brother the tree on occasion, cut out annually the choking mass of "cloth" from its top, removed fading fronds as soon as their decay reached the stage where they were no longer benefiting the tree, cut his coconuts. I could see the hot sunlight flash against the wide blade of the canebill as though it had been a small heliograph-mirror. Fabricius was about a thousand yards away. He raised the canebill empty in the air, and with it made a sudden, cutting, pulling motion downwards; a grave, almost a symbolic movement. Fascinated, I watched him return the canebill to its place, on its hook, fastened to the belt at the left side.

But, abruptly, my attention was distracted to what was going on nearer at hand. Carrington's shout died, half-uttered. Simultaneously I heard the yells of uncontrollable, sudden terror from the two labourers at the tree's foot. My eyes, snatched away from the distant tree-man, turned to Carrington beside

me, glimpsing a look of terrified apprehension; then, with the
speed of thought, towards the tree where one labourer was in
the act of falling face-downward on the ground—I caught the
terrified white gleam of his rolled eyes—the other, twisting
himself away from the tree towards us, the very personification
of crude horror, his hands over his eyes. And my glance was
turned just in time to see the great coconut which, detached
from its heavy, fibrous cordage up there, sixty feet above the
ground, struck Grumbach full and true on the wide pitch hel-
met which he affected, planter-wise, against the sun.

He seemed almost to be driven into the ground by the impact. The axe flew off at an angle past the tree.

He never moved. And when, with the help of the two labourers, Carrington and I, having summoned a cart from the nearby
road-gang cutting bushes, lifted the body, the head which had
been that poor devil Grumbach's, was merely a mass of sodden
pulp.

We took the body down the road in the cart, towards his
newly erected manager's house. And a few yards along our way
Silvio Fabricius passed us, running erectly, his sombre face
expressionless, his stride a kind of dignified lope, glancing not
to right or left, speeding straight to his brother the tree which
had been injured in his absence.

Looking back, where the road took a turn, I saw him, leaning now close beside the tree, his long fingers probing the two
gashes which Hans Grumbach, who would never swing another
axe, had made there, about two feet above the ground; while
aloft the glorious fronds of the massive tree burgeoned like
great sails in the afternoon Trade.

Later that afternoon we sent the mortal remains of Hans
Grumbach down the long hill road to Frederiksted in a cart,
decently disposed, after telephoning his wife's relatives to break
the sorrowful news to her. It was Carrington who telephoned, at
my suggestion. I told him that they would appreciate it, he being the head of the company. Such nuances have their meaning

in the West Indies where the finer shades are of an importance. He explained that it was an accident, gave the particulars as he had seen them with his own eyes—Grumbach had been working under a tall coconut-palm and a heavy coconut, falling, had struck him and killed him instantly. It had been a quite merciful death.

The next morning I walked up towards the fountain again, alone, after a sleepless night of cogitation. I walked across the section of field between the newly-grubbed roadside and the great tree. I walked straight up to the tree-man, stood beside him. He paid no attention to me whatever. I spoke to him:

"Fabricius," said I, "it is necessary that I should speak to you."

The tree-man turned his gaze upon me gravely. Seen thus, face to face, he was a remarkably handsome fellow, now about thirty years of age, his features regular, his expression calm, inscrutable; wise with a wisdom certainly not Caucasian, such as to put into my mind the phrase: "not of this world." He bowed, gravely, as though assuring me of his attention.

I said: "I was looking at you yesterday afternoon when you came back to your tree, over the lower end of the field—down there." I indicated where he had stood with a gesture. Again he bowed, without any change of expression.

"I wish to have you know," I continued, "that I understand; that no one else besides me saw you, saw what you did—with the canebill, I mean. I wish you to know that what I saw I am keeping to myself. That is all."

Silvio Fabricius the tree-man continued to look into my face, without any visible change whatever in his expression. For the third time he nodded, presumably to indicate that he understood what I had said, but utterly without any emotion whatever. Then, in a deep, resonant voice, he spoke to me, the first and last time I have ever heard him utter a word.

"Yo' loike to know, yoong marster," said he, with an impressive gravity, "me brudda,"—he placed a hand against the tree's smooth trunk—"t'ink hoighly 'bout yo', sar. Ahlso 'bout de enterprise fo pineopples. Him please', sar, yoong marster; him indicate-me yo' course be serene an' ahlso of a profit." The tree-man bowed again, and without another word or so much as a glance in my direction, detaching his attention from me as deliberately as he had given it when I first spoke to him, he turned towards his brother the tree, laid his face against its bark, and slowly encircled the massive trunk with his two great muscular black arms.

I arrived on the island in the middle of October, 1928, coming down as usual from New York after my summer in the States. Great Fountain had suffered severely in the hurricane of the previous month, and when I arrived there I found Carrington well along with the processes of restoration. Many precautions had been taken beforehand and our property had been damaged because of these much less than the other estates. I had told Carrington, who had a certain respect for my familiarity with "native manners and customs," enough about the tree-man and his functions tribally to cause him to heed the warning, transmitted by the now nearly helpless old patriarch of the village, and brought in by the tree-man four days before the hurricane broke—and two days before the government cable-advice had reached the island.

Silvio Fabricius had stayed beside his tree. On the third day, when it was for the first time possible for the villagers to get as far as the upper end of the great field near the fountain, he had been found, Carrington reported to me, lying in the field, dead, his face composed inscrutably, the great trunk of his brother the tree across his chest which had been crushed by its great weight when it had been uprooted by the wind and fallen.

And until they wore off there had been smears of earth, Carrington said, on the heads and faces of all the original Dahomeyan villagers and upon the heads and faces of several of the newer labourer families as well.

LIGHT SPIRITS

*Horrific Specters, Comedic Shades,
and Criminous Phantasms in
Vintage Periodical
Ghost Stories*

Also Available

Coachwhip Publications

CoachwhipBooks.com

ARBORIS MYSTERIUS

STORIES OF THE UNCANNY AND UNDESCRIBED
FROM THE BOTANICAL KINGDOM

Also Available

Coachwhip Publications

CoachwhipBooks.com

THE SUPERNATURAL
STORIES OF MONSIGNOR
ROBERT H. BENSON

THE LIGHT INVISIBLE
A MIRROR OF SHALOTT

Also Available

Coachwhip Publications

CoachwhipBooks.com

A HOUSE A-HAUNT

CLASSIC STORIES OF HAUNTED HOUSES,
HORRIFIC ROOMS, AND OTHER GHASTLY ABODES

Also Available

Coachwhip Publications

CoachwhipBooks.com

CATS OF SHADOW,
CLAWS OF DARKNESS

Stories of Were-Cats, Ghost Cats,
and Other Supernatural Felines

Also Available

Coachwhip Publications

CoachwhipBooks.com

TRAVELS THROUGH
LOST WORLDS

THE LIVING DEATH
IN AMUNDSEN'S TENT
DROME

JOHN MARTIN LEAHY

Also Available

Coachwhip Publications

CoachwhipBooks.com

DAYS OF DOOM

APOCALYPTIC VISIONS &
UNEARTHLY NIGHTMARES

OWEN OLIVER

Also Available

Coachwhip Publications

CoachwhipBooks.com

LONELY HAUNTS

Also Available

Coachwhip Publications

CoachwhipBooks.com

www.ingramcontent.com/pod-product-compliance
Lightning Source LLC
Chambersburg PA
CBHW032242010726
47494CB00002B/595